"Cordelia is needed for their version of the ritual." Escobar took a breath. **"We could try to sneak up on them and kill her before it happens. At least it will stop Benedicta, and—"**

"No."

"But—"

Angel vamped. *"No.*

"I don't understand you," Escobar said slowly. "You are willing to die for this cause. But you would rather jeopardize the entire mission—an entire race—than ask one of your men to do the same."

"Cordelia's not one of my men."

"I don't understand you," Escobar said again, more softly this time. "A vampire. . . . They say you're different than the rest, but *so* different? A vampire is supposed to be a monster."

I know, Angel thought. *I am.*
And that hellbeast is not going to hurt Cordelia.

No one is.

They try, they'll meet the monster I am, just before they die.

Angel™

Available from Simon Pulse

The Essential Angel Posterbook

Available from Pocket Books

ANGEL™

endangered species

**Nancy Holder
and Jeff Mariotte**

SIMON PULSE

New York   London   Toronto   Sydney   Singapore

Historian's note: This story takes place in the early third season of *Angel*.

First Simon Pulse edition August 2003

SIMON PULSE
An imprint of Simon & Schuster
Children's Publishing Division
1230 Avenue of the Americas
New York, NY 10020

Also available in a Simon Pulse hardcover edition.
The text of this book was set in New Caledonian.

Printed in the United States of America
10 9 8 7 6 5 4 3 2

The Library of Congress has cataloged the hardcover edition as follows:
Holder, Nancy.
Endangered Species / Nancy Holder and Jeff Mariotte.
p.cm — (Angel)
Summary: Angel, Cordy, Gunn, Wesley, Fred, and Chaz set off for a tropical island to try to save Faith from the nefarious plans of Chaz's wife, Marianna, but the real danger may come from the lawyers of Wolfram & Hart.
ISBN 0-7434-2782-3 (hc.)
[1. Vampires—Fiction. 2. Lawyers—Fiction. 3. Islands—Fiction. 4. Horror stories.] 1. Mariotte, Jeff. II. Title. III. Series.
PZ7.H70326 En 2002
[Fic]—dc21
ISBN 0-689-86210-5 (pbk.)

In memory of my nephew, David Paul "Kawika" "Spooky"
Wilkinson, 1993 Imperial Court of Hawaii Ambassador of
Aloha; and to all our ohana Jones-Holder-Morehouse-
Wilkinson-Reaves, who miss him dearly.
—N. H.

For my family, near and far, through blood and by choice.
Love to you all.
—J. M.

⚜

Jeff and Nancy would say *mahalo* to: Joss Whedon, David Greenwalt, David Boreanaz, and the cast and crew of Angel; Debbie Olshan at Fox and the Simon & Schusterians, Lisa Clancy, Liz Shiflett, Lisa Gribbin and Micol Ostow.

For his agentry and friendship, thanks to Howard Morhaim and his assistant, Flo Felix.

Jeff would also like to thank: Chris Golden, Scott Ciencin, Jack Passarella, and Mel Odom, for showing me the way and helping through the hard parts of life; Tara O'Shea for her witchery, and Nancy; collaborator extraordinaire, for the invite.

Nancy would also like to thank: Debbie Viguié and Dal Perry, fine writers in their own right; Linda Wilcox, Katherine Ramsland, and Karen Hackett for being wonderful friends; Steve Perry, Barbara Hambly, Marc and Elaine Zicree, and David Wise, for being new friends; and of course, my faboo collaborator, Jeff, and his patient wife, Maryelizabeth.

Dearest Michael, thank you for all you do and are.

And thanks to my daughter Belle, who kept asking me, "Why do you have this job?"

PROLOGUE

Northanger Convent, London: 1898

The birds were singing, such lovely singing. Drusilla could hear it even as she stroked their little broken bodies. They had come to her, looking for crumbs to take home to their babies. The way they always did. The way they never would again. The poor little things would probably die without them. Naughty mother birds to leave their babies alone.

Drusilla rose from the ground.

"Mummy, I'm thirsty," she whispered. Mummy didn't answer. No one did. She walked slowly across the stone floor. It should have felt cold under her toes, but it didn't. "Not cold, not cold." At least she wouldn't freeze. But all alone she might starve just like the baby birdies.

She stepped carefully across the body of the mother superior, wrinkling her nose slightly as the smell of stale blood assaulted her. "Food's all spoiled." She pushed one of the sisters with her toe. The woman's body felt stiff. "Father left nothing to eat," Drusilla whimpered.

She heard a stifled sob and she turned toward the sound. She stepped around the other bodies. Beneath the altar, huddled beneath the cloths, was a figure.

She knelt down and came face-to-face with Mary Kelly. The other young woman stared at her with wide, terrified eyes. Mary Kelly was a good girl. Like Drusilla used to be. Like Drusilla tried to be. She had always liked her. Now Mary Kelly was looking up at her and trembling so very hard.

"Shush, little birdie," Drusilla murmured, stroking Mary Kelly's cheek. "It will be all right, little birdie. Mummy's here."

She sunk her teeth into Mary Kelly's neck. She was so thirsty, and as the liquid flowed into her mouth she closed her eyes and felt it spreading through her, making her skin all tingly. Mary Kelly was crying, praying. Slowly her cries grew fainter and her body grew limp in Drusilla's arms.

At last Drusilla lifted her teeth from the girl's neck. Her hunger quenched, she wiped the back of her hand across her lips. Mary Kelly's body slipped from her arms to the ground with a dull thud as Drusilla stared at the drops of blood on the back of her hand.

She stared evenly at Mary Kelly. Her face was pale, her eyes lifeless. "Poor little, birdie. Mother shouldn't have let you go. What will you do with the winter coming? Your wings aren't even grown yet. Fly from the nest. Save yourself. Fly."

Drusilla pushed Mary Kelly, but the girl did not move. Then Drusilla shook Mary Kelly's shoulders so that her head hit the ground, but still she lay quiet.

"Fly, little birdie. Mummy's not coming home. And all the little birdies will starve unless they fly off."

Drusilla's eyes fell on the back of her hand where it grasped Mary Kelly's shoulder. Three drops of blood shone like light, like life. She brought her hand to her mouth and slowly licked at the blood. It was so warm. She bit her hand, shuddering in pain and pleasure as her own blood washed down her throat.

Somewhere a bird sang and she pulled her fangs from her flesh. She looked back at Mary Kelly. Slowly she put her hand against the girl's lips.

"Come on, little birdie. Mummy brought you something sweet to eat."

The girl's lips moved slowly and Drusilla pressed her hand down harder. Suddenly Mary Kelly's eyes flew open. She clamped her lips around the wound in Drusilla's hand and began sucking.

Drusilla stroked her head. "Good birdie. See? Mummy came to feed you."

The pain began to mount and Drusilla began to feel dizzy. Finally it was too much, and with a cry she ripped her hand away from Mary Kelly. The girl's head fell back on the ground. She lay staring for a moment, and then her body began to convulse.

At last her body lay still and her chest ceased heaving. Drusilla stood up and smiled. "Fly, little birdie. You're free now. I gave you wings."

"Drusilla?" a hard voice called.

He was coming. He would kill her little birdie. She glanced down at Mary Kelly. "Or did I kill the little birdie?"

She shrugged her shoulders. It didn't matter. Daddy was calling. She turned and scampered out the door, running to meet Angelus and the golden-haired woman. . . . Was her name Darla?

On the cold stone floor, beneath the altar, Mary Kelly woke up and screamed.

Los Angeles, the Present

Tourists were routinely warned to keep out of Griffith Park's lonelier environs after dark. Taking one of the well-maintained roads to the Greek Theater or the famous Griffith Observatory was safe enough, or so the conventional wisdom held. But the rest of the Los Angeles park—and at four thousand acres, Griffith, the largest city park in the country, had a lot of "rest"—was considered too dangerous for average people to risk wandering about in after the sun went down. Muggers, gangsters, and the occasional mass murderer ruled the night here.

Even ranger Randy Clayton was nervous, and he knew the park like he knew his own backyard. During his six years on duty here he had walked every oak-spotted hillside, every scrubby canyon, every rocky creek. He knew the park's history—knew that a wealthy man with the unlikely name of Colonel Griffith J. Griffith had donated the land to the city in an attempt to buff up his image after he was imprisoned for shooting his wife in the eye. She survived the attack; Griffith's reputation did not.

But familiarity with the park didn't help allay Clayton's

concerns tonight. The Smith & Wesson .38 in his holster and the powerful Maglite in his left fist were somewhat reassuring. Still, the ranger's hand quivered so much that the flashlight's beam flitted like an intoxicated butterfly across his path, and he knew that if it came down to needing to use his still-holstered weapon, chances were good that his right hand wouldn't be much more cooperative. Fear coaxed sweat from him in rivulets, the rancid smell overwhelming the aromas of oak and grass, the tang of the pines up on the ridge, the musky cottonwoods near the creek.

One could be a park ranger for a lot of years without encountering a situation like Clayton faced tonight. A lifetime, for most. Because something had been happening in Griffith Park—*his* park, Clayton liked to think—for the past several nights, something that was both strange and terrifying.

So he hiked into a deep, narrow canyon in one of the park's most remote corners, because every indication pointed to this canyon as being at the center of the—well, he still hadn't been able to put a word to what was going on. The evidence of it was all around him: ground squirrels, Norway rats, starlings, finches, pigeons, possum, a couple of skunks, three big raccoons, even a single coyote, were visible from just this one spot. All dead. All—if he were to bother to take them in for necropsy, as he had dozens of other creatures over the last couple of days—with no apparent cause of death. Their hearts had just stopped, and no one could say why. But Randy, triangulating where the deaths had occurred, had determined that they were centered right here in this canyon. And since they had all died at night, it would be at night that he would investigate.

None of the other rangers had been willing to accept his something's-lurking-in-the-dark theory. They wanted more study, more research, scientists paid by government grants to come in and waste weeks, even months, looking into possible causes. To humor him, they'd taken a hike through the canyon during daylight hours, turning up nothing out of the ordinary. Clayton hadn't been convinced, though. He knew he was right, certainty burned in him like a highway flare. It was just a matter of looking at the right time. He would get to the bottom of this tonight, and prevent any more wildlife from meeting an untimely end.

As he walked deeper into the canyon, rock-strewn slopes and spreading oaks cutting off the last glimmer of moonlight, Randy Clayton felt his determination waver. More than that, he realized he was a little dizzy. The idea came to him that maybe whatever was killing the animals could have the same effect on people.

A little late to think of that, he thought. *I'm committed, now.* He pressed on, opening the clasp on the leather flap that held his revolver in its holster. He shook his head, trying to clear it, and as he did, figures loomed out of the darkness ahead of him.

"That's the guy," one of them said. The voice sounded female, and Clayton's hand darted to his gun's grip. But before he could free it from the holster, another of the shadowy forms lunged at him, faster than humanly possible, and struck out with a heavy fist. Clayton saw stars, then slumped to the ground, mercifully unconscious.

"My God, Angel, did you have to do that?" Wesley Wyndam-Pryce demanded. "I thought we came here to save him, not to pummel him into a coma."

Angel shrugged, surprised at Wesley's outburst. "He was

going for his gun. Anyway I thought it'd be easier for us to work if we didn't have to worry about him seeing us."

Cordelia Chase knelt by the ranger's still form. "He'll have a pretty good bruise, I think. And his lip's cut. You ever give any thought to pro boxing, Angel? Because I think that world could use some fresh blood, so to speak, and you might get a chance to beat up Mike Tyson, which, you know, would be a bonus."

"You sure that's the dude you saw?" Charles Gunn asked her. "Hate to be spendin' all this time with the wrong park ranger while the one in your vision is around the corner gettin' his head bit off or somethin'."

"No, this is definitely him," Cordy replied. "Looks like a duck, smells like a duck." She made a face. "Definitely smells. Although in the literal sense, I think I'd rather smell a duck."

"Flop sweat," Gunn said. "Bein' a ranger out here is no picnic, 'scuse the expression, but most of the time they don't have to sneak around at night by themselves chasin' after . . . well, whatever it is this one was chasin'."

"A Chaos demon, I'm convinced," Wesley said. "The laws of reality itself are warping in this area, and all this dead wildlife is just one of the outward manifestations of that." He slapped his Bavarian fighting adz against the palm of his left hand. "Speaking of which, we'd best get on with it if we're going to defeat it before Los Angeles itself becomes an anomaly in the space-time continuum."

Cordelia snorted a laugh. "Like anyone would notice."

"Be that as it may—," Wesley began.

Angel cut him off. "Shh!"

"What is it, Angel? Did you hear something?" Wes asked.

"Shh!" Angel said again, more forcefully than before. *How can you not understand, "Shh?"* he wondered. He had, in fact, heard something. He raised his Scottish basket-hilt broadsword—still in remarkable condition, considering it had once belonged to Robert the Bruce of Scotland, in the fourteenth century. Angel had acquired it in lieu of payment on a debt, late in the eighteenth, and it was still a fine weapon. He used it to point deeper into the canyon.

"Down there," he whispered. "Sounded like footsteps."

The words had barely passed his lips when the darkness down-canyon came alive. Robed figures burst toward them, r tically invisible in their dark fabrics, their faces shadowed by big hoods. Only the weapons in their hands were distinct: polished metal blades catching what moonlight there was and glinting like fireflies.

Deadly fireflies, charging straight at them.

Angel didn't need to say anything. His friends were trained and ready. Cordelia stood with her legs apart, a short-handled cudgel held in her hands like a billy club, ready to strike. Gunn's trusty hubcap axe was already in motion, weaving back and forth to distract his opponents. Wes's adz was uplifted to shoulder height, and Angel dropped to a half-crouch, reducing his target area to one that he could easily defend with Robert the Bruce's magnificent blade.

Thus prepared, they held their ground as the enemy attacked. The robed figures carried spears, short but heavy, with long metal heads on thick poles. *Good weapons for close fighting,* Angel thought, parrying a thrust with his sword. He swung at the pole, and his sword bit at the wood but didn't break it. The robed one jabbed at him again. This time Angel had to take a step back and bring his blade around in a tight arc to block the blow. The being thrust one more time, and Angel sidestepped the attack, brought his sword up and over the outthrust spear, and rammed it home in the center of the robe. The spear dropped to the ground and the robed figure let out a piercing shriek, then collapsed at Angel's feet. Angel used the tip of his blade to draw back the hood.

The dying creature had bright yellow skin mottled with brown, Angel saw. In daylight he'd look like a banana. "You were right, Wes!" he shouted. "They're Bentlars!"

Wesley was busy swinging his adz, trying to break through another Bentlar's defense. The demon used his spear's heavy shaft like a shield, blocking each of Wes's attempts. Gunn was having no such problem; his massive axe cut through the spears like they were made of balsa wood. And Cordelia, with her shorter, more maneuverable weapon, was plowing through their defenses as well.

"I'm . . . gratified to . . . hear it . . . ," Wesley managed through gritted teeth. Angel moved forward, weaving a silvery web with his blade that confused an approaching Bentlar into lowering and then raising his guard. Then Angel stabbed it through the heart—in a Bentlar demon, Angel knew, the heart was located right about where the navel would be on a human. But since Bentlars laid eggs instead of giving live birth, no need for a navel.

With that one down, Angel worked his way to Wesley's side. Wesley was still hacking away, making some progress on the Bentlar's spear shaft. The Bentlar was forced to keep defending itself or Wesley would certainly kill it, but Angel figured if they waited until Wes broke through the pole, all of L.A. would be caught up in the reality warp.

"It's not a cherry tree, Wes," Angel said. "And you're not George Washington."

"Yes, well . . . ," Wesley replied, still chopping. "I always wondered if . . . there was any truth . . . to that . . . story."

Angel sliced at the Bentlar's arm, cutting the robe and drawing blood. The Bentlar dropped its spear, and Wes swung again, burying his adz in the Bentlar's hard skull. He yanked it free again and looked at Angel. "Well? Is there?"

"How old do you think I am?" Angel asked him. "Washington was born way before me."

"Really?" Wes asked, sounding surprised.

"No," Angel said. "We're basically contemporaries. But I was still human when that whole tree incident happened, if it really did." He parried another Bentlar attack. "Didn't you have some kind of plan for these Bentlars?"

"Oh, right." Wes dropped back a couple of steps and reached into his pocket.

Wes had anticipated that they'd encounter Bentlars, claiming that they were the only type of demon who could generally adapt to life within the reality warp zone of a Chaos demon. They seemed to thrive on it in fact, so most Chaos demons—not that there were a lot of them, at least in this plane of existence—tended to surround themselves with acolytes from the Bentlar species.

So Wesley had come prepared—*a lot more so than that poor park ranger,* Angel thought. As he, Cordy, and Gunn held back the remaining Bentlars, Wesley read an incantation he'd copied from one of his old texts. The Bentlars seemed to know what was coming; after they heard the first few words, they shrank back, giving up their attack and trying to blend into the shadows.

But it was too late for them. As Wesley finished his incantation, the Bentlars suddenly folded like empty sacks and fell to the ground.

"Hey," Cordelia said. "That really worked. Too bad you can't do that all the time. We could hang up these weapons for good and just let you talk a lot."

"Like he don't already," Gunn observed. "Good job, English."

"Yes, thank you," Wesley said. "But we knew Bentlars would be easy if we found them. The real problem is still before us."

"Mr. Chaos," Cordelia said. "The big guy."

"He hates order," Wes explained. "He generates a field of random uncertainty, in which virtually anything can occur, and no rational-minded creature can surv—"

"Remember what I said about talking a lot?" Cordy asked him. "Doing it again. And we already know all this."

Wesley looked a little sheepish. "I suppose I'm just trying to delay the inevitable," he said.

Cordelia wiped her forehead. "Yes, and the longer we delay, the longer my vision hangover lasts. And good old Ranger Smith back there isn't out of the woods yet, you know. Not until the Chaos demon is gone."

"Maybe instead of tryin' to kill it, we should take it down to Venice Beach," Gunn suggested. "Let it see that around here, too much order is the least of its worries."

"Come on." Angel didn't see any value in postponing the confrontation any longer. Every minute they waited, the Chaos demon's sphere of influence grew. "Stay close together, keep each other grounded or you won't be able to cope with the reality warp. If you feel yourself losing control, close your eyes and think of something simple, something you can envision clearly and completely."

"Heard this part, too," Cordelia announced. "Head still hurts. Can we get this over with?"

Angel nodded and they all stepped forward, into the darkness from which the Bentlars had emerged. *In some ways, the dark will help us,* Angel thought. *In daylight we'd be better able to see the reality shifts—well,* they *would be,* he amended. *I'd just be able to see myself bursting into flames.* Since he'd become a vampire, daylight and Angel didn't exactly see eye to eye.

But that optimistic thinking wasn't borne out. The dark of night was just as subject to the laws of physics as anything else, and the closer they got to the Chaos demon, the more those rules were broken. The dark sky became a kind of light green, like mint ice cream, Angel decided, and then it bent and twisted and became the ground they walked on. Stars that had been spinning lazily overhead metamorphosed into a flock of winged snails and then, shooting toward Angel and his friends, became tiny particles of light that passed right through them. The sound of creek water rushing over smooth stones turned red and reared up before them like a dragon taking flight.

Angel held Cordelia's hand in his, and he knew that, somewhere, she held Wesley's and he held Gunn's. When she began to mutate into the smell of musty old books, Angel closed his eyes, focused on the warmth of her hand, and tried to bring her smile into his mind's eye. In this way, step by step, they made their way to the Chaos demon who sat at the center of the reality warp, legs crossed, hands on her knees.

"My word," Wesley breathed. "Do you think that's its true form?"

"No way of knowing," Angel said. "Unless you know someone who's seen one before."

"I might have seen thousands," Cordy said. "Hard to tell."

The Chaos demon looked up at them with a sly smile on its face. Angel knew it was something that couldn't be allowed to live—its destructive potential was too great, its power too awesome—but it looked like a Catholic school-girl, wearing a pleated, plaid skirt, white knee socks, and a modest navy blue sweater. She—it—held a daisy in its hands, plucking out the petals one by one.

"I don't know about y'all, but I'm not sure I can do this," Gunn said.

"We've got to," Angel reminded him firmly. "It'll take all of us, attacking at once. Now." He released Cordelia's hand and thrust forward with the tip of his sword.

At their attack, the Chaos demon dropped the daisy and stood, but instead of standing to the four feet or so that the young girl's form would have reached, it kept going—six feet tall, then eight, then ten. And its shape changed as well, the school uniform transmuting into green and silver scales, twin ponytails becoming eyestalks, the girl's soft brown eyes changing into one of three mouths that slavered several feet over their heads.

"Okay, that's better," Gunn said, and they all struck at once.

Once the Chaos demon was slain, Cordelia's head began to feel better almost instantly. She'd seen commercials for headache remedies that showed tiny demolition crews working inside cutaway heads with jackhammers and dynamite, and lately her visions—sent by The Powers That Be to alert Angel to people in trouble—had felt quite a bit like she had a crew or two of her own working in there. The pain, which had at first been centralized in the head, now took over her whole body, making her nauseous and weak and generally unfit company. It lasted until whoever she saw in the vision was safe from whatever threat had prompted it, and then, mercifully, the pain faded pretty fast.

They were on their way to where they'd left Angel's car when she started to feel human again. The ranger was behind them, propped up against a tree. The zone of mysteriously dead animals was behind them too, and she'd seen something, a night bird or maybe a bat, zip through the air over their heads. *That's a relief,* she thought, *because that whole dead animal thing is just nasty.*

All in all, Cordelia realized, *I feel pretty good right now.* The city and its troubles seemed far away, her friends were beside her, a night wind rustled the trees . . .

. . . so, of course, that's when it hit her.

She went down on her knees in the dew-damp grass. That demolition crew had exploded twenty tons of TNT in her brain.

"Cordelia, are you all right?" Wesley asked her.

"Is it a vision?" Angel wanted to know.

Gunn just put a strong hand on her shoulder and squeezed. She held it for a moment, squeezing back, then used it to pull herself back to her feet.

"What was it?" Angel asked.

"If there are grass stains on these pants," Cordelia said. "I am so going to give The Powers That Be a piece of my mind. Do they have any idea how long I stared at these in the window of Barney's before I saved up enough to buy them?"

"Cordy, the *vision*," Angel prodded.

"Oh, yeah. That. It was Faith. Some bizarre creature was trying to kill her."

CHAPTER ONE

"Where is he?" Angel couldn't keep the impatience out of his voice, and was beyond caring who heard it.

Cordelia swiveled around in her chair, which had been facing the computer on her desk. "He's only been gone about ten seconds," she replied wearily. The strain of the new vision that she'd had in the park, so soon after the vision that sent them there, was taking a toll on her. "But the way you're pacing around you're going to wear a groove in the lobby floor I polished. Remember how gunky it was after we killed the Thesulac?"

Angel remembered. The paranoia demon had fed on the Hyperion Hotel's residents for years, and back in the early fifties, when he had lived here for a while, Angel had just let the demon have his way. Upon returning to the hotel fifty years later, he had finally slain the Thesulac and decided then and there that this place would be the new headquarters of Angel Investigations. Since then he'd temporarily left the team, at which point Wesley stepped up to the plate and took over. They were all back together and on good terms now, and the Hyperion continued to serve as hearth and home.

And yes, he remembered what a pain it had been to clean scorched demon goo off the floors. And the walls.

"Anyway, at the risk of having my head bitten off, so to speak, I could also point out that Wes is the boss now, and if he makes you wait a couple of extra seconds then it's certainly nothing you haven't done to him in the past."

She's right, Angel thought. But he wasn't going to give her the satisfaction of saying so. And probably, waiting another minute or so was not going to make a difference, one way or another. But he'd had to go out of his way already, to bring Cordelia, Wesley, and Gunn back to the hotel in Hollywood, and he wanted to get down to the Yorba Linda Ranch women's prison to check on Faith.

To be fair, he knew, Hollywood wasn't that far out of the way. Griffith Park was north of downtown L.A., and Hollywood was a little south and west of the park, but still north of downtown. Yorba Linda, on the other hand, was all the way down in Orange County, almost to the San Bernardino County line. So he had to more or less pass by Hollywood to get there from the park, anyway.

He was just anxious about Faith, he knew. Because Cordy's vision had shown her in danger. *And,* he thought, *because I wasn't around to help the last Slayer who died.*

Buffy was back now, thanks to Willow-witchery. But she had died, while he'd been off in Pylea, Lorne's home dimension, so there had been nothing he could do about it. He wouldn't stand by helplessly while the same thing happened to Faith.

"He'll be right back," Cordelia insisted. "I thought you went to Tibet to find inner peace."

"I have inner peace," Angel said. "This is only outer tension. My inner self is as calm as a mountain lake."

"Yeah, on a volcano."

"Can I help it if the Tibetan monks turned out to be evil?" he asked.

"Even evil monks ought to know the value of patience," she observed.

"Cordelia . . ." He let the word hang there, sentence unfinished. She got his drift and turned back to the computer screen where she was supposed to be trying to research the creature she had seen threatening Faith.

"Got it," Wesley said, coming in from his car with something dangling from his hand.

"About time," Angel grumped.

"Ignore him," Cordelia urged. "He's testy."

Angel glowered mildly. "I'm in a hurry."

"I understand, Angel," Wesley assured him, approaching Angel with it. "But I thought this was important." He held out the object in his hand—a medallion of some sort, strung on a worn leather cord. The medallion was oval-shaped with a stylized sun in the center, but inside the sun, where an orange juice advertisement would probably put a happy, jolly, sun-face, there was instead a distinctly recognizable skull face.

"Because it's the accessory everyone's wearing this year," Cordelia suggested.

"Because it's a warding amulet from ancient Mesopotamia," Wesley countered. "Given to me by an acquaintance, a shaman from New Guinea, in fact, after I did him a rather immense favor. It's exceedingly rare and quite powerful. It will keep Faith safe from all manner of evil."

"If it's so powerful," came a small voice from up the stairs. "Then why don't you wear it, Wesley?" The voice had a bit of a Texas twang, even after five years in Pylea. Fred. Winifred Burkle appeared on the stairs, a slight young woman wearing a conservative tan sweater and knee-length brown skirt. The contrast with Cordelia, who had changed out of her grass-stained outfit into a revealing V-neck yellow shirt and tight red leather pants, couldn't have been more pronounced.

"Fred's got a point," Cordelia said. "It might have done you some good, like, for instance, when you were shot by a zombie cop."

Wesley nodded. "It might have," he agreed. "But then its power would have been dissipated. I preferred to save it until a time when I thought it would be truly needed. Now, with Faith in peril, seems like that time."

"Because you couldn't have let me have it the time demons tried to lay their young in my scalp," Cordelia muttered, turning back to the computer again.

"One can't just wear it all the time," Wesley said. "According to the legend, if it's worn too much it will use up its energies protecting the wearer from all manner of threats, real and imagined. You might be wearing it on the streets of Los Angeles and it will be busy keeping an elephant from falling out of the sky and crushing you—but then again, what are the chances of that happening, realistically speaking? It's like a battery in a flashlight—if it's turned on, it's losing juice."

"So it needs to be saved until there's a definite threat," Angel said, catching on. "And you're willing to let Faith have it."

Wesley swallowed. He had been no great supporter of the rogue Slayer. The fact that she kidnapped and tortured him may, Angel realized, have entered into that. So it was really quite a sacrifice for him to hand something this precious over to her.

I'd better go before he changes his mind, Angel thought.

"If it's like a battery," Fred said slowly, "there might be some way of recharging it."

"It's possible," Wesley agreed. "I haven't run across any in the literature, but that doesn't mean it doesn't exist."

"I'll work on it," Fred said, starting upstairs again. "Drive carefully, Angel."

"Yeah. Thanks." Angel said. He tucked the amulet into an inside pocket of his black leather duster. "And thank you, Wes," he added.

"Keep her safe, Angel," Wesley said, sincerity evident in his tone. "Please."

"That's what I'm planning to do," Angel said. He walked out of the hotel lobby to the alley where he'd parked his car.

Driving down from Griffith Park, they'd agreed on how to split the workload. Angel would go see Faith. Cordelia and Wesley would get busy on research, trying to identify the threat—although Cordy insisted that it had been so vague, in the vision, that it could have been anything from a ferocious killer demon to a murderous jelly-filled donut. Gunn would hit the streets, to find out if there was any scuttlebutt—a word that had seemed to entertain Cordelia and Gunn no end, when Angel had used it—about anything coming into town that might have its sights set on a Slayer. And Fred—well, Fred rarely came out of her room, but Cordelia offered to bring her up to speed when she had time, in case Faith could be saved by the handy application of some obscure mathematical formula.

Cordy's grown a lot since her Sunnydale days, Angel thought as he keyed the engine, *but that sarcastic streak will never die.*

"He's a bit on edge, isn't he?" Wesley asked after Angel was gone.

"He's not the only one," Cordelia replied. She rubbed her temples with her fingertips, as if she could massage the vision-induced ache out of her head. "I'm just about wiped from tonight's double whammy, and staring at this computer screen isn't helping."

"You could take a break," Wesley offered. "Would you like a cup of tea?"

"I'd like a barrel of tea," she said. "Hit me in the head with the barrel and put me out of my misery. Then you can drink the tea while admiring my deceased but still excruciatingly hot corpse."

"I believe that a corpse is, by definition, deceased," Wesley pointed out.

"There you go, Wes. Bust me on grammar, because that's going to help my mood a whole lot."

"Sorry," he said.

He really is trying to help, Cordelia thought, *so I probably should cut him a break.*

But then again, why?

"Never mind the tea," she said. "You should be getting busy on the reference books, shouldn't you?"

"I should, yes. But it would help if I had something specific to look up. 'Vague shadowy could-be-a-demon form' doesn't appear in any of the indices that I'm aware of."

"I'm sorry I didn't get a better look," Cordelia said for what seemed like the hundredth time. "But it's really not up to me, you know? The Powers That Be are the ones who decide what I see, and when. I pretty much have to just go along with what they want to show me."

"Let's just go through it again," Wesley urged.

"Wes, we've been through it—"

"Just once more. You know sometimes it helps, Cordy. Jogs your memory, shakes loose another piece or two of the puzzle."

"This time I think all that's shaking loose are brain cells."

"Give it a go," he said. "Exactly what did you see?"

"I saw Faith. Close-up, eyes wide. Jumpy-looking. Whatever is coming for her, she's aware of it, and has been for a while, I think. It's got her spooked."

"She's inside her cell?"

"I can't tell," Cordelia said, closing her eyes. She was trying to see the vision again in her mind's eye, trying to recall every minute detail. But the background behind Faith was a dark blur, without detail or form. "It's kind of dark, but there's enough light to see her face. She could be inside or outside. All I can see is her, and the expression on her face that tells me she's afraid of something. I can hear a kind of shuffling, scratching noise, and it's getting closer—she can hear it too, because her eyes move and she looks toward where the noise is coming from. And then that's it—it's over." She opened her eyes again and wiped her forehead with the palm of her hand. "That's all I can remember, except for the lancing pain in my skull when it happened. That part I remember vividly because I'm still living it."

"I know these are hard on you, Cordelia."

She shrugged. "I could have given them up to Groo," she said. The Groosalugg, back in Pylea, would have been able to free her from the visions—and he was the only person she had encountered since Doyle had passed them along to her who could have. But in the end, she had declined the offer, realizing that the visions were Angel's best link to The Powers That Be and the greatest contribution she could make to Angel's cause.

"And you chose not to, which was terribly brave."

"We all do what we have to do," she said. "You chose to hang onto your protective amulet instead of using it yourself. I chose to hang onto blinding headaches and the accompanying nausea."

"Ah, but it's nausea for the best possible cause."

Cordelia took a big breath and blew it out, but there was no relief for the throbbing pain in her head. "Yeah, a good cause," she said. "That makes me feel a whole lot better about it."

"I'm okay, I guess," Faith said. Angel had arrived at the Yorba Linda Ranch too late for visiting hours, but he'd already established false credentials as Faith's attorney so he wouldn't be inconvenienced by such minor details.

When he used that alias then he also got to see her in an interview room instead of simply through a window, talking on a phone, like the first few times he'd visited her here.

"You haven't seen anything threatening you?" he asked.

"Angel, this is prison," she pointed out with a half smile. "Yesterday a girl pulled a knife on me because she said I used some of her leave-in conditioner without asking."

"Did you?"

"Well, you know, hair like this doesn't come without a price," she said, fluffing her dark locks with both hands. "But the point is, everybody in the joint gets threatened on a regular basis. A woman was killed last month because she wouldn't share her mashed potatoes in the mess hall. Couple of her friends found the chick who killed her and they cut her an extra mouth, right across her throat. Now she could eat potatoes twice as fast, if she could eat 'em at all."

"And it doesn't bother you, staying here?" Angel knew that Faith was tough—Faith personified tough, in fact. But she was a Slayer—if she wanted to get out, she'd be out. Humans hadn't built the prison that could hold her against her will.

And, I guess, that really shows how truly strong she is, he thought. *Strong enough to know that she has to pay a price for the things she's done, so she's willing to put herself through this to atone.* He wasn't sure he'd be that strong, if the circumstances were reversed.

Of course, prison had other disadvantages for those of the vampiric persuasion. Like "lights out" coming at night, and the rest of the scheduled activities—including time in the exercise yard—being slotted for those times of day guaranteed to make him burst into flames. Any jail sentence could be a death sentence for Angel.

"Of course it bothers me," Faith told him. "But you know. Girl's gotta do what a girl's gotta do, right?"

"Yeah, I suppose," he said.

"So what was it Cordy saw stalking me? You got a line on it?"

He shook his head. "She said it was really vague. Maybe a demon, maybe a human . . . she just couldn't tell."

"Think she'd be able to tell if she liked me better?"

"I'm sure that's not it, Faith," Angel replied. "She doesn't play around like that with her visions. She takes them very seriously. She has to—I'm worried about her, in fact. They've been getting worse and worse, really taking a lot out of her."

"Maybe that other guy, what was his name—"

"Doyle?" Angel prompted.

"Yeah, Doyle. Maybe he was better suited to them. You said he was a demon, right?"

"Half demon."

"Still."

"I think it was easier for him, yes." Angel glanced around the interview room. A bare metal table with a fake wood-grain surface, three plastic chairs. The room smelled like disinfectant, but it just masked other odors—sweat and tobacco foremost among them, even though there was no ashtray and a big NO SMOKING sign on one of the walls. Two of the walls were glass, and Angel could see Orange County corrections officers watching them without interest. The other two walls were cinder block, painted a kind of light green, almost the same green as the sky had been near the

Chaos demon. He remembered thinking it looked like mint chocolate-chip ice cream without the chips, and wondered if he'd ever enjoy ice cream again.

"Oh, speaking of people who don't like you much," Angel said, reaching into his coat. "Wesley sent this." He drew out the amulet.

Faith took it, turned it over in her hands, examining it. "I guess he doesn't like me," she said. "Am I supposed to wear this? The ladies on the block'll kick the crap out of me just for offending their fashion sense."

"You can take them," Angel said with a grin.

She returned the smile. "Yeah, I can."

"No, it's really valuable," he went on. "It's Mesopotamian, Wesley said. It's ancient. One of a kind."

She looked at it again. "Not hard to see why."

"It has power," Angel explained. "It'll keep you safe."

"From what?"

"From anything that might endanger you, I guess. He says it's very powerful magic."

"And he gave it to me?" Faith asked quietly. She didn't seem to quite believe it, as if she were looking for the catch that must surely come with it.

"He wanted you to have it. Said he was saving it for the right person who would need its protection. That's you."

He thought Faith was tearing up, but she turned her head away quickly, and a shock of thick dark hair blocked his view. "That's . . . really nice," she said, her voice catching a little.

She is *crying,* he thought. *I'll have to tell Wes his gift was appreciated.*

"You okay?"

"Yeah, I just . . . ," She dabbed at her eyes with the tail of her orange prison uniform. "Just got something in my eye, I guess."

"That'll happen in places like this," Angel said.

"Once in a while," she agreed. She turned back to him, blinking away the moistness that remained in her eyes.

"So they're all right?" she asked him. "Wesley and Cordy?"

Angel thought it over for a moment, not wanting to give her the facile response. Wesley had been through some tough times recently—taking over Angel Investigations, dealing with Angel's Darla-induced trip to the dark side, getting shot in the gut, and still being unable to impress his father with any of his accomplishments. But the trip to the demon dimension of Pylea seemed to bring a lot of things into focus for him. There, too, he became a leader, of the rebel forces opposing the wicked rulers of that world. And he excelled in the role.

Pylea had been a strain for Cordelia, too. She had been captured, and taken for a simple "cow"—what the locals called humans—until she'd had a vision. Then she was hailed as their Queen, a role she played to the hilt. Even as the Queen, though, she had to answer to the high priest. She'd been expected to mate with the Groosalugg, who had turned out to be not only handsome but genuinely nice. But Angel had to fight him, and the mating part never happened. Finally they'd all been happy to get home and leave the strange world behind—bringing Fred, a human who had accidentally been trapped there, with them.

He supposed he'd faced some challenges there, too. He had been able to move about under Pylea's suns, but when

27

threatened, he had become an AngelBeast, his inner demonic nature coming to the fore in a big way. Fred had seen him as human and demon, and hadn't judged him, and that had helped him realize the value of both aspects of his personality.

"Yeah," he said finally. "They're good. They're really good. I am too, I think."

"Glad to hear it," Faith said. "I miss you. All you guys, I guess. But you know, especially you." She draped the amulet Wesley had given her around her neck. "I should probably get back to my busy night, y'know," she said.

"I guess so." He noticed that the guards were looking more carefully now, and one of them was eyeing a wall clock. Even fake attorneys weren't allowed to overstay their welcome. Faith had just been trying to give Angel a graceful out, before they came and ejected him. *Something the old Faith would never have done,* he thought. *Showing consideration for others. Maybe prison isn't all bad.* "You be careful, Faith. Cordy's visions are sometimes vague but they're never wrong. You *are* in danger. Just keep your eyes open, and be sure to call me if there's anything I can do."

"I will, big guy," she assured him. "Count on it."

Faith always watched her back in the joint, Cordy or no Cordy. Those who didn't ended up on slabs with tags wired to their big toes. Faith was Slayer-tough and Slayer-trained, better than any ten of the other inmates around her. But even a Slayer could be killed if she didn't pay attention. Faith didn't intend to fall into that category.

She'd been truthful with Angel—beyond the ordinary, day to day dangers of life behind bars, she hadn't been aware of any particular threats. Wesley's amulet notwithstanding, she felt kind of keyed-up after Angel's visit, hyper-aware. She was escorted back to her block, where she lived, if one could call it that, with her cellmate. The cell had two wafer-thin mattresses on platforms, and there were seven cells just like it on this side of a wide, central corridor, with eight more lining the other side. There were doors in both ends of the small building, and a tiny barred window in each cell. From her bunk, with her head on the pillow, she could see a tiny square of night sky out the nearest window.

This night, she lay in the bunk with a blanket pulled up over her, thinking about Angel's warning, and thinking about how unexpected it was to have Wesley, whom she had treated so horribly, do something so nice for her. All around her, the steady breathing and occasional snores of the other women indicated that they had all fallen asleep; she was the only one staying awake into the night wondering how she had gotten so lucky as to have someone like Angel looking out for her, in spite of everything she'd done. Finally, as she was beginning to drift off herself, something moved in front of the window, blocking the few stars she could see.

Suddenly alert, Faith tensed her body, ready to hurl off the blanket and spring into action if anything came at her. Her senses were alive. Since becoming a Slayer, she had felt like she had an extra sense that no one else got to experience, and it warned her when she was in real danger. It was screaming now. In the window she could only see a dark silhouette. It was rounded at the top like a head, but had no more detail than that. Then it moved away from the window. She strained to listen, and heard barely audible footfalls on the gravel outside. A moment later the doors at the end nearest her bed rattled gently. But nothing else happened—whoever or whatever it was didn't come in, didn't make a play for her.

The amulet, she thought. *It warded off whatever that was.*

She knew there were plenty of other possible explanations. There never was any danger; she'd only caught a glimpse of one of the guards making rounds, checking to see that the doors were locked.

But she had sensed the peril outside. That had been something malevolent, and it had been looking for her.

"Thanks, Wes," she mouthed silently.

CHAPTER TWO

On the streets of L.A.'s financial district gridlock ruled the day. The city was legendary for its traffic jams, and they didn't affect just the freeways, sadly. And, unlike the subways and bus routes in other big cities, mass transit was more concept than reality here.

But Lilah Morgan was off the streets now, standing at the floor-to-ceiling windows of a thirtieth-floor conference room, looking down at the cars and sipping expensive coffee from a Styrofoam cup. *For six-fifty a shot,* she thought, *they ought to throw in real china.* She'd been harried all day, worked late, and had finally gotten home. And then she'd answered her phone. It was Nathan Reed's secretary, calling to tell her that she needed to get back for a conference that would be starting at midnight.

She'd showered quickly, changed, wolfed down a late dinner, and made her way back.

And in spite of it all, she was the first one here. She took another tentative sip of the coffee, purchased from a cart in the lobby of the Wolfram & Hart building and still too hot to swallow. She didn't know what the meeting was about, only that Nathan's secretary hadn't left her much time to both get to the office and still look presentable, and she knew that looking presentable was important at W&H, particularly for its young female attorneys.

She accepted it as part of the corporate culture at the firm, and was happy to play the game for all she was worth. She knew that when Nathan looked at her, job performance came in somewhere, for him, after the fit of her skirt and the sheen of her hair. But that was okay—it was an advantage she had over the male attorneys, and she'd never been one to shy away from pressing any advantage. Sometimes, though, Lilah found herself missing Holland Manners. Holland had been evil—no one climbed the ladder at W&H as high as he had without that prerequisite, which Lilah didn't necessarily consider a character flaw—but he'd been fair, she thought, in his estimation of people's abilities. It was too bad he'd been one of the casualties, along with an assortment of the firm's other players, of Darla and Drusilla's wine-cellar banquet. Not that being dead had entirely removed him from the Wolfram & Hart employee roster—he still served a purpose, but he wouldn't be showing up at company picnics anymore.

The conference room door opened behind her, startling Lilah out of her reverie. She turned and set her cup down on the teak surface of the conference table, next to a pad and pen she'd already placed there, and watched Nathan Reed come in. *The man is all head,* she thought, not for the first time. She knew that wasn't literally true—and at Wolfram & Hart, it was quite likely that at some point in the past or future, there had been or would be an associate who did fit that literal description—but the impression that he made upon entering a room was made almost totally with his head. He was bald, his pate a smooth, round surface that looked like a pale bowling ball. His face was owlish, eyes lost behind heavy-framed black glasses, nose jutting beakishly between the lenses. His body was just a man's body in an expensive black suit, but his head made a statement.

"Hello, Nathan," she said pleasantly.

"Lilah, good morning," he replied, full of good cheer, it seemed. Then he turned away from her and held the door for a second person to pass through. This person made a statement of an entirely different kind.

She was stunning. Lilah doubted if there had ever been a room this woman had entered since puberty in which all eyes hadn't automatically turned her way. Anyone who didn't want this woman, she guessed, probably wanted to be her.

The woman's clothing was simple, even a little inappropriate for a high-level conference at a law firm. Under a tan leather jacket she wore a white silk shirt, clingy in the right places and open to the fourth button, displaying an amount of décolletage that would be fine at a nightclub at midnight, Lilah thought, but seemed out of place here. The shirt was tucked into faded blue jeans, which were themselves tucked into knee-high black leather boots with high heels and pointed toes. On her wrist she wore a silver bracelet with turquoise and red-coral stones, and around her neck was a leather choker with Indian-style beadwork.

But whether she wore a designer gown or nothing at all, it wouldn't be the clothes that made this woman stand out. Her hair was pitch black, with the kind of fullness and luster that shampoo models only dreamed about. She wore it pulled back at the sides and loosely knotted at the back of her head. Even from the front, Lilah could see it sway behind her, at about the level of the small of her back. Her skin had a glowing olive tone, flawless and rich. Her eyes were huge and dark, with just the slightest hint of an almond shape, and when she regarded Lilah there seemed to be a mixture of good humor, empathy, and curiosity in them.

A lot of weight for two eyes to carry, Lilah thought. But the woman pulled it off. Her nose was small and perfectly formed, and her lips were full and exquisite.

As she stepped toward Lilah, her lips parted, revealing even, white teeth and a smile that begged to be returned. She held out a hand, and Lilah took it. The woman's grip was friendly but her flesh was cold.

"Hello, Lilah. It's a pleasure to meet you. I'm Marianna Escobar."

As they shook hands, Nathan made himself comfortable at the head of the table. "Thanks for meeting us at this hour," he said, as if Lilah had had any choice in the matter. "I'm afraid it was necessary. Marianna is a vampire," he explained. "A vampire with a very interesting proposition."

"Let's hear it," Lilah said. She had known Marianna was a vamp the moment they'd clasped hands. "I'm always interested in a good proposition."

The three of them sat down at the conference table. Marianna moved, Lilah noted, with quiet grace and confidence. Of course, if she was a vampire, then she was likely much older than the twenty-five or so that Lilah had originally assumed, and could have had plenty of time to gain self-confidence. She sat with her back straight, her hands resting lightly on the tabletop.

"I have come to Los Angeles in search of something quite rare," she began. "And I believe I've found it, with the help of an associate."

"Marianna has a Thoqual," Nathan interjected. Lilah nodded—a Thoqual, she knew, was a demon whose particular gift was for locating particular individuals, whether by smell, aura, or unique energy signature. Thoquals were born with a skill for moving about surreptitiously that would make ninjas jealous, and between that ability and the heightened senses that enabled them to sniff out their quarry even through solid walls, they were unbeatable when it came to finding people.

"Yes," Marianna said, with a pleasant smile at Nathan. "And this Thoqual has confirmed the whereabouts of the individual I've been looking for. But her location has raised some . . . well, let's say, issues."

"Which are what?" Lilah asked politely.

"She's in prison, for one thing," Marianna replied. "And in researching her case a little, I discovered that there is a preexisting relationship with Wolfram and Hart. Now, I know Nathan only superficially—we have a couple of mutual friends, and we've attended the same functions from time to time. But I didn't want to do anything that might interfere with whatever plans Wolfram and Hart might have for this individual, so I brought my proposition to Nathan."

"And I thought it sounded grand, just grand," Nathan said, uncharacteristically effusive. "And like something you would do well to get involved with."

Lilah didn't like the way they were dancing around the identity of Marianna's quarry, but Nathan was her boss. She thought there might be a way to work through the subtleties, though. "May I ask who this person is?"

"Her name is Faith," Marianna replied simply.

"Faith," Lilah repeated. "The Slayer."

"That's right."

"And what do you want with her?"

Marianna held Lilah's gaze. "I want to get her out of jail."

Is she joking? Or insane? Lilah wondered. She turned to Nathan. "What an interesting concept," she said.

"Hear her out," Nathan urged. "I think you'll like this."

"But Nathan . . . we have no reason to want the Slayer out of jail. As long as she's there, she's out of our hair. She's not causing us any trouble. Remember, she double-crossed us. The only reason I'd want her sprung is if we were going to kill her, and even that would be easier with her behind bars. In fact—" She stopped, a different angle occurring to her. "Is that it? Are you going to kill her?"

"Not immediately," Marianna answered. "But soon enough, yes. The Slayer will be killed."

"Well, then . . . you're right, I do like it," Lilah said. "That part, at least." She tried hard to keep an open mind, but the idea of springing Faith ran so contrary to her instincts it was hard. After all the trouble Faith had caused Wolfram & Hart, she wouldn't mind seeing Faith rot in there forever.

"You have to face facts, Lilah," Marianna said. "Faith is

young, she's strong, she's in good health. According to all reports she's been a model prisoner since she went into the system. And our prisons are so overcrowded, authorities have been releasing convicts in droves. Faith will certainly come up for parole, maybe sooner than any of us expect. Her record and her physical attractiveness will sway the parole board, and she'll be released. When she comes out, she'll still be young enough, and she'll still have her Slayer abilities, and she'll definitely have a grudge against Wolfram and Hart."

"A very likely scenario, I'm afraid," Nathan put in.

"My proposal is to get her out early. Exercise some of the pull your firm has over judges and prison officials, and get her released into my custody. I guarantee to have her out of Los Angeles within the hour. She'll be in no position to seek revenge on you or to interfere with your business in any way. Within a week she'll be dead. No more Faith, no more worries about what happens when she eventually does get out on her own."

"There's a certain appeal to that," Lilah admitted.

"I have an island," Marianna continued. "San Teodor. It's off the coast, part of the Channel Islands. Occasionally I sponsor hunting parties there."

"I've been to a couple," Nathan said with a big smile. "They're great fun."

"My specialty is the exotic hunt," Marianna continued. "We've hunted humans, werewolves, demons of various stripes. But one species we've never been able to arrange—"

"Oh my God, you want to have a Slayer hunt!" Lilah exclaimed.

"Exactly."

"Which requires freeing the most dangerous woman in Los Angeles."

"Excuse me," Marianna said sweetly, "but I believe that honor goes to me."

"Lilah," Nathan cut in, "if—no, *when*—Faith gets out, she'll be gunning for us. There's no question about that. Marianna's way, Faith is removed from our lives altogether. No more Faith, no more worries about what happens when she's freed. Or decides she wants to escape."

"Okay," Lilah agreed. "You've got a point." She fiddled anxiously with her pen. *This is crazy,* she thought. *There are so many things that could go wrong. It's never good to intentionally upset the apple cart when there's a Slayer involved.*

But she had been the one who had recruited Faith in the first place, after the Slayer had gone rogue and escaped Sunnydale, and Buffy's wrath, by catching the first bus to anywhere. She'd hoped to point Faith at Angel and pull her trigger, but the stunt had backfired. Now Faith and Angel seemed to have become buddies, and Lilah had spent many a sleepless night wondering at what point Faith would decide she'd had enough prison life and break out. At that point, Lilah figured, her own neck would be Faith's first target.

Besides which, Nathan wouldn't have brought Marianna here if he hadn't been sold on the idea, and it never hurt to climb on board the boss's bandwagon.

"But even if it works, wouldn't Faith's death would just activate another Slayer?" Lilah inquired. *A good attorney considers all the angles.*

"Not necessarily a problem for us," Nathan countered.

"We don't know where that Slayer would be located. Buffy Summers is still running around down in Sunnydale, and she doesn't cause us any trouble. Faith happened to end up here, but that doesn't mean her replacement would."

"Still . . ." The idea of a new Slayer, not confined behind bars, made Lilah extremely nervous. He seemed to sense that she was teetering.

"Let me sweeten the pot, Lilah," he said. "We have a couple of clients. I think you know Cutter Arlington, right?"

She nodded. A long-time client, whose annual billings topped a million dollars. He'd spilled a glass of sherry on her at a party once and tried to dab it up with his own handkerchief. "We've met."

"Cutter and his friend DeWitt Baker, whose financial contribution to the firm this year will actually exceed Cutter's, thanks to a particularly nasty product liability case, are both very keen on this Slayer hunt idea. They've been to a couple of Marianna's earlier hunts, and found them great fun indeed. After Marianna approached me with this idea, I made some phone calls, and found that both men would pay a premium—a big one—to be included in an adventure of this magnitude. Marianna and I have arrived at a revenue sharing agreement. If this goes off as planned, the firm stands to benefit in a direct and significant way. And that, need I remind you, will be remembered at bonus time."

Lilah smiled at Marianna, looking for any sign of the vampire within and not finding it. "Okay, then," she said. "I'm in. I'd only point out one thing, which I'm sure you've already considered, Nathan."

"What's that?"

"If Angel and his friends find out what we're up to, they'll make trouble. That's guaranteed."

"Then we'll simply have to make sure they don't, won't we?" Nathan asked.

And that, Lilah thought, *is the kind of thing they had in mind when they coined the phrase "easier said than done."*

That went well, Marianna Escobar thought. She had expected no different, of course. Marianna had learned, long ago, the art of persuasion. This time she had relied on one of her favorite techniques, that of letting someone else expend most of the effort for her. Nathan Reed couldn't do all the necessary work alone—he'd need a team on a project this complex, and that team had to be sold on the benefits. But by getting Nathan on board early, most of her job was done. And Nathan—being male—was ridiculously easy to manipulate. A few more-than-friendly glances, an occasional touch on the hand or the cheek, and most men fell over themselves trying to give her whatever they thought she needed. Nathan had been no different.

In retrospect, that's what had drawn her to Chaz, at first. Chaz had been her husband, her soul mate, the love of her life. By the time they met, he had amassed a fortune. He had started with some family seed money but had quickly multiplied that many times over. Chaz Escobar had been young, rich, virile, and so handsome it almost hurt to look at him.

And when he saw Marianna for the first time, he hadn't bothered to spare her a second glance.

She was amazed—first, that such a man existed, and

second, that for the first time in her memory, she was in the presence of someone who might attract as many stares as she did. Or more, she thought. His clothing choices were flashier, while still elegant, and drew the eye. They first ran across each other at a party on Ibiza, a real beautiful people, jet-set affair. Everyone had been talking about Chaz, and Marianna had discredited the obvious exaggerations she was hearing. But then she saw him, from the other side of a ballroom almost as big as a soccer arena, and realized that words hadn't done him justice. She had made her way across the vast space and introduced herself.

"A pleasure," he had said. He'd smiled and bowed gracefully, kissed her hand, and then turned away to continue a conversation he'd been having about a big-game hunting trip in South Africa. Marianna couldn't remember the last time she'd been ignored in favor of a conversation about tigers and rhinos, most likely because there hadn't been one.

So she had done the only thing she could—she joined the conversation by bringing up an expedition she'd been on, from which she'd brought home a full-sized polar bear.

Chaz Escobar paid attention to her then. By that night, they were lovers. Within the year, they were wed. For their honeymoon they took a safari in Kenya, collecting ivory that they smuggled off the continent and into the home they were building on San Teodor.

That had been in 1969. By their tenth anniversary Marianna had been killed.

The hotel was quiet when Angel got back, except for the occasional clacking of computer keys. Very occasional.

Cordelia sat in the office alone, the light shining on her hair, and he thought, *She really is beautiful*. He felt a stirring . . . then reminded himself *Hey, Cordy . . .* and the stirring remained.

Hmmm.

He let the feeling sink in. *Okay, it's because she looks nice today, new clothes, whatever.*

And her perfume . . .

He walked up behind her, telling himself he wanted to see what she was working on. *She sure as hell can't type.*

"Hi," he said.

"Gaaah!" Cordelia shrieked. She slammed her hands down onto the keyboard, sending a nonsense message to the screen.

He was abashed. "Sorry, I . . ."

She raised her eyes to heaven in that I-so-suffer way and huffed. "You thought, 'there sits a girl who hasn't actually had her heart stop today, so maybe I can finish the job.'" She swiveled her chair around and crossed her arms decisively over her chest.

The boat-neck top formed a V, and Angel cleared his throat as softly as he could and tried to look elsewhere.

"I was trying not to scare you."

She tried to keep her face stern, but he knew her well enough to see that she wasn't really angry at him. She had a rep to maintain, after all—if not as the Queen of Mean, than as the Princess of Quite a Few Comebacks.

"You did a lousy job of it. Maybe if you tried not to pay me the way you tried not to scare me, I'd be able to put a little something away for a rainy day."

"Hey, your compensation is a matter to take up with

Wes, not me," Angel reminded her, giving her something to push against, rather enjoying this fencing match. "Out of my hands, remember?"

"Yeah, I know." Now she actually smiled at him, competing with the lights in the room. "I just figure it doesn't hurt to get in the occasional dig where I can. How's Faith?" Her tone went flat, as if she didn't really care one way or the other. Angel knew that was her wary, unhappy voice. The fact that she went back to the hunting and pecking served to underscore how neutral she was trying to be. But she had major issues with Faith.

Not that I blame her in the least.

"She seems okay. She asked about you and Wes."

"Because she so cares about us."

"I think she does," Angel told her. "But I still don't know what your vision was about," he added. "She doesn't seem to be in any particular danger."

"She's in danger," Cordelia insisted. "It may not be immediately obvious, but it's there, or I wouldn't have had the vision. I may not always understand them, but I'm pretty sure The Powers That Be don't hit me with them just for giggles."

She got up from the computer with some papers in her hand, moved to a filing cabinet, and started cramming them into folders without really looking at them. Her forehead was pinched; he figured she was in pain, and he was sorry.

"I told her to keep her eyes open," Angel said. "And I gave her Wesley's protective charm."

"Well, the headache is still with me," Cordy replied, slamming the file cabinet drawer, then wincing at the noise. "So the danger is still out there."

43

"Have you been having any luck with the research?" Angel asked, giving the computer screen another glance. She had the "Demons Demons Demons" database up. He highlighted "Lurker Demons" and scanned through the names. *So many demons, so much time.*

"I remembered a couple of details about what I saw stalking her," Cordelia explained, coming over to him. "Big, scaly brown skin, eyeballs with red irises and no eyelids. Not much, but I gave it to Wesley and he thought he'd go talk to Lorne, see if maybe he's seen anything like that lurking around Caritas."

"Good idea."

The Host's karaoke bar had been trashed by their return from Pylea, which had deposited Angel's trusty '67 GTX right in the middle of the bar. But Lorne had spent the last couple of weeks rebuilding, and the night before had been a kind of grand reopening. Just about every demon in L.A. had been present, it seemed. If the thing Cordelia described was really in town, chances were good that Lorne or one of his customers knew about it.

"You finding anything?" Angel asked her, gesturing to the screen as she stood beside him. Her perfume was scented with vanilla.

Buffy wore vanilla, he thought with a pang. *It was her favorite scent.*

"Just enough to really creep me out," she said, shivering, even though it wasn't particularly cold in the room. She looked genuinely disturbed just remembering what she had seen.

She reached around him and tapped the keys. "I was following some links, trying to get a line of some kind on the demon. They were leading me to some sites I haven't been to before—kind of weird ones, to be honest. But I figured, hey, when you're looking for something you've never seen before, it doesn't hurt to look in places you've never been before, right?"

"Makes sense." Angel perched himself on the corner of the desk, arms folded over his chest. Her body radiated heat, making him shift self-consciously. Cordelia was oblivious.

"So I was reading about some particularly revolting demonic mating behavior when I got this Instant Message. It freaked me out because it's in a demon language or some weird foreign language, I don't know what. It's not from anybody on my buddy list, I can tell you that. Here, I saved it for when Wes got back."

Angel figured he must have looked a little crestfallen, because she quickly added, "Or you, of course."

"Of course," he echoed. *She means Wes.*

He looked at the IM she pointed to on her computer screen. Her "weird foreign language" was Latin, and he told her so. "I'm a little rusty," he admitted. "But it looks like a ritualized greeting. It could even be automatically generated, and not written by any individual. Maybe it goes out to anyone who looks at the page you were on."

"What does it say?" Cordelia asked, frowning. "Latin, huh. Y'know, they had a Latin club at school. I figured it was a bigger haven for geeks than the chess club, and you know how *they* are." She sighed. "Who would have thought I'd ever need Latin?" Then she shrugged. "Hey. I don't. I have *you*."

"It's a bunch of nonsense," Angel interpreted, as he made his way through the declensions, remembering his old schoolmaster and how much he had hated the man. Master O'Reilly spent more time slamming his ruler down on Angel's—then Liam—knuckles than he ever did on the lesson.

"Like I said, a lot of vague, polite greetings, well wishes for the health of you and your family and all your heirs, and so on."

"That's not so creepy," Cordelia said, sounding surprised. "It's kind of nice."

"Here's the creepy part," Angel said, scrolling downward. He didn't like this at all, but tried to hide his concern so he wouldn't upset Cordelia any more than necessary. "I can't get the context exactly, but it says something about the Beast of the First Blood." He paused. "Maybe we do need to wait for Wesley."

"Told you." She sounded triumphant, but her voice was soft. He glanced at her, to find her rubbing her temples. "Sorry," she said. "Vision hangovers don't go away with Tylenol."

He tried to hide his alarm; she had enough to contend with without knowing where he was going with his questions. If he was right about what he suspected, Faith wasn't the only one who needed to stay on DefCon 4.

"Cordy, what were you searching that sent you here?" he asked carefully.

She gestured to the screen. "Mostly I stayed in the Demons Demons Demons database," she said after a moment's pause to reflect. "Like I said, running a search on the eyes, since that's the most unique characteristic. One thing kind of led to another. There was a link to something called the Book of the Interregnum. While I was trying to see what that was, the IM came on my screen. I didn't answer—I was so freaked out by it, I just saved it and logged off."

The words sent a chill down his spine. They would send a chill down any vampire's spine.

"The Book of the Interregnum," Angel repeated somberly, thinking, *This is worse than I thought.* "Great. Cordy, I think logging off was probably the best thing you could have done."

CHAPTER THREE

Actually, Angel mused, *there are worse things Cordelia could have run across online.* Angel had heard, for instance, that there was an active Internet *Three's Company* fandom. But short of that, he couldn't think of many things Cordy might have linked to that were more dangerous than the Book of the Interregnum.

He moved away from the desk, wondering how much to tell her. He didn't want to frighten her, but Cordelia was one person he had no luck lying to, or even simply varnishing the truth. She was not one to mince words, and she could cut through deliberate vagueness with that razor-sharp mind of hers faster than a Sholirt demon could eviscerate a camel.

"What is it?" she asked him. When he didn't answer

right away, she shifted her weight from one hip to the other and prompted, "Angel, I don't like the look on your face, even though you basically have three expressions and only one of them remotely resembles a smile. What did I do wrong?"

"Nothing," he said, trying to sound reassuring. *It's not what you did,* he thought. *It's what you might have done— attention you may have called to yourself.*

"That's not what your expression tells me," Cordelia replied. "Your lips say 'nothing' but your eyes say 'oh, crap.'"

And as usual, she's read me right.

Angel crossed the office and grabbed a chair, which he rolled back to the computer. At his gesture, Cordelia sat back down in her chair. She took a breath and lifted her chin as if bracing herself for very bad news. Angel had to admire her courage; Cordelia never, ever backed down from a fight, or backed away from the truth.

If I'm going to tell the story, he thought, *I might as well get comfortable.*

Apparently she realized what he was doing. She looked at him and made a little face, scrunching up her nose and pursing her lips together. "Long story, huh?"

"Long one," he confirmed.

Then he heard footsteps moving down the stairs and across the lobby floor. He listened for a moment, recognized them, and waited for Fred's cautious approach.

"I love stories," she said, hovering in the doorway. "Can I listen too?"

Angel nodded his head, remembering when she had been his only link to sanity . . . and to the self he thought of as Angel. Back on Pylea, she had seen the AngelBeast within him and treated him with compassion, shielding him and protecting him despite the hideous monstrosity he had presented to her.

"Might as well," Angel invited her.

Fred started to sit on the floor, her back against a desk. "There are plenty of chairs, Fred," Cordy pointed out.

"I'm fine like this," Fred explained with a shy smile. "I'm not really so used to chairs yet. Though I am kind of liking sleeping in a bed again, with a pillow. Pillows are one of life's pleasures that you take for granted until you don't have one for a while." She scooted around for a moment until she was comfortable. "What's the story about?"

"It's about a convent," Angel said. "Or at least it starts there."

"Angel's always had a thing for convents," Cordy interjected. "That whole 'sacred and profane' business, I think—"

"This'll go faster, Cordelia, if you skip the editorial asides," he pointed out.

"Sorry." She settled back in her chair, cupping her palms around her knee as she crossed her legs. She had on strappy sandals, and she wore brilliant red toenail polish.

And I'm so preoccupied with that because . . . ?

"Go on," she urged.

"As I was saying. There was this convent—this is back in the old days, Fred, when I was Angelus—"

"Before you got your soul back," Fred interrupted, eyes wide as a child's about to hear a good bedtime story.

He gave her a confirming nod. "That's right. Anyway, Drusilla was a novice in the convent. Darla, who was my sire, had pointed her out to me in the street, telling me that she had the sight."

"By 'sight,'" Cordelia interpreted for Fred, "Darla meant that she's loony as a bedbug."

"Drusilla was always a little bit off, and I pushed her over the edge of sanity," Angel agreed. "But at the time, I guess I wasn't all that sane either." His voice dropped as old memories, and old guilts, took hold. "I made Drusilla—turned her into a vampire. Which made her Darla's granddaughter, in a way."

"This vampire stuff is all kind of incestuous, isn't it?" Fred asked, looking thoughtful.

"More than I like to think about," Cordy drawled, grimacing. "I mean, eeew. It's Chinatown, Jake."

Angel sighed. "I'm going to bed when the sun comes up whether or not I'm done with the story."

"Sorry, Angel. I won't interrupt anymore." Cordy mimed zipping her lip.

Fred copied her. The girls settled themselves for a long tale.

After taking a few moments to collect himself, Angel caught the rhythm of his story again. In the days of his youth, the old men—the town bards, as it were—had told wonderful, engrossing stories all in the Irish lilt, lacing their words with Gaelic even though the English had strictly forbidden the native tongue of the Irish. Angel had spent many an hour in a tavern on a winter's night, listening to the old men spin their tales.

"Now, in the convent with Drusilla—though I didn't know it at the time—was a young, innocent woman named Mary Kelly. She was, I believe, not much saner than Dru, if at all."

"I think it's all those women living together that makes 'em go wacko," Cordelia said. "I mean, can you imagine the competition for the bathroom? Plus, only one guy, and he's a *priest* . . ."

Angel cleared his throat. She moved her shoulders apologetically, said nothing, and raised her brows, indicating that she was happy to resume listening.

"I only figured all this out years later, when I heard the stories about her and put two and two together. After Drusilla became a vampire, one of the first people she made was little Mary Kelly. Dru was so new to the whole vamp thing, I don't think she even knew what she had done."

"You didn't really know either," Fred said loyally.

He made a gesture of protest with his hand; he wasn't going to let himself off the hook "Oh, I knew. I saw an innocent young girl terrified of her gift, and I savored every mental torture I visited on her. I tormented her with a song in my heart."

Fred looked unconvinced. She leaned forward earnestly and said, "Darla found Dru for you, just like she found that Gypsy girl too. She pushed you into proving yourself to her. That you could match her evil for evil. She may as well have driven Dru crazy herself. Right?"

"No, not right." He began to pace, the conversation growing more difficult, at least for him. "Fred, inside . . . I am evil. You saw what I am."

Fred murmured, "I saw what part of you *looks* like. And that's all I saw, Angel."

He was touched. His face must have softened, for Fred glowed at him, and there was a single moment such as there had been on Pylea, where he knew that she completely, utterly accepted him. It was an amazing notion.

"Darla did the same thing to you that you did to Dru," she continued, her voice gentle. "She manipulated you."

"It doesn't matter. Dru was human when I drove her insane," Angel declared flatly.

Fred nodded gently; and it was clear that though she was troubled, it was also clear that she understood . . . and still accepted him.

"Dru and I left, without knowing about Mary, and there was no one to show her the ropes, teach her about what she had become. I think it pushed her over the edge. She left the convent—after feasting on the mother superior, I've heard—and eventually renamed herself Benedicta, Speaker of Blessings."

"No delusions of grandeur or anything," Cordy put in.

"As Mary Kelly," Angel continued, choosing to ignore Cordy, "she had always been interested in religion. This interest continued when she became Benedicta. Except that instead of practicing the religion she had been trained in, she decided to form her own."

"They always do," Cordelia said to Fred. "The nutcases with big egos, I mean. Next thing you know, they're charging for weddings and funerals. We have a lot of this sort of thing in California."

"Only, this was Victorian England, right?" Fred asked Cordelia.

She shrugged. "Vegas, Victorian England. They all want a piece of the religion pie."

"So, this religion," Fred asked Angel, "it had to be about vampires and stuff, right?"

Angel nodded. "It was pretty nuts—at least, that's what the vampires who didn't join said. A mixture of Kabalistic rituals and blasphemous texts culled from all over the world. She was very big on Latin." He pointed almost unconsciously to the computer screen. "Calls herself the Mother Infernal."

"See? Grandeur," Cordelia cut in. She motioned for Angel to continue.

He did.

"She got together with a druid named Bran Cahir and made him her High Priest."

"And there's the priest thing again," Cordelia said knowledgeably. "Can't leave well enough and leave guys out of it. They always have to have some priest or sorcerer or something." Then she winced and said, "Listening. I must have had too many lattes while I was researching. Sorry."

"Maybe you're nervous because, well, I have a feeling this isn't just a nice story," Fred said.

"So. Priest," Cordelia said to Angel.

Angel wearily pressed on. "He's supposedly centuries old, got some kind of magickal way to keep himself alive that doesn't involve being a vampire. Word is they have legions of devoted nuns and acolytes, many, but not all, of whom are vampires. While they were building up, they traveled the world collecting bits and pieces from hundreds of religions and cults and threading all that into their own religion. Benedicta called the hodge-podge the 'Mysteries' and that became, unofficially at least, the name that was applied to her religion."

"Like in *Shakespeare in Love*," Cordelia offered helpfully. "'It's a mystery.'"

"Missed that one," Fred said. "I was still a fugitive back then."

"I have it on DVD," Cordelia told her. "I'll bring it in for you."

Angel doggedly pressed on. "So if you hear anyone refer to the 'Mysteries of Benedicta,' that's what they're talking about."

"And yet, oddly, I've never once heard anyone make that reference," Cordelia said, looking at him. "Imagine that."

"You've led a protected life," Angel countered.

She flared. "Right. *You* get pregnant with demon spawn and then tell me that again."

Fred's eyes grew big and round as she followed the sparring between her new friends, but she remained silent.

Angel could feel the pull of dawn on his body and ignored all Cordy's barbs in favor of finishing his expository narrative.

"Anyway, Benedicta continues adding to her Mysteries, even today. I've run across her path once or twice—never encountered her, just seen the aftermath. The story is, she has spent many years looking for a book—"

"Let me guess," Cordelia interrupted. "The Book of the Interregnum."

"That's right," Angel said.

"Oh, dear." Fred looked frightened.

"And we have a winner," Cordelia said unhappily.

Angel tried to keep her calm. "I've never actually believed in the Book of the Interregnum. As far as I know, it's a myth, like the Holy Grail."

"Or Santa Claus," Fred observed, "or healthy fast food." She was a brilliant woman, but there was a definite childlike quality to her, a sense of wonder that Angel found appealing. He was glad they'd been able to bring her back from Pylea—and glad he hadn't beheaded her there when he had been ordered to.

"Not so much a myth," Angel said. "But that's a story for

another time. According to the legends, if the Book is read aloud, it will summon the Beast of the First Blood."

"That's what that IM mentioned, isn't it?" Cordy was clearly getting creeped out. Angel wished he could spare her all this lengthy explanation; all it was going to lead to was that she might have stumbled onto something very, very bad. "Beast. Blood. I'm not thinking this is a link to a dating service."

"The Beast of the First Blood is—again, according to legend—the creature whose blood is considered to be the origin of the vampire demon blood that transforms dead human beings into hosts for vampiric demons."

There was a pause. Cordelia looked completely shocked, and Fred was taken aback as well. Angel thought about all he had heard about the Beast; it was like the vampire's version of the boogeyman, a story bandied about but not given credence . . . unless one was a cult follower of Benedicta. Angel had met many of Benedicta's followers in his travels. Even for vampires they were uncommonly vicious and very, very savage in their hunting methods.

"O . . . kay." Cordelia tugged at her boat-neck top as if it were too tight. Her cheeks were pale. She was not a happy lady.

"Summon the Beast from where, Angel?" Fred asked anxiously. "Not like Tarzana or someplace, right?"

Angel shook his head. He had no clue. For all he knew, Tarzana might be the profane ground where the Beast could enter this dimension. Or the Hellmouth in Sunnydale. Or the Rite Aid on Wilshire.

"Some other dimension, I guess—nobody's quite sure where, probably because his very existence is pretty much just a collection of stories at this point," Angel supplied, trying to keep them both calm. "The theory is that he was sent away from this dimension by ancient priests, because he was virtually impossible to kill. Oh, and one other thing."

"What other thing?" Cordy inquired, clearly worried by his attempt to downplay it.

Angel rose from his chair and paced the floor for a moment, delaying his answer. He didn't want to say it because saying it somehow would make it seem more real. And he really, really didn't want it to be real.

"The one thing?" Cordelia echoed, her voice growing shrill. "Don't we already have enough things?"

Angel stopped pacing. He faced her.

"Something that is impossible, for all other vampires— he can mate with vampires, and produce offspring."

She and Fred traded glances. Fred balled her fists and placed them against her chest, making herself very small in her little space on the floor.

"But you always said that's impossible," Cordelia challenged him, raising her chin. Her eyes shone with fear.

"I just said that. Weren't you listening?" He didn't mean to snap. *But I'm afraid too.*

"He's the exception that proves the rule," Fred put in. "This Beast, I mean." She was flushing, and Angel knew she was thinking about him and the mating, and he felt badly because that would never happen; and as for mating with anyone, well, he wouldn't go there.

Angel sighed. "Right."

"So what does this Benedicta want with the Beast?" Cordy asked. "Some kind of doomsday scenario? Another end of the world prophecy cult?"

Have you been listening to any of this, Cordelia? he

almost retorted, but he knew the tension in the room was rising because, well, the tension in the room was rising. He smelled their fear, and he was reacting to it.

He said as calmly as he could, "Benedicta is a vampire. She wants to mate with it. She believes that by doing so, she can create a new, more powerful race of vampires—with herself, naturally, as its queen, spiritual leader, whatever."

Cordelia smoothed back her hair and hugged her arms across her chest once more. "Well, you said she was crazy, right?"

"She is," Angel confirmed. "At least, according to all reports." A beat, and then he said, "But that doesn't mean she's not right."

"Is she?" Cordelia asked querulously.

Angel knew that now was not the time to pull punches. He said, "If the Book is real, and if it will truly summon the Beast of the First Blood, and if the stories about the Beast's abilities are true, then there shouldn't be any reason that her plan wouldn't work."

"And that would be a bad thing." She turned to Fred as if Fred needed that made clear.

Cordelia, mistress of understatement, Angel thought wryly. "That would be a really bad thing. You've seen how powerful vampires are to begin with. And they—we—don't have a lot of natural predators, except for the Slayer."

"Slayers," Fred corrected. "Buffy and Faith." She sounded pleased at her retention of information.

"Right now, yes," Angel said to her. "But only one who's really active."

"That being the one who is not a crazed psychopath," Cordelia put in.

"Right." Fred got that. "And there's us, and a few other vampire hunters scattered around. If we were up against vamps who are stronger than Angel by a factor of who knows how much—and if a result of the mating between Benedicta and the Beast is that their offspring can also mate and produce young . . ."

Cordelia moaned as she looked at Angel and Fred. "Then how long will it be before the earth is completely overrun by these things? Who'd be able to stop them?"

"I'd give it five generations," Fred mused, cocking her head as she did the math. "Maybe a little less, depending on length of gestation, how many young each one can reasonably have, how quickly they reach maturity, and a few other unknowns. And keeping in mind that the natural mortality rate is zero."

Angel looked at her with surprise. He tended to forget how she translated almost every situation into a mathematical formula, which her mind could process almost instantly.

"Five generations. That's a long time," Cordelia said a little more brightly.

"To a mortal, yes," Angel pointed out. "To a vampire, an immortal, five generations is nothing. It's how long you'd wait to get a table at The Palm."

Cordelia was silent for a moment, speechless. *That doesn't happen often,* he mused.

Finally she covered her nose and mouth with her cupped hands, as if hyperventilating. *Or praying,* Angel thought. *Either response might be appropriate.*

After a moment she pulled her hands away from her face. "So that's what I fell into the middle of, trying to track down whatever it was I saw in the Faith vision."

"I'm afraid so," Angel replied. "I'm afraid that you've aroused the attention of one of Benedicta's acolytes, since they'd be keeping a close watch on any sites that so much as mention the Book of the Interregnum."

"That's pretty creepy," Cordy said.

"It could be worse," Angel went on.

"How?"

"You might have caught the notice of Benedicta herself."

Well that, Wesley thought, *was a complete waste of time*. He glanced at his watch. It was almost three in the morning, which explained why he felt so tired. *And quite a bit of time, at that*, he amended.

Caritas had been packed. Not as crowded as it had been for Lorne's grand reopening, but a full house nonetheless. Lorne had been in his element—the green-skinned, hook-nosed, lantern-jawed demon played up the Host angle for all he was worth, constantly circulating among the tables, prodding demons to refill their drinks, introducing the karaoke participants and performing readings for those who asked. Lorne was an anagogic demon, which meant that he could read the auras of those who sang for him. It was a talent that kept him in high demand.

But as a result, it had been hard for him to break away for a private chat with Wesley. When the ex-Watcher had first arrived, Lorne had asked him if he was here on an emergency matter, and Wes had told him that he could wait awhile. Lorne had nodded, relieved, and then Wes had been forced to sit around waiting for almost an hour—listening to some truly awful singing, like the Bittle demon sisters whose version of "Muskrat Love" left

Wesley longing for the mellifluous tones of Captain & Tennille, as unlikely as that seemed. He hadn't even known that Bittles could have triplets, or that any creature could have a voice so grating and still survive to adulthood.

After a wait that seemed equivalent to Angel's hundreds of years in Hell, Lorne was finally able to break away and join Wesley at his table, which was blue glass that glowed from within. The Host—clad tonight in an iridescent red suit with a green shirt that almost matched his skin, set off nicely by a yellow silk tie—liked to be surrounded by color. Having been to Lorne's home dimension, Wesley knew why. Color, and music, were in short supply in Pylea.

"What do you think?" he asked Wesley.

"The place looks great," Wes answered. There were brilliant hues everywhere, from the underlit bottles behind the bar, filled with a rainbow assortment of liquids, to the glowing tables, to the demonic clientele itself. Caritas was a sanctuary, which meant that any grudges or feuds had to be left at the door. No one could attack a demon inside.

"Yeah, it does, doesn't it? And my regulars, bless their hearts—well, the ones who have hearts, anyway—have been so supportive."

"That's great," Wesley said.

"But you didn't come to talk about my balance sheet, did you?" Lorne asked. "What's going on?"

"It's Cordelia," Wesley explained. "She's had another vision—immediately on top of the last one. It's really wearing her down, I'm afraid."

"Poor kid," Lorne sympathized. "What can I do?"

"Well . . ." Wesley turned his highball glass slowly on the tabletop. "This one was rather vague. She saw what she believes to be a demon, threatening Faith—"

"Slayer junior?"

"She'd slay *you* if she heard that," Wesley said with a smile. "But yes, her. The thing is, she couldn't see much detail at all on the demon—certainly not enough for us to even get close to making a positive identification."

Lorne took that in, looked intrigued, also a little smug. "So you thought you'd come to Poppa—the guy who knows every demon in the book on a first name basis."

"Exactly."

"What's she got?" Lorne asked. He glanced at the bar, then at the stage—mercifully empty, for the moment. "I can spare a few to listen to the description."

"It won't take long," Wesley said. "Brown scaly skin, eyes with no lids, but red irises. Oh, and it's rather large."

Lorne looked at him expectantly. "Go on," he urged.

"That's it, I'm afraid. That's all she remembers."

"That's it?"

"As I said, not much."

"You weren't kidding, brother," Lorne said. He turned in his chair and pointed at a demon who sat at the bar, sipping from a glass that steamed like dry ice. "Look—brown scales. Not a little guy, either."

"No, I can see that."

"The Bittle sisters? I saw you cringing. Lidless eyes, red irises."

"So what you're saying is—"

Lorne spun back around and leaned his elbows on the table, cutting Wesley off midsentence. "What I'm saying is, you've got nothing. It's like me coming to you and saying, 'I'm looking for a specific individual, somewhere in Los Angeles. I think it has blond hair, and maybe blue eyes. I don't know if it's a male or a female. Think you can point it out?"

"You don't know any type of demon with that particular combination."

"I know a hundred of them. More. That's as common as it gets, in the demon world. They don't all get skin like mine, I can tell you." He turned his profile to Wesley, as if expecting admiration.

"I see," Wesley said.

"Look, you know I'd help if I could," Lorne added. "You've just got to give me something more to work with."

"If she can remember anything else, then, I'll get in touch."

"You do that. In the meantime, if I hear about anything, anyone messing around with Faith or anything, I'll let you know."

"I'd appreciate that," Wesley said. "We all would."

He had left then, calling Gunn, who had dropped him off and was supposed to give him a lift back to the hotel after he did some research of his own. Gunn had hit the streets earlier and drawn a blank, but he'd said he had a few more sources he wanted to check with.

Twenty minutes after making the call, Gunn showed up, driving Wes's car, and stopped at the street corner where Wesley waited. "Hop in, English," he said.

Wesley hopped.

"Anything?"

"I'm afraid not," Wesley said. "I got nothing in there except a massive headache. Now I think I know how Cordelia feels."

"Doubt it, man," Gunn countered, pulling away from the curb. He flashed Wesley a broad smile. "I don't think any of us could take what she goes through. Men just don't have the pain threshold women do."

"I know," Wesley said. "You're right. I'm just feeling frustrated."

"Well, join the club," Gunn said. "I came up with a big fat goose egg myself. There is *no* word on the street. Not just nobody talkin', because when nobody's talkin' there's always somebody talkin' about why nobody's talkin'. But now there's just nobody talkin'. You dig?"

"Yes, well, I think I follow. Nobody's talking."

"You got it."

Gunn drove in silence for a few minutes. He knew the streets of Los Angeles better than Wesley ever would, it seemed. Wesley would have headed for the nearest freeway onramp, but Gunn ignored the freeways in favor of surface streets, made some unexpected turns, and somehow still seemed to be closing in on the Hyperion, all without ever encountering serious traffic.

Of course, Wesley thought, *the hour might have a bit to do with that as well.*

"Heads up, dog," Gunn said as he turned onto a street just six blocks from the hotel.

"What is it?" Wesley asked. He'd been looking at the glowing instrument panel instead of out through the windshield.

"Just saw a shape kinda flit across the street, there up ahead," Gunn told him. "Don't like the looks of it."

"What do you think it is?"

"I think it's trouble."

Gunn brought the sedan to a screeching halt, as the trouble he'd spotted erupted from the shadows on both sides of the street. The shapes they saw, dark silhouettes against distant streetlights, were bizarre, unnatural shapes—even, Wesley realized, to people who spent their lives dealing with things that walk by night.

"You strapped?" Gunn asked him.

"I've got a couple of stakes," Wesley replied. "And I think there's a crossbow in the back seat."

"Best make sure," Gunn said. "Think we're gonna need it."

Wesley noticed that Gunn was looking in the rearview mirror with an expression of considerable concern. He cranked his head around and saw that more of the strange shapes were converging on them from behind.

"What are they?" he asked, feeling in the back for the crossbow. When his fingers came across it he snatched it up, making sure a bolt was locked.

"I don't know," Gunn said. "I'd have said I made out a couple of Howler demons, but then I realized that they were walking on four legs each."

"Howlers only have two legs."

"That's my point," Gunn said. He reached down to the floor by his feet and came up with a short-handled axe.

Wesley looked around, front and back. Gunn was right. Wes had encountered a wide range of demons in his time, both with Angel and as a Watcher, and he'd learned about many more in his Watcher training before being sent on assignment to Sunnydale. But in all that time, he had never seen any of the dozen or more different types of demons who surrounded the car now. He recognized individual features: the ones Gunn had pointed out, the torsos and heads that looked very much like Howler demons, except on the wrong legs; a tall demon that looked like a Klakivan but with yellow fur instead of pale yellow leatherlike skin; a crouching, muscular demon with the curled horns of a Carnisat, but the hooved feet of a Bovissle.

"It's like they've all been thrown into a blender and have come out wrong," he whispered.

"However they got made, they look ticked off," Gunn said urgently. "At us."

"What have we done to upset them?"

"You figure it out, man, you let me know. If you can find me."

"Find you?"

"Yeah, Wes. They outnumber us about ten to one, y'know, and there's enough of 'em that if we tried to run 'em down, we'd get hung up on the bodies about halfway through. I think in this case, best thing we can do is try to run."

The demons came closer to the car. Wesley saw slavering, fanged mouths, sinister claws, fiery eyes.

"Yes, Gunn . . . I have to agree with you." He transferred the crossbow to his left hand and with his right he gripped the door handle. "On three."

Gunn tapped him lightly on the arm. "Forget about waitin' for three," he said. "On one. Let's go!"

Both of them threw their doors open and burst from the car. Wesley fired a bolt from the crossbow toward the mass of demons that closed on them, without even bothering to aim. Gunn had the axe shoulder-high, ready to swing.

But they were surrounded. They both pulled up short. Nowhere to run, too many to fight. Wesley and Gunn stood back to back as the circle of demons closed in around them.

CHAPTER FOUR

A small village in China, 1900

The Boxer Rebellion

The Chinese had finally rebelled against their oppressors, the pale-skinned Europeans. The round eyes sought to destroy all history and tradition and make them forget that they, not the Christians, were the sons of heaven. With opium and their god, with treating Chinese men like slaves and Chinese women like prostitutes, the foreigners were determined to rid China of her true masters and set themselves up as ruthless demigods.

Finally the Chinese people had had enough; they rebelled and fought back. Their hatred and frustration boiled over, and they became a huge whirlwind that descended upon the invaders, much as the locusts in the Christian Holy Book.

Darla never could resist a war.

The fires and rioting that engulfed the buildings surrounding her were nothing compared to the hellstorm raging inside Darla. Though she had driven away Angelus, the vampiric companion she had sired back in Ireland, he had followed the trail of bodies she had left in her wake to this remote Chinese village. Finding her alone in her quarters, he had begged her to take him back.

She had said yes, and then watched him, tested him. He had failed miserably. Oh, her boy, her dear boy . . . *he's vile with contamination, filthy with that soul . . . he can't make a good kill; he's lost his taste for the hunt.*

Though it can't beat, my heart is breaking.

It was her fault. Back in Romania, it was she, Darla, who had plucked the succulent Gypsy girl from her camp and presented her to Angelus. The maiden was a delectable gift, something very special that the two of them could share . . . with Angelus feasting and Darla looking on, savoring the viciousness of her lover. He had shown that girl no mercy.

But the Gypsies sought revenge for the death of their favorite clan daughter. They forced Angelus's soul back inside his body, smothering his pure vampiric instincts with remorse and morality. Angelus went mad from that torture.

I drove him away then, she thought. *I couldn't stand the sight of him, the stench of that soul inside him. I threatened to kill him if I ever saw him again.*

But I haven't killed him. I don't have the stomach for it . . .

or is that cancerous soul somehow infecting me as well, staying my hand when I should destroy him, if only to put him out of his misery? What kind of sire am I, that I should let this happen to my boy, and then turn my back on him?

Her mind in turmoil, she walked through the firestorm with Drusilla and Spike. Angelus had sired Drusilla, and Drusilla had sired Spike, and now they remained with her. They didn't know, at first, what had happened to Angelus. The reek of his soul was not apparent to them, as it was to her.

She had sent him away after he had failed to kill the human infant she had presented to him. It had been a test, and he had failed. *He has tried so hard to be what he had once been—my amazing, ruthless Angelus. He takes fresh human blood again. But only from those he deems evil. Of the pure, the innocent . . . he feels himself to be too much like them, and can not cannibalize his own kind.*

He is no longer my kind.

The door to her quarters opened. With a tiny whisper of hope in her throat, Darla closed her eyes and caught her breath. If Angelus was here to reconcile, if he was ready to drain the child for her sake . . . .

"'Ey, what's all this then?" Spike asked. He was still full of himself, a cock o' the walk with the blood of a freshly slaughtered Slayer singing through his veins. "Darla, are you hurt?"

Drusilla swayed, murmuring with her arms outstretched, "Cor, poor lady, your tears are like sizzling moondrops on the palace floors." Titching her teeth, she swept her skirts out of the way as she sank to the floor beside Darla. "Grandmother, what's the matter?" She looked around the room in a daze of addlepated wonder. "Where's Angelus?"

"Do not utter that name," Darla said between clenched teeth. "He is dead to us, do you hear me? *Dead!*" She glared at Drusilla, and then at Spike.

Drusilla's face fell and she began to sway. "Oh, 'e's dead," she crooned. "My poor sire. Do you know who did it, Grandmother? 'Ave you killed them already?"

"Oughtn't we have felt it, then?" Spike asked Darla. "I mean, Dru being my sire and him being hers, don't we feel something if he dusts?"

Darla transformed to vamp face and rushed him. "If I say it, he is dead. To us."

He raised his brows and held up his hands, giving her a nervous nod. "Dead," he assured her. "As a doornail. The 'orrible lout."

Darla swallowed down the rest of her tears and smoothed her elaborate Chinese dress. Dru held out her hands to help her, and Darla bit off, "I . . . am . . . fine." She jerked herself away from Drusilla's well-meant attempt and faced Spike.

"And don't even think that you are half the vampire he was," she flung at him. "Don't even . . ." She broke down. "Get out of here. Both of you!"

"Spike, the fires are raging and death is playing his mandolin," Drusilla began. "Her tears sizzle." She rippled her fingers at him. "Let's dance on his grave."

Spike grabbed her arm and dragged her away from Darla, toward another part of the room. "'E's not dead," he whispered. "They've had a row, that's all. She's angry enough to kill 'im, is what she means."

Drusilla grabbed her lover's arm and raised on tiptoe, whispering sotto voce, "Then let's hunt him down and kill him. It'll cheer 'er up ever so much."

Spike looked startled. Then he chuckled. "Remind me never to quarrel with you. But no, there'll be no running after the likes of 'im, Dru. Not now, and not ever. D'you understand me?"

"You're jealous of Angelus." She sang the words. "But you killed the Slayer, not 'im. So we'll have tea." She clapped her hands together, then reached them out to Darla. "There was a tea room just down the road."

This time Darla stared down at Dru's proffered hands, and after a moment, she took one. Dru giggled wildly and swung their arms like schoolgirls, then, dropping Darla's hands, traipsed after Spike as he left the building. Darla hesitated on the threshold, taking one last glance at the room where she'd sent Angelus packing for a second time.

He'll find me, she told herself. *He'll take command of himself and come after me. And be my wild lover again.*

She stepped into the street. Orange and red flames shot up like geysers against a sky of black satin and diamonds. Carts blazed. Women screamed. Roosters shrieked as their henhouses went up. By morning the village would be nothing but heaps of cinders. Ashes of buildings, ashes of people. No more dreams. Just death.

I didn't even have death, she thought. *The Master took that from me when he brought me into this life. . . . I'll go back to him, beg him to help me. I'll . . .*

She lifted her chin. *I will do no such thing. I am Darla.*

Dru was prattling about something new; Darla paid her no mind. Her rage and sorrow dulled to an aching numbness; she wasn't sure that her feet were touching the ground. She could feel nothing, not the muddy ground, nor the scorching heat of the flames, hot enough even to warm the cold blood of a vampire. As if in a trance, she allowed Drusilla to pull her along. The mad young girl alternately cooed at her and flirted outrageously with Spike. As Darla had asserted, Angelus had always been the better vampire—more brutal and aggressive. But now Drusilla's mate had no competition.

"Here it is," Drusilla merrily announced, clapping her hands as they stopped outside a hovel coated with soot. "Tea and cakes!"

Spike raised his leg and smashed the door down with his boot. Screams erupted from within the place, and the three vampires glided over the threshold. It had been a public inn, and so there was no need to depend upon a personal invitation in order to enter.

A few trestle tables sat at odd angles from the door; there was a single exit covered with a dirty black hanging decorated with a red crest. The only occupants were an old man and a woman, huddling on the floor in the center of the room. As soon as they saw Drusilla, who had transformed her face, they shrieked with terror and crabwalked toward the door with the black hanging.

With a sharp clap-clap of her hands, Drusilla set her jaw and narrowed her glowing eyes. "We want some tea!" she shouted. "And cakes!"

"And none of that green swill you Chinese drink," Spike added, changing as well. He flung a bench out of his way as he strutted toward one of the tables and plopped himself down in a rickety wooden chair. "Proper tea. Like we drink in London."

"Yeah," Dru intoned. "*Proper* tea."

Darla felt oddly detached from the scene. Under different circumstances, she would have found the terror of the old Chinese couple thoroughly intoxicating. *We would have drunk their warm blood from tea cups, he and I. He would have slaughtered them for me. Slowly. To Brahms.*

He could be so romantic that way.

She took a seat by a mudded hole that served as a window and looked out. Beyond, the village swayed with wild flames that capered and dipped like Balinese shadow puppets. *I always did like a view,* she thought wistfully. *And he always gave me one.*

The tea was brewed, then served; the couple slaughtered and consumed; and with an idle wave of her hand, Darla dismissed her two young friends to run along and frolic. Alone, she sat at the empty window and watched the hellfires. Her tea grew cold; she didn't drink it.

The building began to burn, and she didn't move.

Hours passed, and she knew that if she wished to live until another sunset, she had to find better shelter than this.

She didn't move.

Then she became aware that someone was watching her, and her heart leapt.

Angelus, she thought, thrilled, *restored. My boy, all better and come back to me.*

But she knew even as she turned that she would not see Angelus. And yet, the sight of an ancient Chinese man in black satin robes and a crimson-and-black skullcap, bowing before her, sent her into such a rage of disappointment that she transformed into her vampire face and nearly tore out his throat.

Though shaken, the Chinese man kept his composure, completing his bow and gazing at her straight in the face. He said in English, "Esteemed empress, may you live a hundred thousand years. I, alas, will not."

"You won't last another minute if you don't tell me who you are and why you dare approach me," she sneered at him.

"There is one," he answered, "who can help you."

"Help *me*?" She balled her fists, her nails slicing into her own palms. She realized she was starving again. She shouldn't have shared the old couple after all.

"Help you rid your beloved of his soul," he continued.

With a flourish he raised his arms, moving them in a strange, rhythmic way that had a calming effect upon Darla. As she watched, her features softened, taking on their human mask once more. Her anger did not disappear, but neither did it consume her.

"There is one, in the Sandwich Islands," he continued. "In the territory of Hawaii. He is Lohiau, and he is a brother of mine in the arts of necromancy."

She blinked at him, said nothing. She felt languid, almost lethargic, and after the distress she had experienced, it was a most welcome sensation. *It could be a trick*, part of herself warned her other self.

"How do you know about any of this? Have you been spying on us?" she demanded.

"Most humble pardon. I was in the room when the white-haired one killed the Slayer . . . I ran after him . . . I came to you."

"Why?" she demanded.

"To thank you." He slid his hands into his sleeves and bowed again. "She killed my servant. Life was difficult for me while she lived."

"Ah. As you say, necromancy. You've been dabbling in naughty things." She finally smiled, though it cost her dearly. He smiled back, appreciating her effort.

"I understand what has happened," he said. "One of your family has been forced to take on a soul. A most unfortunate happenstance." He bowed low. "And I say to you, wise empress of blood, please go to Lohiau. He will take that soul away."

She took a moment to find her voice. *If it's true . . . if I can save Angelus . . . my boy, my dear boy . . . .*

"Your reward is my kiss," she said. "Eternal life."

He bowed deeply.

"If Lohiau can do it, I'll come back to you, and I will do it," she assured him. His face fell. "But if this is a false road, I'll come back and break your neck."

He paled. "It is no false road. I assure you of that."

She regarded him. For a moment she was too tired. Too tired to think about Angelus, and changing him, and wanting him, and despising him. She had a vague memory of dying—of beginning to die—of the whore's disease, and then, of bliss and joy and the kill and the hunt. But it was all so long ago, and such incredible effort to remember. Right now a dark tomb and a long rest were what she craved above all else. And yet . . .

"Tell me how to find him," she said. "And how to make him do what I want."

"You must make a long sea voyage," he began.

"What do you suppose they want?" Wesley whispered.

"My guess would be dinner," Gunn replied. "But I could be wrong. Could be more of an early breakfast."

"Very comforting," Wesley said.

Then the first of the demons charged and there was no more time for discussion. A demon—Wesley would have sworn that it was a Kailiff demon, except for its fire-engine red skin and a pair of tusks that sprouted at the sides of its nose—gave a low snarl and rushed at Wesley, muscular arms outstretched. Wesley fired a crossbow bolt at it, but the demon dodged; the bolt missed its heart and lodged instead in its shoulder. Slowed but not stopped, the creature came on, grabbing Wesley's jacket and throwing him to the ground. Wesley kicked, his foot making contact, and the demon grunted in pain.

Gunn, meanwhile, was occupied with demons of his own—Wesley could hear, but not see, the sounds of a pitched battle taking place.

The Kailiff-looking thing lunged at Wesley again, even as the ex-Watcher reloaded the crossbow and fired another bolt. This one sank into the flesh of its left biceps, causing it to whimper as it tugged the bolt out. Hot green blood splashed Wesley and the street. Still the demon came, dropping to its knees on Wesley's ribcage. Wesley raked the crossbow over the demon's face, cutting cheek and forehead. The demon howled with rage and closed its right hand over Wesley's throat. Other demons moved in now—Wesley could hear the shuffle of their feet, see their silhouettes looming around him, even as the world faded toward black.

Very powerful, he thought with some surprise. *More so than I expected, certainly . . .*

When the first demon to make a move headed for Wesley, Gunn half turned to swing his axe if the crossbow didn't stop it. But two other demons, just beyond arm's reach, had been waiting for that move. As soon as Gunn's attention was diverted, they hurled themselves at him. He caught the motion from the corner of his eye and spun around, bringing the axe up—but a fraction of a second too late. One of the demons sank long claws into his chest, as if trying to carve right through to his heart. The other snapped at his throat with pointed teeth that looked like a mouthful of rusty nails. Gunn swung the axe, striking tooth guy in the jaw. The demon lurched backward, blood spouting from its face. But the one with claws in his chest dragged them down Gunn's torso, drawing long furrows. He felt himself weakening already from the loss of blood, and maybe from shock setting in. *Don't get it,* he thought. *We shoulda been able to take out at least half of these guys before they brought us down.*

With the last of his strength, he lashed out with the axe again, chopping off the hand that was buried in his torso. The demon that had been attached to the hand let out a long scream and backed away, cradling its bleeding arm in its other hand. But before Gunn could celebrate, three more took its place.

Fangs and claws tearing at him, Gunn dropped to his knees.

At first, Wesley thought their rescuer was a fever dream, the product of his imagination as he slipped into unconsciousness and death. Certainly, the man cut an unlikely figure.

He appeared from above, as if he had flown in under his own power, like a comic book superhero. *Very unlikely, though,* Wesley thought. *He probably jumped from a rooftop.* He was a huge man, one of the biggest Wesley had ever seen. He was shirtless beneath a black leather vest, zipper pulled halfway open to reveal a massive slab of chest. The exposed arm muscles looked like they had been shaped by effort and hard work, real manual labor rather than hours in a gym with a personal trainer. His neck seemed as big around as Wesley's thigh. Tree trunk legs were clad in black leather leggings with straps and pockets that seemed to hold—as did the vest—a variety of weapons and equipment. In spite of the man's size and agility, Wesley realized he was not young—his black hair, combed straight back from his forehead, was streaked with gray, and his rugged, dark-skinned face was lined with wrinkles.

But none of that seemed to matter to the man. With a war cry, he waded into the midst of the demons. A sword appeared in his hand. Wesley realized it was electrified somehow, because it sparked when it made contact with demon flesh. The man wove a glittering, flashing web with it. Everywhere it moved, demons fell away. When two of them began to pelt him with debris from the street—hubcaps, a metal trash can, a spare wheel ripped from the back of a luxury SUV—the man took a tiny weapon that appeared to be a homemade handgun from one of his pockets, and fired tiny darts at them. When they struck the demons, the projectiles exploded, and those demons were no longer a threat.

The Kailiff-like demon released Wesley's throat almost as soon as the man appeared on the scene. Wesley had the vague sense that it had recognized the man from the way it immediately responded with obvious trepidation to his dramatic entrance. By the time Wesley scrambled to his hands and knees, shaking off the aftereffects of the demon's attack—*those ribs will be sore for a while,* he thought—the man had made short work of the demonic horde.

Wesley helped Gunn to his feet. His friend had suffered a serious wound. Gunn's sweatshirt was in ribbons, soaked in blood. "We need to get you some medical attention," he said solemnly.

"I'll be okay," Gunn countered. "I just need a complete transfusion. After about three months of bed rest, I'll be good as new."

"Right," Wesley said. "First stop, emergency room."

"We can't go anywhere yet," Gunn said with urgency.

"Why not?"

"I wanna see who that guy is."

Wesley looked for the man who had come along in the proverbial nick and saved their proverbial bums. The street, still empty of traffic, was an abattoir, littered with dead or dying demons and demon parts. A slaughterhouse stench assailed Wesley's nostrils, a smell that made him think of spoiled meat slowly cooking over a fire built from logs of human hair. Finally he spotted their rescuer kneeling beside one of his downed opponents. The man's eyes were downcast, almost as if he were grieving. Or praying.

As he watched, the big man regained his feet and came toward them, a smile spreading across his face. "You probably were not expecting this," he said. His voice carried a slight accent. *Definitely European,* Wesley thought. *Maybe Castilian.* "On the other hand, most Angelenos do not carry axes and crossbows in their cars, to my knowledge. So perhaps you gentlemen are not what you appear to be."

"We have encountered demons before," Wesley answered him. "As, clearly, have you."

"Usually not such tough ones, though," Gunn added. He kept an arm across Wesley's shoulders, for support. "I mean, they're usually bad, but not *bad* bad, if you know what I mean."

"It is safe to say that you have never done battle with any quite like these," the man said. "Very few have, and survived."

"But you have," Wesley observed.

"Oh, yes. I have."

"How? Where?"

"I am afraid I must offer you my most humble apologies," the man said. "For I am at least partially responsible for the existence of these beasts. I hope they have not damaged you too badly."

Gunn tried for a laugh, but Wesley felt him wince as he did. "No, we'll be just like new," he said. "Nothin' that can't be fixed with a Band-Aid and some of that red stuff, you know? Stings when you put it on?"

"Mercurochrome," Wesley suggested.

"That's the stuff," Gunn agreed.

"You . . . you created these demons?" Wesley asked the man, not quite believing what he had heard. "What, you . . . you *bred* them or something? Summoned them?"

"I beg your forgiveness," the man replied. He cocked an ear, and only then did Wesley notice the distant wail of approaching sirens. "Perhaps we should talk. Somewhere else."

"Yes, let's," Wesley said. "I know just the place."

CHAPTER FIVE

"My name is Chaz Escobar," the stranger announced in a booming voice. It sounded to Angel almost as if he were on stage. Wesley and Gunn had brought the guy in with them a few minutes before, and now they were gathered around the lobby to hear his story. Even Fred had come downstairs, clad now in an ankle-length nightshirt, her hair tousled from sleep. As soon as she'd seen the condition of Gunn and Wesley, she'd gone for a first-aid kit and started tending to their wounds. Wesley's introduction of their rescuer, complete with a brief recap of the battle, had been nothing short of breathless. "As I told your associates, Mr. Wyndam-Pryce and Mr. Gunn—"

"We just call them Wes and Gunn," Cordelia interrupted. "No Mr. needed."

"Nevertheless," Escobar continued graciously, "they have proven themselves as men before me . . ." Cordelia and Fred exchanged bemused looks at that line, Angel noted. ". . . and are therefore worthy of all the respect I can show them."

"Proved ourselves?" Gunn asked. He sat up a little straighter on the banquette, but winced as he did so. Fred pushed him back down and continued to minister to his wounds. "'Bout all we did was bleed and fall down."

"Most humans would have run like babies at the sight of those creatures," Escobar argued. "You did not. You held your ground and faced them. Like men."

"Again with the men stuff," Cordelia said under her breath. Angel shot her a warning glance. He wanted to hear the guy's story. And, given Escobar's size and general demeanor, he wanted to hear it without ticking the guy off.

"Yes, I suppose we did that," Wesley said.

"But . . ." Angel wasn't quite sure how to phrase his comment. "You . . . smell human to me, Mr. Escobar."

"I am human." It was clearly a point of pride with him.

Angel took that in as he scrutinized Escobar, trying to detect some other-than-human quality about him. He had saved Gunn and Wesley, true, but Angel knew full well that the road to hell was paved with intentions that might not be as honorable as they appeared to be.

"Then how were you able to defeat the demons so easily?" he asked pointedly.

"Yeah," Cordy put in, challenging him. "You're big and all, but Wesley and Gunn are no novices to the whole demon ass-kicking thing, you know."

"I am sure they are not," Escobar replied, all European

grace and discretion. Then he returned to the bragging pit, adding, "But I had an advantage that they did not."

"Which is?" Angel prodded. *At this rate, we won't find out until the third act.*

"As I told them at the time," the man said, "I am, in part, responsible for the existence of those creatures. Therefore, I know their weaknesses as well as their strengths. And they know and fear me."

Angel pondered that. *Which part are you responsible for?* he wanted to ask him. *Responsible in the way I was responsible for Drusilla? Or did you actually sit down with a set of plans, like Dr. Walsh back in Sunnydale, when she created Adam?*

"Maybe you should start from the beginning," he told the man. It was not a request, and from Escobar's expression, he didn't think it was one. He inclined his head as if to say, *All right, no more beating around the bush,* and took a breath.

"I shall, Mr. Angel. Thank you." Escobar had refused to take a seat, even though everyone else was sitting on a desk chair or one of the lobby's banquettes, or in the case of Fred, on the stairs. He remained standing, and once again Angel was put in mind of the old men in Ireland and their love of weaving a good story, letting out a bit at a time, gauging the proper moment to spin a few more threads.

"I am in Los Angeles in search of my wife, Marianna Escobar. She is a lovely woman." His face radiated love, desire, and passion. He reminded Angel of Ricardo Montalban playing Khan on Star Trek. "The sunrise in the morning, the sunset at night, the call of a bird in the springtime, all pale next to Marianna."

"Aww," Cordelia said. As a quiet aside, she muttered, "Gag me." Angel tossed her another stern glare, to which she shrugged.

Still Escobar didn't seem to have heard. He went on. "Sadly, though, she is a vampire, as well."

O . . . kay. Didn't see that coming, Angel thought.

"That'll put a damper on a relationship," Gunn observed.

"Indeed," Escobar said flatly. "We were wed long ago, when we were both quite young. We had many things in common—youth, energy, a certain amount of money, and a love of the hunt were among them. That passion, particularly. Together we went everywhere, hunted every kind of wild beast you can imagine. When we ran out of those that were legal, we moved on, I am embarrassed to admit, to those that were not. Endangered animals, protected animals—their illegitimacy merely served to heighten our desire to bag them as trophies."

"Oh my God," Wesley said. "That's . . . that's awful."

"I know that now," Escobar admitted. "But for many years, my twin passions—Marianna, and the hunt—obscured that sad knowledge from my view. We roamed the planet, everywhere we went adding new trophies to our collection. On San Teodor, an island off the California coast, we built a magnificent estate to contain our trophies. During our travels, though, we became aware that there was a shadow world unknown to most humans, populated with those—like yourself, I believe, Mr. Angel—that most would call monsters."

"Just Angel is fine," Angel said.

"It's a Cher thing," Cordelia added.

"It's really not," Angel corrected. "Please go on."

"As we ran out of new species to hunt, Marianna and I became more and more intrigued by the rumors of these other beings—demons, werewolves, vampires, what have you—that walked the earth. A whole new range of creatures to hunt, we believed. New challenges, new opportunities. Where we had been growing stale, suddenly a new world opened up to us. Our marriage, which had been atrophying along with our hunting skills, blossomed anew.

"But then one horrible night in Lima, Peru, the unthinkable happened. We had been married less than ten years—our anniversary was approaching, and it was that milestone we celebrated in the Andes Mountains that week. And we celebrated by hunting ñaqaq, the Andean vampire."

"There are Andean vampires?" Fred asked from her perch on the stairs.

"Oh, yes. There are many varieties of vampire—"

"All descended from the same root, though," Angel clarified.

"So they say," Escobar said. "The ñaqaq are somewhat unique in that they don't actually drink blood. The legends say that they are beasts who take the form of men, mesmerizing their victims and draining off their body fat."

"Kind of a supernatural liposuction," Cordelia suggested. "People in L.A. would pay to meet them."

"Indeed. Once the body is drained of fat, the victim returns to her home and dies. We believed that one of these beings would make a fine addition to our trophy collection. And, as you know, I'm sure, traditional vampires are very difficult to display, since they have a tendency to explode in a cloud of dust when they're killed.

"Unfortunately the legend wasn't entirely accurate, this time. The ñaqaq—like Angel, I presume—do indeed drink blood and not body fat. And while we were expecting the frighteningly countenanced being of the stories, this particular ñaqaq, who turned out to be quite a handsome fellow, befriended Marianna in a tavern while I was searching for a local guide. They shared a few drinks, and then he told her that he had some good area maps in his car. When they went outside, he turned on her, and bit her. You know what happened then, no?"

"She became a vampire," Wesley said.

"Correct."

"And you couldn't bring yourself to dust her?" Gunn asked. Angel knew that Gunn had been forced to stake his own sister when she had been turned, and that it was that experience that had made Gunn the driven vampire hunter he was.

"No," Escobar replied. "I couldn't. I kept her well-fed, and protected myself, so that she couldn't turn me, and took her back to San Teodor, where I worked to find a cure for her. All my resources and energies, which had previously been put into hunting, were now devoted to hunting for some magickal cure for her condition. In my search, I gathered many different varieties of demon and monster, and . . . I am chagrined to admit . . . I experimented on them, hoping against hope that they would point the way to a cure.

"Eventually my fortune began to dwindle. I couldn't allow Marianna off the island to hunt, so I had to constantly travel to the mainland and find sustenance for her."

This was the second reference he had made to providing

for her, Angel noted. The man was every bit as bad as his vampire wife, in many ways. "People," he said simply. "You provided her with people."

Escobar looked mortified. "People. I brought them back to San Teodor and let her have the pleasure of the kill, so her meals were always fresh. For that she was . . . grateful."

He made a deal with the devil, Angel thought. *Or rather, with the devil's spawn.* He had been an evil vampire; he sincerely doubted Marianna Escobar felt anything resembling gratitude. More likely the demon inside her dead body realized that Chaz Escobar was still in love with his wife, and played on his emotions like a violinist on a Stradivarius.

I knew how to do that, too. God, how I played Drusilla, pretending to be her confessor, driving her mad . . .

. . . And my own sire, Darla, she played me so well. She had me twisting in the wind. In everything I was her toy, her slave . . .

Escobar was still speaking, and Angel stirred himself from his reverie to listen.

"Eventually she came to me with an idea. Since we had stocked San Teodor with a variety of unusual creatures—hybrids I had created in my lab, as well as live specimens of many different types of demons, humans, and other beings—we could invite human hunters to the island. They would pay handsomely for the privilege of hunting our creatures, which would replenish our coffers. And Marianna could avail herself, from time to time, of our guests, who would be said to have perished in hunting accidents. It was a nearly foolproof system, and it worked well for many years. While I aged, and Marianna—" His voice caught. "Marianna stayed young and beautiful."

"Nearly foolproof, you said," Wesley observed. "Which means something happened."

"Something did happen," Escobar said. "As time passed and I became older, Marianna began to turn against me in spite of my best efforts. She wanted me off the island, out of her life. I refused, of course. I had devoted my life to finding a cure for her, and now she didn't want one. Finally she persuaded our creatures that I was their enemy, and they joined forces against me. With her help they drove me from my own home, from my island—our island, I should say.

"For almost a year I have sought a way to get back to San Teodor and restore my control of the creatures, who have become, effectively, Marianna's personal army. It is only there, in my lab, that I can hope to ever reverse her condition and bring her back to life."

Angel was given pause. Poor Escobar, doomed to failure; Angel was sure that if there were a way science could reverse vampirism, it would have been found long ago. He was no scientist, but he had known several, and none of them had come close. *What could a hunter do?* He wouldn't have the faintest idea where to begin.

Then he thought of Lohiau, and Maui, and thought, *Not even a magician can cure a vampire of his curse . . .*

"And you still want to, after what she did to you?" Cordelia asked, again drawing Angel back to the present. "I know most guys have a hard time with rejection, but that's a little extreme."

"I would give anything to have her back in my life," Escobar replied baldly. "And human again, so that we may grow old together as we once planned."

And now Angel thought of Buffy. For one full day, the beautiful Slayer—*my soul mate*—had been back in his life, and he had been human. The touch of her, the smell, the taste . . . *mint chocolate-chip ice cream, the sun on my face, the salt on her skin as I made love to her* . . . all had been so precious. So miraculous. But he had given it all up, let it go, to save her life.

He understood Chaz Escobar very, very well.

"But now I have learned that Marianna is here—in Los Angeles. And I thought that perhaps, away from the island, she would be more vulnerable. If I could find her, maybe I could get her away from the creatures and take her back." Escobar's voice trailed off, to misty places where men harbor feelings they do not share . . . at least back in the day, when Angel had been human and emotions were thought to belong to the fairer sex, while men had only occasional use of them.

"So let me guess," Gunn said. "Those guys who attacked us tonight—that's her private army?"

Escobar lowered his head as if in deep remorse. "That is some of them. A small portion of the whole, I am afraid. As I told you, I was able to defeat them because I know them so well, and they were frightened at the sight of me. If there had been very many more of them, the result would have been quite different, I assure you."

"It was quite impressive to us as it was," Wesley said.

"Thank you," Escobar responded, beaming with pride at the compliment. Angel was struck by the way the man seemed to wear his ego on his sleeve, making no attempt to hide his pride. It was almost childish; not many people were so open with virtual strangers.

But then, he realized, *he already knows a lot about us, and knows that we move in the same world he does. I guess there's a common ground.*

"Why do you think they attacked Wes and Gunn?" Angel asked him.

"I cannot be sure," Escobar said, "since it has been so long since I have had their confidence. But I would guess that they perceive Mr. Wyndam-Pryce and Mr. Gunn as a threat, for some reason."

"A threat to Marianna."

"Correct. She is a headstrong and determined woman, and if something stands in the way of what she wants, she will do whatever it takes to remove that. Apparently she felt that these two stood in her way." He gestured to Wesley and Gunn.

"Just them?" Fred queried. "Or all of us?"

"That, I cannot answer. But I would suggest keeping your guard up, just the same."

"We usually do," Angel said confidently. The others nodded, looking professional and accomplished; but privately, he thought, *What have my people gotten involved in?* "But do you know what she wants? What we're in the way of?"

"There is only one thing I know that Marianna wants here in Los Angeles," Escobar said. "One thing she has talked about for many years." He took a breath. "A hunt she would like to sponsor."

Angel looked at him, waiting for him to fill in the blanks. The man did not disappoint.

"A Slayer hunt. And I believe there is one of those here in the area. If you have some connection with the Slayer, then that alone would be enough reason for Marianna's minions to target you."

No one spoke for a moment. Then Cordelia said, "Oh, *great.*"

Okay, Angel thought, *this is not what I expected.*

Chaz Escobar had climbed into the front seat of the Angelmobile with him and proceeded to say . . . nothing.

The man went absolutely silent. He stared ahead as they drove away from the hotel, merged onto the freeway and drove with the traffic. The silence startled Angel; on the other hand, it was nice—nice that the man was taking a breather, and giving Angel a chance to process everything that was going on.

Then Escobar said, "Does it upset you?"

Angel took his eyes away from the road. "Sorry?"

"All the talk of curing her." The hunter looked at Angel. "Of making her what she was. Human. Does it bother you? He stared hard at Angel, as if trying to take his measure. "Or does it give you hope?"

Angel glanced back at the road, signaled left, changed lanes, and said, "No. Neither one."

Chaz took that in. "Would you like to be cured?"

I was . . . cured, Angel thought. But he said, "I don't think you can do it, not medically anyway. I think once the body dies . . ." He hesitated. "You're aware that a demon is inhabiting her body?"

"Yes."

Angel let his silence be his answer.

"But there's you," the man said. "You're more than a demon inhabiting a corpse." Before he could respond, he continued, "I know that you're a powerful warrior in the battle between good and evil. Who is to say that my

Marianna was not destined for such great things? That something happened and she is what she is by mistake?"

That would be a very big mistake. Of course, The Powers That Be are far from infallible.

"Or that *I* am destined for great things?" Escobar continued softly. He stared straight through the windshield, at the lights and the darkness, as if seeing a big, bold landscape starring himself. As big as Chaz Escobar's life was, it was obviously not big enough.

I have been to other dimensions, Angel thought. *I've been to hell and back. And let me tell you, "great things" is a highly overrated concept.*

But Angel kept driving.

He had nothing more to say.

There was no point.

As he walked into the Yorba Linda facility for the second time in one night, this time with Escobar, Angel hoped it wasn't going to become a habit. He had a great deal of respect for Faith's decision to serve her time and pay her debt to society, but the place gave him the willies just the same. Even if it hadn't meant a virtual death sentence, prison would have been unbearable for him. Since his mortal youth, he had been someone who needed to be able to move around at will, set his own schedule, make his own rules. Becoming a vampire had changed some of that, put constraints on him that took a lot of getting used to. But prison? Death might be preferable.

Once again Faith was brought into the interview room to see him.

"I'm getting a lot of visits from my 'attorney,' considering

I'm not on trial or appealing my sentence," she said by way of greeting. "Some of my bunkies are starting to think we've got something going on."

Angel indicated Escobar. "Expert witness for the defense," he said. "This is Chaz Escobar. And this is Faith, the Slayer we talked about."

Her pretty brown eyes opened wide at Angel's identification of her as a Slayer. "He knows?"

"He knows more than that."

"I know about Miss Chase's vision," Escobar said. "And I think I know what it means."

"Yeah?" Faith leaned slightly forward.

"I fear that my wife may try to break you out of prison." He looked very grave, and Faith had to chuckle.

She sat back from the table and put her hands on her thighs. The warden noticed, and craned her neck in Faith's direction as if to say, *I'm watching you*. Faith could tear her head off if she wanted to.

"Is she a member of Amnesty International or something?"

"Vampires not so Anonymous," Angel shot back.

"That can't be good," Faith replied nervously, glancing at Escobar.

"Puts a strain on the relationship," Angel offered.

"Marianna—my wife—sponsors hunts," Escobar said. "For profit, and her own amusement. And she has long dreamed of holding a Slayer hunt. She is in Los Angeles now, and I believe that she has set her sights on you as the object of that hunt."

Faith was quiet for a moment. Then she said, "But she'd take me out of here first, right? Not just hunt me where I am. Because I'm pretty much a sitting duck, you know?" She smiled weakly.

"I am quite sure that she would remove you from these premises," Escobar replied, equally blunt. "Even though she could hunt you in here, her clientele could not. Likely she would take you away to someplace wild. Ordinarily I would suggest our island home, but she knows that San Teodor is the first place I would look for her, so perhaps someplace else. I cannot say for sure where."

"Still," Faith said, pacing around the room now like a cornered lioness, "I can defend myself to a certain extent in here, but it's kind of a trap, right? I mean, I can't run, I can't hide. All I can do is fight. One vampire, no prob, I can take her out—"

"I would prefer that you didn't do that," Escobar interrupted.

Faith grunted. She spread her hands and moved her shoulders in that old Faith way Angel remembered. "Hey, sorry she's your wife and all, but a girl's gotta have priorities, right? If it's her or me, it's her."

"Some people tried to do this to the other Slayer, Buffy Summers." Angel filled Escobar in. "They all ended up dead."

"Yes, of course." Escobar looked at the floor, then sighed and nodded, agreeing. "However, she may not come for you herself—and if she does, she may not be alone."

"Who's she gonna have with her?" Faith looked less than pleased. Angel gestured for her to listen to her visitor.

"It could be any of a variety of creatures," Escobar said. "She has at her disposal a small force of demons, part-demons, mutated humans, and the like."

Faith made a sour face. "You guys must have some great family reunions."

"I am afraid that we are . . . estranged, at the moment. I hope to rectify that, which is why I would like to keep her—well, not alive, of course, but undead—for the time being."

She regarded him for a long moment. "You know, you're lucky I've seen Chuckles here with Buffy, so I know that whole human/vamp thing can work out, at least in the short term. But, um, rectifying, well, that's really tryin' to pull your hat out of your—"

"I will do it," he said flatly.

"We'll work on the outside to track her down," Angel promised her. "And if you think you're safer outside, we can break you out."

"I've been out," Faith reminded him. "I'll take my chances in here, unless things get really hairy. Maybe you guys'll get her and it won't even be an issue."

"We will do our best," Escobar said. "You have the word of Chaz Escobar on that."

"Well hey," Faith replied, with one of her mock-joyful grins. "What more could a girl want, huh?"

CHAPTER SIX

About twenty minutes after Marianna Escobar swept out of the Wolfram & Hart conference room, a delivery was made to Lilah's office: a dozen long-stemmed red roses and a bottle of very fine single malt scotch. The note read: *Glad you're on my team. Marianna.*

Lilah wasn't sure what to make of the gesture. In her professional life, she had received few bouquets, although as a lawyer for W&H, she had ordered quite a number of them, mostly for funerals. The roses were perfect, each an exquisite work of nature, but the scotch was a work of art. Smooth and expensive, it went down easily.

Thanks, I needed a drink, she thought, as she poured herself a second shot. *As a matter of fact, I could down the entire bottle and still quake at the thought of setting Faith free.*

She had just lifted the glass to her lips when her office door opened and Gavin Park strolled in. *As if he owned the place,* Lilah thought, greeting his rudeness with a blank stare of complete disdain.

"We also drink on the job?" he said aloud, raising a brow at her.

She shrugged, turning her back to him as she angrily drank the liquor . . . sipping it, however, instead of belting it back the way she really wanted to. What she did was none of his business, although he was trying every trick he could to edge her out and take her job.

He walked over to the flowers and said, "Nice. Ouch!" He'd pricked himself on one of the thorns. She wished they'd been sprayed with mulfac extract, which was a remarkable preservative manufactured by demons who lived in the former Yugoslavia. It also killed humans instantly.

Lilah smiled coolly at him. "They're from a client thanking me for my services."

"Oh, I'm certain of that," he replied dryly. Then his expression changed to one of insincere embarrassment as he added, "Oh, you mean, a *law* client."

She didn't react, although inwardly she seethed. *I really can't stand this guy,* she thought. *He has no grounds for his attitude. He's got no talent, no brains, and he's not even that easy on the eyes. He loves to try to intimidate me, but he's a joke. Now Lindsey . . . he gave me a run for my money. Saved my life, too. But that's another story.*

"So. Marianna Escobar," he drawled, glancing at the gift card that had accompanied the roses. "Freeing a Slayer. Bold move."

She put the cap back on her new bottle of scotch, making a point of not offering him any, and said, "And you would know about bold moves. Trying to frighten Angel out of that hotel with health-code violations. Brrr. What daring."

"*Safety*-code violations," he corrected. "And that's why I'm here."

Lilah didn't follow, but she didn't want to admit that. So she took a moment to place the bottle of scotch in her private bar. Gavin displayed a noticeable lack of high-level status within the firm, if he thought he could rattle her with a comment about drinking alcohol at work. Most of the upper echelon did.

We have to, to do the things we do. Not that I'm complaining. I knew this job was dangerous when I took it.

"You need a reason to get Faith out of jail." He gestured to himself. "I've come up with one."

"We're going to shut the prison down because there are cockroaches?" Lilah sniped, folding her arms across her chest and leaning against her desk, a gesture designed to communicate her contempt for him.

He ignored her comment. "We've got guards and judges on the payroll, of course." She seethed inwardly, denying herself the immature pleasure of snapping at him for lecturing her. "But we still need a plausible reason for springing her."

"Time off for good behavior," Lilah suggested. It was what she'd been pondering; it made as much sense as any other reason she could come up with.

He shook his head. "Too complicated. And too time-consuming. We'd have to wait for the parole board to convene, then buy a majority of the board members off, and so forth." He copied her posture, crossing his arms and leaning against her desk, violating her space and her dignity. "I figure we'll just get her released to a rehab facility."

"Rehab." She was underwhelmed.

"Run by Dr. Marianna Escobar," he added. "I can create all the documentation we need, to fool anyone in the system that we need to fool."

"So can . . ." *I*, she was about to say. But she only meant "I" in the sense that she had the clout at W&H to delegate such a task to the appropriate underling of her choice. She was good at hacking, but not that good. Apparently Gavin himself was better.

The other attorney took her silence for what it was—an admission that he'd won a round—*but what a puny victory, he's so pathetic*—and he preened a little as he unfolded his arms and walked around to her desk. He opened her lower right-hand drawer and pulled out her laptop. Attorneys of her stature rarely displayed computers on their desks. It smacked too much of elbow grease and clerical busy work, when what important clients paid for was intellectual genius and strategic brilliance.

"I've taken the liberty of creating a set of documents, which I'll import here to your system." To her displeasure, he flipped open the lid of the laptop, pressed the power key, and as she watched, smoothly typed in her ultra-secret, well-protected password.

Pursing her lips Lilah walked around the desk and hovered over his shoulder. The documents that were appearing on the screen—a transfer request, a bogus dossier on Marianna Escobar, Ph.D., Director of the Pasadena Behavioral Institute, even a set of Yellow Pages featuring a tasteful, well-designed ad for Escobar Treatment Facility in Pasadena—appeared with lightning speed.

She left here less than half an hour ago, Lilah thought. *When did he have a chance to put all this together?*

She could tell he was itching for her reaction, but he would never ask her for it and she would never give it. Instead she straightened and said, "You didn't need to use my computer for this."

"I know. It's just that when it gets sent, I didn't want to leave a trail to my machine. In case there are any surprises."

Fuming, she snickered, "It's a laptop, Gavin. It won't be traced to me anyway." But she wasn't certain of that. When it came to penetrating high-tech firewalls and tracking internet signatures, she was out of her league. In fact she had no way of knowing if he was sabotaging the entire operation, then leaving a guidepost to her, specifically to get her in trouble with the Senior Partners.

I'd do the same thing, if I knew how, she thought. *It's not like the old days, when we played real people off each other in the streets, with real weapons and real action.* She sighed inwardly, wistful for the rivalry she'd enjoyed with Lindsey McDonald. Theirs had been a battle on all fronts—physically, mentally, and psychically. Lindsey had won their war, but then he'd handed her his victory with his evil hand and sailed off for unknown waters because he'd finally had enough of the paper chase. *Gavin's just . . . officious and boring, Lindsey had dash.*

"I need my desk back," she announced. "Are you about finished?"

Gavin raised his head up from the keyboard. "Oh, no, Lilah. I'll be here all night." He smiled pleasantly, as if instructing a child. "It's going to take a lot of falsifying records and computer docs to fool the criminal justice system. In fact"—he reached in his suit pocket and fished out his cell phone—"why don't you order us something to eat? Working always gives me an appetite."

She glared at him. "Call one of the secretaries. That's why they're here."

"It might be better if we handle it ourselves. Come now, you can lower yourself to dial for takeout." He smirked at her. "We all have to make little sacrifices now and then."

Lilah snatched his cell phone from him. Then she threw it to the floor and stepped on it with the stiletto heel on one of her very expensive Bruno Magli pumps.

"Whoops. Another little sacrifice," she said, gazing at him levelly.

"Whoops, another typo," Cordelia sang out.

Wesley stopped himself from asking her to move aside so he could do the typing himself. *If you teach a man to fish, he won't starve. I can't teach her how to behave—I'm not sure anyone can—but I can encourage her to develop her clerical skills. Then, one day when all the demons have been vanquished, she'll still be able to find meaningful work.*

"That other word there, it's also a little . . . wrong," he ventured, pointing to the screen.

Squinting, she said, "Where? What word?"

"'Ho' should be 'who,'" he said cautiously.

She moved her shoulders. "There are just too many keys on these keyboards. For example, who is ever going to type one of those curly things you put over *n*'s in Spanish?" She gestured to the guilty key.

"Ah, perhaps someone who speaks Spanish?" Wesley suggested.

She tried again. "Or . . . or percent signs."

"Accountants?"

"All that stuff just clutters it up for regular people." She huffed and pressed another key. Then another. Boldly she sped up, then grimaced and hit the delete key to start over. She prepared to pounce on another word; her attack put Wesley in mind of the Phantom of the Opera taking on Bach's Toccata and Fugue in D Minor.

Gunn had left to take Escobar back to his Westwood condo. Even the seemingly indefatigable hunter had to rest sometime, and Gunn wanted to check the streets for the other half of his vast family, i.e. his homeboys. Gunn was the connecting link between two very different kinds of demon hunters—one set was Angel Investigations, and the other a street-toughened posse.

Angel had excused himself to get some pig's blood out of the fridge.

"'Whoever seeks, let them look with their eyes for the Book,'" she read aloud. It was their contribution to the thread Cordelia had inadvertently joined the last time she was on the DDDd. "'Like sands through time, the pages turn for the Seeker of the Book.'" She slid a glance toward Wesley, narrowing her eyes. "You know, Wesley, I think someone's been watching too many soap operas. That sounds very 'like sands through the hourglass,' if you know what I mean."

"Thankfully I've no idea what you're talking about." He sniffed and pulled himself up. "I've never watched daytime drama in my entire life."

Cordelia snickered. "You're such a liar. You spent an hour in the *Luke and Laura* chat room last Thursday."

"I did not . . . how do you know that?" he asked, fascinated despite himself. He hadn't realized she was proficient enough to check for computer cookies.

"You press this key here," she told him. "It makes a list of all the Internet activity for the last twenty-four hours. I happened to open it and boom, your evil little secret was revealed."

Wesley couldn't hide his grin. "But Cordelia, I didn't spend an hour in the Luke whatever chat room. Someone did, obviously, but it wasn't I."

"Then . . . who . . . ?" Her mouth dropped open. *"Angel?"*

"Yes?" Angel asked from the doorway with his cup in his hand.

He walked into the room and they both blinked at him. Clad in his black duster, he seemed to walk in slow motion as he approached. The coat didn't exactly make the man, but it certainly did not detract.

"How's it going?" the vampire asked, leaning in. Scanning, he brightened. "Oh, good. Luke and Laura . . ." He caught himself. ". . . are the names of old friends of mine."

Cordelia sang, "Busted," just as the familiar red letters "IM" appeared in a box in the upper left-hand corner of her screen.

"Here we go," she whispered. *I'm looking for information about this Book,* she wrote. "That's what set 'em off last time. Wesley, you're gonna have to spell 'Interregnum' for me."

"I will," he said, leaning over her shoulder. "Very slowly."

Meanwhile, from the shadows, Fred came halfway down the stairs and half raised her hand. Her eyes were wide and her forehead creased. She said, "Angel?"

"Yes, Fred."

He left Cordelia and Wesley at the computer and approached the skittish young woman. *I wish we could have brought her back to a safer world,* he thought sadly. *Before she was transported to Pylea, she had no idea that Los Angeles harbored waking nightmares.*

"How's it going?" she asked, her Texas twang pro-ᴜnced. It tended to get thicker when she was nervous or worried.

He hesitated. She seemed so fragile. And yet Fred had slain Pyleans and demons and okay, she was still writing on the walls and afraid to come out of her room, but all in all, she was recovering . . . fairly well.

"Bingo," Cordelia called. "And, oh, pooh."

The screen froze.

"I'll have to reboot," Cordelia said.

Then the lights went out.

"Not liking this," Cordelia said unhappily.

"Me, neither." Fred's voice wobbled with anxiety. "Does anyone have a flashlight?"

One flicked on. In the dim light Cordelia beamed the flashlight over the others. "I think the last time this happened, we were attacked by exploding mummies."

"No," Wesley cut in. "That was the time before last."

"Oh, right. It was some Howler demons, wasn't it?" She frowned thoughtfully. "Or was it those demons who wanted to steal our spleens?"

Fred shivered. "Books. They can be dangerous, you guys. I read out of that big book and sent myself to . . . well, you know." She mumbled half to herself, "They weren't spleen thieves, but they did cut people's heads off."

"I know." Angel reached out and touched her forearm. "We'll make sure you're safe."

She patted him back, and the touch felt good. Not a lot of people touched Angel. Nor were they usually touched by him. "It's just, well, golly." She giggled. "Bad memories."

"It'll be okay. If it can be," he amended.

"That's certainly comforting." She sounded very sincere.

"Better douse the light," he told Cordelia. "In case we're being, you know . . ."

"Attacked?" she asked, as she turned off the flashlight and handed it to him.

Angel winced, fearing a loud reaction on Fred's part, hearing none. *I don't give Fred enough credit,* he thought. *I'm not sure I could have survived alone in Pylea for five years. But she managed it.*

Angel gave her the flashlight and said, "Turn this on if I tell you to, okay?"

"Yup."

Then he fanned out, listening carefully for the movements of Wesley and Cordelia. He could see very well in the dark, but with the fanning, both of them had moved out of sight. After a couple of moments, Angel located his trusty axe, which he had been planning to sharpen during the daylight if he had insomnia, and called softly, "You guys armed?"

He got two breathy yesses. The *s*'s were sibilant as rattlesnakes.

"It's an old hotel," Fred added, as if trying to convince herself not to panic.

Angel crept. Cordy and Wesley crept. Much with the creeping.

I wonder how Gunn and Escobar are doing, Angel thought as he made his way back to Fred. *Hope Gunn comes back in one piece.* When he reached her side, he said, "I'm going to check the fuse box."

"Do you want the flashlight? Oh, vampires can see in the dark," she remembered. "Like cats and owls."

The lights flicked on. Gunn stood at the entrance to the hotel with his hand on a light switch.

"You guys playin' flashlight tag?" he drawled. "'Cause that's not a good idea when you're packing weapons."

Cordelia came back from down the hall. Wesley emerged from Angel's office. Angel took a quick inventory: Wes had his Bavarian fighting adz, Cordelia had a sword, and Fred still had the flashlight.

"The . . . the lights went out," Fred announced, as everyone moved into relief mode and gathered back together.

"Yeah, that's what switches are for," Gunn observed with a smile no one else shared.

"I checked the switch," Angel told him.

"Somebody foolin' with your fuse box?"

"No sign of anyone," Angel replied. "Cordelia just did something on the computer and—"

They all turned to look at Cordelia who shrugged, looking unhappy. "Maybe the Book of the Interregnum doesn't want to be found?"

"Could be something like that, I guess," Angel said.

"A special kind of firewall," Fred chimed in.

"I'll look into it," Wesley suggested.

Angel nodded and looked questioningly at Gunn, who walked down the steps. "No problem with Escobar. Condo's nice. He's got TiVo. And man, does he have weapons. Sure does like to go into the 'manly man' routine."

"No kidding." Cordelia rolled her eyes. "Makes me kind of wonder about him, if you know what I mean. Guys who have to talk about their guyness like that. Not that I'm prejudiced," she added. "I think it's wonderful when people discover their gender identities. Like Willow has."

"Well, let's boot up, see if we can reconnect," Wesley suggested. "No time like the present."

"Yeah, since we waved, we might as well shout hello," Cordelia retorted.

Everyone filed into Angel's office. Cordelia swallowed and sat back down while Wesley rebooted the computer.

"Retracing our steps," Wesley said. "I'm looking for this . . ."

"*B-o-o* . . . Let's see . . . *k*, where's *k*, yes, *k*. Book!" Cordelia said triumphantly as she painstakingly typed in the letters. Then she took her hands off the keyboard and pushed herself backward in the chair. "Hoping it doesn't, you know, explode this time instead of blowing out the power."

"They were pancreatic demons," Wesley said thoughtfully. "They wanted our pancreases, not our spleens."

"Giving us the phrase, 'watch yo' pancreASS.'" Gunn moved his shoulders.

On the screen, Latin appeared in an IM window. Wesley translated under his breath, then looked at Angel, who had come up behind him and Cordelia. "Angel, this person is asking if we are fellow seekers of the Book of the Interregnum."

"I'd say we have a match," Angel murmured. "Tell him yes."

Cordelia took a deep breath. "*Y-E-S.*" Like a symphony conductor, she pushed the return key.

They all waited a moment. An answer came back. Wesley cocked his head. "She says she has pages from the Book of the Interregnum."

Angel came around to examine the screen. "*She.* Which we can tell because of the declensions in Latin."

"Indeed," Wesley said. He turned his attention from his computer screen to Angel. "It could be Benedicta."

Fred half-raised her hand. "Or that macho man's wife? Marianna?"

Angel studied on the screen. "Tell her you have some pages too." He paused. "This could take a lot of . . . spelling."

Wesley said, "Cordelia, I don't want to insult you . . ."

"No problem," she said breezily, pushing her wheeled chair back from the desk and surrendering the keyboard to Wesley. "I don't want to get carpal tunnel anyway. Or some hideous virus."

Fred laughed. "Oh, Cordelia, you can't really get a virus from a computer like you can from a person . . ." She looked at the others. "Sorry," she said, smiling helplessly. "I keep forgetting who I'm hanging out with. What you guys are into."

Wesley took the con. He thought a moment, then said to Angel, "Let's arrange a rendezvous."

"Oooh." Fred made a face. "Whoever she is, she probably doesn't want to hang out with us . . . but she would want the pages. Gotcha." She snapped her fingers.

Cordelia considered. "If it's either one of those two vampire women, then she's fairly upscale, so I'm thinking we should meet her somewhere that would be very comfortable for her. How about Saks? What?" she added, at their looks. "It's where I'd go if I were a vampire." She gave Wesley a look. "If I were a better paid vampire."

Gunn snickered. "Saks. A department store."

"It's as good a public place as any," Cordelia shot back.

"It's also closed at this time of night," Wesley pointed out. He said to Angel, "I think we should strike as soon as possible." Angel nodded, and Wesley continued, "It should be some place crowded, so she—or they—can't ambush us. And somewhere neutral to them."

"And to us," Angel finished.

The three looked at each other, then said in unison, "Caritas."

"Which I know how to spell," Cordelia announced huffily.

"You'll be paid more when we make more money," Wesley retorted over his shoulder.

"Well, that'll be when hell freezes over, which it probably will someday, so at least I have a shot at a decent standard of living."

Wesley gave her a look. "You are scarcely living in a dump, Cordelia." He continued to type.

"And you have a lot of nice clothes." Fred smiled at her. "I wish I had the nerve to wear the kinds of things you wear."

Cordelia preened, then folded her arms and said, "I live in a nice apartment because it's haunted and I have nice clothes because Angel bought my friendship with them."

"And it didn't come cheap, I'd like to point out," Angel asserted. He and Cordelia nodded together. "Not that I, you know, kept track."

"You'll get paid more when everyone else does," Wesley said again.

While they squabbled, Angel picked up the phone and checked Escobar's number, which he'd written on the back of one of his Angel Investigations business cards. Cordelia had designed the hand-drawn angel logo, which had been mistaken for everything from a lobster to the face of former Beatle Ringo Starr.

There was no answer. A voice message system came on with no prompts for the caller and no identification of the owner of the voice mailbox. *He's careful,* Angel thought. *That's probably why he's lived this long.*

"We met today," he said. "You have my number. Call me back." He disconnected.

Cordelia appeared in the doorway. "Okay," she said. "We've set up a meeting at the karaoke bar for two hours from now."

Angel frowned. "Two hours? That's cutting it close."

She looked at him. "Close, for . . . ?"

"Dawn." He looked at her, noticing for the first time the dark circles under her eyes and the ashen cast to her skin. She was exhausted. He was worried about her; the visions were taking a terrible toll on her.

"Then she won't try any funny stuff," Cordelia said, not sounding confident. "If she's a vamp."

"I was planning to go . . . ," Angel said, then glanced at Wesley as if for permission.

Wesley nodded, much more at ease with his role as their leader than he used to be. "I was planning to send you. But not alone. We've already run into her minions before. Just because no one can fight on the premises doesn't mean there won't be forces of darkness afoot in the street."

"I'm goin' too," Gunn said.

"Fine." Wesley nodded. "I'm going to stay here in case our blackout was no coincidence."

Angel patted his coat pocket for his car keys. "Then let's go," he said to Gunn, who picked up his customized fighting axe from beside the main doors and hoisted it onto his shoulder.

"I'm cool," he said.

"I'd feel better about this if we knew with whom we're dealing," Wesley said as they headed for the door. "Whatever this Book is, we're the ones who should have it."

Cordelia sighed. "We'll wait up."

"Good." Angel turned to leave.

From the stairs Fred called, "Angel?"

He looked up at her. "Yes, Fred?"

"Um. Be careful." She flashed him a faltering smile. "'Cause if anything happened to you . . . oh, golly." She swallowed hard.

"I'll be careful," he promised her.

"'Loving you is easy 'cause you're beautiful,'" a Shastgul demon crooned to the crowd. He stood alone on the stage, bathed in lights and unbelievably hideous, but with a voice like an angel.

"And it's a beautiful night when you walk in, honey," Lorne said to Angel from his perch on a stool at the bar. "Whassup, as the kids say these days?" He grinned at Gunn, who cleared his throat and looked patronized.

Angel scanned the room. "Looking for someone."

"Lots of someones in this city," Lorne drawled, narrowing his big red eyes. "You people have a penchant for the vague. Not an asset when you're looking for answers." He gestured to the bartender, who nodded and pulled down a glass from an overhead rack. "Have some O pos. You look pale. Gunn? Care for a beverage?"

"You see anyone unusual in here tonight?" Angel asked as Gunn shook his head at the Host.

"The understatement, it's so . . . piquant," Lorne observed, as the bartender passed the glass of blood to him. "Want some cayenne in this?"

"You're as bad as Cordelia," Angel said distractedly. "She put some cinnamon in it once. Gritty."

Angel nudged Gunn, and the two scrutinized the back of a lone patron sitting far across the room with his or her back toward the bar. It looked to be a man, or a good-sized demon, wearing a black leather coat not unlike Angel's own, and a knitted cap down low over his head.

The Host traced Angel's gaze and wagged his finger. "Remember, Angel, there is no fighting. This is a sanctuary for all my patrons, even those who need singing lessons and a personal stylist."

Just then the lone patron rose and strolled casually toward the exit.

"Let's go, dog," Gunn murmured at Angel.

Angel immediately followed, ignoring Lorne as he said, "Happy hunting."

The stranger moved faster; Angel kept up and Gunn trailed closely behind. Then the figure broke into a run, pushing open the emergency exit and racing out into the service stairwell. Footfalls clattered as he—Angel was now certain that he was pursuing a man—half ran, half stumbled up the stairs, trying to put as much distance between Angel and himself as he could.

It was no contest; Angel was beside the guy before he knew what was happening. He pushed him out of the shadows and up against the cement wall. Gunn joined the altercation and yanked the man's hat off his head.

"Okay, we've made contact," Angel said, "and . . ." He trailed off.

The man he had hold of was Chaz Escobar, who said nothing, only shrugged apologetically.

"Man, you big liar," Gunn flung at him. "You told me you were going to watch *Gosford Park*."

Just then the door opened. A building security guard looked startled, then highly suspicious. He said, "What are you guys doing?"

"Nothing," all three men said.

"I'd better check, make sure everything is all right," the guard said. He gestured to Chaz Escobar's coat. "Please, open your coat."

Gunn muttered, "Yo, bro, check it out," and pointed toward the open door.

Angel said, "Yeah, I felt it."

The first streaks of gray were lightning the sky. Dawn was coming. If Escobar was carrying anything unusual that might lead to questions, the guard was going to pose a problem.

I'll just knock him out, Angel thought, but Escobar passed muster. The guard grunted and pointed at Angel.

"Now you."

Angel had concealed a few stakes in his coat sleeves; other than that, he was clean.

"Hey, man, I'm cool," Gunn assured the other man. "I would never pack at Caritas."

The guard looked unimpressed. Gunn sighed and lifted his red sweatshirt, revealing a wicked fine blade from Angel's arsenal at the hotel.

The guard gestured to it: "That's mine," he announced, extending his hand palm out.

"Hey, man, we're not in Caritas now," Gunn argued. He slid a glance toward Angel. "Getting light out."

Angel sighed. "Just give it to him."

"Cool." Gunn made a fist and rammed it into the face of the guard. He went down, and they went out the door.

Vampire, friend of same, and hunter strolled down the street. Angel regarded the sky again, then gave the Spaniard a hard look.

"Want to start explaining? Quickly?"

Escobar looked frustrated. "Do you really have the pages?" When Angel said nothing, Escobar shrugged. "I need the Book," he said, "so I can put an end to your kind."

CHAPTER SEVEN

"I can see that I have some explaining to do, Angel," Escobar said.

"You sure do." Angel had stopped on the sidewalk, fists clenched at his sides. "And do it fast, before I run out of patience."

"I have deceived you," Escobar said, somberly. "I apologize, and beg your forgiveness."

"We'll have to wait and see about that part," Angel said.

"I understand. May we walk?"

"What do you mean, walk?"

"I prefer to be on the move," Escobar said. "My senses are sharpest and my mind clearest when I move, and I need to explain something to you that is difficult for me."

Angel shrugged. He had started out almost trusting Escobar, mainly since the guy had first shown up saving Wesley and Gunn. *But from some of his own home-grown monsters,* he remembered. *So maybe that trust thing wasn't the best idea.* Now, though, after finding out that Escobar had been the one who IMed Cordelia, Angel was far less inclined to take anything he had to say at face value, even though Escobar couldn't have known who she was.

"I have lied to you," Escobar announced after they had covered most of a city block.

Except that. That I believe. "About what? Everything?"

"No, not all."

"Just a side note, Escobar, but this walk can't be a long one." Gunn gestured toward the sky. "'Cause, flames, y'know?"

"I understand, Mr. Gunn." The Spaniard sighed. "I will get to the point. I thought it best not to be fully forthcoming with you, because when I met you I could tell that you are a vampire."

"Which has what to do with it?"

"You will see." He waved his hand in an imperious gesture to be quiet and listen. "I am—as I implied to Miss Cordelia earlier this evening, via the internet—interested in the Book of the Interregnum." Escobar's normal exclamatory tone was gone, and Angel almost had to strain to hear him over their footsteps and the light pre-dawn traffic of the city.

"So the thing really exists," Gunn said softly. "Damn."

Angel said to Escobar, "You want to summon the Beast of the First Blood?"

"I do," Escobar admitted. "But only to kill it."

"If it could be killed, it would have been done long ago," Angel countered. "By the priests who banished it."

"They did not know how," Escobar explained. "They had to work fast to figure out how to banish it, hoping to rid the world of a plague that had taken root during their watch. They didn't have the benefit of thousands of years of further experimentation and study, as I have."

"So you've actually come up with a way to finish it off, once and for all?" Gunn glanced at Angel, who shrugged noncommittally. He took this with a huge grain of salt—boatloads of it, in fact. He was pretty sure the Book of the Interregnum was nothing but a myth, and the idea that Chaz Escobar would have come up with a way to kill the Beast of the First Blood when no one else ever had seemed far-fetched, to say the least.

"As I told you, I have traveled this planet from end to end, corner to corner," Escobar said. "Hunting, seeking prey—but also, particularly since Marianna became a vampire, seeking knowledge. I have met many, many people with a variety of skills and abilities, and have sifted through myth and legend, sacred texts and whispered rumors, and have, finally, reached some conclusions of my own."

Gunn cocked his head. "So what happens when you kill the Beast? What do you accomplish?"

Escobar stopped walking now, and stood with his back to the window of a closed dry-cleaning establishment. "It will sever the power of the Blood in all vampires, across the earth," he said.

"Meaning what?" Gunn demanded, his voice rising.

The hunter took a beat. Then he raised his chin and said, "Meaning they all will become extinct. No more vampires. Ever."

Including me, Angel thought. He took that in as best he could, but truth was, he had long ago given up on trying to imagine himself truly dead, truly gone. On another level, as a warrior for the cause of good, he had to rejoice at the thought of an end to all vampires.

But all he said was, "Including Marianna?"

"It is my fervent wish to restore her humanity before this comes to pass," Escobar replied. "But if I cannot do so, then yes. Including Marianna."

Gunn whistled.

"How sure are you about all this?" Angel asked him. "I always thought the Book was just a story."

Escobar started walking again, and Angel glanced once more at the sky, now a flat, leaden color. *Have to wrap this up quickly,* he thought, *and get under cover.*

"Not at all," Escobar assured him. "I have some pages from it in my possession. Enough to prove the Book's existence, and to indicate that my ultimate purpose can be achieved. I just don't have enough to summon the Beast."

This was a new twist. Actual pages from the Book meant it was real—or that Escobar had been the victim of a clever con game. Every legend about the Book agreed on one point: There was only one copy, had only ever been one copy, and every attempt to duplicate the Book had ended in death and destruction. According to the stories, acolytes in a twelfth-century monastery had tried to copy the Book, and just before getting to the end of it, the place had been caught up in a horrible conflagration. The entire monastery had burned to the ground, most of the monks died in the fire, and the manuscript—the result of six years of labor by a dozen sets of hands—was totally consumed.

Somehow, though, the original Book, from which the monks had been copying, was untouched. The few survivors wanted nothing to do with the thing, calling it a tool of the Devil.

Just stories, Angel had always thought. *To scare the innocent.*

If it exists, then the Beast can be summoned.

If the Beast can be summoned, maybe it can be killed.

If Escobar is right.

So many ifs, with no guarantees. But, Angel thought, looking again at the sky, *if all the ifs play out right, then vampires can be eliminated from the planet. Humans would no longer have to fear the dark, be hunted for their blood. That would be big. That would be important.*

"Well, then," he said. "I guess we'd better find that Book."

"But Angel," Wesley said. "That would include you, right?"

Angel shrugged. "I'm a vampire. So, yeah."

They were back at the hotel. Escobar had gone his own way, and Gunn had immediately alerted the rest of the gang about what was going on. Angel was exhausted and very much wanting to go to bed, but nobody was letting him. They had convened in the lobby. Cordelia and Fred sat on the circular couch, Angel facing them; Gunn and Wesley paced, as if the energy of their emotions compelled them to keep on the move.

"You can't die," Cordelia said. Her expression was morose, her tone urgent. "You just can't. You're . . . you're Angel."

Angel sighed as he gestured his surrender "Cordelia—I know how you feel. I'm not so happy about the dying either. But . . ."

She gave him a patented Cordy Look of Indignation. "Right, you know how I feel, because you're so good at that whole empathy thing."

"Cordy," Fred whispered, distressed.

"No, I do." He frowned, distressed that he was not conveying his real emotions to her. *So* not *good with the empathy thing . . .*

"You'd miss me. I'd miss all of you. Except that I'd be dead—deader. And hopefully you wouldn't be."

Stopping by the weapons cabinet, Gunn snorted. "You got that right, bro," he said.

Wesley tapped the lobby counter as if all the talk was something to be gotten through as quickly as possible, because it was stupid.

Angel pressed on. "So I don't know how much that missing you part would be a factor for me."

Oooh, lame.

"See? So you should pay attention to our feelings, and not your own." Cordelia humphed at him and looked at the others for support. To a human, they appeared to side with her, by the nods and earnest looks shot Angel's way.

"I might go to hell again," he mused. "If I really died."

"Glad you're thinking this through," Gunn grumbled.

"But the flip side, Cordy," Angel argued, looking hard at her. "No more vampires, at all. Anywhere. *Ever*."

"Vampires are pretty nasty," Fred ventured, half-raising her hand as if she had to seek permission to speak. "Not counting you, of course."

"Thanks, Fred." Angel smiled kindly at her. She was dear. Wacky, but dear.

"Yeah, they are," Gunn said, taking the floor as he, resumed pacing." And you know I always vote for killin' 'em when there's a choice." He stopped dead in his tracks. "But I agree with Wes and Cordy—I think you gotta take another look at your options here."

"There aren't any options," Angel said, stuffing his hands in his pants pockets and shrugging. "I've devoted myself to helping humans. Maybe I'm trying to absolve myself of guilt for the wrongs I've done. I'm just trying to help people. And getting rid of all vampires would help people—not much room for argument there."

"It's not just about you any more," Cordelia pointed out, crossing her arms and legs, very much pulling away from him with her body language. "You work for The Powers That Be. We all do."

She gestured with one hand to the group at large. "You don't just take out vampires, you do what they need you to do. Demons, evil doctors who can take themselves apart, possessed kids—you do it all. One-stop shopping for the supernatural terrors that surround us."

"Who's to say the Powers didn't put Escobar in front of me?" Angel replied reasonably. He walked to the counter; Wesley drifted away, and Angel leaned against it. "They sent you a vision of Faith in trouble. Faith is in trouble from Escobar's wife, who is a vampire. It all ties together."

"Well, my vote is with the others," Wesley said, raising his chin and giving him a look that nearly rivaled Cordelia's in intensity. "You do the world a lot more good here than you would not here."

Angel was moved. He and Wesley had been through good times, bad times, and times where they had had no time for each other. Personal feelings aside, the fact that Wesley valued his presence on the side of good meant a lot.

"Look," Angel argued, still needing to make his point, "my not being here wouldn't really change all that much, in the greater scheme of things." He shrugged as they began to protest. "Sure, there was a time that I worked alone, pretty much did everything myself. But now there are all of you. You're a team. You can fight demons and win. You can go up against just about anything the world can hand you, even without me."

"Nuh-uh," Cordelia began.

And there was another moment . . . another of what Angel was beginning to think of as "perfume moments," when he was aware of Cordelia's scent, and her aliveness, and the fierce sparkle in her eyes as she insisted that she couldn't do without him.

Covering his reaction, he continued, "And there's still the Slayer. Slayers, plural, with Buffy and Faith both out there. I wouldn't be leaving the world defenseless. But I'd be eliminating one of the major things that has to be defended against."

"Angel's right," Fred chimed in, looking earnest as she gazed around the room. "If you look at the numbers there's no other way to take it. The sheer volume of vampires in the world, constantly feeding—they must be taking more lives in a year than Angel could possibly save if he lived . . . well, forever. But I guess he would live forever, really." She was thinking it through as she went, her scientific mind clicking off postulations. "But he can never, as one person, catch up to the damage a world full of vampires can do."

As the others shifted uncomfortably, she continued, apparently oblivious to their pain. "Especially if the Book is real, and Benedicta could manage to get her hands on it and summon the Beast, instead of Escobar doing it. If Benedicta summons it and mates with it, then the vampires you all have been dealing with up to now would be like children compared to what you've been up against."

She was beginning to run out of steam. "The best way to make sure she doesn't get it is to help Escobar get it first, and to let him eliminate all vampires, including Benedicta.

"And Angel."

Then her eyes misted and she swallowed hard to keep from sobbing. "But that's just the math," she added. Her eyes welled and she threw up her hands, saying in a rush, "I don't want you to do it either, Angel. There's more at stake than just math."

"We can't let there be more at stake," Angel countered. He regarded his friends—his family—making a mental snapshot of this moment. *They care. They don't want me to die.*

He said firmly, "The math is right. The rest of it is just our personal feelings, which can't get in the way of the greater good."

"Why not?" Cordelia demanded angrily. "Why the heck not? We work hard for the Powers. We bust our butts. We take on anything they send our way and we do a good job and we help a lot of people. If we want to be selfish for once, I think we're entitled."

"That's right," Gunn added.

"It's the magnitude of it we have to consider," Angel said. "Like Fred pointed out, I can keep helping people one at a time or I can do one thing that will help, over the span of my potential existence, maybe millions, even billions. And then you have to realize, I could be killed tomorrow. I'm still a vampire. A big splinter can take me out. A ray of sunlight. With that as a reality I pretty much have to go for the big splashy finish."

They were all quiet for a moment, reflecting on what he had said.

Then Wesley broke the silence. "Do we know that Escobar can really deliver? And that he isn't actually in league with Marianna? Or with Benedicta?"

"We can't know anything about him for a fact," Angel agreed. "He's lied to us before. But I think we have to take him at his word, and keep a close eye on him at the same time. When—if—he summons the Beast, I have to be there. And if he doesn't kill it, then I will."

"Can you?" Wesley asked him point blank, and Angel respected him for it. For not pulling punches, and for asking the hard questions. Wesley had more than proven himself as a tough strategist, in this world and in Pylea.

"I will," Angel repeated. "There's just one thing—until all this happens, Faith is still in danger. And if I . . . go, then it's that much more important that she is still around to carry on the fight. You've still got the vision hangover, Cordy?"

"Check, boss," she said glumly. As if to underscore her answer, she rubbed her temples. Seated beside her, Fred patted her shoulder and pulled a sad face.

"So the danger is still out there. We have to divide our efforts—we need to find the Book of the Interregnum, before Benedicta does. And we have to make sure that

Faith is safe. I think I probably have the best chance of finding the Book, so you guys need to keep tabs on Faith, okay?"

"Delighted to," Wesley said. He didn't sound delighted at all.

For Faith, the day was progressing much like all the days before it, and like the ones to come would most likely be as well. Change wasn't exactly the watchword at the Yorba Linda Ranch. Routine was. And routine had never been something at which Faith had excelled, which made the whole prison thing a bit of a challenge.

Maybe that's the point of prison. Challenge.

Since Angel had been to see her a week ago, nothing had changed. Nothing on the inside, anyway. During the late afternoons she and the other babes in chains spent a couple of hours in the yard. Some of the women exercised or lifted weights. Some played sports—basketball was big, and there were a couple of soccer teams, on the theory that round balls didn't make terribly deadly weapons. Others simply walked or jogged around the enclosure.

Faith tended to spend a lot of time standing near the twenty-foot fence, looking beyond it at the rolls of concertina wire that surrounded the second fence—the one that separated Yorba Linda Ranch from the rest of the world. That was what she did today, as well. Watching the world—that small part of it that could be seen from here, trees and grass and birds and clouds in the sky—and trying to make a decision.

I'm going nuts waiting for whatever is going to happen, to happen.

Angel had told her about Buffy's death and return. When she had heard that Buffy was dead, the temptation to leave this place was strong. Buffy had died before, which had activated a Slayer named Kendra. Then Kendra died, activating Faith. So Buffy's more recent death probably didn't activate a new Slayer, since she was already out of the Chosen loop.

Which meant that, while Buffy was gone, Faith was the only Slayer. Every night during that time, her dreams had been uneasy, her waking moments fraught with indecision. She had committed to staying in jail for the duration of her sentence, except when she'd been out on brief but necessary business. If she took off on her own, she would not only break her promise to herself, but she would be sought as a fugitive. Staying in L.A. would be impossible, and even Sunnydale might not be far enough away. Could a Slayer really function if she were hunted not only by the bad guys but by the good ones as well?

In the end she had decided to try to stick it out. Angel's friends had no real reason to trust her, but they'd agreed to let her know if there was any major crisis requiring the services of a Slayer. They had probably agreed because even Angel was going away, and with Buffy and Angel both out of the picture, Southern California was wide open to the forces of evil. So Faith stayed put at Yorba Linda, and somehow the world continued to turn. Then Buffy came back from whatever hell she'd been in, and Angel came back from Tibet, and Faith felt relieved. She'd made the right choice.

But now, if that guy Escobar was to be believed, someone was trying to get her out again. And this time the purpose was to kill her. She didn't like the first idea, and she was definitely opposed to the second. Yorba Linda Ranch was a pit, but it was home, and she had no plans to leave it any time soon.

She saw figures moving on the horizon, and figured them to be her bodyguards. Wesley had brought down some of Gunn's homeys to watch over her, and he'd done some magic spells and even spent a couple of days in the field with the troops.

Musta bugged him bigtime, she thought. She fingered his amulet, which she kept stuffed in a pocket, and thought about what a weird deal she had going on with him. *God, I tortured him so badly. I have no clue why he hasn't broken in here himself and shot me in my bed.*

Well, actually, I do. He's a decent guy.

An inmate didn't survive long at the Ranch without maintaining a hypersensitive alertness to her surroundings. Even standing by the fence looking out, Faith knew that there were two people crossing the yard toward her—the steady crunch of their feet on the sandy floor, the determined pace of their approach—everything pointed to people who were not inmates, who carried the weight of authority. That they were coming for her, she had no doubt; that they were guards and not cons she was equally sure. She let them get to within a dozen feet before she turned to face them.

And was surprised. One of them was a guard, but the other was the warden. Faith had a surprising amount of respect for Carola Westin, considering that the woman's main purpose in life was keeping other women behind bars. She was a rarity in the world of corrections officers— even women's prisons were generally under the charge of men, and there were only a small handful of female wardens in the state. Carola Westin had a reputation, among them, of being fair and levelheaded. But along with that reputation there was a corollary—don't try to mess with Westin, because she doesn't take any crap.

"Warden," Faith said, nodding briefly to the guard that accompanied her. He was male, a veteran of the Orange County Sheriff's Office, and someone that Faith didn't like or trust.

"Hello, Faith," Warden Westin said cheerfully. "You'll have to come with us."

"Come where?" Faith asked. *What's going on?* Her Slayer senses went into overdrive. She had to lick her lips to keep herself from bolting.

"Your things are already packed and waiting for you," the warden continued, pointedly not answering the question.

"I don't care about my things," Faith said "I just want to know where I'm going."

"You're being released," Westin told her.

"Released? Like, cut loose? Free?" *Okay, trouble. I smell it.* "I'm not anywhere near eligibility for parole."

The woman smiled. "No, I'm afraid it's not quite that attractive," she said. "But it should be interesting just the same."

"You going to tell me what it's all about?" Faith asked. She leaned toward the warden as she spoke, and realized that her tone was probably a little harsh. The guard's hands clenched on the shotgun he carried, and Faith knew that in the tower, there was probably a sniper with a bead on her right this second. It didn't pay to make sudden moves toward the warden.

"I'm not sure I even understand it all myself," the warden said. "Some sort of experimental rehabilitation program. They're taking prisoners who have good behavior records from institutions all over the state and putting them in a kind of work-study facility. They say there'll be career training, work experience, placement services, all geared toward reducing recidivism and making sure that you ladies can find gainful employment after your term is served."

She smiled, but it didn't reassure Faith. "You know what happens when ex-cons can't find work—they end up back in the system within three years, most of them. Usually less time than that. They tell me this is a model program designed to combat that, to turn the statistic inside out. I have to support an effort like that."

"Have you heard of this program before?" Faith asked. She didn't trust it for a second, considering the timing, with the Escobar woman wanting to break her out.

"No," the warden said. "But that's not surprising, given the nature of bureaucracy. I've seen the paperwork. It's all on the up and up."

"If you haven't heard of it," Faith pressed, "how'd they pick me?"

"I'm sure they have access to all our records," Warden Westin replied. "It's not all that surprising. You're a good candidate, Faith. Just go along with it, and I'm sure it'll be a terrific opportunity for you."

"Do I have a choice?"

"No," the warden said seriously. The eyes of virtually every woman in the yard were upon them, and she seemed more than a little nervous about the exposure. "I'm afraid not. Let's go, now—the transport is waiting for you."

To a few shouts and hoots aimed her way—nothing too pointed, since no one in the yard was sure of what was going on—Faith allowed herself to be led from the yard into the control building, where the warden's office and the inmate processing rooms were located. Out-processing turned out to be much faster and more efficient than in-processing. As the warden had told her, what little she owned—a hairbrush, some rudimentary cosmetics, a couple of books—had been packed into a bag for her.

A sealed envelope contained personal items she'd had on her when she turned herself in, but that envelope was handed over to a uniformed guard, not to her. She wouldn't get that back until she was freed. She remained in her prison uniform. She had to sign a couple of forms, but most of the paperwork was between the warden and the guards who were picking her up. She'd never seen either of them before, but that wasn't unusual—while it seemed sometimes like she'd encountered every cop in Southern California, the reality was far from that.

Then it was done. The warden shook her hand warmly and wished her good luck, and the guards put handcuffs on her and led her out a door to a covered loading dock where a van waited, white with a state seal on it and bars over the windows. Inside the van, in the front passenger seat, a beautiful woman with long black hair sat, watching Faith with a sly, secret smile on her face.

"Who's that?" Faith asked, tensing up at the unexpected sight.

"Don't worry about it," one of the guards said. These guards were both male, both strong, and heavily armed. Faith didn't like the brusque response. She tugged, surreptitiously, at the handcuffs, to see how much effort they'd be to break.

When she did, she felt shooting pains up and down her arms. She stumbled.

"I wouldn't try anything," the guard warned her. "The cuffs are enchanted. You're not going anywhere."

Enchanted? Shit!

She opened her mouth to scream, but no sound came out. Her voice was gone. She struggled with the cuffs, but succeeded only in causing herself more racking pain. The guards hustled her into the waiting van and slammed the door. Faith tried to open it, but she was too weak to even get the door open.

The woman in the front seat turned to her with a big smile. "Welcome, Slayer," she said. "It's so nice that you could join us."

Faith tried to respond, but her voice still wouldn't work. Furious and frustrated, she just sat back in the seat. *These cuffs will come off sometime,* she thought. *And there'll be hell to pay.*

"One moment," the woman in front said to the guard who sat down behind the wheel. "One last bit of paperwork with the attorneys. *Your* attorneys, Faith," she added. She climbed from the van and went back inside the processing center. Faith could see her through a window, talking with Warden Westin and two other people, a tall, glamorous woman and a lean Asian man.

She had no idea who the guy was, but she recognized the woman. She'd never forget that face.

Lilah Morgan, of Wolfram & Hart.

If that was her attorney, then she was really in trouble.

CHAPTER EIGHT

Leaping from the shadows, Chaz Escobar rushed Angel with a machete as Cordelia, crouched behind a metal column, sprang into action.

Like that chick on *Witchblade*, she made her weapon seem like an extension of her arm as she lunged, parried, and whacked the hell out of one of the columns in the basement. Steel clanged against aluminum and Angel grimaced at the grating sound. He couldn't help his distraction: Back in the day, his little sister tormented him by trailing her fingernails down the piece of slate their mam used to teach them letters.

I told her I'd kill her every time she did that. Eventually I did.

Escobar tried to take advantage of Angel's attention hiccup, swinging the machete at Angel's neck, but Angel tucked and rolled, knocking Escobar onto his butt like a weightless Styrofoam boulder. Jackie Chan–quick, he yanked the machete out of Escobar's hand as he planted his feet firmly beneath himself. As he rose, he whirled around and, holding the machete like a *kendo* sword, angled it over Escobar's throat.

Escobar chuckled and raised a hand in defeat. "Okay, *macho*. You win."

Coming up to them Cordelia muttered, "Hope I didn't nick it." She examined her blade as Angel held out his hand to Escobar. The Spaniard took it, hoisting himself to a standing position.

"Never spare your weapon," the man said to Cordelia.

"Words you live by," she drawled, "I'm sure."

His eyes flashed and he smiled appreciatively, as he said, "Ah, *chavelita. Estoy un pocquito enamorado de ti.* You have a certain . . . flair." He slid his glance toward Angel. "*Ay, perdón.* You two are not . . . ?"

"No, we're not," Angel assured him, at the same time that Cordelia said, with false sincerity, "Why, yes, we are." She glared at Angel. "We *are*, Angel, *okay?*"

"Oh?" Then Angel got it: She didn't want Escobar to be on the prowl for her. "Oh." He nodded vigorously and swept her into his arms. Her back was warm and damp from the exertion, and he noticed that she fit comfortably against him. *More than comfortable. Hey, liking this.*

"We are. We're very . . . are," Angel continued.

Cordelia flashed Angel the smashing, brilliant smile that she usually reserved for when someone gave her something. In this case, it was an excuse not to be Escobar's next quarry.

"Good. So you know I'm . . . protected. From being poached. Or poached on."

"Alas," Escobar said mournfully.

"Not that I'm not flattered," she added hastily, giving him a slightly less smashing, brilliant smile. "'Cause, boy, if I weren't already taken . . ."

Angel got that too. Cordy was a good businesswoman and she would never go so far as to offend someone who had money, at least just to prove a point. "Everything is good here," she said, deftly spinning the conversation into a safer direction. "Let's go eat." Escobar had promised to take them to Morton's for dinner. Though he had no particular desire to eat, Angel was accompanying the group anyway. These days, he had a lot to discuss with Chaz Escobar.

Cordelia started up the stairs, followed by Escobar, while Angel put away his and Escobar's sparring weapons. The hunter was a good fighter, quick on his feet, and very aggressive. Any endangered species that crossed the man's path was likely to become more endangered in a very short time.

"Hey, Wesley," Cordelia chirruped, then added, "who is looking . . . not happy. Even though we're getting a free meal. And not a free happy meal, may I add. Sit-down restaurant free meal."

"There's no such thing as a free meal, Cordelia," Wesley snapped.

By then, Angel had reached the top of the stairs. Wesley's face was tired and drawn. In the past week of intensive work researching the items Escobar needed for his ritual, he had already taken Angel aside a number of times and asked him to reconsider his participation in what he referred to as "the Extinction Project." Angel was moved by Wesley's refusal to concur that getting rid of all the vampires on the planet was worth his, Angel's, life. But that didn't lessen his own determination to make that happen.

"Gunn just phoned. He has located the mummy of the sacrificial Virgin of Nuremberg mentioned in the Book," Wesley said, with less than joy. "It seems that the cousin of a demon who frequents Caritas is using it as a roadside attraction in Cabazon. For five dollars tourists can take a look at it before going further down the highway to take in the breathtaking experience that is Dino-land."

"Don't make that snobby British face," Cordelia chided him. "You guys charge five times that for people to gawk at big rocks."

"Stonehenge is not just 'big rocks.' It's an astronomical calendar, and those large stones are called dolmens."

"Dolmens are a kind of Greek food, and gosh, mummy found, and I'm suddenly not very hungry," Cordelia said glumly. Trudging past Wesley, she muttered, "I hate it when you find the stuff he needs."

Escobar beamed at Wesley. "*Muchissimas gracias,*" he said, clapping the former Watcher on the shoulder. "The mummy's very important to the ritual. You used a protected phone, sí?"

"Sí." Wesley put his hands in his pockets and glanced down, not sharing in the moment. "Of course."

"What about the Mead Bowl of Loki?"

Wesley shook his head. "Negative on that one. I've not found a single lead. I'm certain it's got to be a skull. Human, of course."

"Of course," Cordelia called from the stairway.

Wesley continued. "The Norse were very big on drinking from the skulls of their vanquished foes. And as for Loki, he's the god of fire, and . . ." Wesley trailed off. "No leads, as I said."

Angel blinked as he felt a dim memory pressing on his consciousness. He said, "What's the Mead Bowl for?"

Escobar gestured for them to walk to the lobby. Evidently he assumed they were still going out to dinner. But by his demeanor, Angel was fairly certain Wesley was going to drop out too.

"It holds the soul of the Beast," Escobar informed them.

"Rather like an Orb of Thesulah," Wesley said, "which they used for you, that first time. When Willow restored your soul."

"An Orb . . . ," Angel mused. "And a fire god. I wonder if that could be another name for Pele's Chalice." He looked at Wesley. "Can you check it out?"

"Certainly."

"After dinner," Escobar said. "We need to take some time, have some pleasure."

Wesley slid a dark glance toward Angel. "If you'll excuse me, the notion of pleasure eludes me whilst I research how to best kill my friend." He inclined his head. "I'm afraid I won't be joining you for dinner tonight either."

Angel gave him a nod. Escobar looked dashed as Wesley walked back into Angel's office and sat down at the computer. Angel said, "I think we'll reschedule." Fred had already indicated her wish to stay in her room and scribble on the walls.

"Como quieres," Escobar said. "As you wish." He gave

Angel a wave and added, "I'll go now, leave you for this evening. If Wesley finds something . . ."

"We'll let you know." Angel added, "I'll send Gunn to pick up the mummy." Cabazon was a straight shot out on the I-10 from Los Angeles, just past Palm Springs. Not a long trip if traffic was light.

"If he needs cash to buy it . . ." Escobar began.

"We're good," Angel cut in.

He watched Escobar go out the front door. Then he glanced at Wesley, seated at his desk. The light from the computer gave his face a morbid glow; Angel knew that the circles under his eyes and hollows in his cheeks spoke of his sleeplessness, and not his commitment to the Extinction Project.

Angel took the stairs, walking down the hall. He rapped softly on Fred's door. It was not shut, only pulled loosely toward the jamb, and soft weeping trailed over the threshold. Angel gently pushed the door open a crack.

Cordelia and Fred were seated on Fred's bed. Fred was cradling Cordy's head on her shoulder, and both of them were crying. A box of tissues sat between them.

"It's not right. I should grab him and take him back to Pylea," Fred moaned.

"Me too," Cordelia sniffled. "Plus I'm a princess there. I could order him to, like, stay there and be really happy."

Angel sighed and moved away from the door.

He felt very alone as he continued down the hall toward his suite. He had no words of comfort to offer any of his friends. Despite the fact that Cordelia, Wesley, and Gunn spent every day and night of their lives dealing with the supernatural, they themselves were all too human: Life for them was either true life or death. For most vampires, there were grayer shades. For him . . . no answers.

I'm a dead man walking with a soul, and that's not supposed to happen. So if all vampires cease to exist . . . what part of me dies? Maybe if we knew, it would be easier for them to do this.

Opening his door and walking inside his rooms, he wondered if Escobar was being straight with him even now. The man had been caught lying, and lying big; and then, though he professed to love his vampiric wife, he was ready to kill her entire species.

Gunn did it, he reflected, opening his fridge for a dawntime snack. *He loved Alonna, but when she changed, he staked her.*

Back in the day, Darla tried to change me after the Gypsies gave me back my soul. She practically went to the ends of the earth to save Angelus from an eternity of torment. Was that her version of love, or was she just trying to reclaim what she saw as rightfully hers?

Did Buffy and I experience true love? She was my soulmate, but Darla was my obsession . . . wherever she is, I think she's still my obsession . . .

Angel undressed and crawled wearily into bed. He closed his eyes and saw again old days, old memories, and very old wounds . . . . He imagined what he had left in his wake back in China, when he had abandoned Darla . . . *when I truly accepted that I was—that I am—the only one of my species . . . a vampire with a soul . . .*

I've got to take another shot at getting out of here, Faith told herself, as Lilah Morgan glanced in her direction. The lawyer from hell—*well, maybe the lawyer on her way to hell, hopefully soon*—smiled her trademark "I'm the bitch of the world" smile and said something to the Asian man. He looked over at Faith, giving her a once-over, and the Slayer muttered under her breath, "Take a picture, dirt bag. It'll last longer."

The two attorneys turned their attention back to Faith's kidnapper, shook hands, and gathered up tons of paperwork. Always with the paperwork. *I wonder how thick the file gets when someone sells them their soul.*

The woman moved toward the door and Faith tensed, her mind racing. Okay, she'd veered down the wrong path for a while—*like, most of my life*—but the fact remained that she was Chosen and her Watcher had trained her well. *I've got the strength, I've got the reflexes. I just gotta strategize a little. Buffy was always on me for acting without running through the play. What would she do in this sitch?*

Faith couldn't help her bitter laughter. *She'd never be in this sitch. B's never gonna end up in jail, moron.*

Yeah, but she's fallen into enemy hands all kinds of times . . . even my hands . . . and she always got free, okay, except for that last time, when she died. . . . .

The woman walked toward the vehicle and Faith's lips parted in surprise. She blurted, "She's a freakin' vampire."

The driver chuckled. "Well, yeah," he said. Then he went vamp face. "So am I."

The woman approached the van, opened the door, and climbed in. She half-turned to address Faith. "Lilah Morgan sends her regards," she said. "You'll be seeing her again soon. On San Teodor."

"I'm so lucky." Faith batted her lashes at her. "And San Teodor is the name of her priest?"

The woman moved her shoulders, which were muscular in the way of chicks who worked out, but not enough to be played by Kurt Russell in the movie. "You'll find out soon enough. Well, not that soon."

"Oooh, sounds like a road trip," Faith said brightly.

"Boat trip," the woman responded. Looking past her, Faith realized that the windshield and side windows of the van were heavily tinted, the glass cutting the sun's rays and protecting the driver and passenger.

Wonder if Angel knows about that, Faith thought. *Handy.* Not that it mattered much; the sun had already dropped behind the horizon, and only its last rays tinged a sky in which the moon was rising.

The driver chuckled, and Faith thought seriously about the pleasure she would get when she shoved a wooden stake through his heart and watched him erupt into a cloud of black dust.

Wesley's got guys outside, she reminded herself. *They'll bust me out.*

The vampire woman's cell phone went off, and she took the call. "Wonderful," she said, then disconnected.

She smiled at Faith. "The men guarding you have been eliminated," she announced. "Now there's nothing preventing me from taking you to San Teodor. Unless Chaz hears about this . . ." She grinned, as if that were what she hoped.

Faith said nothing. She was very sorry about the guys who had just given up their lives for her. *I'll get out of this, make it right for their families,* she vowed.

She'd heard the name San Teodor before—Chaz

Escobar had told her that it was the name of the island he had shared with Marianna. He hadn't thought that his ex would take her there, though—too easy to find her, or something like that.

But she is anyway. Which means, maybe, she's so tough she doesn't care if he finds her.

She's not the only one who's tough. She'll find that out.

CHAPTER NINE

The Sandwich Islands, 1901: Maui

After they left the excitement of China behind, Darla sent Spike and Dru on to other adventures. She preferred to conduct her quest for Angelus's freedom alone; she didn't need the additional pressures of dealing with a madwoman and a young, vigorous male vampire, whose oversexed presence only served to emphasize how far Angelus had fallen.

When at last the square-rigger landed in Honolulu Harbor, she savored the island of Oahu for a few nights, then hired another, smaller vessel to transport her to the island of Maui. The trip was so short she didn't have time to kill any of the sailors, which was only a mild regret.

It was paradise. The moon was a huge, milky coconut

color, gleaming above fields of sugar cane. There were miles of cane on vast plantations, waving in the soft trade winds. The cane barons were the sons and grandsons of missionaries, who had subjugated the local people and stolen the land from the Hawaiian Crown. The most recent Hawaiian monarch, Queen Liliuokalani, had been deposed in a coup. The United States had failed to come to her aid, and now her subjects were treated no better than slaves.

The planters felt no guilt or shame over their ignoble acts, but they did suffer over bringing their pale, easily-burnt brides to these islands. At these latitudes the sun was intense. Their women dried up in it, becoming old before their time. Thus it was completely acceptable that the exquisite Miss Darla Masters of Virginia retired during the bright hours of the day, and refreshed herself with company in the cool, fragrant night.

She had been on Maui visiting the sugar plantation owners and enjoying the admittedly limited social activities, for three weeks. During that time she had sent innumerable messages to the hidden lair of Lohiau, the chief of all the local magick users, called kahuna.

The locals murmured stories under their breath about Lohiau. They said he could do things no other kahuna could boast of. He raised the dead and he commanded the little people—the *menehune*—to do his bidding. He was feared and loved in the same breath.

And so, Darla thought, as she lounged in a fabulous palm garden illuminated with crackling torches and sipped a glass of pineapple juice and rum, *we share something in common. I, too, am loved and feared in the same breath. Often.*

That night, she was once again the guest of the Doreintz family. She had been to their vast plantation a number of times, and though the patriarch, Thomas Doreintz, had initially disguised his interest in her by issuing invitations to all the wealthy island families for a dinner party, it was well known that he was courting Darla to be his new wife. The old one had worn out, withered, and died.

To emphasize her dewy freshness, Darla had had an evening gown cut from her jade Chinese dress, the heavy beading encrusting the low bodice. Her hair was swept up and back, revealing her long, white neck. Her skin was the color of ivory. The other women were envious; despite all their efforts to protect their complexions, over time each one sported freckles and tans.

She liked being wanted and it was always great fun to play with her food in the dance of flirtation; however, she was not at the party for pleasure . . . exclusively. After all, there was no way to avoid sensual delight in such perfect surroundings. But she had sailed to these islands to save Angelus, and finally, it appeared that her efforts were about to pay off.

A string quartet began playing as the Hawaiian servants glided among the guests with silver trays carrying goblets of champagne. All the luxuries one could wish for were imported from England. Even the Hawaiian Royal Jewels came from Britain, as did the suffocatingly hot black velvet livery sported by Doreintz's servants. It amused Darla to see the women of this place enduring corsetry and heavy clothing because they wished to be stylish.

Everyone wants to be a European, she thought. *They're all such sheep. The Chinese had the right idea, trying to rid their country of Western influences. The Hawaiian people are dying out because of Western influences.*

As if on cue, a tall, burly Hawaiian male appeared before her with one of the trays, which was lavishly filled with delicacies. He held it out to her, and murmured, "I come from *him.*"

She had been waiting for this meeting all evening. Now she raised a brow and smiled lazily at him, though inside she trembled with victory. *At last. I'll save my boy.*

"Later tonight, Mr. Thomas, he watch hula on the beach," the man said in heavily-accented English. "He ask, you go."

"The hula is a forbidden dance," she drawled. "Ladies most definitely do not watch it."

He smiled at her. "You go."

Darla did go, Thomas's hand clasping hers as if they were promenading down a wide, Parisian boulevard. A handful of other ladies snuck down to the shore as well, protesting and giggling that they really oughtn't to be there, it was so very scandalous. Not only was the hula illegal, but it roused primitive emotions in the male of the species. And one couldn't have *that* . . . .

Silhouetted by a bonfire built on top of the sand, a brown-skinned man with leaves in his hair pounded on a gourd over which had been stretched a piece of sharkskin. Another man stood beside him, intoning a pulsing chant.

The sole dancer was a young woman—Darla judged her to be sixteen or so—who was scantily clothed in a skirt made of large leaves. She wore anklets and bracelets of white flowers, and a crown of the same flowers in her hair.

As the man sang in the strange, foreign tongue, the girl raised her arms and began to sway. She was beautiful, and Darla was appreciative. However, the maiden's movements put her more in mind of a cobra bobbing for a snake charmer than a dance of any sort.

Beside her, Thomas put his hand to his mouth, covering a yawn. He frowned slightly and said, "So sorry, m'dear. I'm suddenly a bit tired."

Darla murmured, "Think nothing of it." Covertly she glanced at the other spectators. Others were yawning. Eyelids were drooping.

The dancer caught her gaze and held it.

Well, well, Darla thought. *This is enchanting . . . truly.*

One by one, the others sank to the sand, asleep.

The dancer clapped her hands . . .

. . . and Darla was transported to a sunken grotto, lit with smoky torches and decorated with hundreds of statues of grotesque figures.

In the center of a lava basin that bubbled and steamed, stood a statuesque figure cloaked in a feather robe and wearing a mask of coconut shells inlaid with mother of pearl.

"Most impressive," she told him.

Lohiau—for it had to be he—bowed deeply from the waist. "Such a compliment, coming from your lips, does me great honor." His upper-class English accent was impeccable.

"Are you British?" she asked him.

He raised a brown hand, clenched it, and laid it across his chest. "I am one hundred percent Hawaiian," he proclaimed. "I was educated in England. The experience nearly killed me."

She grinned. "I can understand that. I've had a number of near brushes with death there myself."

"I thank the tiki that no harm came to you." He gestured to the bizarre statues covering the walls and floor of the grotto. They were dark, made perhaps of lava glass or burnished wood. Their heads were huge, their features elongated and ugly. Beneath the heads, stubby bodies twitched and bobbed as if awakening from a deep sleep.

Then the tiki nearest her skirts, a squat, man-shaped thing, hopped toward her. From behind the animated statue, a tiny, elflike creature appeared, took her measure, then skittered off into the shadows. Another peered at her, and then another, clambering and jostling over the rocks and darting around the tiki.

"Those little folk are *menehune*," Lohiau told her. "Our little people."

"Hawaiian faeries," Darla translated. "Are they as mischievous as the English ones?"

Lohiau shrugged. "They are not kind, if that's what you mean." He clapped his hands, and perhaps a hundred of the unpleasant little creatures scattered, losing themselves in the gloom of the grotto. Darla thought she detected a faint odor of sulfur in their wake.

Once they were gone, Darla dispensed with further pleasantries and got down to the business at hand. "Angelus," she said. "Can you manage it?"

"I really can't say," he replied, equally blunt. "Who has ever heard of a vampire with a soul?"

He vanished from the bubbling crater, then reappeared standing directly before her. "I do not flatter myself, vampiress. I am a strong and powerful sorcerer. But even I have my limits."

"You came highly recommended," she informed him.

"I know." Though he still wore his mask, she could hear the smile in his voice. "To answer your question, however, I have been studying the matter. There is something I will need to attempt the capture of Angelus's soul. Once I have it, I have good hopes that I will succeed."

She made a show of sighing and toyed with the large black pearl dangling from her neck. "Let me guess. This 'something' is enormously expensive. And you want me to pay for it." *Perhaps I can persuade Thomas to purchase it for me. As a wedding gift. For a wedding night that he will not live to see.*

"It is priceless," the kahuna corrected her. "It cannot be bought."

When he said nothing more, she snapped, "Then . . . ?"

He walked a little distance away from her. The torches roiled and smoked as he passed by, a testament to the magickal forces. "My country has been stolen from its rightful owners." Beneath the feather robe, his broad shoulders tensed. "I work day and night with sorcery to take it back, and give it to my people." He turned to her. "Long ago my ancestors gave the *alii*—our royalty—a sacred vessel. It is called the Chalice of Pele. It was in Iolani Palace when the invaders occupied it and imprisoned the queen. I have no idea where it is now."

"And this Chalice . . ." She began.

"Is necessary for the ritual to take away his soul. I have been unable to locate it. It's on Oahu, somewhere among the spoils they stole from us." He touched his chest. "I am Hawaiian, and cannot freely mix with the haole."

"The white people." She shrugged. "What about me? I'm very pale, as you may have noticed, but I am a vampire."

"But you can move among them without detection. You've been doing it here for weeks."

"You've had me watched." She was amused.

"Of course. You have a reputation, Darla. You're very dangerous."

"You know how to flatter a girl."

He raised his chin. "The Chalice is my price."

Simply to wring the last little bit of sport from the meeting, Darla pretended to hesitate. The man tensed, and she was delighted. At last she said, "Very well."

Then she turned to the shadows and said in a cold voice, "Come out, Angelus. I know you're here."

The next moment was a chasm of silence, and then her boy emerged from the blackness. She was appalled by the stink of his soul, and the haunted, tormented look on his face.

"How long have you known?" he asked with his Irish lilt.

"That you followed me here from China?" She made herself stay calm—or at least, sound calm. In truth she had only just sensed him—here, now—and she was filled with rage and joy and a hundred different emotions. "It doesn't matter."

"You see," he said hoarsely. "You see how it is with me, Darla. I want this as much as you do."

She hardened her face. "You should want it more than that."

He took a step toward her. "Ah, darlin', don't be cruel to me. If it had happened to you . . ."

"Don't." She glared at him. "It didn't." She threw back her shoulders and turned to the kahuna. "I will find it. But keep him out of my sight."

After Darla swept out of the grotto, Lohiau removed his mask. Though the Hawaiian sorcerer claimed to be fifty years old, he looked young enough to be Angel's brother, had Liam had one. Angel felt a kinship with the kahuna, who had shown him nothing but kindness and compassion for his predicament, while Darla could not conceal her disgust.

Lohiau said, "Spot of tea?"

"Thanks, if you have something Irish," Angel said.

The other man laughed. "You can't taste the difference in varieties of tea. You're a vampire." He studied Angel. "Or is it the fact of the conflict you Irish have with the English that you'd care for something from your native earth?"

Angel nodded. "Old loyalties die hard," he confessed. "I'm not really Irish anymore, I suppose, but I think of myself in that way."

"If I live until these islands sink into the sea, I'll remain Hawaiian," Lohiau told him. "How I hate these damn Americans." He ran both hands through his hair. "If your sire finds that Chalice, I'll blow them all to kingdom come with it. After I damn you back to hell, of course. Snatch back your soul and turn you into a ravening beast."

"Much obliged." Angel smiled crookedly.

"Although I do wish you'd reconsider. I could give you shelter here, and a cause worth fighting for. After you change, I doubt you'll care much about justice."

Angel shook his head. "I have one care, and one care only. And that's Darla."

Lohiau looked thoughtful. "I can understand why, my boy. She's exquisite." He unhooked his feather robe. "Well, then, I'll pray to the tiki that the Chalice safely finds its way into her hands. And then into mine. With any of that famous Irish luck, you'll be a bloodthirsty monster in no time."

"One can hope," Angel glumly replied.

"And she did find it," Angel concluded. He had wandered back down to the hotel lobby, to find Cordelia and Fred seated on the round couch with Wesley, the three of them sharing a half-gallon of chocolate chip cookie dough ice cream and a bottle of rum. The three had been spellbound by his story, and now that he was finished, none of them looked very happy about what they'd heard.

"So what you're saying is, that the Mead Bowl of Loki may very well be the Chalice of Pele," Fred said slowly.

"And we are not talking about Pele the soccer player," Cordelia put in.

"Goddess of Fire, Hawaiian," Wesley said vaguely, sounding more like an entry from the Demons, Demons, Demons database on Angel's computer than his usual snappy British self. "They used to sacrifice virgins to her."

"I'm glad that's an outdated practice," Fred said.

Cordelia turned to the young woman. "Not so much. Wes used to have this girlfriend who almost got sacrificed but turned out not to be a virgin. . . . I'll be quiet now." She gave Wesley a sad smile. "Sorry." Sotto voce, she said to Fred, "Virginia couldn't handle our dangerous lifestyle. So Wesley broke up with her."

"Oh." Fred pulled a sad face. "That's so sad."

"And yet, noble," Cordelia asserted.

Wesley cleared his throat. "You were saying that she located the Chalice. What did she do with it?"

"Gave it to Lohiau for the ritual to take my soul away."

"Did it work?" Fred queried.

Deadpan, Angel replied, "Yes. And I stand before you a ravening beast."

"Golly, I need a score card to keep track of all the times you've been damned and redeemed," Fred murmured. She looked very impressed.

Cordelia shook her head to assure Fred that Angel was joking, took the carton of ice cream from Wesley and jammed her soupspoon into it. Angel remembered the single day—and night—with Buffy, when he had been human again. But try as he might, the taste of ice cream eluded him. The taste of chocolate as well.

But the taste of Buffy's lips on mine . . . I'll remember that until I'm dust.

"We're collecting all the stuff Escobar needs awfully quickly," Cordelia said, licking her spoon. "And I haven't seen one shred of proof that this Benedicta chick is still alive, or anywhere nearby. I think that's a false herring."

Wesley muttered, "*Red* herring."

"My herring's fine," she retorted halfheartedly, as if making barbed jokes was beyond her. "So, yay about the Benedicta part anyway, right, Angel?"

"Yay." He shrugged. "I guess it would be too much bad news all at once."

The phone rang. Cordelia got up and grabbed the one on the lobby counter, saying, "Angel Investigations. We help the hopeless." Then she listened gravely. "When? That's all you've got? Okay. Thanks," she said finally, and hung up.

She faced the group. "About too much bad news," she said. "We have some more."

"What?" Angel asked, half rising, his mind playing out a dozen scenarios.

Cordelia said, "Faith's been released from prison. Our stoolie just watched it happen."

"Why is that bad news?" Fred asked innocently.

Cordelia sighed heavily and ran her hands through her hair. "Because she got sprung by Wolfram and Hart. Our informant on the inside just saw the paperwork."

"That is bad news," Fred said, grimacing.

"There were also some initials. On the paperwork. M. E.," Cordelia added.

"Marianna Escobar," Wesley concluded. "Gunn's men . . ."

Cordelia shook her head.

Wesley paled. "And the hits just keep on coming."

Angel headed for the door. "We've got to go after her. Save Faith."

Dashing after him, Cordelia rounded in front of him and waved her hands in his face. "Whoa. Down, boy. We don't know where they took her."

"That doesn't matter," he said as he yanked open the door.

She started to say something, then nodded. "Let's go." She looked back at Wesley. "Fort?"

"Holding it." He looked upset. "Faith was my watch," he said. "I was to keep tabs on her."

"Don't, Wes," Cordelia said. "You did your best."

"I'll hold the fort too," Fred said. She rose from the couch and crossed to Wesley. "I'll hold with you. Maybe we can hack into the prison records," she suggested.

Wesley smiled faintly at her. Then he glanced back at Angel and Cordelia. "Go quickly," he urged them. "The trail will get colder and colder."

As he and Cordelia headed for his car, Angel gritted his teeth until they hurt. "God, I wish I still killed people," he said.

"Tell me about it," Cordelia replied. Then she stopped, turned on her heel, and headed back to the hotel. Puzzled, Angel caught up with her.

She pushed open the door, startling Wesley and Fred, who had already started work.

"Why didn't your amulet work?" Cordelia asked Wesley.

Angel frowned. *That's a good question.*

Benedicta, Speaker of the Mysteries, Queen of Damnation, raised her hands from the fire pit and smiled as the skull of another of the abominations crumbled in upon itself. The magickal flames were hellfire hot, reducing everything laid into them to cinders in less than the blink of an eye.

She and Bran Cahir had created a miniature temple beneath the city streets of Los Angeles. Above them, the busy trains and subways of Union Station rattled and vibrated. It was quite easy to capture passengers as they hurried down the tunnels toward the trains and the Metro, like picking fruit from trees.

In addition to gathering food, her acolytes had been collecting the hideous malformations created by the hunter, Chaz Escobar, and brought to Los Angeles by his vampiric wife. The few misshapen creatures who were capable of thought and speech, she had tortured into providing what information they could about the couple. She had already learned why he was seeking the Book of the Interregnum—his inquiries were what had brought him to her attention in the first place. She wasn't certain if he meant to end all vampiric life on earth, as he claimed, or if he hoped to place Marianna on the throne of the earth, once that lady mated with the Beast.

Thus it was that she, Benedicta, had a personal interest in their respective quests—his to find the Book and the rest of the arcana needed for the Rite of Raising—and hers . . . what was Marianna Escobar's quest about? Why was she in Los Angeles? To kill her human husband, or to continue their game of cat and mouse?

"I wonder if she knows about the Book," Benedicta said to the disintegrating skull.

Behind her, Bran Cahir, the ancient Druidic sorcerer, clasped his hands around her waist and nuzzled the nape of her neck. The centuries had not been kind to Bran—he was a wizened piece of leather, with tiny, beady eyes and yellow teeth.

He had once been her savior. In an utter paroxysm of terror, she had had no idea what she was after she rose from the cold floor of the convent. Staggering through the slaughter, tripping over the bodies of dead nuns who would not rise, she had gone quite mad. When she came to herself, Bran had found her in the grove, and taken her back to his cave. He had administered strong potions to her and brought her back to self-awareness. With the skill of a chess master, he plotted every move she should make to grab and wield power, until she was one of the most feared and revered vampires in existence.

"And now we are all in the city of angels, and of Angelus," she mused. "You and I, Bran, and Marianna Escobar, and her mortal husband."

Bran moved her black gown away from her back and began kissing each delicate point of her spinal column. "We are all here, but not all of us will survive being here." He whipped his head to look over his shoulder and snapped, "Yes?"

An acolyte—she had been a little Goth street urchin on Melrose Avenue that they had picked up a few weeks before, enticing her with food and then with propaganda—approached with trembling steps and dropped to her knees before him. Her gaze moved hesitantly to the stone altar, upon which dozens of statues, large and small, of an assortment of vengeful goddesses glared down at her. Then she turned her attention to the fire pit, and shuddered.

"They have found more of the creatures," she said, eyes downcast. "My lord asked to be informed if that happened."

"Yes." He bent down and held out his hands. "Thank you."

His voice was gentle, his smile kind. The young girl inhaled sharply, her eyes huge in her gaunt face, and she placed her hands trustingly in his.

He hauled her to her feet, held her, and bared her neck for Benedicta. The queen vampire savaged the girl's neck, draining her so fast the child had no time to struggle.

As Benedicta walked away, wiping the blood from her face, Bran hoisted the body into the fire pit, where it exploded, then was gone.

Benedicta sighed with pleasure as the girl's blood filled her system.

"I love L.A.," she said.

"We'll make this city the seat of your new empire," he told her, offering her his arm. "But first we'll burn it to the ground."

She smiled brilliantly, and together they swept out of the chamber.

CHAPTER TEN

The road trip to Cabazon yielded something that was very ripe, but it wasn't fruit.

The mummy stank. But then, most mummies did. Royal pharaoh or virginal Incan sacrifice, the fact of the matter was that mummies were nothing more than dried-up dead people, and dead people smelled.

No gross-out, just true, Gunn thought, as he and Wesley carried Miss Nuremberg 1867 into the hotel. *Fact of life in the demon-killing biz.* Anyway, Lorne's friend's cousin's roadside stop in Cabazon didn't smell much better— mummy or no mummy, there had been some plastic toilet stalls in that parking lot that hadn't been emptied this decade.

Fred was working on the computer keyboard, but she turned and watched as the two men staggered through the front door with the prize.

"Damn, she's bloody heavy," Wesley grunted. The Virgin had come dipped in resin, complete with her own carrying case—an old, weathered box that had a bunch of writing on it in Spanish, but which had something to do with food and *super-lotería*.

"You need to work out more, dog," Gunn jibed. "I'm having no problem. So, Angel ain't checked in yet, and still no word on Faith?"

"That's right." Wesley took small steps backward down the stairs into the main area of the lobby. The former Watcher had filled Gunn in as while they got the mummy out of Gunn's vehicle.

As they set the box down, Gunn cricked his back and neck while Wesley knelt beside the box and pried it open. He made "hmm" noises while he checked out the thick coating on the body.

Then Fred glided away from the computer keyboard on the lobby counter. Gunn felt a familiar warmth in his gut as she drew near. Girl was hot. Okay, maybe a little crazy, but she was starting to smooth out her rough edges, get over being a prisoner on another planet or dimension or whatever for five years.

"Bingo," she said excitedly, then gave Gunn a quick, shy smile and a wave and added, "Hi." To Wesley, she continued, "I got into the police records. The guards who signed Faith out have all been placed on administrative leave."

"That was fast," Wesley mused. "Wolfram and Hart are nothing if not efficient."

"Wolfram and Hart," Gunn echoed, grimacing. "They the ones who got her out?"

"It would appear so," Wesley said, shifting his weight to his haunches as he examined the mummy.

"That sucks." Gunn frowned at the group. "Remind me why haven't wired that place to go up?"

"Because we are the good guys." Wesley made a face at the mummy and tilted his head sideways.

"Well, all's I'm sayin' is, we are the stupid good guys."

"She's in terrible condition," Wesley continued, "but she does appear to be authentic."

"We gonna tell Escobar we have her?" Gunn asked.

There was a long and pointed silence.

"Um, Angel said we should," Fred murmured.

Wesley and Gunn gazed at each other levelly and Gunn realized something that made him feel better about the Extinction Project: Wes was not completely on board with it. *Just like me. We're collecting the stuff Escobar says he needs, but by no means is it a given that we are handing it over to him. Angel may not realize it, but Wesley and I could be mutineers when it all goes down.*

I am so good with that. Rock it, English.

They gave each other a nod. Gunn said quietly, "Let's put this in the elevator for now, just to get it out of the way. Stupid machine don't go down to the boiler room, and I'm not carrying this thing down all those stairs."

"Right."

"And it's too late to call anybody, especially a human being," Gunn added.

"Right." Wesley

Fred creased her pretty face and said, "But Angel said we should let Señor Escobar know as soon as pos—"

"Not right now." Wesley's voice was gentle but firm. "Gunn's right, Fred. We'll call him . . . in the morning."

Fred opened her mouth, closed it, touched her pretty, curly hair, and looked very uneasy. But Gunn knew she wasn't going to overrule them and make the call herself. He could see that as she scratched her cheek and crossed her arms, silently watching as he and Wesley pushed the mummy across the floor.

Gunn's backside was to her. *I've been working out, wonder if she notices*, he thought, then ticked his glance across the box to Wesley. *Check out the upper body. For all my dissing him, he's been working out too. Wonder if she notices that.*

They finally shoved the mummy into the elevator and closed the doors, and Fred went back to the computer. The stinky mummy took up most of the room in the elevator. But it didn't take long to stash her in a corner and then Wesley fretted about whether maybe they should have put her in the boiler room after all, where there were weapons. If somebody wanted to come after the mummy, it would be handy to have bludgeoning tools, swords, bazookas, those kinds of things, nearby. Gunn told him there was no way he was moving that dead girl again and Wesley got his turn to give him some stuff about him needing to put in more hours with the free weights if "this minute amount of activity" had worn him out.

When they came back upstairs, Cordelia and Angel had returned. Angel was on the phone and Cordy started filling the guys in on some new developments.

"We got nowhere, despite driving all over Los Angeles," Cordelia said. "But I remembered some more details of my Faith vision."

"The one that turned you Catholic," Gunn teased, but no one got it. "Faith," he said. "Vision. Faith vision. Religion."

She frowned blankly. "Anyway, what I realized was that in my vision, I could smell the ocean, and there were palm trees. And I saw part of a coastline. Very beachy."

Angel looked over from the receiver, evidently on hold. "And I was thinking about what Wesley said about the Mead Bowl maybe being Pele's Chalice, which is probably still on Maui with Lohiau."

Cordelia ran her hands through her hair. "Or maybe it's San Teodor I saw. Or some other island-y place. We don't know."

"Like Disneyland," Fred offered. "They have an island." She frowned. "But no ocean smell that I can recall. It's been a long time since I was there."

"Girl, ain't you been to see the Mouse since you got back from Pylea?" Gunn asked. "I gotta take you there."

Fred beamed at him. "Wow. That would be wonderful."

"I've never been," Wesley protested, "and no one's offered to take *me*."

"You can come with us," Fred said happily. "We'll have a company outing. When I worked in the library, we got discount tickets to all kinds of places."

She looks adorable when she's all giggly and excited. Alonna would have liked her, Gunn thought sadly.

"So anyway, Angel's looking for Lohiau," Cordelia said. "Talking to sorcerer types and magicians and stuff. No one's heard anything about him for a long time."

Angel hung up and said, "I'm going to try faxing Maui again." With a whoosh of his coat, he vanished back out the front door.

"Okay, because the fax machine we have here in the hotel is broken?" Wesley asked Cordelia as he watched Angel leave.

"He doesn't want to leave a trail, supernatural or electrical or anything else. We used a couple different fax machines at Mail Boxes Etc. on our way back from the prison."

Cordelia put her hands in her back pockets and swiped at a piece of resin on the floor. "If he doesn't locate Lohiau soon, we just might be ordering red-eye tickets for Maui and continuing the search on site."

"He's that determined to go?" Wesley asked. "On a hunch?"

"Excuse me, on a vision?" Cordelia was miffed.

"Who wouldn't want to go to Maui?" Fred asked dreamily. "Beaches, mangoes, and . . ."—she looked at the others, her expression growing concerned—" . . . lots and lots of sunshine."

"Exactly," Cordelia said. "More sun than we have in Los Angeles, even."

There was a moment of silence. Frowning, Gunn ventured, "Angel think about that? That he ain't exactly Coppertone guy?"

Cordelia shrugged. "When I asked him about it, he said that Lohiau forced the *menehune* to build tunnels all over the island. So he can still do the underground railroad thing."

"Tunnels?" Wesley asked. "Whatever for?"

Cordelia shrugged. "The kahuna was very secretive. Plus, rebel for Hawaiian independence, so he had to have a lot of places to hide from the authorities. So, tunnels, just like here. Only maybe not so sewery, one would hope."

"Maui's got possibilities," Gunn cut in. "You gotta give Angel that."

"Or you could give it to *me*. Hello, vision girl, saw the beach, the palms, smelled the ocean smell?" Cordelia raised her hand.

"Still . . ." Wesley said slowly. "Going all that way when he can't even find Lohiau. Did Angel consider the notion of 'divide and conquer'? That getting him away from us may be exactly what Escobar—and Wolfram and Hart and their unknown client—want?"

Gunn nodded. "We're being pulled in a lot of different directions. We've got a lot of distractions. Findin' enchanted objects and worrying about computer messages and now Faith's gone."

"Maybe she got tired of being in prison and made another deal," Cordelia suggested, her voice hardening. "I wouldn't put it past her."

"But why would Escobar want to separate us? I mean, Angel's helping him. And if he wanted to kill Angel, he wouldn't have to go all the way to Hawaii to do it," Fred said reasonably. "He didn't say anything about needing the Chalice of Pele. He wanted the Mead Bowl of Loki. And we're still not absolutely positive they're the same thing."

Wesley looked grim. "The appearance of Wolfram and Hart makes it even more confusing. We don't know who they're working for. It could be Chaz Escobar or his wife, Marianna the vampire."

"Or Benedicta the vampire," Fred suggested, half raising her hand.

"Unless that part's made up," Gunn said. He got up and wandered over to the weapons cabinet, as if looking for something new that could really slice and dice.

Wesley made no answer. After a time he said, "Did Angel consider who would go with him and who would stay here?"

Somberly Cordelia raised her chin and squared her shoulders, offering herself in service to the cause. "I think I should go. I've been to Maui before. A lot of times. I know my way around." She cocked her head as she continued in her very serious voice. "Well, okay, only around the resorts. But some of them are really big. They cover miles." She grew wistful. "They have their own beaches. It's so lovely there. The shops . . ."

Gunn turned his attention from the swords and the axes and stared at her, saying very slowly, "Cordy, sometimes I can't believe we were born on the same planet."

Wesley slapped his knees with his hands and stood, all business and English efficiency. He had been working hard; there were circles under his eyes. They all had. They were not frosty or fresh; and worrying about Angel was also taking its toll.

"Well, before we go off half-cocked making decisions about this, I think we should do some research."

Cordelia groaned. "More with the computer?"

"No," Wesley rejoined, with a weary half-smile. "More with the microphone. Let's have the Host take a look at our auras, see if he can lend us a new perspective."

"I'll be in my room," Fred announced, sounding nervous.

"Hey, no, you should come, too," Gunn urged her, reaching out a hand toward her.

"No, that—that's okay." With that, she turned tail and fled up the stairs.

"But . . ." Cordelia watched her go. Then she said to the

others, "You know, it doesn't matter, guys. We can predict Fred's future. If we can't get her to Caritas, we for sure aren't going to get her to Maui."

"Still holding out for Disneyland, though," Gunn said, half to himself.

"Hey, honey, looking deelish as always," Lorne greeted Angel as the vampire did the coat thing across the crowded floor of Caritas and joined him at the bar. "In to hum a few bars for *moi*?"

Angel replied, "You got a fax machine?"

"Okay. Confusion is reigning." Lorne adjusted the flamboyant red-and-purple tie of his even more flamboyant purple suit. He had on matching purple suede shoes. There was a shrink named Ira—all the Beautiful Demons went to him—who knew the most faboo shoe stores in L.A. "I have a fax machine, and a karaoke machine, and it doesn't seem to me that you would bother coming all the way here to use the former."

Angel was scanning the crowd. He said, "You've got a spell on it that protects it from being traced, right?"

"Oooh. Undercover Angel tonight, are we?" The Host fanned his fingers over his chest and waggled his eyebrows. "Doing something dangerous? Dragging my club into it?"

Angel looked at him. "Yes."

"In that case," the Host said sarcastically, "it's in my office. And you know where my office is. When your car demolished this place on our return from my homeworld, I believe one of your fenders took out my office."

"Thanks." Angel walked off.

"My pleasure," Lorne called after him. Then he sauntered off to the bar and said, "Julio, darling, make me a Sea Breeze."

Julio got to work. Onstage, Mordar the Bentback was crooning "Fly Me to the Moon" to an appreciative audience of demons. Lorne smiled fondly. With that voice, Mordar should take a trip to Jupiter, at least.

Just as Julio said, "Here you go, boss," and passed the beverage to his employer with his flipper, the colorful blue-and-red interior of Caritas . . . wobbled.

Lorne blinked his handsome red eyes and squinted. There it was again—a kind of blurring of his surroundings for perhaps one instant, and then all popped back into regular focus.

He looked around. No one else seemed to notice.

A red bottle fell off the mirrored shelves behind the bar and clunked to the floor.

And Mordar was singing the same phrase over that he'd sung about the first time three seconds before.

While Lorne took all this in, Angel reappeared, coat, coat, coat, tucking some papers into his pocket. He bobbed his head at Lorne and mouthed, "Thanks."

"Hey. Wait." Lorne departed his bar stool and headed the vampire with a fashion statement off at the entrance to the club. "Did your fax go through?"

Angel shrugged. "Your machine said I had a successful transmission."

"Please. There are some things men should not discuss in public," Lorne quipped. Then he leaned in toward Angel and said, "Dorothy, there's been a rift in the Force." He waggled his fingers. "Like a glitch in the time/space continuum, if you know what I mean. Which you would if you watched *Star Trek: The Next Gen.* I'm guessing someone tried to intercept your fax."

Angel looked more angel-y than ever, dour and concerned and dashing all at once. "By who?"

"*Whom*, angelcakes. And the answer is, I have no idea. I'm not even sure how to go about finding out."

Angel kept looking at him.

"But we can try," he added brightly.

"Good." Angel gestured to the crowd. "Is it one of them?"

"Won't know until I hear them sing." He gestured to an enormous female demon seated alone in the corner. "The fat lady, too." He sighed. "It's going to be a long night, I can see that."

Angel looked grim. "They're all long," he replied.

Bran's new finder spell had worked. Somewhere in the world, someone had just made an effort to locate another of the sacred items connected with the First Beast.

He and Benedicta were in the underground chamber, she lounging on a bed of skin and bones, resting and relaxing. Being the head of a religion taxed one so. Blinded acolytes chanted in the shadows, reciting a prepared text from an ancient Sumerian grimoire. They probably did not realize they would hasten the end of the world by a year each time they sang a verse.

Before Bran, the luminescent visual echo of two sheets of white paper glowed in the center of a sphere of magickal blue energy. The sphere crackled and shuddered, then was still as Bran raised a leathery, bony hand and spoke in ancient Gaelic, ordering it to halt.

While Benedicta nibbled at the neck of a handsome male acolyte, Bran snapped his fingertips together. Bone clicked against bone and the ghostly images floated closer to him. He waved a hand over his eyes to improve his sight and scanned the lines of text.

"It's someone named 'A,'" he said. "Looking for a kahuna named Lohiau. I'm not sure why."

Benedicta thought for a moment. "Lohiau . . . that name's familiar. Yes. He was the leader of a rebellion in the Hawaiis. Darla had a thing with him, or so the gossip went. It was all quite bizarre. No one knew what she saw in him."

"What she saw in him was power." There was an edge to Bran's voice that he hoped he managed to conceal. He was quite aware that Benedicta no longer looked upon him with lust and admiration, as she once had. She had completely forgotten that when he had found her in the oak grove, she was quite insane. He had taken care of her, tutored her, made her what she was today—a queen. Now, in her glory, she clearly felt that she had outgrown him.

The reason he looked so grotesque now was that he had expended large amounts of energy protecting her from enemies. The magick he had originally used to preserve his life had been drained to a large extent to preserve hers, and his body had suffered a breakdown at the cellular level as a result.

She had had so many enemies over her lifetime. Even Darla's beloved Master had taken her on once, feeling threatened by the charisma she exuded. He had been worried that some of his followers would decamp, particularly after Angelus had humiliated him upon first meeting.

Angelus. A. Bingo.

After all, he's here in Los Angeles.

But what does he have to do with Lohiau? Do the two know each other? Darla must have introduced them.

I'll have to look into this.

Benedicta rolled over on her stomach and clapped her hands together twice. Her attire disappeared. Smoke rose from the bed itself, then gathered and took form, and the phantom shape of a Grecian body slave materialized into being. The slave began to massage her back. She sighed, rippling with delight.

The apparition began to weep big red tears of blood. Bran knew that he hated being held captive in this bed of death while his family moved on to paradise. But he was too good at working out her kinks to be released from captivity.

Bran watched for a moment. Then he sighed and went back to his work.

He flicked his wrist and the second inchoate visual of the secret message came into focus. "This might be interesting. An oblique reference to 'M. E.'" He pondered. "It could be Marianna Escobar."

He scratched his chin, realizing too late that his razor-sharp fingertip was slicing through the desiccated skin on his chin. Seeing it, Benedicta grimaced with distaste.

I have this face because of you! Enraged, Bran pointed a finger at the body slave, who immediately disappeared. He whirled around and jabbed two fingers in the direction of the blinded acolytes, and they fell down dead.

"What do you think you're doing?" Benedicta shouted, raising up on her palms.

"Now you listen to me." Bran crossed to her side and grabbed her shoulder. Then his hand grabbed and cupped her chin, forcing her to gaze up at him. She transformed, hissing at him, and he eased his hold on her chin. "Listen," he said silkily. "Listen to me, Mary."

"Mary Kelly," she said dreamily. "Sister Mary Kelly."

Her eyes were practically spinning. The madness that he could control with magick still rumbled beneath the surface like a volcano. *Like those damn infernal blowholes in Hawaii, always going off at without warning . . . .*

"Who is your lord?" he whispered.

"You."

"And who is your master?"

"You."

"Who do you want?"

"You."

"Then prove it," he ordered.

It had been a long time since he had done this to her, and he hadn't been certain that he could still control her mind. But she submissively lay back down, this time on her back, and held her arms out to him. Her dazed smile was inviting, wanton. He climbed onto the bed and took her. Savagely.

Left to her surface consciousness, she would not have permitted this violation. He had grown too repulsive for her embrace.

She had no idea that he could do this to her.

After he was finished, he closed her eyes with the flat of his hand. She lay still as death. She would be like that for a while, docile and biddable, in her unbeating heart still a good convent lass. Her dreaming mind was back in London, at the convent, before Drusilla changed her.

He left her there, exiting the chamber and locking the

door behind him. Then he rubbed his hands together briskly, creating skin, and draped it over his features and up and down his hands and arms, like a mask and a pair of opera gloves. It was tiring to parade around like this, just as it had been tiring to maintain the protective sphere of influence around Benedicta back when she had been more vulnerable. There had been a time when the presence of the skin had made it possible for her to bed him, but that, too, had deteriorated with the years . . .

To facilitate the "legitimate" business interests they maintained as a front, as well as to perform research and some of the necessary paperwork that came with running a church, they had rented several floors of an office building near the Museum of Tolerance in Beverly Hills, and he thought about going down there to stand in the recreation of the Nazi death camp. The surroundings helped him think better. But he should move fast on this new wrinkle, the pages someone had sent to Lohiau.

Idly he walked into one of the computer rooms and craned his neck over the top of a cubicle. The young man at the keyboard visibly paled when he saw Bran. For a moment Bran thought he had caught the man slacking on company time—downloading pornography or playing a computer game—but then it dawned on him that the look of terror was also one of recognition. The human knew who—and what—stood in front of him.

That didn't please the ancient druid.

"I—I was going to come to you," the man blurted. "I've just found something."

Bran said nothing, only arched one brow expectantly as the man babbled on. "I got behind a firewall. It was well-constructed, but . . . well, anyway, I—I managed to get the address of the computer the queries about the Book came from."

"The ones Mr. Escobar answered," Bran observed, "pretending to be us." They'd figured out that much.

The man nodded, his head bobbing so quickly Bran wondered if it might pop right off his neck. "The password belongs to someone named Cordelia Chase." Then the good lad added, "She works for a place called Angel Investigations."

Bran touched his forehead. "Angelus. A." He smiled at the man. "You've done wonderful work."

The man dabbed his own forehead with a tissue. He'd been sweating profusely during their entire conversation. "Yes, sir. Thank you, sir."

Still smiling, Bran came around, grabbed the man around the back of the head and under the chin, and snapped his neck.

"Loose lips," he said, winking at the corpse. "Wouldn't want you to mention this to anyone else. Just in case we have spies or traitors in our midst."

He leaned over the barrier to the next cubicle over. A young woman cowered inside, weeping silently. When she realized he was looking at her, she became hysterical.

He sighed, pointed at her, killed her.

"I simply wanted you to take care of my mess," he said, wagging a finger at her. "So," he said, in a loud voice, "do I have any volunteers for little light office cleaning?"

Within five minutes, there were no traces of the two bodies, nor of any of their personal effects. The surviving humans would live to see another day, if only because they were very good at hacking.

I wish more demons would get computer literate, he thought. *Then we wouldn't have to outsource to humans at all.*

He sat in the woman's vacated cubicle, cracked his fingernails, and began typing rapid-fire on the keyboard. He felt good. He felt smart.

Cordelia Chase, he typed in.

"Let's see who the hell you are," he murmured, "and what on earth you want with the Book of the Interregnum."

CHAPTER ELEVEN

At Los Angeles International Airport, Cordelia gazed longingly at Angel's big, fat, juicy boarding pass as he got ready to leave the checkpoint. Back before her parents had lost all their money, she had taken for granted their many trips to Hawaii, sometimes for as short as a weekend. Five hours over, five hours back. Sometimes it took that long to drive from Los Angeles to San Diego, when the traffic was bad.

We stayed at the best hotels, ate at the best restaurants. Mom and I thought nothing of going down to the gift shops and charging a small fortune in jewelry and designer beachwear.

"Don't worry, I'll be fine," Angel assured her, misreading her expression. "It'll be dark all the way, and still dark when I get there."

She felt about two inches tall and shrugged off her attack of the poor-me's.

Back then I was the Queen of Mean, a total bitch. I thought I was happy when all I was, was powerful. In high school, lording it over people who were not as socially advanced as I was.

Okay, better to be nice, but couldn't I be nice and rich?

"I don't think you should go," she said bluntly. "We don't have enough information." Taking a breath, she added, "You're kind of splitting on us, Angel."

"Cordy, I just have this sense," he said. "This is what I should do. If I can rescue Faith . . ."

She sighed. "Well, you're the boss. Only not, because Wesley is. But you know what I mean."

He gave her a hug, which surprised her. He wasn't big on gestures of affection, at least not spontaneous ones. Then he picked up his small suitcase—Angel had traveled light for centuries—and walked into the security checkpoint.

"Take care," she murmured.

In the evening, Benedicta liked to walk.

Bran was with her, promenading the streets of Los Angeles, his false skin a burden that was wearing on his reserves of magickal energy. As soon as he could, he would need to bathe in a pool of blood and promise yet more sacrifices to his dark gods.

I wonder how many human beings I have offered to my masters, he mused, as Benedicta bent over a flower. They were in a place called Griffith Park. The moon glowed across her black, black hair and he stirred for her.

There was a rustling in the bushes, and both of them turned as one to see what it was.

Something lurched from the foliage. It was a ruddy ocher color, and it appeared to have seven legs covered with scales and ending in cloven hooves. Its body was a misshapen, bulbous mass topped by a massive head that resembled nothing so much as a claw.

Bran flicked his wrist, sending a blue fireball at it, and then another. They landed easily, causing bad burns. The creature roared and then hobbled back toward the bushes. Bran set those on fire, too, and the creature reared back, tumbling end over end to the ground.

The sorcerer walked toward it, saying over his shoulder to Benedicta, "Let's see if my finder spell works on it."

"What is it?"

"An aberration. A demonic mutation," he guessed.

He knelt on one knee beside the creature and intoned the litany of the finder's spell. Then he said, "Who ruled you?"

From the inert creature's body rose a glowing sphere, and in the sphere, the face of a beautiful vampire formed *en profile*. Her eyes were dark and flashing, her lips lush and inviting. Bran found her enchanting.

Benedicta said, "That's Marianna Escobar. Do you remember her? Some of our minions captured her and changed her." She chuckled. "And then she killed them."

"What does she have to do with the Book?"

Benedicta exhaled. "Obviously if her husband is looking for it, then . . . look, Bran," she interrupted herself. "The Slayer."

Inside the sphere Marianna's face was joined by that of the dark-haired slayer named Faith. Though not as active as she once had been, her name still crossed the lips of many a demon, many a vampire. After all, she had rejected the side of the light in favor of the forces of evil. There was much to admire in such a young lady.

The sphere grew to the size of a small car—*preferably a Porsche Boxter,* Bran thought, knowing Benedicta's tastes as well as he did—and Marianna's profile altered until she was facing the Slayer. Then the Slayer's head lowered, and as their forms took shape, Marianna stood over Faith, who was chained by her legs to a wooden floor. Her arms were pulled tightly behind her back, huge chains wrapped around her wrists and bolted to the floor as well.

"She's her prisoner," Benedicta mused. "She's captured the Slayer."

"But what has that to do with the Book?" Bran persisted.

Benedicta smiled at him. "Let's find out."

He prepared to enlarge the sphere. Benedicta put a silky hand on his forearm, and said, "Find out where they are, Bran, and we'll go to her."

"Yes. I'll take some acolytes and—"

"I want to go too. I'm bored," she announced.

How could one become bored in Los Angeles? he thought, but he didn't voice his opinion.

"I'm not sure you should go," he said carefully, with no desire to incur her wrath. "We don't know what she's doing with the Slayer, and—"

"I am the Keeper of the Mysteries," she reminded him. "I am the Mother of All the Damned, including Marianna. And think of how delighted my acolytes would be if I could torture an actual Slayer to death before their astonished gazes. Find out where she is, and take me to her," she insisted.

177

An hour later, en route to San Teodor, Bran stood at the bow of a richly appointed, rented yacht and remembered the days when he would travel all over Britain by galley. That was in the days when magick was part of the everyday world, and there was no need to cloak necromancy and sorcery from the local authorities. The modern world, for all its conveniences, was very inconvenient for those who conjured.

It still being night, Benedicta joined him. She was swathed in crimson and black, and she looked beautiful. Her skin was the color of ice, down to a tinge of purplish blue at the hollows of her cheeks and across her forehead. She had painted her lips blood red, and her black hair tumbled over her shoulders and down her back. She could have been the model for the Grimm brothers' Snow White . . . as seen from inside her crystal coffin.

She still did not remember their tryst, had no idea that he had tasted her flesh, loved her, died inside her.

She said, "If Marianna tries to keep me from taking her Slayer, I'll smash her to bits."

She had become fixated on that, nearly forgetting the larger goal of assessing why Marianna's face had appeared to them in a finder's spell about the Book. Though irritated with her, Bran let her go on for a while, and then said, "First we'll try reason," he reminded her.

"I am her mother superior in this world," Benedicta informed him, balling her fists. "She must do everything I say."

"We need to find out what she knows about the Book."

Just then, a strapping man dressed in black, a bulletproof

vest strapped across his chest, approached the couple gingerly. Bowing and scraping, obviously speechless in the sight of his dark mistress, he finally managed to tell them that Marianna Escobar's own private yacht had been sighted.

"Prepare to board her vessel," Benedicta ordered. Then she smiled at the man and said, "And come with me to my cabin. *Now*."

She glided past Bran with the man in tow. Though Bran was humiliated by her utter disregard for his feelings, he was more philosophical about her actions.

She may be incredibly old in years, but she's still a wanton young girl at heart. She has needs. As do we all.

He turned to another acolyte and said, "Make way toward Marianna Escobar's yacht." He repeated the coordinates the first man had given them.

"Aye, sir."

From below decks came the sudden shrieking of a man in unbelievably agony. It lasted for perhaps a minute, then was abruptly cut off.

He looked out to sea with a little smile on his face. *She has her needs. Which are fleeting and quickly satisfied.*

But I will still be here even after we raise the Beast of the First Blood. I will always be here.

He stood at the bow and spread forth his arms. With a few words in Welsh, he caused the ocean beneath the yacht to become as clear as glass. Fish and seaweed and kelp swam and floated below the hull.

With a splash over the side, the savaged body of Benedicta's momentary lover floated into Bran's field of view. Then a shark zeroed in on it, and it was gone.

I always see everything she does. I know what she thinks, Bran reminded himself. *And if, after the Beast is raised, she is too much trouble, I know how to kill her. I'm like that shark . . . if there is blood in the water, I will swallow her up.*

And I will rule that Beast, and I will be the king I always should have been.

Before his long trips to and from Tibet, Angel hadn't flown in an airplane in a very long time, and he still wasn't entirely fluent with the new realities of air travel. While the other passengers settled in, grabbing blankets and pillows, ignoring the safety instructions on the video monitors, he gawked a bit, trying not to be obvious but fascinated nevertheless. The rumbling sounds did not comfort him, nor did the takeoff; but once airborne, he began to adjust. He leaned back against his chair, wishing he had sprung for first class, but contenting himself with the fact that he'd gotten a bulkhead-facing seat on the aisle. At least he could stretch his legs.

He didn't exactly doze, but he did let his mind wander, and suddenly it was if he was waking from a very long dream.

What the hell am I doing? he thought. *What was I thinking? I can't leave the others back in Los Angeles without me.*

Too late now. They are back there without me. And, contrary to popular culture hackjobs about vampires, I can't turn into a bat and fly home.

As the long hours passed and the plane flew through the night, Angel tried to manage his anxiety. No can do.

Has someone been controlling my mind? he wondered, alarmed. *Is my head clearing because I'm leaving their sphere of influence?*

Then it didn't matter, because the flight attendant was announcing their descent into Kahului Airport. Around him, tourists were muzzily waking up; slack-key guitar music from the plane's speakers filled the air, and Angel glanced anxiously at the open window to make sure the dawn had not run ahead of the plane.

Safe.

He was glad he hadn't packed any pig's blood for the journey when the agricultural department asked him to wait while they searched his luggage. Weapons had been out from the get-go, of course. Now he supposed he must seem a little suspicious, dressed from head to toe in black and carrying only a small bag. The last time he had worn a Hawaiian shirt, he had been posing as "Herb Saunders," trying to stop a mobster from leaving Los Angeles.

I asked about the tour boat to Catalina to stall him, he recalled. *I had no idea then that there was another island in the Channel Islands called San Teodor, or that demons were being bred and tortured there. A lot was different back then. Doyle was still alive. . . .*

Fresh anxiety washed over him as the inspectors finished pawing through his stuff and waved him on. *I couldn't keep him alive. What about Cordy and the others? Have I abandoned them to the same fate?*

"Sir?" asked a large, black-haired woman standing just outside the exit doors of the airport. She was holding an armload of fragrant leis. "Are you ill?"

He blinked at her. "Thanks, I'm fine."

"You gotta make sure you put on lotta sunscreen," she ordered him. "Or you gonna wind up in the hospital with one sunburn."

He nodded. *I must be the palest guy she's ever seen.*

The sun began to tug at him, and he knew he had to find shelter. He said to her, "Where's the nearest motel?"

"'Cross da street." She wagged her finger at him. "You be careful. That one sun, it would fry you to crisp."

You got that right, Angel thought. "That's a nice lei," he said, pointing to a loop of plumeria draped across her arm. "How much is it?"

"For you, free." She wrinkled her eyes at him appreciatively. "You're a nice man. You take care, honey."

She gestured for him to duck down so she could put the lei over his head. He did, and then she kissed him on the cheek in a traditional Hawaiian greeting of aloha. Her eyes widened and she drew back, startled.

"You're freezing. You sick, honey."

"I just need some rest," he said. "I need a place to stay."

"'Cross da street," she told him again.

He adjusted the lei and picked up his small bag. "Thanks," he said again.

"Mahalo."

As he turned and walked away, he realized he was going to have to find Lohiau's tunnels soon. *I'm drawing far too much attention.* On the other hand, that could be good, if the gossip about a cold, white-skinned tourist reached Lohiau. *Back in the day, he had ears and eyes everywhere.* The *menehune.*

Then he was across the street and at the small reception desk of the Island Breeze Airport Motel, paying a small fortune for what he discovered was an even tinier room. He walked down the interior corridor just as the sun cleared the water; he didn't see it, but he felt it.

The room was small, but serviceable. He stripped the thin blanket off the bed and covered the draped sliding glass door with it, just in case. He rinsed his face in the sink in the bathroom, then stretched out. For the first time in a long while, Angel slept.

And he dreamed.

CHAPTER TWELVE

The Sandwich Islands, 1901: Maui

Darla had dressed for the night in a long, formal muumuu of crimson and black, the train dragging across the floor of the cavern as she walked with proud joy toward Lohiau. In her hands she held a bowl made of koa wood inlaid with shells. Smoke poured from the bowl and when she handed it to Lohiau, it uttered a small moan of pain and sorrow.

"It's still alive," she said to the kahuna. Her gaze ticked toward Angel, and he wasn't certain if she was referring to Pele's Chalice, or to himself. "They didn't know what they had. They kept it in a museum."

Her laughter skittered up and down Angel's spine. She

was luminous, her blond hair wound into a chignon atop her head, tendrils grazing her cheeks and the nape of her neck. God, he loved her.

But God had nothing to do with Darla, nor she with Him.

With great ceremony, Lohiau bowed deeply to Darla. He raised the bowl above his head, gathered breath into his lower abdomen, and began to chant. Darla gazed at Angel, hungry for him, loathing him. Angel saw that in her demeanor, in her expression. But she still wanted him.

My soul . . . Angel thought, torn. *It will leave me. I'll be a beast again. I'll kill, and I'll butcher. I'll delight in inflicting pain.*

But I'll be with Darla again. We'll love, as we did. We'll ravage, as we did.

Lohiau continued to chant. Throughout the grotto, strange skittering noises signaled the arrival of the *menehune*. Angel looked down at the circle of them gathered around him, huge, yellow eyes glowing with anticipation. Across the grotto Darla's magnificent body heaved with passion and longing.

The chanting continued for perhaps an hour. Something in the grotto stirred and came alive: a miasma of evil, something dark and unloving and thirsty. It was like a thickness in the air, an extra layer, and Angel heard a series of sharp clicks, like teeth, or talons sharpening each other.

"It's here, Angelus," Darla said excitedly. "It's here to undo that curse. To take away your soul."

"What is?" he whispered.

"The thing that lives in the Chalice." She smiled brilliantly. "It's going to work. Oh, my dear boy . . ."

Other voices joined in the chanting, smeared, sinister sounds that rose and fell across the melody line that Lohiau carried. Angel began to sway; his stomach rolled, and an intense pain filled his unbeating heart. It spread throughout his body, wrapping its fingers around his spine and shaking it so hard that Angel braced himself for the pain of its snapping in two.

"It's going to rip it from you," Darla said. She looked at him eagerly. Her chignon had come undone and her beautiful, silky hair flowed freely down her shoulders. "I know it hurts, but don't fight it, Angelus."

The chanting rose. The grotesque statues lining the walls and crevices of the grotto began to undulate. Smoke rose from the cavern floor, and from Lohiau's pool. Around him, Angel smelled hot, steaming blood, heard the screams of terrified humans.

I'm going to make up for lost time, he thought gleefully, flexing and unflexing his hands. He could feel his teeth sharpening and lengthening, the vampiric ridges on his face bursting from his smooth human visage. *I'm going to cut such a swath through their kind. . . ..*

I'm on my way back, Darla.

The demon you love is being unchained. The demon . . .

. . . is not me.

His eyes widened.

The demon is not Liam. Is it me she loved at first sight, or what she could have if she changed me?

The chanting rose; the ceiling of the grotto shook. Chunks of damp stone jittered and shook, then fell like bombs to the floor. Fissures formed, and from them, more *menehune* skittered free, like swarms of spiders, jabbering and shrieking in a frenzy.

Smoke rose from the fissures, but this was of a different nature; it stank of sulfur and rotting flesh and it had a shape: horns and a hideous, gaping maw filled with teeth; above the mouth, eyes of black flame that spun and roiled.

"It's going to eat your soul," Darla cried. She turned to it. "I don't know who you are, but take it away from him. Do it! Now!"

The shape rose, filling the cavern. Angel stood still, wincing from the stench. Though he would never show it, he was terrified. Yet he stayed rooted to the spot . . . and realized that there were so many rings of *menehune* staring up at him, pressed so tightly against his legs, that he may as well have been bound at the ankles. He couldn't have moved if he wanted to.

The face bore down on him, grinning. The mouth opened. Echoes bounced off the walls: the word "hunger" in languages he did and didn't speak.

Wind blew across his own face, an icy slap. His eyes teared with cold as he stood unmoving. The *menehune* chittered; the tiki statues babbled incoherently. Somewhere in the cacophony, he heard Darla urging on the monstrous face, begging it to devour his horrible soul.

Then everything stopped. As if with the snap of a finger, the face vanished. The sounds died. The smell was gone immediately. There was no smoke, no black flame, no wind.

Lohiau sank to the floor. The Chalice of Pele rolled from his grasp and clattered onto the lava floor. A single *menehune* jumped inside, and then another, and they all giggled and shrieked as they made it rock back and forth, like a child's play yard toy.

Darla looked around. "What happened?" she cried. "What *happened*?"

In a voice scarcely above a whisper, Lohiau rasped, "It didn't work."

"*What?*"

She ran to the Chalice, kicking *menehune* out of her way as she retrieved the bowl, dumping out the *menehune* as if they were leftover pieces of rice. With a shriek, she hurled it across the grotto with fearsome vampiric force.

"No," Lohiau protested.

The bowl didn't break, as Angel expected. Instead it ricocheted off the wall and clattered to the floor. There was no sign of pain, no moan of sorrow.

"It's dead," Lohiau murmured. "The Bowl is dead."

"And so are you," Darla hissed, rushing him. She flung him onto his back and straddled him. "How could you do this to me? To *us*?"

Angel took a step toward her. "Darla . . ."

She threw herself off the kahuna. Tears streamed down her face. "Don't." Without another word, she got to her feet and left the grotto.

Angel stood over the man, whose nose appeared to have been broken in the fall. Lohiau was gasping; he caught his breath and looked steadily up at Angel.

"If you want to kill me, I'll understand," he said.

Angel shook his head. "I don't."

"You might." Lohiau fixed his gaze on him, did not waver. "It was going to work. I stopped it."

"Then you can do it again," Angel ordered him. "Now."

"I won't." Lohiau awkwardly raised his hand and felt his nose. He inspected the blood on his fingertips. "My life, my work . . . it's all about freedom. I will not take your freedom from you, my friend. You'll have to find someone else willing to enslave you to darkness again."

Angel let himself go vamp face as he bent over the fallen shaman. "I am darkness. I live in darkness. The light will kill me."

"You have light in you now, along with your darkness. That's what makes you a shadow, Angel."

"Change me or I'll kill you."

The kahuna moved his head, gritting his teeth from the pain. "You won't. You want that soul. I can tell. I saw it in your eyes. You don't want to become Angelus again."

"You're wrong," Angel insisted. Then his shoulders jerked with dry sobs and he sank to his knees beside Lohiau. "You're wrong . . ."

"You know I'm right. The goodness in that soul wants to live, Angel. And though it's true that I have murdered people in my bid to free my country, I try very, very hard not to kill good people." Slowly, as if he wanted very badly to be understood, he said to Angel, "You are a good person."

Angel snorted with disgust. "That goes to show how little you really know, you fraud."

The kahuna looked at him and raised his chin as if challenging him to do his worst. "Then let's say you have the capacity to become a good person."

Angel covered his face with his hands, feeling the vampire ridges, the sharp fangs.

"You're wrong," he said again.

The yacht is a beauty, Bran thought, watching in admiration as they drew closer to it. A classic windjammer-style schooner harking back to the late nineteenth century, she looked to be nearly a hundred feet in length. The sails were currently furled to her three masts. Her railings and deckhouse were mahogany, and the brass fixtures and appointments were bright enough to gleam even in the moonlight. Though late Victorian in design, she had obviously been updated with all the luxuries and comforts of the twenty-first century, to judge by the microwave and radio array mounted on the stern. He felt a sudden swell of admiration for Marianna—ruthless vampire though she might be, she certainly had a sense of class and style. And, after all, as Benedicta's consort, he was certainly no stranger to ruthless vampires. There were times, and this was one of them, when he wished that Benedicta's influence over other vampires extended farther than it did—even as far as she believed it did.

Marianna was obviously aware of their approach, for as Bran's vessel drew closer, he saw her standing in the bow, holding one end of a massive iron chain. The hasp at the other end of the chain was fastened around the neck of a monstrosity that looked, from this distance, to be a hybrid of some unholy sort, maybe a cross between a Tayleous Demon and a Red Erebus Fiend. Before he could be more certain of its ancestry, he saw its mistress jerk its chain sharply. The crossbreed responded by generating a crackling ball of magickal energy balanced on its three horns, which it then launched toward Bran's ship.

"Hard to port," Bran ordered the demonic captain, who gave the order. As the yacht turned, Bran raised both his hands and invoked Crom, one of his personal gods, though Benedicta would never know he had personal gods. As far as she and all their followers were concerned, he had no other deities but she.

The fireball plummeted into the clear water, hitting the shark that had just finished devouring Benedicta's lover. Such was the circle of life. The nearby fish and kelp were destroyed as well, the entire mess transformed into a startling mass of cinders that roiled in the water before it dissolved into the sea.

Knowing there would be nothing gained in harming Marianna, Bran rather jovially lobbed a fireball back at her. Rather than simply dodge the projectile, she yanked on the chain of the crossbreed. It stumbled in front of her just as Bran's fireball found a target—the side of the creature's face. The creature shrieked with pain and pawed at its ruined flesh. Marianna clearly could have cared less. She shook the monster's chain and hit it in the midsection. Half in agony, half in submission, it lurched out another fireball and sent it toward Benedicta's yacht.

Benedicta sniffed. "Clearly she does not know who we are."

Or care, Bran thought. Now *this* was a queen. Whereas his queen . . . was perhaps his queen no longer?

His mind spun at the idea.

"This is ridiculous," Benedicta snapped. Then, before Bran realized what she was doing, she threw back her head and shouted to the skies. Immediately the black night burst into a heavy rain.

She shot straight upward into the torrents, still screaming orders to the elements, and a wind took her over to the other yacht. Bran invoked the gods to give him wings as well, but in the few seconds between realization and reaction,

Benedicta had Marianna pinned around the front of her body, her huge double rows of fangs bared against the throat of the other vampire.

Marianna's minions, both hideous creatures and normal-looking humans, stopped everything they were doing and watched.

Bran landed on the deck beside the two females, as Marianna blurted, "Take the Slayer if you want her, damn it."

Benedicta held her fast. Then her left arm shot sideways and she ripped the arm of an advancing human out of its socket, a wicked Borgian stiletto still grabbed by the now-dead hand.

Geysers of blood erupted from the human's shoulder as she—for it had been a female—sank to the deck. Blood gushed everywhere, mixing with the freezing rain, and Marianna's monsters began to howl for it like hyenas after a fresh kill.

Then Benedicta hoisted Marianna from her feet and whirled her around in a circle, knocking several approaching demons off balance. Bran was most impressed by—and also alerted to—the fact that his lady's ruthlessness in battle was still the stuff of legends.

I began to take her for granted, he realized. *By holding her in contempt, I've been underestimating her. I wonder if she knows what I've been thinking? If she actually knows about my violations of her, and permits them?*

"I want to talk to you," Benedicta informed the other vampire, as she flung Marianna to the deck and wrenched the stiletto from the human hand lying on the deck about ten inches from her left boot heel. She put one four-inch boot heel on Marianna's back and leaned down, angling the stiletto across the back of Marianna's neck.

"I'm guessing that this is dipped in poison, and that your little acolyte hoped to end my existence with it. Two can play that way, you stupid little bitch."

"You . . . you're Benedicta," Marianna whispered. "My Lady, I submit."

"As if you didn't know who I was." Benedicta was remarkably limber, now, still with her boot planted on Marianna's back, she leaned forward from the waist, dipping down like a vulture, and whispered into Marianna's ear. "My followers *made* you. Your life belongs to me. If I choose to end it, it is over."

"What do you want?" the other vampire asked dully. Bran was impressed in spite of himself. Benedicta's influence was something to behold.

"A nice Chianti," Benedicta replied. "And some warm clothes. But I'll take a place to talk." She went vampface, and allowed her long talons to skewer Marianna's neck on either side. As the female screamed, Benedicta yanked her head back and stared into her eyes. "Do you have such a place?"

"Be-Belowdecks."

Her talons were like pincers as she put Marianna on her feet once more. "Bran, come," she commanded, without so much as a backward glance at him.

A lesser man would have taken her dismissive tone of voice personally, made plans for payback. *I am a chess master and a politician,* he reminded himself. Still, a man could only take so much.

Marianna staggered down the narrow companionway to a small passageway. Benedicta came after her, and then Bran. Both he and his mistress took note of the coppery scent in the air . . . Slayer's blood. A rich and fabulous delicacy. Bran's body rushed with excitement. To kill that Slayer would be a glorious end to a very busy night.

Benedicta glanced at him over her shoulder and smiled evilly at him. Again he was shocked by her quickness and her apparent intellectual capacity. He felt as if he had been dreaming while she had been becoming smarter.

I wonder . . . is this an artifact of being with her? he thought. *Is she draining me of my energy, even then? Using me up?*

There was a strangely proportioned creature in front of a slatted wooden door, a white-fleshed human shape covered with what looked to be closed eyes. He wore a sort of a toga loosely draped around his body, and a hammerlike weapon lay across his muscular chest.

Marianna snapped her fingers and the monstrous thing inclined his head. Then he opened the door and walked in first, shutting the door behind himself. After perhaps a full minute, he returned, shook his head, and allowed his mistress to enter the cabin.

It was a beautifully appointed stateroom dominated by a bed, a floor-to-ceiling mirror, a torture rack, and a conference table. Only Bran and the monster's reflections showed in the mirror.

"Please, sit down," Marianna said, all graciousness. The wounds at her neck had already started to heal. "May I get you some refreshment?"

"That would be nice," Benedicta replied.

Bran remained silent.

Marianna snapped her fingers and the white-fleshed monster left the room. Marianna folded her hands on the shiny conference table.

"What may I do for you?"

Bran took over. As Benedicta's advisor, it was appropriate for him to do so. "Your husband is in Los Angeles. Why?"

She smiled with pride and genuine affection. "To kill me, I suppose. He has a thing about being married to exotic prey."

"You two are seeking the Book of the Interregnum," Bran continued.

Marianna blinked at him. "The Book of the what?"

He said nothing. But Benedicta leaned forward and said, "He has pages from it."

Bran flashed with irritation. There was no reason to reveal more information than what might serve them. Benedicta was overstepping her role. His old contempt for her rose to the fore and he had trouble controlling his expression, aware as he was that he should have taken a seat with his back to the mirror, so that neither vampiress would have the advantage of seeing his reflection. On the other hand, he had a good feedback system with the mirror, a way to check to see if he appeared to be as genuine and direct as he needed to.

I must be getting tired, he thought, *or losing too much magickal energy. I never had to worry about these things before.*

Marianna looked massively confused. "I honestly have no idea what you're talking about," she said. "I don't know about that book."

As a druid, Bran had been trained to look at situations from many angles, and to consider that upon occasion, people spoke more than surface truth. So he said, "It's something that we want. Intact. And we know that your husband has parts of it."

Then Benedicta cut in. "Why do you have the Slayer?"

Marianna appeared to hesitate. Then she said, "I bought her. I'm going to offer her up to friends to hunt."

"Won't her own friends come after her?" Benedicta asked, then slowly smiled. "But then, that would just add to the sport, wouldn't it?"

The two bloodthirsty women shared a moment. Marianna said, "Indeed it would. In fact I'm preparing for an assault by them just in case. You see, one of them has visions, and—"

"A Seer?" Benedicta half-shouted. "One is a Seer?"

"Is it a male?" Bran asked hopefully.

Marianna frowned. "Why? Does it have to do with that book you mentioned?"

Bran realized they had to lower their voices, keep her calmer and more forthcoming. He looked at Benedicta, signaling her to let him handle this. Her eyes were shining like spinning chips of outer space. Impulsively she stretched her hand to him and murmured, "Oh, Bran," and he heard memories of the day in her silky tone, when she had been his willing Galatea and he, her Pygmalion. He had literally brought her back to life when she had been little more than a mad image of her former self, lurching through the oaks and weeping incoherently.

"It's a girl," Marianna said eagerly, seeing perhaps a way to ingratiate herself with the Speaker of the Mysteries of all vampiredom. "Her name is Cordelia."

At that moment, more things clicked into place than Bran could possibly have hoped for. *Cordelia Chase, who has been looking for the Book on the Internet. Who works for Angel Investigations.*

He turned to Benedicta, who once had looked upon him as her lover and rescuer, and said, "Would you have a problem with that, my queen?"

"Of course not. I would have preferred a male, but . . ."

"What?" Marianna demanded. She launched into Spanish, which Bran spoke. "What are you after, why do you want her?"

"*Calmate*," Bran soothed. "You have a fine young Slayer, and you're hoping that her friends will come to rescue her. But here's a thought, lovely lady. Why don't we mass our forces and return to Los Angeles, mount an attack, and take them all?"

Marianna hesitated. "They don't know that it was I who took her. They think it is a law firm called Wolfram and Hart."

"We know that firm well," Bran said. Benedicta nodded in agreement, flashing him a secretive smile. "Surely the enjoyment of your sporting aficionados would be enhanced with the addition to your hunt of some more . . . exotics."

"And I already have cargo," Marianna argued.

She has the Slayer aboard. "Let this boat go on to its destination, delivering her. You can come back on ours."

"But if Angelus found out . . ." Marianna said.

"He probably already knows," Bran asserted. "In fact . . ." He stopped a moment. Closed his eyes and called to his gods for Seeing, pressed his palms together, and pulled them slowly apart.

No luminous sphere appeared this time, but a fluid membrane of pure green energy vibrated between his palms. The sensation was of dozens of rats scrabbling over his skin.

In the membrane, he saw a pale, white form slowly descending into a tunnel. *That's disappointingly vague,* he thought. Then, as he watched, the form became a crisp image, and there was a garland of flowers around his neck. In his hand he held a used airline ticket stamped: AGRICULTURAL INSPECTION PASSED, KAHULUI AIRPORT, MAUI, HAWAII.

It was Angel.

He smiled at the two women. "Angel will not be a problem," he said. "The wolf has left the flock unguarded."

"Wolves live in packs," Marianna observed. Then she smiled slyly. "Has he?"

CHAPTER THIRTEEN

1899, an Oak Grove on the Outskirts of London

"Her hair was black as a raven's wing, her lips were red as rubies, and her cheek was white as snow."

She glanced up at him, her eyes glittering with a fevered light. He wasn't entirely sure whether the red of her lips was natural or just the blush of fresh blood, most likely that of the slain boy beside her.

He tipped his head to the side as he studied her. She seemed very young, but looks were often deceiving with her kind. Her sleeve was torn and streaked with blood. She quivered, wary as a cornered animal.

He crouched down gently, extending his hand as he would to any wild creature. It was a gesture of warmth and invitation and with it he had lured many an animal to its death. "And she was fair to behold."

"Whom are you referencing?" Her teeth glistened in the moonlight.

He smiled. Snow White she was not, though she looked the part. "It is you of whom I speak."

She glanced uneasily at the dead boy beside her. "Nasty boy. Nasty boy tried to touch me."

He nodded slowly. "And you killed him."

She shook her head fiercely. "He's sleeping."

Looking closer at the body he could tell that she had ripped his throat out, probably after drinking him dry. "Ah yes, I can see that now."

"Who are you?"

"I am called Bran Cahir. I am at your service."

"Are you going to try and touch me?"

He glanced at the smooth flesh of her arm where her sleeve had been rent. He licked his lips slowly.

"No, not today. You have much to learn of the world and who you are."

She edged slowly toward him, her back slowly leaving the protection of the oak tree under which she had sat. Fate had led him to the grove, led him to her, he could feel it. She crept closer and closer, her eyes gleaming. He braced himself as he could feel her desire to attack grow.

She threw herself forward, face changing and fangs extending.

With a wave of his hand he sent her crashing to the ground, whimpering and cowering. He let her lie there for a moment before moving to her side.

She shuddered as he touched her hair. It must have

been glorious once; now it was just a tangled mass clotted together with bits of twigs and dried blood.

They sat there for several minutes before she finally lifted her eyes to meet his. He smiled slowly, gently, and she at last smiled back. Good, he could teach her. He closed his eyes and felt the future that they could share.

When he opened his eyes again she was gazing at him in wonder. She touched his face slowly. He stood up, drawing her with him.

"Come, my dear. The sun will be up soon."

"You're not like me?"

"No, I am not."

She gestured to the body lying at the foot of the tree. "And you're not like him?"

"No. I am something—different."

She nodded slowly, digesting that information.

"Time to go."

"Where?" she asked, even as she allowed him to begin to lead her.

"Home. I have centuries of wisdom to share with you."

Wesley returned from his patrol of the hotel garden and said, "All quiet on the western front."

"That's east, bro," Gunn told him.

"I loved that novel," Fred said. Wesley and she shared a smile, and she added, "And the movie, wow."

"Dug the movie," Gunn said. He hitched his axe over his shoulder and gestured to the curving stairway. "See you two in about half an hour."

Wesley glanced at his watch and nodded. "And Cordelia . . ."

". . . is back from the elevator," she responded, "where Miss Creepy is still lying quietly in her packing crate, taking up all the space and emitting a decidedly cheeselike odor. We should be glad no one is taking advantage of our helpless and vulnerable position to stage an attack on us, right?"

"I don't think anyone is gonna attack us," Gunn predicted, stopping and looking at her over his shoulder. "I think we're below the radar of anyone who would care that Angel's out of town."

"I'd be insulted, but I'd rather be breathing," Cordelia muttered. "Hey, we're badasses, too, right? We kick butt all the time."

"One would think, however, that an attempt to take the mummy from us would be attempted," Wesley mused.

"Maybe Mr. Escobar will just ask politely." Fred wandered over to the computer. "Maybe he's off killing his wife and he'll call us about the mummy in a little while."

"One can hope," Wesley assured her.

"That's one way to cut down on alimony." Gunn smiled sourly and went up the stairs. "I'm going to patrol upstairs for a while."

"This is a no-fault state," Fred called after him. "Alimony is not usually the case."

"Unless you're in *this* town. L.A. means big money." Cordelia moved her hands, seeing the scene all too clearly in her mind. "He's some movie director, off for months at a time while she stays home. To . . . work out a lot and go to really great restaurants and to shop," she added dreamily. "At all the boutiques on Wilshire. Look at me, such a loser, I can't go to Maui, and I can't get divorced in Los Angeles."

"You're not even married," Fred said, chuckling. Then she raised her brows in dead-on, earnest sincerity. "But you could be, if you wanted, just like tha—"

Simultaneously, all the windows on the ground floor shattered as huge shapes hurtled through them and invaded the hotel. Some landed on two legs, others on four or more. They growled and shrieked and as they rushed Cordelia, Fred, and Wesley, their colors gleamed wildly in the soft light: electric crimson and iridescent blue and phosphorescent green.

"They're under a protection spell!" Wesley shouted, as he raised to pick up his Bavarian battle adz. He began to chant in Latin as he raced toward them.

"Gunn!" Cordelia bellowed. "A little help here!"

She had had her sword at the ready. She took it in both hands, standing *kendo* style to find her energy, as Angel had taught her, and then began to fearlessly advance. With a shriek, Fred picked up the computer, thought the better of her choice of her weapon, and looked around for something else to damage hellbeasts with.

"Gunn!" she shrieked.

Eventually she spied a Peruvian blowgun Wesley had recently purchased from the lost-and-found at Caritas. All weapons had to be checked at the door, and the owner had never returned.

She joined the fray as Wesley took on a four-legged monster covered with armored plates and hooves that sliced up the floor as it advanced and retreated on the former Watcher. Its face was crablike, decorated with a fan of pincers, but the eyes on its stalks were clearly human. Fred was revolted, and not a little terrified.

Still, she checked the blow gun for its ammunition—a poison-tipped arrow—and blew with all her lung capacity at the creature. It shrieked and staggered; taking advantage, Wesley arced his adz over his head and brought it down heavily, slamming the blade into the creature's neck area. Its head drooped forward but did not detach. Red blood spurted from the wood, splatting on Wesley's forehead and the bodice of Fred's peasant blouse. His counterspell had worked.

"Gunn!" Wesley shouted.

Cordelia had just successfully stabbed a biped with a human torso and frog-leg lower half. Her sword had found a vital organ, for the creature limply batted at the sword, then fell to its knees, then collapsed forward, its own weight pushing the sword clean through its body.

"Got your back!" Gunn shouted from the stairs. "Had some excitement of my own up here."

He aimed a flamethrower and released a death-dealing stream of flame, barely missing Fred as it incinerated a creature that had come up behind her. The monstrosity was at least ten feet tall, and as it went up in flames, the hotel fire sprinklers came on.

Wesley shook water out of his eyes and tightened his grip on the wooden shaft of the adz. Cordelia said, "On your left," and together they advanced on another attacker, this one a bulbous object that rolled toward them. Stuck onto its exterior were several small animals—a cat, a squirrel— that must have gotten in its way here as it rolled, tanklike, to the hotel.

"Whom do you serve?" Wesley yelled at it, whacking his adz into it.

Cordelia yelled, "How about maybe the Humane Society?"

Wesley finally hit it in the right place; with a high squeal, it shook and trembled, then began to deflate.

"Die, hairball, die!" Cordelia shouted at it.

Amazingly enough, a number of the animals that had glommed onto it now worked themselves free, and in the case of the cat, turned tail and raced for cover from the sprinklers somewhere in the lobby.

The creature itself became a distended puddle of sticky dead thing, and Wesley wrinkled his nose and said, "This looks like something we're going to have to clean up."

"Someday, my maid will come," Cordelia said, raising her right foot. As she did so, she lifted the sole of a formerly wonderful pair of sandals from the glop. "And she'll bring me some more shoes."

Moving away, she and Wesley both raced to Fred's side, as she battled against a female monster sprouting three heads. The head in the middle was human and vampiric; the other two were batlike, pitching and flailing in utter panic.

Cordelia said, "I'll take the right head."

"I've got the middle."

From the corner in which she'd taken refuge, Fred said nothing, only blew into the blowpipe—she had located a pile of poison-dipped darts and was making liberal use of them—aiming, and hitting the head on the left. The entire creature shrieked and staggered backward, landing on its backside. The head Fred had shot lay limp while the vampiric one clacked its fangs in furious imitation of a windup toy, while the other bat head chittered and wove like a cobra searching for its beloved snake charmer.

Then Gunn uttered an expletive not allowed on prime-time shows as something rammed him from behind, and he crashed over the banister and hit the floor hard. The flamethrower skittered away from him.

"Gunn?" Cordelia shouted, weaving her way toward him. She belted an oncoming wraithlike creature in the face and elbowed a small vampire with the grace and poise of someone who had been waiting since five A.M. to take on the well-toned soccer moms at the Nordstrom half-yearly sale. "Gunn?"

Something that she couldn't even describe had straddled Gunn and was whamming him across the face over and over again. What scared her most was that Gunn wasn't fighting back, and each time the thing hit him, his head rolled with the punch—no resistance, no grunt, no nothing.

What if he's dead?

"No!" she screamed, renewing her efforts to reach his side. She became a battle machine, hitting, kicking, gouging, doing whatever it took to reach her friend. She tackled the bludgeoning thing; as the assailants collided, Gunn was taken with them, rolling over onto his stomach.

The spigots were going nuts; part of Cordelia was glad to know the sprinklers worked; *that jerk from Wolfram & Hart had that on his list of safety code violations, the big liar—*

And then the bludgeoning thing was straddling Cordelia, and began to beat her with the rhythm and force of a demolition ball. She crossed her arms over face and tried to protect herself. But there was so much strength in the creature that as it swung at her again, it knocked her right shoulder from the socket.

For all that she had been through in the battle—the hits, the punches, the kicks—the pain was unbelievable. She heard a thin, high-pitched wail, and realized it was her own voice.

God, I hope it knocks me out soon, she thought.

And it must have read her mind, because it did.

Fred, her darts all used, stayed tucked into the corner beside a potted palm and a mirror. She noted the number of the attackers who did not register a reflection. The raiding party was comprised of vampires as well as demons and humans, then. She tried to think of some other attack she could use, some way that she could be helpful. But she knew her physical strength wasn't enough to be effective against vampires. Perhaps she should try to stay under cover, so that when their assailants had finally gone, she'd be able to find Angel, call for help. She tried to make herself miniature, tried to blend into the corner.

Even so, her eyes grew wide as four human-looking creatures in black and red robes caught hold of Wesley and threw him against the mirror, shattering it. The shards dug into his back and as the scent of his blood hit the air, both his captors transformed into vamp face. The one on the right yanked back Wesley's neck and prepared to sink its fangs into his carotid artery.

Then the entire room blazed with blue, crackling light. The water shut off immediately, and the vampires who had hold of Wesley released him so abruptly that his knees buckled.

From her safe haven, Fred watched three figures glide through the carnage. A man with the oddest skin stood to one side of a regal woman dressed in black, and another in more stylish red leather pants and a baby T-shirt. The creatures around them bowed and scraped, or scurried away.

They floated a few inches above the ground, and finally they arrived a few feet in front of Wesley. He blinked rapidly—Fred thought he was trying to keep himself from passing out before he had a chance to speak to them and find out what they wanted.

"You may have the two men, Marianna," said the woman in black. "All we want is the Seer."

"Watcher," he corrected her. "I was a Watcher . . ."

But no one appeared to be listening to him. So, like his friends, Wesley succumbed to the arms of darkness, and fainted. And Fred, caught in the steely grip of utter helplessness, watched as they lifted him up and took him—took all of them—away.

CHAPTER FOURTEEN

Where are Fred and Cordy? Wesley thought, and not for the first time.

He had been terribly beaten, as had Gunn. But they were still alive. Since Marianna Escobar had killed others—Faith's Yorba Linda lookouts, for instance—there was a reason for that.

And probably not one that would make me feel better.

As the small plane descended, Wesley could see only one cluster of buildings on the island, close to the northern tip. Bright moonlight revealed the rest of the landscape, covered with chaparral not unlike the hills around Los Angeles, and streaked by a few dirt tracks that must have been Jeep roads cut into the back country. The buildings, encircled by what looked like a ten-foot wall, looked to have been mostly built with local materials—adobe made from the island's own earth, most likely. They were the same dun color as the bare ground that surrounded them, but with the red tile roofs so common on Southern California's mainland. There was a dirt airstrip just outside the compound, its lone runway reaching almost to the surf line.

"It looks like we're landing," he said.

Gunn fixed him with a steady stare. His face was bruised and his eyes nearly swollen shut. "Good," he muttered. "My arms are killin' me."

"Same here," he agreed. Before being put on the plane, their wrists had been bound in front of them with plastic cuffs.

The plane had only eight seats, including the pilot's and copilot's. Two of the remaining six were occupied by Marianna Escobar and a demon companion, a male that looked human except for pale green spots underneath his first layer of skin and bright green claws instead of nails at the ends of his fingers. Wesley couldn't classify it, and he had no idea if or how he could kill it, given his present condition.

"We're goin' down," Gunn said as the plane began its descent.

The small plane's landing was bumpy but professional. By the time the craft came to a stop in the cloud of dust it had raised, a shaggy-looking demon in a pickup truck had pulled up beside them, the truck's headlights boring tunnels into the night.

Marianna climbed out of the plane and went straight to the passenger side of the pickup. Her demon companion, whom she addressed as Clete, looked back at Wesley and Gunn and crooked a long, clawed finger at them.

"Let's move it," he said in his gravely voice.

Outside, Clete and the furry driver hoisted both of them into the truck's bed. The night air was fresh, scented by the chaparral but with a hint of salt water.

The driver resumed his position while Clete and the flight crew crowded into the pickup's bed with Wesley and Gunn. They drove up the dirt road and through the high walls of the compound.

Floodlights mounted on the walls splashed illumination over the whole scene. Most of the buildings were low-slung; the largest one, which was immense, was clearly someone's house. *Marianna's, I expect,* Wesley thought. *She carries herself like someone who is accustomed to a certain amount of luxury.*

The massive, carved wooden front door was six steps up from ground level. Two gigantic tusks—*each must be at least seven or eight feet long,* Wesley noted—flanked the door, points directed toward the sky. *I can scarcely imagine the animal those must have come from.*

Above the door was an enormous skull that Wesley guessed must have been from the same beast. An elephant of phenomenal size, or perhaps a mammoth or mastodon of some sort, he assumed.

Marianna tripped lightly up the stairs and the door was opened at her advance by a servant standing beside it that Wesley could only glimpse in the shadows.

"Nice place," Gunn whispered. "If you like dead stuff."

"We like Angel," Wesley replied.

"Yeah, well, he's dead but he ain't, you know . . . dead."

"Shut up," Clete snarled. The others climbed down from the truck bed and headed toward one of the other buildings. Clete and the furry demon tugged Wesley and Gunn from the truck. "Inside," Clete said.

The furry one hustled them up the stairs. Clete brought up the rear. Inside the door, Gunn stopped short and Wesley nearly ran into him.

The front room was a cavernous showplace, a museum-quality collection of hunting trophies from around the globe.

"You got to really, really like the dead stuff," Gunn observed quietly, "to want to live in a place like this."

Wesley didn't answer, because he could think of nothing to say that would even begin to be appropriate. There were two doors leading off this grand entryway, one on each side. Directly opposite the front door was a staircase that swept up in both directions, curved toward a landing halfway up and then continued from there as a single piece. The ceiling was at least three stories high. And there were animals everywhere. The dead kind.

A gigantic polar bear, rearing up on hind legs, stood against the wall at the base of the stairs, right beneath the landing. On shelves mounted at various levels around the room Wesley saw wolves and foxes, a bobcat coiled to spring, a Canada lynx, a wide variety of birds, including a golden eagle, a Cooper's hawk, and a snowy owl, and dozens of other specimens of mammals and birds he couldn't identify. On marble bases scattered about the floor were larger land animals: a bison, a lion, a gazelle, a pair of ibexes, a Rocky Mountain goat, a silverback gorilla, and a Bengal tiger.

Intermingled with the animals were a few creatures that were less well known to the public at large. Outside their nightmares, at least. Wesley shuddered when his gaze fell upon a werewolf, but he realized quickly that it was a female and quite a bit smaller than Oz. Paired with the polar bear was another snow white animal, more human-looking and yet more wild at the same time. Its face was fleshy, its expression dour, even sorrowful. *A yeti?* Wesley wondered. He didn't see what else it could have been.

Whatever taxidermists did this work are skilled indeed at their grisly task, Wesley thought. Every animal in the room looked alive, frozen at a moment in time, but with the potential to leap or fly or growl or run without notice. Their fur or feathers were immaculate, as if anything as groomed as they might have been in the wild. Glass eyes glinted in the light like the eyes of living creatures from an overhead chandelier that was made from an assortment of antlers. The overall effect was unsettling.

"Yes," he finally said in response to Gunn's comment. "I believe you're correct. Whoever lives here does indeed like dead stuff."

Marianna had disappeared as soon as she'd entered the house, her servant with her. Clete and the furry one led Wesley and Gunn through the doors on the right into a formal dining room decorated with more of the same. In this room, though, the dead animal motif was interrupted somewhat by tapestries—*quite old, at that,* Wesley thought—depicting hunting scenes. They didn't linger here, though, but passed through another door into a kitchen big enough to feed a regiment, and then through that into a hall, where the décor distinctly changed. Gone were the paintings, the wallpaper, the stuffed animals.

Present were bunker concrete, filth, and smears of blood on the wall.

Muffled through a thick wall, they heard something scream in agony.

Gunn and Wesley traded glances. Wesley said to Clete, "Where are we going?"

Clete grinned evilly at him. "Holding cells. Until the hunt."

Gunn sighed. "Shoulda known, English."

Wesley nodded grimly.

Cordelia had no idea how long she had been unconscious, bound, and gagged, but she was awake now, and not loving that. Nor did she have any idea where she was, except that it was not the laughin' place, as they said in Fred's beloved Disneyland. This place had horned gods with enormous teeth and so many goddesses one could say she was in a goddess harem.

Bone was the main motif of the decorating style— human bones, demon bones, big weird bones, and little teeny bones. They were scattered everywhere. On the big altar in front of her, blood was the color scheme. Preferably thick and dried.

And even less than she was loving her surroundings was she loving what was surrounding her. Sometimes Hell turned out shoddy work: Her new best friends included a demon armed with one set of talons far larger than the other; an Ehrongliss with a missing third horn, and a whole lot of generally hideous hideousnesses gone hideously wrong.

So it was with some relief that all this was taken from her when someone yanked something over her head and knocked her out.

She awoke once more to the smell of fresh blood. She saw a man about six feet tall, wearing a white muslin robe over what looked like a very fine black silk cassock. The sleeves were monkishly long and the hem dragged on the floor. For all she knew, he had no feet.

Beside him, in truly breathtaking regalia, stood a woman who would have been dwarfed by the man if not for her regal bearing. Her hair was gathered up on top of her head and twisted into a knot. Holding it in place was an ornate silver skewer from which hung dozens and dozens of miniature silver skulls. Their jaws were hinged, and as Cordelia watched in revolted fascination, they opened and shut their mouths at random intervals, revealing rows of golden fangs inlaid with rubies or really good imitations of them.

The stiff, black lace collar of her gown reached the tip of her towering of hairdo, then fanned out on either side of her head. Her face was chalk white, her lips brilliant red. Her eyes were ringed with very black liner and her lashes were so long they just had to be fake.

She had to be the CIC—Chick in Charge—and Cordelia wondered if she could work some of the old Queen of Mean charm on the woman. Then she realized that the reason she, Cordelia, had been silent for so long was that there was a gag in her mouth.

In equal, although ungagged, silence, the couple stared at her. Then, as Cordelia watched in horror, some kind of struggling, writhing victim-in-a-bag was carried to the altar, and at the snap of the woman's fingers, thrown into what Cordelia now realized was a fire pit.

Roughly, her gag was removed. It was in her mind to scream, but instead she managed to swallow hard, lick her lips, and say, "I'm guessing this isn't exactly the moment for me to say, 'Tag, you're it.'"

To her shock, the unholy couple bowed deeply.

"We are honored by your presence, Seer," the man said. "We shall begin your rites of purification immediately."

"Oh, how . . . unnecessary," Cordelia managed to reply. "Seeing as I am so very pure already." *And if my friends back in Sunnydale could hear me saying that, they'd be on the floor in hysterics.*

The man continued, "For our purpose, you must be as pristine as the driven snow, both in body and mind."

"Oh, big problem then," Cordelia said, wrinkling her nose in a friendly way. "Because, well, let's move on to my mind. I'm so much a product of my time. TV." She waved her hand and shook her head in dismay. "So much sex and bad language. And I'm just totally addicted to it. The more unpristine, the better."

"However," the man continued, as if she hadn't spoken, "if we cannot purify what is there, we will erase it completely. Or throw it out."

"Throw it *out*?" she repeated shrilly. "Excuse me, throw it out?"

"Your body . . ." The man gave her a rude once-over, which she did not appreciate. She saw the flicker of nasty, undriven lust on his face and glared at him. However, she said nothing about it. She wanted no further discussions on throwing out anything of hers, no matter how impure.

"The Rites of Purification and Cleansing will be painful," he went on, which Cordelia took to mean, *Yay, I'm a major perv and I get to torture you*. "We had hoped for a male Seer, in part because it is possible that your female body will not be able to withstand the ordeal."

And thanks yet again, Doyle, for passing the vision gift on to me.

"But when you are as cleansed as is possible, you will know joy and fulfillment beyond all previous capacity to understand." He beamed first at her, and then at the Queen Amidala wanna-be at his side.

Now his voice grew low, the way the voices of villains got in TV shows when they were about to blow the big secret. "You will be filled with the essence of the Beast of the First Blood, and then you will join the Speaker of the Mysteries in Sacred Union." He gestured to the woman, whose eyes glittered with excitement. The skulls on her hair thingie clattered and clacked.

"Um, no offense, but I really prefer men in the sense of uniting," Cordelia said apologetically. "Oh, but maybe I'm making an assumption here," she blurted. "Because, well, I just assumed that, um, 'she'"—Cordy made air quotes—"is a woman."

As both of them stared at her, Cordelia prattled nervously on. "I'm . . . open-minded, of course. Because, like, I *love* Willow, for example. Not in a big lesbo way, but . . ."

The woman raised her hand. She didn't speak, didn't make any other motions. But instantly Cordelia was caught in a field of energy that made her shriek with pain. It was like being hit with dozens of Tasers all over her body. Her bones rattled from the pain; her nerve endings were being held, one by one, over a welding gun. She felt as if her cells might burst apart at any moment. Her eyes throbbed as if someone was trying to push on them from the inside as well as the outside, with only a thin membrane to keep them from exploding.

Everything sizzled, and *hurt*—teeth, fingernails, even the tattoo at the base of her spine.

Oh, my God, make this stop, she pleaded silently, because she couldn't speak. She couldn't even remember how to speak. Within the crackling field she shook from head to toe, but it was as if her someone were holding her too tightly, not allowing her to shake as hard as she needed to find release.

All at once it was over; all the agony and the shaking. She lay on the floor, shaking.

"Don't you *ever* speak in our presence again," the woman commanded. Then she turned her back on Cordelia, who had begun to flop like a fish as the terrible aftermath of her torture overtook her muscles and tendons, making everything misfire badly.

"Prepare yourself. That was a mere taste of what is to come," the woman said, sweeping out of sight.

The man lingered behind. He knelt beside Cordelia and said, "You see how it is with her. She must be obeyed."

"I thought . . . it was an honor to meet me," Cordelia finally managed to rasp.

"It is. *I* understand what an honor it is." He touched her cheek. His finger was like a branding iron, but she didn't have the energy even to flinch. "Listen to me, girl. You will be cleansed. And if the Raising works, you will be filled with the Beast. You have very little power to control your destiny. But remember this: I was kind to you. And she was not."

Then he made some vague hocus pocus-y motions with his hands and pulled a cool glass of ice water from his sleeve. He held it out to her, and she drank avidly, whimpering when the last of it had slid down her throat.

"Are you saying you're not loyal to her?" Cordelia asked. Then at his horrified expression, she lowered her voice and said, "Are you planning, you know, a mutiny?"

He looked pityingly at her. "I am very old," he told her. "You have no idea how old. And I have survived this long in part because I am a master chess player. You do understand that I'm not referring specifically to the game of chess, do you not?"

She looked down at her hands. Her cuticles were bleeding. Her palms were sliced and bruised. "I'm superficial, not stupid," she said dully.

"All right, then." Again he moved his hands. This time, a small white tablet appeared between his fingertips. "This is a concoction that will help to dull the agony of what is to come. Open your mouth."

Cordelia hesitated. *What if it's a trap? What if it does something really, really bad to me?*

"Bran?" called a voice from a not-too-distant distance. It was the Shebitch of the Mysteries, or whatever he had called her. "We have to get ready to receive all our acolytes."

He looked at Cordelia. She gazed at him, and finally parted her lips. It was probably just off-brand aspirin. He slipped the pill into her mouth. Immediately things began to get very hazy. She felt horribly dizzy, as if someone had thrown her off a cliff.

Muzzily she heard the clanking of chains, and the woman's voice in a blurry, slow-down speed.

Then something very, very hideous walked up to her. It was joined by another, this one carrying very heavy chains with what looked like ice tongs at one end. Wicked-huge ice tongs.

The woman said something again, and ice-tong guy bent down and placed Cordelia's feet together. Then he opened the tongs and positioned them on either side of her feet.

Then he inserted the tongs into her flesh.

As she writhed and shrieked, the two creatures dragged her out of the altar chamber and down a long, cold corridor. At the end was a metal door with a grate in the center of it. The other one opened it while the one with the tongs waited.

Once the door was open, the tong holder walked into the room, dragging Cordelia, who screamed and sobbed behind him on the floor. He unclamped the tongs, allowing her ruined feet to slam against a cold cement floor, stepped over her, and joined his companion at the door.

When the door was shut, the room—or rather, the cell— was pitch black.

Cordelia had a change of heart about Bran's pill:

Oh, my God, I hope it does kill me.

In her office at Wolfram & Hart, Lilah took another swig of her single malt scotch.

Nathan Reed had just laid a whammy on her and Gavin Park.

He had summoned them both into the penthouse conference room, smiling pleasantly as they took seats at the polished ebony table, and said, "You two are going to San Teodor."

Lilah spoke first. "Yes. To make sure the hunt goes well."

He took that in. "You're also taking something with you."

She and Gavin looked at each other, then back at him, and Lilah crossed her legs above the knee, waiting expectantly.

Nathan pressed the intercom on the phone and said, "Bring the Book in."

A few seconds passed, and then the doors to the conference room opened.

What Lilah saw next would stay with her for the rest of her life.

Two very tall figures in heavy black robes walked into the room. Their heads were bent down and shrouded with hoods. But their hands were chalk white. Signs and sigils had been etched into their flesh, the scars raised and prominent.

Ornately carved poles rested on their shoulders, and between the two of them, they carried a large box that looked as if it had been carved out of large pieces of bone. It was fitted together so that each joint appeared to be a femur, and the top of the box was curved like a slab of human ribs.

The figures carried the box to the conference table, then moved swiftly away, retreating back the way they came.

"This," Nathan said, "is the Book of the Interregnum."

"You're kidding," Lilah murmured, then covered her shock with a look of inquiry. She slid a glance toward Gavin, who was doing no better.

"We have a very special client," Nathan continued.

"Marianna Escobar?" Gavin followed, eager to show Lilah up.

Nathan smiled at him. "Well, she's very special too, of course. But I'm referring to Benedicta, the Mother Infernal."

Lilah's jaw dropped. "I didn't . . . I thought she was a legend."

Nathan wandered over to the box. He pressed on the curved lid and it popped open. He gestured for them to come toward him. At nearly the same time, both Lilah and Gavin complied.

"No legend. Very real. Look inside."

Lilah looked into the box. And saw . . .

Bavaria, 1310
"Das Biest!" the monk shrieked as he raced into the church. The back of his habit was aflame; as he ran, it caught fire; within seconds he was a pillar of flames.

Outside a wind whipped up and batted the church. The stained-glass windows blew inward in horrifying explosions. From the vaulted ceiling high above, stones shook loose and crashed down on the congregation as they began to scatter, shrieking in panic. The floor cracked; pieces jutted up, and at least a dozen people tumbled down into the flames and smoke of a fiery pit that roiled with the stench of sulfur.

At the altar, the priest fell to his knees and began to pray. The roof ripped off.
Within seconds, the building exploded.
And a huge shadow consumed the fiery inferno, and . . .

Lilah pulled away. It wasn't so much the vision that made her do it, but the horrible feeling that had accompanied it.

She felt sick down to her soul, ill in a way she could not describe. Never in her life had she felt so overwhelmed by such incredible evil . . . and she had been in the presence of the Senior Partners.

This was worse. Far worse.

This was the worst.

As she fought to compose herself, Nathan shut the box. Then she realized that Gavin was lurching into the private bathroom, about to be sick.

At least I didn't throw up, she thought smugly.

"Marianna Escobar has been doing some of our dirty work," he said, "although I'm sure she doesn't realize it. She's removed a Slayer from action, and she captured Cordelia Chase—who is a Seer, in the parlance of the Book—and she's also entertaining several of our wealthiest clients. And paying us for that privilege."

"Did she find that?" Lilah asked, avoiding looking at the box.

Nathan chuckled. "Oh, no, we've had this for centuries."

Lilah had only seen the barest surface of the items Wolfram & Hart had in storage. Ancient texts, magickal scrolls, legendary objects of every description . . . Nathan had once shown her an ornately carved box that contained the asp that had slain Cleopatra, and explained that it could be used in a ritual to induce lust or a very different ritual to cause permanent paralysis. The going price, to have the firm take it out of storage and allow its use, was fifteen million dollars.

"There are, of course, pages of it scattered around the world between an unknown number of individuals. But the binding, and the largest selection of intact pages, has been

Wolfram and Hart property since the fourteenth century. Shortly after the Beast of the First Blood was banished from this dimension, in fact."

Confused, Lilah said, "Why do you want us to take it to San Teodor?"

He waved a hand for her to be quiet as he continued. Abashed she lowered her chin.

"Safekeeping," he said simply. "Even though Benedicta is paying us a lot of money for this book, we don't want to give it to her until we're certain she can put it to good use. She's promised to work with the firm once she's brought the Beast of the First Blood back into this dimension and mated with it."

Gavin nodded. "So you're withholding it until you're sure she can do it."

Nathan beamed at Lilah's enemy, and Lilah was too sick to care. "Exactly. The Summoning Ritual must be performed during a full moon, but other than that, there's no time pressure. So we'll wait until we know she has everything she needs, and then we'll hand it over."

"There's a full moon in just a few days," Lilah said.

He nodded.

"And if she tries to simply take the Book, it won't be here," Gavin finished.

"We'll have it," Lilah said quietly.

"On San Teodor," Nathan confirmed. He beamed at the two attorneys. "Questions?"

Neither spoke.

"Excellent," he said, then checked his watch. "And now, you have a plane to catch. To San Teodor."

CHAPTER FIFTEEN

Marianna stood in the library, a heavy cut glass tumbler with a shot of sixty-year-old scotch in it in her hand. *Chaz's drink,* she realized, *the one he always had when circumstances required him to be sociable with people he didn't know well.* That description certainly applied here, so she upheld the tradition.

She had met all thirteen clients at least once before, but she knew none of them well. Certainly there had been a time, long ago, when she had been a socialite, and nothing excited her like a party full of strangers. One never knew what the night would bring, what fascinating people one might encounter.

But the life of a hunter, she knew, required a different set of skills: the ability to keep one's own company for long hours, even days or weeks at a time; the gift of stillness; the facility to think like one's prey, to hear what the animals heard, and to see through their eyes. The more deeply a hunter became immersed in the hunt, the less she cared for the company of other humans.

Noticing Marianna in the doorway, Lilah Morgan approached her, drink in hand.

"Lilah," Marianna said, kissing the air near the attorney's cheek. "How wonderful to see you. Isn't it exciting?"

"You have such a fabulous home," Lilah said. "And I've been getting to know some of your guests. Interesting mix."

Before either one of them could say more, Gavin Park joined them. "Just as Lilah understated your beauty before the first time we met," he said to Marianna, "no one adequately prepared me for the magnificence of Villa Escobar. My compliments."

"Thank you, Gavin," Marianna said. She caught Lilah rolling her eyes and sensed a rivalry between the two lawyers that would be good to keep in mind. *One never knows when that might come in handy*, she thought. "I appreciate your coming. Both of you."

"Who would want to miss this?" Lilah exclaimed. "A Slayer hunt. It's a once in a lifetime thrill, I can assure you."

"Even if your life is very, very long," Marianna agreed.

"I've just been getting acquainted with D'Leethis Iridiwanny," Gavin said. "Did I pronounce that right?"

"I believe so," Marianna told him. "The Enciardan, right?"

"Yes, that's the one," Gavin said. "Fascinating fellow."

"I didn't realize demons were invited to participate," Lilah said. "I thought this was a humans-only event."

"Actually just the one," Marianna said. "D'Leethis can usually pass for human, he loves to hunt, and he had the price of admission."

"Plus he's a personal friend of Nathan's," Gavin said. "And I think he'll be transferring his legal affairs to me when we get back to Los Angeles."

Again the eye roll. It seemed to be an unconscious response Lilah had to nearly everything Gavin said. *But then,* Marianna thought, *almost everything he says is a conscious attempt to get her goat.*

She let her gaze wander around the room at the wealthy men and women—mostly men, as only three women had signed up—who had each paid five million dollars to spend the weekend on San Teodor with her. *Sixty-five million dollars in two days.* That would not only keep her comfortable for a while, it would keep Wolfram & Hart obligated to her for a long time to come.

Faith's trip had been full of surprises, to say the least. She'd been locked in the hold of a small boat by Marianna and her crew, but en route there had been some kind of interruption. After a short while, the boat had started again, but when they had finally arrived at San Teodor, Marianna and a couple of her hench-creatures were gone, presumably on whatever craft had stopped them.

Now she was in the big house again.

This prison cell was far more upscale than her bunkhouse at Yorba Linda Ranch. It was like the old Sunnydale days, when the mayor had gotten her her own cool place— fancy bed, fancy bathroom, big honkin' walk-in closet.

However, still a prison cell.

There were no bars on the windows, but the glass was unbreakable. Maybe if she'd had command of her full power, it wouldn't have been, but they had kept bracelets on both wrists that sapped her of strength. The door was a foot thick and solid steel—even at full strength, it would have stopped her. There were always two armed guards— demons of some sort—outside the door, and others that she could see patrolling the grounds outside the windows.

Then someone approached the door and said, "Stand back, or I'll unload this Uzi into your chest."

Sounded like a good idea, so she moved away from the door.

It opened.

And in fell someone she knew very well . . .

"Wes!" she shouted.

. . . And someone she didn't.

Lorne was not loving how deserted the hotel was. He knew Angel had left for Hawaii, but where were his four pals? And why had they had such a huge, destructive going-away party without inviting him? There didn't seem to be a window or a stick of furniture that had survived intact.

He thought about belting out a stirring rendition of taps, but he decided to keep a low profile—*as if I could, with this nose, ba-dum-dum.* So he walked through the lobby, attempting to make as little noise as possible, acutely aware that where Angel trod, trouble usually followed.

That's when he heard the weeping.

He cocked his head and began to follow the sound. It came from upstairs.

This is like a bad horror movie, he thought. *And to think that as soon as the hero in one of those things creeps through the haunted, deserted, incredibly scary, apparently empty hotel to investigate a noise, I lose patience and go to the lobby to pump more butter flavoring on my popcorn. And here I am, imitating bad cinema.*

Then he realized who was crying, and made a beeline to Fred's room.

Sure enough, she was sitting on the floor with her back against the bed, rocking herself like a frightened little girl.

Lorne crossed swiftly to her side and crouched beside her, talking her hand and patting it as he said, "Fred? Freddy? What's wrong? Where is everybody?"

She registered his presence, wiped her nose, and shuddered out one more sob. "We got attacked," she said. "Cordelia, Gunn, and Wesley were taken prisoner."

"But not you," Lorne observed.

She gave him a look. "There was so much confusion. I learned a lot about survival tactics back on Pylea."

"That's okay. That's good," he assured her. "Who attacked you? What did they want?"

She crossed her arms and rubbed her shoulders. "I wanted to go to you, tell you," she said. "But I . . . I didn't know where Caritas was. Plus, the city." She looked miserable. "But I should have phoned. But I . . ." She gestured to her room.

"You couldn't leave. Oh, you poor kid." Lorne took her hand and gave it a squeeze. "How long have you been in here?"

"I'm not sure," she admitted. "Seems like a long time."

"You must be hungry. Come on, we'll go downstairs together and I'll make you something to eat. I'm a very good cook," he assured her. "I was the only one who could make a Krvetchalk that Numfar would eat. You've met Numfar, right? The Fred Astaire of my family."

Despite her predicament, Fred giggled. "The dance of shame."

"If he ever comes to this dimension, I'll start entering him in ballroom dancing competitions. There is fabulous prize money to be won."

Gently he pulled her to her feet. His face became more serious and he shepherded her toward the doorway to her room. "Who were they?" he asked.

"Benedicta, I think. And some icky-looking sorcerer."

"That would probably be Bran Cahir," he pondered. "They usually travel together."

"And I think Marianna Escobar. She took Charles and Wesley, and the other two took Cordelia."

The Host raised his eyebrows. "Did you call Angel?"

"No," she said. "I . . . I didn't know the number."

"Don't fret," he said. "We'll call right now."

"Done," said a voice from the doorway.

It was Chaz Escobar, with a cell phone in his hand.

"Today we might actually die," Faith told the others.

Gunn grunted. "Not loving it when a Slayer says that."

She grinned at him. *Liking this guy.* "You can take it."

They had let the guys rest for a whole day. Now sunset was coming on and just like condemned prisoners in any industrial nation, Faith and the boys had been stuffed with lots of protein—steak, shrimp—and lots of carbs—potatoes, garlic bread, and peas.

Faith hated peas.

When Faith was finished—all three making an effort to put away as much as they could, knowing they'd need the fuel later—she felt almost human despite her restless sleep of the night before. *And around here,* she thought, *almost human is a lot more than most of the locals can say for themselves.*

After their dinner was done, there had been a knock at the door and then several muscular demon guards entered, weapons at the ready. "Time to go," one of them said with a sinister, multifanged smile. "Hope you got your running shoes on, kiddies."

Gunn got quickly to his feet and parked himself directly in front of the big demon. "Take these cuffs off me," he said, "and I'll show you where you can stick your running shoes."

"Don't worry, punk," the demon replied casually. "The cuffs'll be coming off soon enough. But by then you'll be a lot more interested in running than in fighting, I'm pretty sure."

"Look, we know the drill," Faith interrupted. Her fuse was short, and she had no patience for displays of bravado. Better to save the energy for when it was really needed. "Just get us out there and turn us loose."

The big demon shrugged and walked out of the room. "Follow him," another one growled. They followed, Faith in her power-inhibiting bracelets, Wesley and Gunn back in fashionable plastic.

The demons led them back through the big house and outside to a waiting blue van whose paint had been oxidized by the sun and salt air.

She slid onto the middle bench seat. Wesley scooted in beside her, but kept his distance, as if he didn't want their legs to touch on the ride.

It's not like I'm going to bite you, Faith thought. *Or do anything else to hurt you, for that matter.*

But she didn't say anything about it. She felt bad about what she'd done to him, even though at the time she'd thought it necessary to get what she wanted, and was glad that he didn't seem to be dwelling on it. She wondered if she should bring it up, but thought that might be a bad idea. They'd need each other, in the hours to come.

Instead, hoping for some kind of truce, she said, "Hey, Wesley. Thanks for the amulet." She tugged it out from beneath her shirt and showed it to him.

He smiled—the first smile she'd seen on him since he had turned up in the sitting room. "You're welcome. Not that it's done you much good, I suppose."

"Hey, I'm alive, right?" *For now, at least,* she added silently.

Gunn sat next to Wesley on the bench, so Wesley had to slide over a little closer to her. When the van started up and cornered to head out of the compound and into the wide open spaces beyond—*the killing ground,* she guessed— centrifugal force shoved them together so that their thighs brushed. She noted, with some small satisfaction, that Wesley didn't flinch away.

CHAPTER SIXTEEN

"Wh-What are you doing?" Cordelia asked through a fog of sleep. She had been drugged, she realized suddenly—fighting her way out of it was like trying to climb the sides of a well that had been greased with Jell-O. She knew this had been going on for at least days, and possibly weeks. Each time she awakened, something different was being done to her.

It was no different this time.

Benedicta was the one doing the something this time, smearing something on her face and neck and chest that was wet and clammy, and the touch of it had awakened her. It was better than the pain, which had awakened her on so many other occasions. . . .

"Shh, it's nothing." Benedicta's voice was calm and soothing, as if she were talking to an infant at bedtime. "It's just part of the ritual."

"Ri-Ritual?" Cordelia tried to sound decisive in spite of her grogginess. "I don't need any ritual."

"Life is all about ritual." Benedicta dipped her fingers into something just beyond Cordelia's range of view. She couldn't see much—a wood-beamed ceiling, white stucco walls, a plank table halfway to one of them. But she couldn't change her position to look at the rest of the place.

I'm tied up, she realized, suddenly angry. *She's got me tied up!*

"Suppose you're getting ready for a date," the vampire continued. "You apply your make-up to appear young and fresh; you brush your hair to make it shine; you dress to expose your breasts and hips. You remind your date that you are of childbearing age, that you can mate with him, and carry his children."

"Hey," Cordelia snapped, "I do not dress like that. And I sure as hell don't go on a date hoping to get pregnant. Although," she added, "it happened once."

Benedicta smiled pleasantly. "That's nothing but a form of ritual magick." Then she ran her two fingers in a line, down from the outer corners of Cordelia's eyes to a point parallel with her upper lip.

Cordelia felt the cold substance on her fingers. *Some kind of paint, maybe.*

"Bearing a child is the ultimate magickal act," Benedicta said. "Creating new life. Why do you think the Frankenstein story has such a powerful resonance for people? Ever since there have been people, there has been magick, and the quest to create life where there was none has been one of the most common goals."

Cordelia was suddenly fully awake, struggling against the bonds that held her. She whipped her head from Benedicta's cold-fingered grip. "Oh, God," Cordelia said. "That's what you want, isn't it? Angel told me about you. You want to bring that—that Beast of the Boiling Blood or whatever it is into our world so you can have babies with it. Little bloodsucking babies that you think will make you the queen of everything!"

Benedicta's hand flashed more quickly than Cordelia could follow, and she heard the slap against her cheek even before she felt it.

"How dare you imagine that one such as you could begin to understand my motivations?" she snarled. "You are unclean, impure, and repulsively mortal. I can barely stand to touch you . . . your skin so warm and flushed, your chest pulsing with that . . . that heartbeat. If the ritual didn't require it, I wouldn't."

Now Cordelia was really incensed. *If I could break these ropes,* she thought, *I'd stake you so fast your head would spin.*

"Me, repulsive? Me? You want to see repulsive, take a look in the mirror. Oops, sorry, you *can't*! Because you're undead, an abomination, an unnatural thing! You're not a woman at all, so don't pretend you know what we think or how we feel!"

Benedicta glared at Cordelia with barely restrained fury.

Um, maybe I pushed a little too far, Cordy thought. *I am still tied up, after all. And she's already demonstrated a short temper.* But instead of attacking her, Benedicta turned away and stormed over to the table Cordelia could barely see. She picked something up there and carried it behind her, out of Cordelia's view, back to her. Stopping directly in front of Cordelia, she revealed a hypodermic needle. One of the big ones.

Cordy bit her lower lip to keep from saying anything or shrieking, not wanting to give Benedicta the satisfaction. But the vamp barely even glanced at her face. She bent over and Cordy felt the needle bite into the flesh of her arm, and within moments she was tumbling back down the well, back into the darkness . . .

Oh, God, Angel, where are you? Where is anybody?

Angel paced across the concrete floor of Lohiau's bunker as he listened to Escobar, cell phone pressed tightly to his ear, an overwhelming sense of dread coursing through his body. He'd given up many of the physical sensations of humanity when he became a vampire, but fear wasn't one of them.

I've failed them. If I had been in L.A.—

The news that everyone had been taken had hit him hard. First Faith, now the rest . . . it seemed as though everyone close to him had to pay for that dubious privilege, sooner or later. And the closer they were, the more often they had to pony up.

Focus, Angel, keep it together. Focus. You don't know they're dead yet. In fact they're probably not. Fred says they were taken alive, not just killed and left behind.

He forced himself to listen to what Escobar was saying. He'd found something—

"—one of Wesley's notebooks. It was in one of the drawers in an overturned desk. It almost appeared as if the desk had been placed that way to hide it."

This was a lucky break. Watchers were trained to keep journals, and his fall from grace with the Council hadn't stemmed that tide. He wrote about everything: cases, discoveries, his emotions. Finding the notebook was the next best thing to finding Wesley.

I just hope we can turn up the rest of him.

"What did it say?"

He reached the wall of the bunker and turned, pacing back towards the other side. His movement disturbed a gecko, which scurried across the room, no doubt seeking a less traveled place to rest.

Angel remembered a story he'd read about the Hawaiian geckoes, how there had been only four or so species on the islands before illegal escaped pets had doubled that number. Apparently some of the newer species ate the older ones, and geckoes that had been common in years past had been driven inland.

It made him think about the way that vampires and demons preyed on humans, their superior strength and abilities pushing back the weaker race, killing them, terrorizing. Of course it wasn't likely that the geckoes felt much terror. Still . . . .

If he succeeded in helping Escobar with his plan, he would be able to eliminate one race of invaders, and possibly redeem himself in the process. It was a worthy goal, even though he wouldn't be around to see the results. . . .

"It looks like he was researching the ritual."

Angel's focus sharpened, he stopped pacing. "Yes?"

"The raising of the Beast of the First Blood. The one Benedicta has her foul heart set on. It must be done during a time of the full moon—"

Angel looked out of the narrow opening that acted as a window for the old World War II bunker. It had been designed as a gun emplacement, a watchtower to take out ships at long distances. The range of the guns enhanced by the bunker's placement high on Haleakala, the huge volcano that was the island's largest landmark. Lohiau had showed him where huge bolts had held the guns to the open concrete platforms.

The concrete walls were covered with drawings of tiki now, as well as other arcane drawings that the old kahuna had used to protect his safe house.

As he stared down at the ocean, the constant breeze that traced the contours of the island parted the clouds, and Angel saw moonlight break through them, casting a reflection on the waves below. The moon was nearly full *now*.

Escobar confirmed it. "Three days from now. The Chalice must be protected at all costs, Angel. *We* must be the ones to perform the ritual, whatever the cost. *Comprendes?*"

The tension, the guilt that Angel was feeling manifested in his words. "I'm willing to sacrifice *myself* for this—but not them. Do *you* understand?"

Escobar sighed. "What will you do?"

What indeed?

Could Angel convince Lohiau to risk the Chalice by giving it to him to take to Escobar? Would the magician be willing to let such a powerful talisman out of his sight?

Were he still Angelus, things would be so much simpler—kill the old sorcerer and take it. Of course, were he still Angelus, he wouldn't be worried about his friends.

Angel paced the room again.

"I'll call you back," he said, "and let you know."

"Let us be careful, eh, Angel? The stakes are high. The highest they can be."

"I know."

"Buena suerte, mi compañero."

"And to you," said Angel, breaking the connection.

Just then, Lohiau approached, as if he had been waiting for Angel to conclude his conversation. Angel quickly filled him in.

The magician frowned. "Did you mention the Chalice by name?"

Angel nodded, puzzled.

Lohiau sighed. "I thought as much. There was a great shift in the *mana-loa* a few seconds ago. I traced the force lines—"

The kahuna waved his hands, and a feathery trace of blue light shone in the air, like a three-dimensional depiction of metal filings around a magnet, surrounding Angel's cell phone.

Then Lohiau pointed at a large shell whose interior had been polished until it shone. Within the shell appeared smaller versions of the lines, along with other icons: water, a rock bisected by a crack, buildings. Lots of buildings.

"The other side of the trace is in Los Angeles," he said. "It would seem that a very powerful magician has been running a spell to find the Chalice. Any mention of it on a modern technological device triggers a locator beacon."

Angel saw the implication right away. "They've traced me."

The kahuna nodded. "Indeed." He pointed through the firing slits on the west wall of the bunker.

Angel scanned the area and within seconds he saw the shambling bodies of the undead working their way toward them.

Here to take the Chalice. And me too, if they can.

Well it's not going to happen.

Angel looked around the room for a weapon. In these days of airport security checks, bringing his favorite sword hadn't been a possibility.

Lohiau closed his eyes for a moment and held his hands together. Then he grunted softly, and blinked at Angel. "The ones who have been seeking Pele's Chalice have been led by *this*."

The magician waved his hands, and a ghostly figure appeared in the center of the shell he'd used before, tiny trace lines pointing out toward the jungle.

Angel took a closer look.

It was a large blue-skinned demon with a huge head and a large set of wings. The creature's head was its most fascinating feature. It was grotesquely large, with a huge bulge over the forehead as if the demon's brain had expanded, spongelike, stretching the skull from within. Piggy red eyes gleamed from underneath the obscenely bulging brow of the creature.

Angel didn't recognize it at first. Then—

"Is that a mind-splitter?" he asked.

The kahuna spoke. Over the years his precise British accent had been tempered, mellowed, by life in the Islands. But he still chose his words with care, Angel noted. "Indeed, so it seems to be. It's been tracking me for weeks, trying to pinpoint my location."

Not good news.

Splitters were particularly nasty demons. They were experts at possession and reanimation, and could split their vital force off into tiny splinters, in order to control large groups of people or things. This was their greatest advantage. They could overwhelm superior numbers by splitting themselves into smaller and smaller portions, using each to animate the dead or control a living mind. There was a point of diminishing returns, of course, but the things were *dangerous*.

As the two of them watched, the first splitter was joined by a second.

Uh-oh.

The splitters did have a weakness: when their will had been fragmented into their maximal distributions, their bodies were weakened, less capable of defending themselves. But if there were *two* of them, one could disperse while the other one maintained its full powers for defending both bodies.

One of the demons looked right out at them and gestured with a gnarled claw. The image in the scrying shell vanished, dissipating with an audible pop.

The vampire turned toward the magician. "Weapons?"

"The second door on the right. I'll be here seeing what I can do to hold back the tide, as it were. We'll teach those haole demon bastards to mess with me on my island."

The magician grinned and joined his hands. Hundreds of the diminutive *menehune* rushed past Angel as he headed through the doorway Lohiau had indicated. The little creatures looked angry, and Angel was glad they were on his side.

As the little things skittered through the slits in the bunker wall, Angel made his own way down a short corridor in the opposite direction, and then turned right at the second doorway. The steel door to the room was shut, but Lohiau kept it well oiled, and Angel tugged it quickly open, moving inside.

It was darker within, but Angel needed very little light. Stacked on the walls around him was a hodgepodge of weapons. There were none of the European edged weapons he favored, but in the corner was an old *katana*. It was probably brought to the island by an immigrant at some point in the past; Hawaii had a large Japanese population, after all.

Angel grabbed the sword, unsheathing it quickly. He was not a real fan of two-handed swordplay, but he figured the weapon would do for the moment. It looked serviceable; someone had kept it in good shape.

He snatched several wicked-looking spears off another rack, and picked up a bola that looked like it had seen better days.

He went back to Lohiau, who gestured to the slits in the wall.

"The *menehune* have engaged the enemy. The splitters have raised some of the undead, and they're converging on this place."

Because of the finder spell, Angel realized.

"The undead won't last long. They are called for a night, and when morning comes, they must cease work."

Well. That didn't give them much time. Angel considered their options; after sunrise he wouldn't be much use either. "We'll have to try and finish them now, before dawn."

Lohiau nodded. "Yes. If we can."

The Hawaiian sketched another symbol on the floor, and began to chant.

From the weapons area came the sound of footfalls and pounding drums. As Angel turned in the direction of the sounds, spectral warriors materialized in midstride. They were dressed in ancient Hawaiian garb—loincloths, feathers, and fearsome masks. They were huge, and muscular; they pounded drums and carried huge spears and shields. Though they appeared to be human their feet did not touch the ground.

The kahuna jostled Angel. "*Huaka'i Po*—Night Marchers. Don't look into their eyes. I doubt they could catch *your* soul, but let's not take the risk, eh?"

Angel moved to one of the slits and peered out. "Where are the splitters? If we cut one of them down the battle's half won."

The magician pointed toward a stand of trees to the left of the slope that led down to the ocean. "There. Go carefully but quickly, Angel. I have another trick for them, but it will take some time to prepare."

Angel went outside.

A furious battle was raging between the *menehune* and some undead whose faces were slack and wasted, and whose bodies were rotted from the grave. Body parts were flying left and right as the Hawaiian little people hacked at their enemies, but it wasn't all one-sided.

One of the small people flew past Angel and crashed into the wall beside him. The little creature's head burst like an overripe melon, cutting off the its high-pitched shriek.

The first of the Night Marchers joined the fray, immediately knocking the line of undead fighters backward, stabbing, hacking, and bashing with spear and shield. But the destroyed corpses reassembled themselves and attacked again.

They were joined by even more bodies, some looking fairly fresh. Angel wondered what graveyard had been defiled to get so many corpses. Some gravedigger was going to be mighty unhappy tomorrow when he arrived at work and saw all the empty holes.

The demons had laid out a fairly organized picket of attackers. To get to them, he'd either have to circle around by going far down the slope and fighting his way uphill, or doing the same thing upward.

Not enough time. He'd have to fight his way through, that was all there was to it. Angel picked the thinnest section of fighting and jumped down from the bunker wall, narrowly avoiding a flying skull.

Katana in hand, the vampire used his superior speed to join ranks with the *menehune*. He slashed at a fresh corpse that looked like a tourist, complete with huge patterned shirt and camera, and felt his blade penetrate to the backbone, hit, and snap the weakened ligaments there, cutting it in half. He quickly spun the blade back around, pulling it in to cover his high line.

Angel kept his focus midrange, keeping his head down to extend the range of his peripheral vision. The key, one of his martial arts instructors had told him more than a normal lifetime ago, was to look at your feet. The change of focus made it easier to track multiple opponents: looking down took the one hundred and eighty degree cone of predator vision and expanded it to greater than three hundred degrees.

Of course it didn't pay to spend all of the time looking down, once you had closed with the enemy. But it was a start.

Two shambling zombies swung shovels at him and he flipped the *katana* over into a two-handed grip, dropping his spears for the moment. He used the extra leverage to slice through the thick wood that made up the shovel handles. The Japanese sword was sharp indeed.

Just because he didn't favor two-handed sword fighting didn't mean he couldn't do it.

A time and place for everything.

Angel dodged a rock thrown by a laughing skeleton—at least it looked like it would have been laughing if it had vocal cords—and leapt forward, past the initial skirmishers. Zombie reinforcements rushed at him and he sheathed his sword, pulling out the two spears.

He gripped them as one, overlapping slightly with the business ends out to each end, giving him the equivalent of a double-ended spear. Bone crunched and organs ripped as he slashed his way through the reinforcements. He had to hurry, now, to get through the attackers before their masters realized his intentions.

He pushed forward, avoiding a thrown blade with a dodge no human could emulate. The blade flashed past, a blurred steel shadow, moonlight refracting brightly as it tumbled just past his right ear.

Close.

He needed to finish this, and soon. His inner sense of timing told him there was less than an hour left before sunrise. It had taken him longer than he had planned to get this far. Angel jumped high in the air, avoiding several attackers, and then he was past the trees.

There.

Ahead of him were the two blue-skinned demons. One lay still, no doubt focusing on the many undead he commanded in the battle. The other watched Angel approach, fangs glistening and eyes gleaming.

The second demon wore a breastplate made of bone with what looked like Nordic power symbols on it. He carried a double-edged axe in one hand that looked wickedly sharp, with cutting edges that had to be at least two feet long. A thick iron-banded handle extended from the center of the axe head, terminating in a huge, spiked pommel.

Angel's first thought—*such a big-headed monster couldn't move an axe that large very fast*—was quickly proved wrong. The demon leapt forward with a speed that surprised the vampire; the only thing that saved his head was an instinctive parry that managed to get one of his spears chopped in half instead.

Angel dropped to the ground and executed a turnaround from one of his many martial arts, swinging the spear that still had a sharp edge around to gut the blue demon. Would it have blue guts as well?

He didn't find out.

The demon twisted away from the swinging spear, just avoiding the tip, flipping the shaft of his axe back to tap Angel's weapon as it passed. The blow knocked the spear out of his hand, sending it across the small clearing.

Turns out splitters are pretty good fighters.

After more than two hundred years it was good to know that there was still much to learn in the world. Although, truth be told, he would rather have found out this particular fact some other way.

Angel poked the broken spear at the demon, smacking it right under the bony breastplate, and shoving forward with all his strength. It was like using a pool cue on a bowling ball. The demon let out a sound like a steam whistle and thrust forward with the armored pommel of his axe.

The point took Angel under his own rib cage, tearing flesh and knocking him backward several body lengths.

He couldn't trade blows with this creature, that was certain. It was faster, stronger, and at least as well trained as he was.

Not a good situation.

The vampire's fast healing kicked in, and his wound began to close as he considered what to do. He found himself wishing that Gunn, Wesley, and the others were there right now. A little teamwork would definitely help. Thinking of his friends, Angel was desperate to finish this. He had to get back to L.A. *now.*

He rushed the demon, whipping the *katana* out and around, executing a perfect slash as he rolled forward, apparently to his own doom. The demon sidestepped avoiding the slash, and stepped forward to chop Angel in half—

—which was exactly what the vampire wanted. He grabbed the bola he'd been carrying on his belt and swung it quickly around, the three balls whirling through the air as he tossed the primitive weapon at the demon's ankles—

And they hit with a *clunk*, trapping the demon's ankles, and the creature started to pitch forward, right toward the vampire's sword.

Except that Angel had forgotten about its wings. They spread quickly, and the fall turned into a leap into the air. A rapid *whump whump whump* and the demon was flying over the vampire, taking one hand to rip apart the rawhide cord that made up the bola while preparing to swing his ax with the other.

At that moment, Angel could almost hear Cordelia saying, "This is *so* not happening!"

But it was.

The vampire rolled to his feet, taking a two-handed grip on the *katana*. Maybe he was going to finally die after all, not quite the way he'd expected, but here it was. Fine. He was going to get at least *one* piece of that demon to take to hell with him.

The blue demon grinned, huge incisors overlapping thick blubbery lips, a harsh bubbling laughter boiling out of it as it swooped at Angel—

Until it *screamed* a horrible bellow and froze, its wings utterly still—and not in an aerodynamic way. Suddenly it crashed to the ground, dropping its axe and clawing at its stomach.

It was probably a toss-up who was more shocked, Angel or the demon. But the vampire didn't let his surprise slow him down. He stepped forward and chopped the demon's head off—or at least *most* of the way off; the sword couldn't cut completely through the demon's thick neck, and go stuck in its backbone.

Angel picked up the dying creature's axe and ran toward its twin, which was just starting to stir on the ground. It had figured out that its protector was out of the picture and was coming back to take care of business.

But Angel didn't give it the chance. He ran forward and swung the axe down with all his strength, lopping the grotesque head off. The expression on its face as the head landed in the dirt next to its body and stared up at him was horrible, but Angel couldn't help taking some pleasure in it.

The splitter is split. How about that.

Angel looked up.

And not a moment too soon.

Dawn was imminent. Streaks of sunlight split the night sky as effectively as he had decapitated his adversary. He hadn't noticed in all the fighting.

He ran toward the bunker, running past the remaining *menehune* and Night Marchers.

He made it with maybe a minute to spare.

Lohiau sat on the floor where Angel had left him, looking a little older. The kahuna looked up at him. "Nicely done. And just in time, too."

Angel shrugged. "We make a good team."

The magician nodded. "Yes." He paused for a moment, then continued. "You know, I was thinking, Angel, that it might be a good time to visit the mainland."

Angel nodded, surprised but relieved. It very dangerous, but it was the logical course of action. Lohiau stayed here, it was only a matter of time before Benedicta took him out . . . and got the Chalice.

"I think Benedicta needs to learn that the tiki still have teeth," Lohiau continued. "And besides, I can't bloody well stay here, can I?"

Angel regarded him seriously. "It's going to be worse over there."

Lohiau actually smiled. "I'm counting on that. I haven't had a good fight since the Revolution."

Which failed, Angel added silently.

CHAPTER SEVENTEEN

When Cordelia awoke, she noticed that her feet didn't hurt. They were about the only part of her body that didn't. The torture she had undergone earlier in order to make her a "pure vessel" had left the rest of her throbbing in pain. She wished she could slip back into unconsciousness, but the pain was too great for that. She wished she had a bottle of Motrin. Failing that, she would settle for a bottle of Jack Daniel's. Anything to stop the hurting.

She was lying on the floor of her small, grubby cell. *So if I'm supposed to be so pure, why keep me in a pig sty?*

Cordy managed to stand, realizing as she did so that her feet had been healed in some miraculous way. *Bran must have done it,* she thought.

Before she could speculate any more about that, Cordy

heard the scratch of a key turning in the door's lock. She half jumped, half fell to the wall next to the door.

The door opened in a wash of harsh yellow light. A vampire—she couldn't see his face, but she'd seen enough vamps over the years to recognize something in the way he moved—stepped in, holding a tin plate full of steaming, unappetizing slop that vaguely resembled canned chili. A machine gun—an Uzi, maybe; she didn't know; Gunn was the firearms expert—was slung over one shoulder. He stopped and looked about the cell. Cordy got ready to slam the door against him.

The vamp put his free hand against the door, bracing it against her push. "You're hiding behind the door," he said. "What, you think I just crawled out of the grave yesterday?"

Cordy stepped into view. "You're too smart for me," she agreed. The vamp grinned unpleasantly, showing crooked yellow fangs. Cordy smiled back and slapped the hand holding the plate of swill from beneath, driving it up and plastering it against the vamp's face.

The vamp howled, dropping the plate and clawing the hot chili stuff away from his eyes. Cordy drove one heel against the side of his knee the way Angel had taught her. She heard the bone break, and the vamp collapsed, screaming in renewed pain.

She grabbed his machine gun and pulled it free—it was much lighter than she expected it to be—and raced into the hall. Her every movement blazed with pain, but she couldn't think about that now. A single naked bulb in the ceiling showed her another door at the hallway's far end. *That must be where they brought me in from the temple.*

She ran to it, pulled on it. Big surprise; it was locked. Cordy backed off several feet, raised the machine gun, and fired at the lock.

And nearly killed herself. The recoil sent her staggering back, and a stream of bullets hit the door, the wall, the floor, and almost hit her—she heard a couple whine past her ears like full metal hornets. But when she regained her balance, she saw that she'd successfully blasted open the door.

Unfortunately that too had been the wrong move.

Cordy realized too late that this wasn't the door leading to the temple. Instead it opened into another cell—a bigger one than hers, and chock full of demons.

I make a lousy action hero, she thought.

The demons poured from the cell—at least a dozen, maybe more. They were incredibly ugly, even for demons. *Oh, my God,* she thought. *They've gotta be part of Marianna's demon groupies! Bran and his vampires must have captured them!*

They charged past her, paying no attention to her save for one who grabbed the gun out of her grasp. Cordy was hurled aside against one wall. The impact, combined with the pain she was already in, nearly made her black out. She slid down the wall and sprawled like a broken doll.

Dimly she heard someone shout "Down the hall!" Someone else cried "There they are!" and then she heard gunplay, combined with screams, snarls, and other sounds of battle. They all seemed to be coming from a long way away. Cordy managed to open her eyes and saw that the fight was actually taking place less than fifty feet from her, down the corridor. A group of vamps were attempting to force the demons back. Kicks and punches were being thrown, blades, axes, and truncheons viciously wielded.

A flicker of what seemed to be lightning dazzled her momentarily. When her sight cleared she could see Bran standing in the midst of the battle. He gestured this way and that, and electrical bolts crackled from his hands, enveloping demons and hurling them aside.

Wow, she thought, still dazed, *the Force is sure strong in him . . .*

Then Bran, the battle, the corridor—the whole world—receded at tremendous speed from her down a long dark tunnel, leaving nothing but night.

Once again Cordy floated up out of a sea of black. She blinked, and suppressed a moan. She was in even worse pain than before, if that was possible.

"You fool! You *idiot!*"

She realized she was back in her cell. There was no sign of the vampire guard. The door was still open, but she knew there was no way she could make a break for it now even if she was alone—which she wasn't.

Benedicta, looking very beautiful in a Snow White sort of way—save that her expression was more like the Wicked Queen's right now—was there with her. She paced back and forth, raging at Cordy. "They got away!" she shouted. She raised clenched fists, shook them at Cordy.

I should be afraid, Cordy thought. But she wasn't. There was nothing left in her except weariness.

Bran stepped through the cell's open door then, stepping up beside Benedicta. He frowned. "Don't kill her.

We had already extracted as much information as we were going to get from those captives."

He came forward and put a restraining hand on Benedicta's arm. "We have located the Chalice. That's wonderful news. Now we can tell Wolfram and Hart to deliver the Book. Once we have those items, we'll be ready."

Not the mummy? Cordelia wondered. *Or did they take it when they attacked us?*

"She dared rise against me." Benedicta raised a hand and vamped out. Cordelia winced and prepared herself for the big chompola.

"We need her. She is our Seer."

Benedicta calmed herself, de-vamping, though not without effort. Then she smiled at Cordy, and said, "Oh, I won't kill her. I'll just make her *wish* I had."

The look on her face made Cordy realize that there was still fear left in her.

On foot, San Teodor seemed a lot bigger than it had from the air. While it had appeared fairly flat, at ground level it was apparent that there were canyons and cliffs and narrow valleys in which to take cover. But there weren't any tall trees or cover thick enough to hide Faith, Wesley, and Gunn if the hunters decided to get airborne. As long as they were also at ground level, Gunn figured, they had a fighting chance.

Although if there's one thing I'm not used to, he thought, *it's having to run and hide in a place where there's no buildings.* With the exception of their brief excursion into Pylea, all his battle experience had been in Los Angeles, where the urban sprawl went on forever. This landscape was al stunted bushes and low growth, dirt, rocks, and lizards. *About as far from my native habitat as it gets.*

The van had dropped them off after driving them about forty-five minutes into the boondocks. Along the way Clete, the demon who had been on the plane with them, had explained what they could expect. "What it is, is, you're gonna take off running. Right now there's another van taking the hunters, thirteen of 'em, to another drop point, five miles from yours. You won't know which direction they're in, and they won't know which direction you're in. But there's a lot more of them, and they have guns. You guys might get lucky enough to find a big rock, but that's all you're gonna get in terms of weapons."

"So much for the virtue of fair play," Wesley sighed.

Clete laughed. "You ever seen a pheasant armed with a shotgun? A marlin using ninety pound test and a boathook? You three, you're just more prey, that's all."

Wesley exploded with rage. "We are not just animals to be hunted! We're human beings!"

Clete turned to them and tapped the claws of his right hand against one of the pale green spots on his cheek. "I'm not," he reminded them. "So that argument don't carry much weight with me."

"We could pay you," Gunn attempted, knowing it was an empty promise.

"You don't have any cash on you," Clete countered.

"We got plenty, back in L.A. Just get us out of this and we'll make it worth your while."

"Somehow I don't think you're as loaded as Marianna is," Clete said. "Besides, I don't want a lot. My needs are taken care of fine."

Faith's turn. She was direct and to the point, and her voice carried a whiff of icy arctic wind. "Just keep one thing in mind: When we finish with the hunters, we'll come for you first."

Clete faced front again, making no reply. Another ten minutes passed, and then he dropped them off at a spot in the road that looked no different to Gunn than any of the other miles of road they'd covered. Of course moonlight did that—distorted the muted, flat grayness of night, making it hard to distinguish between one hillock and the next.

That had been an hour ago, and miles of cross-country running away. They had watched him drive off, Faith successfully managing not to take off after the smug bastard and rip him to shreds.

Then they debated for a few moments, quickly reaching the consensus that it didn't matter where they went so much as that they put distance between themselves and the drop-off point, which was the only place they had been known to be. None of them trusted Clete's version of the "rules." He'd said the hunters would be dropped with no knowledge of where their targets were, but they had no way to know if he was telling the truth, and every reason to assume that he wasn't. And strobe lights and spook-eye headsets would expose their prey to them even more easily than if they'd been hunting by daylight.

Somehow, Gunn thought, *I don't get the sense that this is about making it hard for the hunters.*

Only ones this is supposed to be difficult for is us.

He stopped running, bent over, and put his hands on his knees while he caught his breath. A moment later Wesley noticed and stopped as well. Faith went on for another dozen yards before she halted.

"What's up?" she asked.

"I just wanna ask a question," Gunn said. "How do we know we ain't runnin' right toward 'em?"

Wesley inhaled deeply, held the breath for a moment, then blew it out as he considered. "Well, I guess we don't. We only know that we're running from the point at which we were dropped off."

"Right," Gunn agreed. "So maybe now would be a good time to start tryin' to come up with a plan. Again."

"I have the same plan as before," Faith offered. "We find the hunters and we kill them."

"They're human, Faith," Wesley said quietly.

Faith looked hard at the ground. "I know," she said. "But so are . . . you."

There was a strained moment between them.

Then Wesley said, "We won't be able to kill them."

"Maybe you won't," she retorted, lifting her head. "Man, Wes, don't be such a wuss. You start out thinking things like that, you might as well roll over the minute they spot you."

Wesley put a hand to his gut subconsciously. Gunshot wounds died hard, and Wes's had been a beaut. "As our driver pointed out, they have guns. We don't. Perhaps the difference is a minor one to you, Faith, but having been shot, I have to say that it's a fairly substantial consideration to me."

She shook her head dismissively. "Anything worth doing is worth a little risk."

They had another silent stretch, which Gunn could watch but get nowhere into because he had not been there when she had tortured Wesley to get Angel to come after her and kill her, put her out of her misery. He did know it was taking a hell of a lot for Wesley to deal with being stuck in some cheesy Jean-Claude Van Damme movie with this chick, who was still half-insane and hey, Slayer to boot.

"So . . ." Faith pressed.

Wesley said, in that high-handed tone he could get, "It's more than a little risk, I should say."

Gunn stepped up. "I'm with English on this one. By 'plan' I was thinking more like, one that would get us off the island without gettin' shot, sliced, or diced. That whole death-dealing-blow thing is a life experience I'm happy to skip."

"I could live without repeating it as well," Wesley added. "Irony intended."

Faith walked back to where the two men stood. *She's hardly winded,* Gunn thought with amazement. *She's been running for an hour—maybe not flat out, 'cause for her flat out woulda left us in the dust—but running hard. I can barely catch my breath, and for her it's a walk in the park.*

'Course, I been beaten half to death. But hey, I'm young.

"So do you have a better idea?" she asked. "If we hide, they'll find us. We could probably dodge them for a day, maybe two. But the island's not all that huge, and they'll track us down eventually."

"If we could work our way back to the airstrip, perhaps steal a plane . . ." Wesley suggested.

"You know how to fly one?"

Wesley hesitated before he answered. "In theory."

"Great," she said. "Theory will get us drowned in the Pacific, unless we're unlucky enough to reach land and end up smeared all over the 405." She looked at Gunn, who shook his head.

"I only fly as a passenger," he said. "Not really all that fond of it then."

"What about a boat?" Wesley asked. "Surely this island must have some boats, right?"

"I saw some from the plane, but they were back by the compound and the airstrip," Gunn replied. "Didn't notice any others."

"That's not a bad idea, though," Faith said. "We work our way to the coast. If we see a boat, great. If we don't, maybe a tour boat or some other ship will pass close enough for us to signal or even swim to."

Gunn shrugged. He didn't have anything better to offer. He wished he'd watched more *Gilligan's Island* as a kid— he remembered that Gilligan and the gang had been stuck on the island for a long time, but that they finally got off it. It was that last part, the getting off, that he wasn't too clear on, though. *Priorities were all screwed up,* he thought. *I should've paid more attention to the important things in life.*

Kahului airport was the only one that ran direct flights to the mainland, but it hadn't been built to accommodate vampires during the daytime, particularly early in the morning.

The airport was made up of several separate buildings, including the inter-island terminal, a building for the baggage claim, and a long two-story main terminal with the standard accordion ramps to send passengers to and from their aircraft.

Lohiau let him out in front of the interisland terminal and Angel carefully navigated his way from under the tarp to a shadowy area under the overhang. The vampire wore a low fedora that the kahuna had scrounged up, and a long duster, collar pulled up to minimize his exposure.

The number of people made it easier to blend in. Angel did get a few strange looks at his long coat and hat, but the reflected sunlight had already reddened his skin somewhat, and he figured the sunburned look would explain his outfit to anyone who cared to inspect him that closely.

Lohiau had said he would meet him at the main terminal by the United Airlines desk, so the vampire made his way there, finding a bench under a potted palm. After a few minutes, the magician came walking up.

"Ah Angel, I see you managed to make it indoors without blowing up. Well done. Or *not* well-done, eh?"

Angel shook his head at the humor but smiled in spite of himself.

Now, as they boarded the plane, the magician closed the three blinds closest to their seats, and one across the aisle. Buying all twelve seats had been expensive, but the extra control over the window coverings was worth it. Soon enough, the airplane filled up with chattering tourists, wailing infants, a small clutch of black-clad nuns, and a few business types with expensive suits and smug faces. It wasn't long before they were in the air winging their way back to L.A.

Angel forced himself to be calm. All he could do now was wait.

After being dropped off, the thirteen hunters had fanned out. No one knew the precise location of their prey, of course. But they had one advantage—they'd been dropped near the northeast corner of the island's coast-line. Since it was unlikely that the Slayer and the other two were trying to swim to the mainland, that eliminated two directions from their search. Moving toward the southwest, spread just wide enough to keep track of one another, the thirteen of them were able to cover a wide swath of territory.

Then Marianna Escobar roared up in a Jeep, dressed in full hunter's regalia.

A Slayer, she thought. *All those millions in fees aside, I can't resist one or two cracks at her.*

Well, this is a surprise, Faith thought. *No two ways about it. I'm having a blast.*

Yeah, she was stuck on some godforsaken goat resort of an island with two of the people she liked least on Earth, being hunted by a vampire big game huntress, a demon, and some rich jerks who who'd seen *The Most Dangerous Game* one too many times, but *Hey, baby—welcome to my life*. She was free again. Maybe that freedom wouldn't last the night, maybe her head would wind up mounted in some sicko's trophy room, but you know what?

It was still better than prison.

Anything was better than prison.

Faith jogged on down the winding arroyo, the dust she kicked up silver in the moonlight. The hunters would have to be deaf, dumb, and blind not to see her trail, but she'd decided she'd had enough of this. There was no chance of her reaching those boats anyway, even after leaving Wesley and Gunn behind; she might as well try to take some of her enemies out before they—

Only the reflexes of a Slayer kept Faith from being skewered by the arrow. It flashed out of the darkness, a tiny quarrel probably fired from a wrist-mounted arbelest, and she barely managed to sidestep in time. She spun, half-crouched, waiting for the follow-up attack.

It wasn't long in coming. This time a bolo whirled toward her, the heavy leather balls on either end of the rawhide thong spinning in deadly orbit. Faith was still slightly off balance from dodging the arrow, and she couldn't avoid this attack entirely—one of the golfball-size spheres struck her in the temple.

The strike would have shattered an ordinary person's skull; it half stunned Faith, dropping her to her knees in the dry riverbed. Dimly she sensed her attacker leaping toward her. Instinct took over and Faith dropped flat.

Marianna Escobar sailed over her, one leg extended in a deadly flying kick. The vampire hit the ground, absorbing the impact easily and spinning to her feet in one smooth and savage motion. By that time Faith was on her feet as well. They faced each other in defensive crouches, each sizing the other up.

"That all you got?" Faith asked. "Next time I'll send my crippled old grannie instead of me . . ."

Marianna grinned. "I was afraid this would be too easy. I'm glad to see it won't. I've heard so much about the thrill of killing Slayers—I didn't want it to be over too soon."

"It will be," Faith said, "for you."

She stepped forward, hurling a combination spinning kick and backfist at Marianna. The huntress ducked, blocked, and struck back. Her knuckles slammed into

Faith's chin and sent the Slayer hurtling the width of the arroyo, to slam painfully against the far rocky wall.

Faith regained her feet immediately. Marianna laughed. "Don't misunderstand me," she said. "It will be easy—just not *too* easy."

"You know what?" Faith asked. "I think I'll leave the snappy banter crap to Buffy and her loser friends. Not my style." And she launched a withering attack of kicks, punches, and strikes at the vampire. Marianna was good— she avoided most of them. Most, but not all, and Faith laughed as she clocked her opponent squarely, sending her staggering back.

"Oh, man, I have missed this!"

She lunged at Marianna, who leapt and tucked into a forward roll that landed her behind the Slayer. Faith spun about to face her, and saw the vampire snap both fists open and shut twice. With a *chunk* two deadly looking blades extruded from forearm sheaths, each extending about ten inches beyond her knuckles.

Faith shook her head in mock pity. "Somebody's read *way* too many comic books," she said.

Marianna lunged, wrist blades glinting in the moonlight as she swung one high, one low. Faith jumped, flattened in midair and let one razored edge pass over her while the other slashed underneath. Then she slammed into the vampire, her momentum knocking the other off her feet and sending them both rolling over a sudden drop in the riverbed. They fell perhaps fifteen feet, thudding painfully against the rocks.

Marianna rose first. Both the blades had shattered in the fall, leaving only jagged stumps which she retracted. She was no longer smiling. Faith looked up in time to see the huntress's face go vamp, yellow eyes glittering, fangs visible in a snarl.

"Guess the thrill of the hunt's wearing off," the Slayer said.

She rose to a crouch as Marianna picked up a rock the size of her head, and backflipped out of range an instant before the stone crashed down where she had been.

Marianna roared, a bestial, enraged sound that any tiger would envy. Faith leapt out of the gulch, landing on the flat and dusty ground surrounding it. Not too far away was a manzanita bush. She moved to it and broke the trunk off near the ground, looking about warily as she stripped away the branches to leave a long and tapering length of hard wood that the lunar radiance colored purplish black. Faith gripped it, hefted it. A little makeshift, but she'd made do with worse.

"Come and get it, jungle girl," she murmured.

The ground was fissured with cracks all about her where the last seasonal rains had flash flooded their way to the sea. It was like a miniature Badlands. Faith turned slowly in a circle. She was standing in the center a roughly triangular "island" perhaps ten yards apart at its widest point. Marianna could come at her from any direction, but Faith didn't doubt her ability to nail the vampire in time. She waited for the attack.

Which didn't come. After several minutes the Slayer moved warily to the embankment's edge and peered over. The full moon illuminated things quite clearly. There was no sign of Marianna. Faith walked the tiny mesa's perimeter, her gaze searching every shadow and hiding place.

The vampire was gone.

The Slayer relaxed slightly. Though she would never admit it, Marianna's full-tilt gonzo lust for the hunt had been somewhat unnerving. If the rest of the hunters were that into it, the chances of coming through this alive, she thought, were slim indeed. She shrugged. "It's *still* better than prison," she said. Then, gripping the stake, she moved out.

CHAPTER EIGHTEEN

Los Angeles spread below the plane as Angel talked to Lorne on the air phone.

The Host assured him that Fred was fine—still scared and upset, but mostly because she hadn't been able to stop the abductors. Physically she was fine.

"But there just seem to be the *strangest* ripplings in spacetime, you know," Lorne told him. "I've registered at least three temporal anomalies in the last *day*. I'm starting to feel like I'm on *Deep Space Nine*, not in my own adopted city!"

"Okay," Angel said distractedly. "I'll call you later."

He hung up.

Lohiau looked at him questioningly. Angel shrugged.

Then they were off the plane, heading down the escalator, and Chaz Escobar was on his way up to meet their plane.

"Angel," he said, his voice the envy of a nighttime deejay. "Do you have the Chalice?"

"This is Lohiau," Angel said pointedly.

The two men shook hands, taking each other's measure.

Lohiau said, "Yes, we have it."

Escobar smiled. "Excellent! Then we have everything we need to proceed."

Angel frowned. *No way am I proceeding.*

His *friends* were all out there somewhere, at risk. He still felt set up, still didn't trust this guy.

He said to Escobar. "I thought you only had a few pages of the book. You suddenly find some more while I was gone?"

And while my friends were being kidnapped? Where were you when they were captured—gathering pages while they provided a distraction?

Escobar was studying Angel's carry-on and Lohiau's satchel.

"I believe I can proceed without the entire Book. I have reviewed the few that I have, and I have, in the past, seen several others. A few more have been described to me in great detail. I'm confident that with the Chalice, and the other things you retrieved, we can summon the Beast of the First Blood."

Lohiau laughed, a soft feathery chuckle. "Mr. Escobar— you are a hunter, are you not?"

The hunter looked in the rearview mirror at the kahuna, his brows lowered. "Yes, you could say that. A very good one."

"Well I am a kahuna—a practitioner of magic, and I'm not too bad at it, either."

The Hawaiian paused for a moment and then continued. "And let me say this: One of the cornerstones of summoning magics is that you must be very, very careful. Particularly when the creature that you call is as deadly as the father of all vampires. I don't know about you, but I'm not sure that I'd trust a second-hand set of instructions to give us the precise intonation, the exact symbols we need to protect ourselves against such a creature."

Escobar's nostrils flared and his face reddened; he replied, his tone one of measured control, "I have seen things you have not, and my memory is *excelente*. And too, kahuna, I am not afraid to die. Ask our friend Angel, if you doubt that."

Escobar paused as he came to a sharp turn, executing it as precisely as he was measuring his words. "I am a hunter. I know how to kill—and believe me when I say that all I need to work for this spell is the summoning. The killing part, I need no help with."

Lohiau looked over at Angel and they had a moment of mutual understanding. Escobar was shuffling his deck with a few cards missing. But Angel needed to keep an eye on him. If Escobar had had anything to do with the disappearances of his friends, Angel wanted very much to keep him near.

"You should move into the hotel," Angel said.

Angel had no intention of letting the man near the Chalice or any of the other ingredients he needed for the ritual until he was surer both of him and of his ability to do what he claimed he could do, but he didn't have to tell him that.

Escobar nodded.

At the next light Escobar made a U-turn and headed back down the way they had come. They drove back toward the 405 and headed north. After a time they exited the freeway and the car made its way up a steep hill, negotiating several sharp hairpin turns that even Angel, with his developed sense of direction, didn't think he could repeat.

"You live in the heart of a maze," said Lohiau after the second or third turn.

Escobar laughed. "*Exactamente*. My prey cannot track me, but the reverse is not true."

They came to a stop in front of a swanky condo complex. Escobar triggered the gated garage entrance and they drove inside. After the gate closed again, they got out of the car. Angel was exhausted. It had been more than a day since he'd taken any blood; had it been a normal day he'd have been tired. As it was he could hardly move.

They took the elevator to an exquisitely furnished apartment, all done in Art Deco—Angel's favorite decorating period—and he and Lohiau took in their surroundings. A cherry wood workbench ran the full length of one wall, and was devoted to weapons. A small forge with a crucible had been set up on a concrete slab near the doorway Escobar had gone through. Angel approached, and could see a silvery residue within. A series of casting molds sat to the left of the setup, for various sizes of bullets.

Silver bullets.

A rack sat on top of the bench, about halfway down, and it was filled with wood. There were a surprising number of varieties: oak, cherry, teak, ebony, even purpleheart. A planer had been set in a vise nearby, and Angel could see that the setup was used as a wood grinder for making stakes.

Serious Designer Stakes "R" Us.

Escobar took his hunting very seriously indeed.

After the hunter had gone, Lohiau, who had been going through some stretching exercises, approached the vampire. "If the Beast of the First Blood is killed, is there not a chance that all vampires, every son or daughter of the beast, will die?"

"That's the general idea."

The kahuna paused, worry etched on his face, not quite sure how to say it.

"But you'll die too."

"All vampires."

"I have given what took place with you, Darla, and me a lot of thought over the years since it happened," the magician said. "At times it has troubled me that I interfered with your path, even feeling as I did that your higher self, your *Aumakua*, the trustworthy spirit that you would call your soul, wished to remain joined with you. But now, seeing you more whole, more joined with your higher self, I see how you have grown together, and I am pleased."

He paused.

"Though I must say, the thought of a sunrise without you—particularly like our adventure today—is not the most enjoyable thought."

Angel half smiled at the kahuna. "The Gypsy who cursed me with a soul succeeded in giving me more pain then he could have imagined. For a long time all I wanted was to give it up, to lose the guilt, and go back to being Angelus.

"But after a time, I started seeing how I could atone. There's so much . . . damage in this world. My soul has helped me see that. Best part is, though, I'm doing my best not to be the cause of any." Talking like this made Angel uncomfortable, but he needed to say one more thing

"So, thanks. For what you did."

Lohiau gave him a long, hard look. "I suppose there still are some good magicians in the world," he said, "as well as good people." The magician paused. "Maybe goodness itself is the endangered species."

If Escobar's plan worked, Angel knew that his name would be on that endangered species list. But he was going to do everything in his power to see that his friends weren't.

Escobar returned with several bundles of what looked like military flak vests. "New composite ceramic armor plates," he said, throwing them into the enormous pile of gear. "They'll stop assault rifle rounds, and do wonders with demon claws."

The three carried all the items to the limo. Angel hesitated when Escobar told them to put them all in the trunk.

"And if we're attacked . . ." Angel said leadingly.

The big man tapped the top of the limo's roof. At the center, there was a circular panel, sitting flush with the roof. Angel hadn't noticed it before.

Escobar reached into the car and pushed something. The panel popped up, maybe three inches. Underneath, Angel could see a nozzle of some kind. There was a clicking sound, like a piezo-electric cigarette lighter, and a tiny flame appeared front of the nozzle.

"If I press the *other* button," he continued, "the twenty-gallon tank in the trunk will squirt napalm in a circle around the limo, the radius making maybe thirty feet."

Angel stared at the flamethrower nozzle. "Nice toy," he said, getting into the car. He thought of Gunn's war wagon.

Gunn could have cleaned up his neighborhood in a matter of weeks with a thing like this.

"Get us to the hotel, fast," Angel said, as Lohiau got in beside him. "The mummy's still there, right?"

Escobar nodded. "I moved it, however, to the boiler room. It is well hidden."

"We're going to move everything out of town," Angel told them both.

"Got a place in mind?" Lohiau asked him.

"I've done much training in the desert," Escobar offered. "I have a small place deep in the Mojave."

Angel considered. *One of the deadliest places on the planet . . . especially for a vampire.* "Good as place as any," he said.

Because there's really no good place.

As Escobar pulled the car into the street, he felt a tingle of anticipation course through his body, and it was all he could do to keep his hands on the steering wheel. The Chalice was in the back of the car with the scrawny Hawaiian, and they were on their way to pick up the mummy. With those items, plus the portions of the Book he had acquired, he was certain he could pull off the ceremony. Killing the Beast of the First Blood would be the ultimate triumph of his life as a hunter—there could be no greater game than the father of all vampires. And though he had not been able to restore his beloved Marianna's humanity, at least he would have his revenge on the bloodsuckers who had taken her from him.

There was nothing that could get in his way now. The road ahead was clear.

At the first corner the stoplight went yellow and then red, and he pulled the vehicle to a slow stop. The street was quiet and dark, with heavy overhanging trees and hedges cutting the lights from nearby condo complexes. He glanced at Angel, sitting in the passenger seat. The vampire was agitated, apparently feeling the urgency of getting to the mummy and making sure that it was safe from Benedicta. Escobar shared the urgency, but he wasn't about to run red lights to get there—the last thing he needed was a police officer taking a close look at this car.

He allowed his attention to drift for just a moment as they sat—and in that moment, the night came alive.

The window next to Escobar shattered. The glass was triple-ply and reinforced with a web of steel filament, so anything that could break through it with one blow was powerful indeed.

"Drive!" Angel shouted.

Escobar stomped on the accelerator and the car lunged forward, but in the next moment clawed hands reached through the broken window and tore into his flesh, yanking him from his seat. He held on to the wheel, pulling the powerful vehicle into a spin. It jumped a curb and came to a stop against a hedge.

He felt himself tugged from the car, shards of glass cutting his skin, and when he landed in damp grass someone piled on top of him, all pounding fists and gouging claws. He still couldn't even see his attackers.

Distantly he heard a car door open. *Angel,* he hoped. *I can use some reinforcements, and Lohiau doesn't look big enough to hold his own against a troop of cub scouts.*

He caught one of the fists that punched him in the ribs, and twisted. His attacker fell back, and Escobar managed to gain the upper hand for a moment. In a shaft of light that filtered through the hedge's closely packed branches, he recognized the beast. It was one of his own, one that had remained loyal to Marianna. In that moment he saw that the shadows were thick with them—the car was surrounded, Angel was out of his seat but locked in combat with several of the creatures, and others were reaching in through the broken window toward Lohiau.

"Stand down, all of you!" he shouted, knowing as he did that it was a long shot. "I am Chaz Escobar, your lord and master!"

A four-armed beast with a massive cannonball of a head clasped two of his meaty fists together and slammed them into Escobar's ribs. Escobar grunted and fell sideways.

They are not only Marianna's troops, but they were no doubt lying in wait for me. He tried to roll back to his feet, but two more of them slammed into him, forcing him back down onto the grass.

Enough of this foolishness. He endured their blows as he reached into an inner sheath and withdrew a hunting knife with a long blade and a serrated top edge. Once it was firmly in his grasp, he twisted away from the creatures who pummeled him and brought it up in a sudden jab. The blade sank into monster flesh, and he twisted it once before tugging it out, the jagged edge ripping at muscle and tendon as it emerged. The creature let out a howl of pain. Escobar kicked it and it fell into one of the others, giving him the moment he needed to gain his feet.

The car was a virtual armory, complete with flamethrower,

but he and Angel were both out of the vehicle and surrounded by Marianna's monsters. From the back seat Lohiau couldn't work any of the weaponry, and Escobar figured the kahuna was probably huddled over the Chalice, chanting some protective spell.

Still, Escobar wasn't without weapons at any time. Now that he had some room to work with, he tucked away the knife, which was still dripping green goo, and took out an automatic pistol. An orange-skinned creature with bony ridges over his eyes charged at him. He squeezed the trigger, and his first burst blew open the orange thing's chest. It fell toward him, but he batted it away with his free hand and fired over it at several other beasts advancing on him.

He caught a glimpse of Angel holding his own, fists and feet a blur of motion as he battled to keep the creatures away from the car. Then Escobar's attention was riveted by another group coming at him. He spun and opened fire, spraying them with bullets. Two went down but the others still came, and his hammer fell on an empty chamber. He hurled the gun to the ground and braced himself for their attack. A clawed hand raked his ribs, but he was able to sidestep and dodge most of the impact. He let the creature slip past him and brought up an elbow, slamming it into the thing's temple. The beast fell, stunned. Escobar kicked it away from him and met the next one, its massive arms swinging wildly. One of the fists glanced off his cheek and he saw flashes of light. His feet gave way beneath him and he stumbled. The creature came on, forcing him down, enormous fists hammering him over and over. He tried to go for his knife again, but the barrage was too great. He felt the world going dark.

Escobar had always known that it was risky, creating the monsters he had. As long as they had sworn fealty to him, he'd been safe from his own creations. But once Marianna had turned them against him, he'd been in danger. He had believed he could always control them, or defeat them by knowing their strengths and weaknesses. Somehow she had persuaded them to lose their fear of him, and that had turned the tide. He was beaten.

A strange blue light filled the air before him. *So this is death,* he thought. *The brilliant tunnel of white is a fiction. It is all blue, the glow of a black-and-white television seen through someone's window at night. And that sound, a looping wail, rising and falling, what can that be?*

He was almost ready to give in, to let the creatures who drove their fists into him win the day. But seeing the odd blue light, hearing strange sounds, he decided he was not quite ready to admit defeat. He caught the pounding fists of one beast in his own hands and forced it off of him, using it to block the reaching claws of still more creatures.

As he did, he saw that the blue glow was in fact coming from his car. Lohiau sat with door open, working his hands in the air, and the glow emanated from him. As it reached the monsters, their actions slowed, as if they were suddenly enveloped in a thick, gelatinous liquid. Two dozen homicidal beasts were reduced by the old man's magicks into a sideshow. Escobar gained new respect for the kahuna in that moment. *The old man is good for something after all, it seems.*

"Come," Lohiau shouted. "This won't last long, and we don't want to be here when the police arrive."

Now Escobar realized what the sound was—not something

otherworldly at all, but the all-too-mundane sound of approaching sirens. Someone had doubtless heard his gunshots and summoned the authorities.

Angel was just finishing a couple of the beasts and heading for the car. The temptation was great, now that the monsters were all moving at molasses speed, to take a couple of last shots at them. But he knew the old Hawaiian was right—they needed to be on their way. They had important business, and dealing with the police would just eat up valuable time.

He sidestepped the last of the slow-moving things—*my own creations, reduced to this,* he thought with a degree of sadness, and slipped back behind the wheel. He backed the big car away from the hedge, brushing broken glass from his window as he did, and flashed a smile at Angel.

"I apologize for the delay," he said. "Marianna must have had them staking out my home, awaiting my return."

"That's my guess," Angel replied.

"I doubt very much they'll bother us again."

"Let us hope not," Lohiau croaked from the rear seat. "We'll have plenty of other foes before our work is done, I guarantee you."

"No doubt." Escobar glanced at Angel again. "The hotel?"

"The hotel. And this time, don't stop."

They had started gathering an hour ago—vampire followers of Benedicta's from all over the globe. In the underground temple, there were hundreds, and thousands more were on their way.

The moon would be full tomorrow night, and Benedicta, Queen of the Mysteries, had resolved to summon the Beast that very night.

Though she didn't actually have the Chalice yet, she knew that Angel did have it, and he was either en route from Hawaii or had landed already. That fool, Lohiau, had caused some interference with some warding spells, but Bran had nearly penetrated them.

Bran had also phoned Wolfram & Hart and told them to courier the Book to her before dawn.

She and Bran had had copied pages of the Ritual in their possession for months. What Escobar and Angel had not realized was that the power lay not in the incantation, but in the actual Book itself. It was the native evil of the Beast of the First Blood, which permeated the pages that would summon Him from his banishment, not speaking the proper words in the proper sequence.

And . . . they had a Seer.

Seated on her throne of bones on a raised dais facing the altar, Benedicta smiled at Cordelia Chase, who had been suitably attired for the Ritual in a plain gauze robe. She was bound to the altar and barefoot.

Then Bran entered the room, looking somewhat concerned.

As their vampire followers broke into applause at the sight of the great Druid, he smiled at them all and raised his hands, then hurried to the dais.

Dressed in a black robe with silver epaulets, he approached her diffidently—since they were not alone, and she, not he, was the leader here—and whispered into her ear, "I've penetrated the kahuna's warding spell. Not only did they land in Los Angeles, but now they've left it. They're on their way to the desert."

She blinked, her mind racing. "We can stop them with magic . . ."

He shook his head. "Not from this distance. Lohiau is powerful. I need to go there."

"I'm coming with you," she said, rising.

He looked alarmed. "No. Stay here. The acolytes are gathering . . ."

She glared at him. "Tomorrow night is the full moon. I want that Chalice in time.

"I'm coming with you." She stared at Cordelia Chase. "And so is she."

CHAPTER NINETEEN

Escobar, Angel, and Lohiau drove like demons; the land-scape changed almost minute by minute until they hit high desert and their windows looked out on sagebrush, creosote bushes, and Joshua trees.

Then . . . utter desolation.

Escobar turned off the highway

A couple of miles in, he pulled in front of what looked very much like Lohiau's bunker back on Maui.

Cradling the Chalice, Lohiau got out first, then Angel. The kahuna looked at the sky.

He said to Angel, "It's going to be dawn soon. You need to get inside." To Escobar he added, "Please start unloading your weapons. They've penetrated my spells. We need to assume that she knows exactly where we are, and that she'll be coming for the Chalice and the mummy."

Angel started carrying weapons from the trunk, selecting a long sword for himself. Escobar carried his own mini-armory with him at all times: guns, knives, stakes. About the only thing Angel hadn't seen him with was a howitzer, and he wouldn't have been surprised if he had one mystically hidden on his person somewhere.

Lohiau refused to carry any visible weapons. He held Pele's Chalice in both of his bony hands. But he was far from defenseless.

Tall Joshua trees with spread branches, gleamed silver in the moonlight. Angel dodged spiky wands of ocotillo, and smaller, many-thorned cholla, and the others followed in his path.

"I need to be invited in," Angel said over his shoulder as he reached the bunker's entrance. Then he looked behind Escobar to the moonswept desert.

Plumes of silver-shaded sand lifted into the air. It looked as if the desert were being grabbed up like a blanket and shaken very hard.

Lohiau looked too. He murmured, "She's here. Benedicta's already here."

The three took that in. "What do you think she has, in terms of weaponry?" Angel asked Escobar. "Or forces?"

"Quién sabe? I am not certain," Escobar replied quickly. "She has most certainly brought Bran Cahir, and he is a warlord of much repute." He gestured at the horizon. "One would assume they have many troops at their command."

"I'm guessing you don't mean human troops."

"I sense nothing human over there, Angel," Lohiau said, "but many bodies." He looked at Escobar. "We were attacked back on Maui, and we were able to deflect her. We won't be able to last forever, though. If you really think you can do it, you'll need to perform the Ritual as soon as you can."

"There's a canyon near here," Escobar said without turning his head from the direction of the moonlit and flumes. "We can defend its mouth better than we can this open plain. Since they will have superiority of numbers, so we need to turn that to our advantage by making them come at us a few at a time."

"Sound strategy," Angel said.

They got back into Escobar's vehicle and drove across the desert. Dawn was coming.

And so was Benedicta.

The mouth of the canyon was almost a tunnel, sheer sandstone walls rising on both sides and nearly closing at the top. It was a couple hundred yards before the walls fanned out and the canyon grew wider, spreading on both sides of the wash that bisected it until it became open enough for the cabin.

Angel leaned against one of the walls, looking back toward the road, back in the direction from which Benedicta would come. He saw a glow in the distant sky, growing nearer by the minute. *The sun?* he wondered. *Already?*

But no—it didn't come from the east. It came from the south.

"It's Benedicta's troops," Lohiau told them, his voice cracking a little. *Even he's nervous*, Angel thought. *Not at all reassuring*. He trusted the kahuna's abilities, and Escobar talked a good talk, but he wished he had Cordy, Wesley, and Gunn by his side.

And about a thousand fighters.

Angel watched it come, and realized the Hawaiian was right. Like a hundred giant fireflies, or sparks drifting from a monstrous bonfire, creatures floated through the dark sky, illuminated from within by whatever magic allowed them to fly. They were humanoid, as far as Angel could tell, but as they neared, their individual glows blurred most details and all he could make out were vague shapes cutting quickly through the air.

At least a hundred of them.

And because they were airborne, they were covering ground much more quickly than Angel and his comrades had.

"We need to protect the Chalice!" Angel shouted. He kept his back to the wall at the right of the canyon's mouth and faced the oncoming horde. "No matter what, don't let them get to Lohiau!"

"Don't forget the mummy," Escobar added grimly, laying it at his feet while he drew weapons from hidden holsters. "It's still in my car."

The sky brightened as the creatures neared. By the time they were close enough for Angel to make out individual features through the glow, the desert had become daytime-bright. Angel could hear the whooshing sound they made as they cut through the air, speeding toward him. He braced himself, raising his sword to striking height. Around him, the others tensed, ready for battle.

Then the enemy struck, coming from every direction at once. Some flew overhead to where the canyon's walls widened and swooped in from that side, others squeezed through the narrow gap overhead, still more hurled themselves at the mouth. Angel swung his blade, cleaving his first foe from shoulder to ribs. As he yanked it free, the beast's glow faded and Angel saw that it was a stunted, gnarled creature, vaguely man-shaped but with arms that nearly reached the ground and massive, powerful shoulders that were more apelike than human. It collapsed backward, replaced immediately by three more of its kind.

"They're Collusites!" Escobar shouted.

"Got it," Angel replied, his breaths short and shallow as he slashed at another one. Collusites were subterrestrial demons who could easily be enchanted into doing the bidding of powerful sorcerers. With almost no will of their own, they were ideal cannon fodder—strong, with no hesitation about dying and no reason to disobey commands.

And there were a lot of them. Two more went down beneath Angel's sword, but more came on. They swung maces and hatchets and swords of their own—at one point Angel found himself parrying four weapons at once, his blade whipping back and forth so fast it was just a silvery blur before him. The bodies piled up in front of him, blood soaking the ground beneath his feet. Still, they came on.

Behind him, at the canyon's other end, he heard the report of automatic weapons. *Good idea after all*, he thought. Conventional bullets could kill Collusites—they were strong, but not immortal.

Angel lunged at the nearest demon. The tip of his blade slid between its ribs, and he twisted the weapon before withdrawing it. The Collusite snarled and collapsed.

"Thank you, Angel," Escobar breathed at Angel's back. Angel glanced and saw him aiming a handgun at the flying demons.

"I hope you have a lot of ammo," Angel said, battling more.

Escobar shrugged. "I believe in being prepared, but I am a hunter, not a soldier. I expect to need one, two shots at the most, to bring down my prey." He took aim and fired, proving his point once more.

"Honor doesn't do you much good when you're not alive to enjoy it," Angel observed.

He caught a glimpse of Lohiau with the Chalice on the ground between his feet, working his hands feverishly in the air. Strange blue light glimmered where he gesticulated.

The Collusites still came, reinforcing the ones who fell.

We can't keep this up much longer, Angel thought. *All they have to do is keep picking us off one by one. We need a better plan.*

Escobar seemed to reach the same conclusion. "There are too many!" he shouted, despair evident in his tone. "How will we—?"

"Keep fighting!" Angel cut Escobar off so the hunter wouldn't ask the question he couldn't answer. "We'll come up with something!"

Then he felt the backs of his legs bumped by something skittering past him, toward the oncoming Collusites. He hazarded a glance.

Menehune.

With guttural war cries, the *menehune* waded into battle. Collusites took to the air to dodge them, but the *menehune* responded by tossing one another skyward, or building ladders by standing on one another's shoulders. Every time a Collusite demon descended to attack, the miniature forces swarmed it.

After what seemed like just a few short moments, the remaining Collusites retreated. Lohiau's small soldiers massed around him, prepared to defend their kahuna should the enemy return.

"Benedicta has not backed off," Lohiau told them. "She has kept her distance through the battle, and she remains in place."

"Perhaps we should take the battle to her," Angel said.

A shimmering glow in the air, not far off, caught Angel's attention. It wasn't the return of the Collusites, but something else. Something new. "I don't think that'll be necessary," Angel said.

After a few moments the glowing spot resolved itself into the image of Benedicta herself. Angel could see the desert through the image; it was almost as if she were projecting herself onto a paper-thin screen that hovered in midair. As they watched, the image moved her mouth and sounds came out.

"Well fought," she said. She glanced in Lohiau's direction. "But it's over, you know."

She's right, Angel thought. He picked up the Chalice and said to Escobar, "Blow this to bits."

The man paled, but raised his handgun nevertheless.

"Stop!" Benedicta shouted. Her voice echoed off the canyon walls, the sharpness of her command like the report of a bullet.

The image of Benedicta began to waver and fade, and another image replaced it in the shimmering patch of light.

Benedicta's voice remained, though, as strong as ever. " offer a simple trade. Pele's Chalice for what you see before you."

And as the new image swam into focus, Angel recognized Cordelia—arms bound, face painted with weird symbols, eyes wide with fear.

"Angel?" Cordelia cried plaintively.

Standing on Marianna's porch, Lilah savored the downtime.

San Teodor was almost a vacation—the closest she'd had in some time, at any rate. But she couldn't quite let her guard down. She had to keep an eye on Marianna and the W&H clients here for the hunt, and she knew she couldn't turn her back on Gavin Park for a minute. Attorneys were often compared to sharks, and in Gavin's case that analogy was particularly apt. He swam silently through the waters of people's lives, always on the scent of blood, and his attack, when it came, was often fatal.

She sipped from a glass of white wine one of Marianna's creatures had poured her—they made excellent servants, it seemed, since they took instruction well and didn't have, as far as she could tell, much individual will—and watched the phosphorescent waves tumbling over the beach in the distance. Suddenly—perhaps because the shark comparison had just popped into her head—the surf took on a threatening demeanor instead of the relaxing, soporific effect it had had moments before. She felt a chill come over her, as if a cloud had passed in front of the sun.

When she turned around, Gavin Park was standing just inside, watching her. She shivered, trying to control it so he didn't notice.

But his eyes missed nothing. "Cold?" he asked.

"Just a passing thought," she replied. "I'm fine.

"That's good." He smiled at her; there was no joy in it. *Maybe a flash of hunger,* she thought. "You should be enjoying this time away from the office."

"Are you?"

"I always enjoy myself, wherever I am."

Probably so, Lilah thought, *since you're the kind of man who would find pleasure in repossessing the homes of elderly widows.*

Which, now that she thought about it, had been fun the one time she'd done it, early in her career. Not precisely a repossession, since she had not been a banker, but the end result was a widow and her three children under twelve living in their car, and a hefty fee paid to the firm by a landowner who was able to build a mini-mall on the site of her former home. The ruthlessness Lilah had shown then had brought her to the attention of Holland Manners, and he had taken her under his wing and started her up the ladder.

"I just got a call," Gavin said, "from Nathan."

Lilah was caught off guard. *Why did Nathan call him, and not me?*

"Seems Angel's on the run with the Chalice. She followed him. She wants us to bring the Book to her. In the Mojave Desert," he added.

"Oh, so she's killed him," she said, and was surprised at the wistfullness she felt. As with Lindsey, life would be a lot less interesting without Angel around.

"Apparently they're having some kind of standoff. But the outcome is obvious, isn't it? Angel won't last against her."

"No, he won't," she murmured. Sighing, she squared her shoulders. "Well, assuming that time is of the essence . . ."

"It is."

"The Beast of the First Blood," Lilah said. She could barely believe Benedicta was so close to pulling it off.

"The Beast, the mating. The offspring." Gavin smiled his disturbing smile again. "I've always been amused by how much we humans think we know, and how little we really do. Once the spawn of Benedicta and the Beast arrive, we'll learn fast. We'll learn the real meaning of horror. We'll learn what fear is all about."

Lilah regarded him for a moment. "You're genuinely enthused by that idea."

"Of course. Aren't you?"

"I'm enthusiastic about being on the winning side when it happens. I'd hate to be on the losing side."

"The very best the losers will be able to hope for," Gavin agreed, "is a quick death."

"The very best the losers will be able to hope for is a quick death," one of them had said. The demon Marianna Escobar called Zed understood that.

Though he was to all appearances merely a hideous mutation, he had once been a man. His name had been Michael Cover, and he had been part of a large and loving family back in Northridge, which was outside of Los Angeles. A long time ago, Chaz Escobar had injected him with some demonic DNA, just to see what would happen.

A nightmare had happened.

But he still had family there.

And he'd be damned before he would let any of them die a quick death . . .

Unnoticed, he snuck out of the main house and headed for the stable. Another mutant, Arle, was as usual chained up in the stable.

First Zed unchained him with the keys left just tantalizingly out of Arle's reach.

Then he told them what he knew.

The two of them moved out.

CHAPTER TWENTY

Hours before, in the day's first light, Wesley, Faith, and Gunn had caught a glimpse of their hunters as they topped a rise in the distance. With the sun at their backs the enemy had been silhouetted against the horizon. Faith had happened to turn around at the right moment, and had come to a dead stop, looking back toward them.

"There they are," she said. "We should take them down."

"If we could divide and conquer, I'd agree," Wesley said, breathing heavily. "But it looks as if they're keeping within sight of one another. We could certainly get one—perhaps three—of them, but the others would see us and gun us down."

"Might be better than running like scared kittens," she replied bitterly. Wesley knew how she felt—none of them enjoyed being hunted. There was a distinct sense of power-lessness—one could not choose one's own destiny when a more powerful force called the shots, but could only react. He knew they were still making their way toward the shore, to see if they could find a boat and a way off the island, but he couldn't escape the feeling that they were perhaps being herded in that direction like so many wayward cattle.

When the group of silhouettes vanished, coming down the slope toward them and therefore out of the light, he turned to the others.

"What do you think? An hour behind us?"

"Less, dog," Gunn replied. "Half and hour, maybe forty-five minutes, tops."

"But they're moving more slowly than we are," Faith said.

"Than we *were*," Gunn corrected. "I can't keep up that pace, though. I'm still just human, unlike some of y'all."

I'm with you, Wesley thought. He didn't say it, though. *wouldn't want to prompt a lengthy diatribe from Faith about how weak I am.*

His legs throbbed, and he knew that if he stopped moving, even for a little while, they'd stiffen and protest. His lungs burned with the effort of running. Faith had found them and told them of her encounter with Marianna; then they'd snatched a couple hours of sleep while Faith stood watch.

The island wasn't big enough to elude them for much longer. There would be a reckoning.

"We crossed that ridge," Wesley pointed out. "So they must have found our trail at some point and are following it."

"Then we just have to stay far enough ahead of them to keep out of rifle range," Faith observed. "If they have binoculars or telescopic sights they might have seen us already."

"For all we know, they put homing devices in our baked potatoes last night," Gunn suggested. "They might just be runnin' us to exhaustion for the sport of it."

Faith tossed one more glance back, though the hunters were now completely invisible against the shadowed side of the hill. "*Someone* might as well be having a good day." She started to jog again. Wesley and Gunn exchanged weary glances and limped after her.

Since then they hadn't seen any other sign of their pursuers. The day had worn on; they had rested and Faith had patrolled alone.

And then . . . night began to come on again.

They'd come near enough to the coast that the birds who passed overhead were more often gulls than ravens, and Wesley could taste the faintest tang of salt air on the breeze. There was, of course, no guarantee that they'd be able to find a boat anywhere outside of Marianna's compound.

But at least the first part of the plan seems to be working, he thought. They were much closer to the compound than they had been.

He pushed away the knowledge that, if there was no boat when they reached the sea, they'd be up against a figurative wall, eliminating that direction as an escape route when the hunters came. As they certainly would.

Once again it was Faith who stopped short, throwing her arms to her sides to halt the others.

"What's up?" Gunn asked her, his voice quiet.

"Look," she replied, pointing to a spot well ahead of them.

"Do they have us boxed in?" Wesley asked. *They couldn't have gone around us so quickly,* he reasoned. *But they could have split into two groups from the start.*

"Yo, what is that?" Gunn said, able to see straight over Faith's head. "Somethin' white."

"Could be anything," Faith said, squinting into the darkness. Wesley knew that her eyesight was far better than his. He could see only a field of tall grass with some rocky outcroppings at its edge. "Some big old weird thing they created outta toilet paper or something. I say we attack," Faith said eagerly.

"I say we jump into the bushes," Gunn drawled. "Damn girlfriend, low profile, remember? There's all kinds of guys tryin' to kill us on this island. We just leap into battle, we might as well send up a flare."

"Yeah, but we can't run forever," Faith argued. "Sooner or later we're gonna have to take a stand."

She's always so aggressive, Wesley thought reprovingly. *Ready to leap into the fray. Now Buffy, on the other hand . .*

. . . is not here and this line of thinking will get us nowhere.

"Hey, English," Gunn murmured, "weigh in."

"He's not the boss here," Faith shot back with a sort of snicker.

Wesley raised his chin. "Sorry to disappoint, Faith, but I am."

"Wha-at??" She looked at Gunn. "You believe this?"

Gunn said simply, "He is." Ignoring her, he gazed at Wesley. "What do you want us to do?"

His gaze still on the advancing shapes and the white thing, Wesley replied, "I would have suggested that we jump into the bushes, but since we've taken so much time to have this chat, I believe we've been spotted." He gestured with his hand. "And that big white thing is a flag of truce."

"Oh, *right*," Faith sniped, her voice dripping with sarcasm. "And all these guys are really sorry they were mean to us and want to take us clubbing."

"Show Wesley respect," Gunn said quietly.

"Okay, because he wants us to just stand here like sitting ducks while these guys break out the rocket launchers—"

"Shut up," Wesley said.

She whirled on him. "Or—?"

"Hey, don't turn your back on the enemy. You're point," Gunn said to her.

"Maybe I got enemies in more than one direction," she said evilly.

Gunn glared at her. "Damn, sister, what's your problem?"

"Her problem is that while she's trying to be a better person, she has good days and bad days," Wesley bit off. "I suppose, given the fact that her survival is being threatened, she's simply reverted to type."

Faith opened and closed her mouth several times. Her fists clenched. Ignoring the warning signs of a psychotic Slayer on overload, Wesley looked past her—and beyond his past with her—to the matter at hand.

"They're advancing toward us," he announced to the others. "Rapidly."

"Thanks, Faith," Gunn snarled, "for doing your damn job."

"Hey," she began, but as the apparent truce matter drew near, she crouched into an attack stance and flexed her shoulders and trapezius muscles, like a barroom boxer loosening up for a good brawl.

Wesley did the same. Gunn moved his neck and muttered, "Damn, if we even had some spears or something."

"Now you're talking," Faith said. "Weapons. Don't leave home without 'em."

"I hear that," Gunn drawled.

Two warriors, Wesley noted, letting go of the personal to get on with the inevitable—fighting for their lives.

It took a moment for his eyes to make out what the Slayer was pointing at, across the overgrown meadow. But he was eventually able to see a cluster of figures making its way though a ravine and heading in their direction. He couldn't see much detail from here, but what he could see caused him to believe that these shapes weren't human— they moved differently, for one thing, some shambling, others almost hopping or skipping along, instead of walking. And there was a greater size differential than one would expect to see in a similar grouping of human beings.

"What do you think? They surrendering to us?" Gunn asked. "Why would they do that? We wouldn't have even known they were there."

"I doubt they're surrendering," Wesley replied. "A white flag means truce, not surrender. Perhaps they just want to parlay."

"And maybe they're trying to trick us into thinking that," Faith said. "They're some of Marianna's monsters, I'd guarantee it. The flag's just to get us to drop our guard so we'l let them get close, and then they'll tear us apart." She paused for a moment, a grin that Wesley found vaguely sinister flashing across her face. "Or try to."

"Do you think they've seen us yet?" Wesley queried.

"Doesn't matter. I say we let them. I say we let 'em think the flag's working. When we get close enough, then we'll surprise them and move before they do. I've been running too long—I want to fight something else. Marianna's gone home.

"Monsters sound like fun."

Angel yanked Escobar's gun from him and held it to the Chalice himself.

He said to Benedicta's image, "If you've done anything to hurt her—"

"She's fine," Benedicta interrupted. "For now. I suggest that instead of making empty threats, you take the steps necessary to keep her that way."

He said nothing.

"Angel, no," Escobar whispered urgently. "You cannot."

"Angel." Lohiau's cultured voice was low. "If she wants the Chalice so badly . . . it could mean that she has the Book of the Interregnum."

In an agony he muttered, "I know."

"So we can't give her—"

"I know!" he snapped.

Benedicta's image smiled at him. "You're going to do it, aren't you?" she purred. "You're going to trade."

Angel had, of course, no intention of making a deal with Benedicta. The vampire was evil incarnate as far as he was concerned. But at the same time, he had no intention of letting her kill Cordelia.

So he agreed to a deal. He, Lohiau, and Chaz Escobar would spend the day in the bunker, since crossing the open plain by daylight was completely out of the question and, short of a helicopter, there was no vehicle that could cross such rugged ground to pick him up. Benedicta had time, anyway—she didn't need the Chalice until the full moon, which was rising that night. And Angel wouldn't hand over the Chalice and mummy until Cordelia was safely returned.

The truce negotiated, Angel and his companions got to the bunker and made sure it was heavily fortified. Escobar told them it had been built to withstand a nuclear explosion, and Angel believed him.

They pulled in all the weaponry and Lohiau performed dozens of warding spells.

Angel asked the hunter, "You got a phone?"

Escobar did.

Angel made a call.

Working out equations on the wall of the Caritas stockroom, Fred jumped when the door opened. She still didn't like doors, unless they closed the world out. Her safe haven, her cave, hadn't had any doors.

But Lorne came through, holding out a telephone to her. Phones, like music, had been nonexistent on Pylea and her relationship with them was much like the one she had with doors. She preferred them when they weren't in use.

"It's for you, sugar," Lorne said gently.

What if it's one of the bad guys? What should I say? What should I do?

"Do I have to . . . ?"

"You want to," he replied. She took the phone from him, eyeing it like it was a three-headed demon dog on a very short leash. "H-Hello?"

"Fred." It was Angel's voice on the other end and she sagged in relief.

"Oh, good, you're alive," she blurted anxiously. "I mean, you know. As alive as you can be."

"Listen closely to me, Fred. I think Wesley, Gunn, and Faith have been taken to San Teodor. You need to get to them. It's one of the Channel Islands. Do you know where the Channel Islands are?"

"No." She waved a hand as to erase that, and tried again. "Not really." She swallowed. "I mean, vague idea." She lowered her voice. "I was hoping it would be Disneyland, Angel."

"Find Wesley, Faith, and Gunn, Fred. Go look for them."

She blinked in horrified astonishment "*Me?* I—I don't— Angel, I can't—"

"You and Lorne can do it, Fred, I have faith in you."

"Um . . . ." It wasn't horrified astonishment; it was astonished horror.

"You can do it."

"Wh-Where are *you*?" she quavered, gripping the phone the way, back in Pylea, she used to grip the shock collar around her neck. Like if she held it tightly enough it wouldn't hurt her.

"I'm in the desert. If—*when*—you find them, tell them where. I need them to come to me. Do you understand? I'll give you directions."

"When—"

"Fred, do you understand? Stay with me here. It's really important."

"Oh . . ." she wailed, scrambling for a pen and paper. She'd dropped the one she'd been using on her bed upstairs in her scramble to grab the phone.

"Good. Make sure you get all this, because I'd hate for the human race to die off because my batteries didn't last. Now, from San Pedro, they need to go east."

Keeping careful track of all he was saying, she found a pen on the counter. There was no paper, though.

"Take the fifteen . . ." he continued.

"Getting it," Fred assured him, as she began writing the directions on the wall.

Now Escobar leaned his back against one of the reinforced walls, sitting on the dirt with his hands resting on his upraised knees. The mummy lay on the ground next to him, her wrappings beginning to shred from the rough handling.

"Does this place have room service, Angel?" he asked, a wry smile on his face. "Because I could use a little something before we sleep. Paella. Gazpacho. Some wine."

"I could use a snack myself," Angel grumbled. "So don't push me."

Escobar looked at him as if unsure whether or not he was joking, and dropped the subject.

Angel decided to try to get some sleep while he could, but as soon as he closed his eyes, Lohiau spoke up. "So tonight, when we make the trade . . ." he began.

"No trade," Angel interrupted.

"No trade?"

"Of course no trade. We can't give Benedicta the Chalice or the mummy."

"But you agreed . . ."

"I would tell Benedicta anything to keep Cordelia alive," Angel explained. "Now I know Cordy will be safe at least until we meet with Benedicta tonight—she knows that if she hurts Cordelia, she'll never get her hands on the Chalice."

"But when it's time to make the exchange?" Lohiau asked him.

"Then I dust Benedicta and take Cordelia. Problem solved."

"She may not prove so easy to kill."

Angel shrugged. "That's never stopped me before." He shut his eyes then, and in a few moments was sound asleep.

While Faith, Gunn, and Wesley had debated, the creatures had drawn ever nearer. There appeared to be five of them, and they were some of the Escobars' ghastly handiwork, misshapen creatures of every size and deformity. The white flag was being carried by an individual who looked vaguely familiar. Wesley realized it was one of Marianna's house monsters, a creature whose sole function seemed to have been the cleaning of her floors.

What could only be described as a large squid-like being slithered over the ground behind the flag bearer, and it raised a clutch of tentacles rather like a stereotypical Native American in a John Wayne film giving the sign language symbol for "how."

"Don't hurt us," the squid said softly. Its head had fallen

back, revealing a sort of mouth. Wesley was sickened by the sheer grotesquerie of its existence, but stayed on his guard as he scanned the party for anyone who looked as if they might want to be a hero by making an end run on himself, Gunn, or Faith.

"We want to join you," the tentacled thing continued.

"Yeah, right." Faith raised a fist toward the creature. "Join *this*."

Gunn gazed at Wesley, who said nothing.

"We're being hunted down to be slaughtered," Wesley said. "I sincerely doubt you're up for that."

"Cheerful spin on it," Gunn muttered.

"*Accurate* spin," Faith flung at the tall, streetwise warrior. She added for the squid's benefit, "Just so you know I'm the Slayer. And I can break you in two for the barbecue, if I want. I don't know about these guys, but I love calamari."

"My name is Arle," the squid-thing said. His voice sounded oddly human—much more human than he looked, in fact.

"I'm Gunn."

"This one"—Arle waved a tentacle at a broken-faced, oddly-occulated mess of a life form that Wesley couldn't quite figure out what had happened to—"is called Zed."

"Two of the guests have a book with them," Zed said without preamble. "It's going to raise a new kind of vampire."

After a pause, Wesley said carefully, "Are you referring to the Book of the Interregnum?"

"Excuse me, leading the witness?" Gunn jibed.

"When we should be gutting the witness?" Faith added.

The two traded a look of consensus.

"We don't know," said the squidish person. "All we know is that Zed heard two guests talking about this evil book." He added, "They're lawyers."

"Lilah. Gavin," Wesley mused, putting together the pieces. He looked at the others. "We should have guessed. Wolfram and Hart have had it all along."

"So you want to help us?" Wesley asked them.

Zed nodded. "We have . . . some of us had families. And we . . . we were human."

"You'll have to fight," Gunn said. "Maybe die."

The thing actually smiled. Then he added, "They're going to the Mojave."

Faith grinned wildly. "No, they're not," she said, cracking her knuckles.

CHAPTER TWENTY-ONE

New hunters had joined the others.

Marianna had sent out armed patrols looking for her missing creatures, Wesley realized.

The first patrol they encountered spotted them, and—apparently with instructions along the lines of "shoot first, ask questions later"—opened fire before their targets were actually within range.

Faith saw the first puff of smoke from one of the guns, even before the sound of the rifle's crack covered the distance, and made a downward-pushing motion with her hands.

"Hit the dirt!" she shouted.

Wesley obeyed immediately, hurling himself facedown to the ground and cutting his right palm on a sharp-edged

stone. *First blood,* he thought. That shot didn't land anywhere near them, but it wouldn't be long before the patrol
had their range.

"Anybody have guns?" Faith demanded.

Arle held up empty tentacles. "We aren't allowed access
to them," he said.

"Yeah, well, no trigger fingers, I can see that," she
replied. "Guess we'll have to do this the hard way." She
flashed a grin at Wesley and Gunn. "Which also happens to
be the fun way."

"I like the way this girl thinks," Gunn said.

"She's great," Wesley agreed. "In the most homicidal
sense of the word."

"Here's what we're going to do . . ." Faith interrupted,
glaring at him "We stay low and spread out. Then we take
them out."

"Some of them are friends of ours," Arle said. "We just
wanted you to stop the attorneys from taking the Book."

"You have friends who are shooting at you," Faith countered.

She rose to a squat and took off down the hill toward the
guns. Wesley and the rest followed her, spreading out as
she'd ordered, trying to stay below the level of the thick
chaparral. As they moved out, he heard a couple more gunshots, but they seemed to be shooting blindly, and none of
their shots had any effect.

Wesley was beginning to wonder if the patrol had
moved away, or if they'd somehow managed to miss each
other, when he spotted a lizardlike creature standing
beneath the moonlight, head held sideways and tilted
slightly so that his eye, which was on the side of his head,

could see. The creature's long tongue snaked from its mouth and then whipped back in, and Wesley was certain the thing had seen him as well.

It started to raise a gun in his direction.

He briefly considered raising the alarm, but then decided that discretion might be wiser—if he could stop the lizard creature before an alarm was raised, then his own companions would be able to move in closer before being detected themselves. If he started shouting now, though, then battle would be joined all the way around.

He charged the thing. As he neared it, the lizard lifted the gun to its shoulder and squeezed off a wild, panicked shot. *So much for discretion,* Wesley thought. He hurled himself over the last bit of shrubbery that separated him from the lizardy thing and plowed into it before it could get off another shot.

Wesley bounced off it and fell backward into the brush. *Remarkably solid,* he thought. Shaking his head to clear it, he saw that it was supported not only by two powerful hind legs, but also by a tail that was as big around as an alligator's and was resting against the ground to give it extra stability. It raised its weapon again. *Point blank range this time,* Wesley thought. *Even with what is probably poor depth perception, it can hardly fail to hit me at this distance.* He was hopelessly entangled in the brush, with no chance of moving away in time to save himself.

Which was when Gunn exploded in the lizard creature's face, all flying fists and feet. The lizard went to the ground under the ferocious assault, and when it was still, Gunn turned to Wesley and extended a hand.

"Cold-blooded," he announced, pulling Wesley to his feet. "Gets a little sluggish when the sun goes down."

"Yes, well, thank you just the same," Wesley said. He brushed off his clothing, though it was hopelessly soiled and torn by this point.

Around them they now heard gunshots and cries of pain and rage. "Sounds like the rest of 'em got here," Gunn observed.

"Then I suppose we should help them out," Wesley said. Before they could move, they heard Faith, above the din, laughing out loud. "Whoever she's facing is probably most in need of help, however."

"And they'd be on the wrong side," Gunn agreed. "Come on, let's get a piece of this fight before she finishes it."

The prearranged location for the swap was an isolated spot in the east Mojave.

Angel, Lohiau, and Chaz Escobar brought Pele's Chalice and the mummy to a rocky plain, a line of smoke trees billowing from a wash at one edge, their aroma rich and pungent in the cool night air. At the other end of the plain, perhaps fifty yards away, stood Benedicta, Bran, who held a semi-automatic rifle in his hands, a few of their minions, and Cordelia.

Strips of leather encircled Cordy's body, holding her arms tight against her sides, and a studded leather gag was buckled across her mouth. Her face was painted with a strange blue substance that seemed to glow in the darkness. She looked like she'd been prepared for a ritual.

Just above the cliffs on the far side of the plain, Angel could see the pale disk of the full moon climbing into the sky.

She never intended to turn Cordelia over, he realized. *She needs Cordelia for the Ritual, as well as Pele's Chalice.*

She's not getting either one.

If Cordelia was somehow needed for the Summoning, Chaz must have known the same thing, and had never mentioned it. He'd already vowed to keep a close eye on the single-minded hunter, but that confirmed the need to do that. Chaz had been hanging back, fighting when necessary, but mostly letting Angel pull the elements together. He'd make his move soon, and Angel would be ready.

Angel's plan was to carry the Chalice into the center of the plain, dragging the mummy behind him. There he would meet Benedicta, leading Cordy. As soon as Cordelia was walking freely toward his side, he would hand Benedicta the Chalice.

When she took it in both of her hands, he would trigger a stake in a spring-loaded harness up his sleeve, lunge forward and thrust it into her heart. There would certainly be some trouble with Bran and the minions, but he didn't think it would be too serious once Benedicta was gone. She was their leader, the brains and the heart of the operation, and without her he figured the others would fold rapidly.

"Angel," Benedicta said, her voice flat and without emotion. "You have the items in question?" She'd added the mummy almost as an afterthought; Angel had no idea why.

"Right there." He gestured to Lohiau, as usual the bearer the Chalice.

She smiled. "As you can see, I brought the Seer."

"I'll meet you in the middle, then."

Benedicta shook her head—a barely perceptible motion, in the silvery moonlight. "Slight change of plans," she said. "You take the Chalice and the Virgin to the middle of the plain and set them down. Then I will turn the Seer loose, and she can walk to you. If she makes a move toward the Chalice, Bran kills her. If not, then when she's past it, I'll start toward it and pick it up. After you leave the items, you wait on your side until I have retrieved them and am back on my side. Nice and tidy for everyone."

There goes that plan.

"Except for a couple of things," Angel countered. "I don't want Bran holding that gun. He can't kill me, but he could accidentally shoot my friends if he's nervous or something goes wrong. And I don't take the Chalice or the mummy in until Cordelia is on her way—no way am I letting go of it while you still have her over there."

Benedicta seemed to think his arguments over for a moment. Then she smiled. "You disappoint me, Angel," she said. "I thought you wanted to do business. Kill the girl," she instructed Bran. He started to raise the weapon.

"No!" Angel held out a hand toward the kahuna, who stood behind him. "I'll do it your way, Benedicta," he said. "But if you double-cross me, I guarantee you that I'll make your death slow and painful. You know I can do it."

"Spoken like the Angelus of old," Benedicta said, her smile warmer now. "I don't think we're so different, you and me. Perhaps later we can share some blood and talk about the old days."

"We don't have anything to talk about," he said. Lohiau still hadn't put the Chalice in his hand, so Angel hazarded moving his gaze away from Benedicta for a moment to see where the old man was. "The Chalice," he hissed.

But the old sorcerer was on the move, heading up the side Angel wasn't facing, up the wash under cover of the smoke trees. The Chalice was carefully tucked under his arm.

"Lohiau!" Angel shouted. "What are you—?"

Discovered, Lohiau began to run. Angel started after him, but Lohiau flailed a hand back in his direction, and the tendrils of brush under his feet snaked up around Angel's legs and tripped him. As he fell, Angel saw that Chaz Escobar was also entangled.

"Lohiau!" Angel called again, desperately. "Get back here!"

But Lohiau didn't turn around, or acknowledge Angel's plea. He scurried across the rocky expanse, toward the waiting Benedicta. As he dashed in her direction, Angel heard his voice.

"I foresee your victory, Benedicta," he declared. "And I would always prefer to be on the winning side of any conflict." He shot a glance over his shoulder, back toward Angel and Escobar. "I didn't attain this advanced age by fraternizing with losers," he added. "Accept my gift of Pele's Chalice, and my oath of loyalty to your cause."

Benedicta graced Angel with her broadest smile yet, her fangs glinting in the light of the rising moon. He struggled against the tentacles of brush, but they held him as tightly as those leather straps did Cordelia.

"Accepted," she said, taking the Chalice from the old wizard's hands. "A pity for you, though, Angel," she said. "Now I have the Chalice and the Seer. And you?" She tossed off a mocking shrug. "You seem to have nothing at all."

"I still have the Virgin," Angel said, cocking his head toward the mummy.

"You have something, or someone, wrapped in decaying fabric. Perhaps it's a mummy, but it's not the Virgin of

310

Nuremberg. We liberated her from that hellhole ages ago. Replaced her with one we took from an Egyptian museum in Chicago." She shrugged, a pitiful expression on her face. "Sad, isn't it?"

Angel was nonplussed. *The mummy was a false herring, as Cordelia would say.*

Lilah and Gavin hurried to their company jet. Gavin clung tightly to his briefcase, which, Lilah knew, contained the Book of the Interregnum.

She shivered.

It's so evil.

As the moon gleamed above their heads, Marianna accompanied them to say good-bye. She had no idea what was in Gavin's briefcase.

"I was hoping we'd be here for the end of the Slayer hunt," Gavin said. "Seeing Faith's head on a stick is something I've often dreamed of."

"Perhaps by the time you come back, it'll be mounted and hung on the wall of the trophy room," Marianna replied sweetly.

"I'm invited back?"

"You both are, anytime," Marianna assured them. "If you'd like to escape the city for a little while, maybe do a little creature hunting. My door is always open to you."

"That's so nice," Lilah said, trying her best to sound appreciative. *Human blood is probably hard to come by out here,* she thought. *Marianna probably invites everyone she meets, just in case she gets the munchies.*

The airstrip was only a couple of minutes from the house, and the plane was warmed up and waiting for them when they arrived. Looking out toward the water, toward California, Lilah could see the moon, huge and bloodred on the horizon. *Full tonight, of course. Perfect for Benedicta's ritual. Perfect for summoning the Beast of the First Blood.*

"We'll be sure to take advantage of that most generous offer," Gavin was saying. *Sucking up to the host—one of his specialties. As soon as the door is closed on the airplane he'll be telling me what an awful shrew she is.*

Two can play that game.

As she climbed down from the jeep, Lilah launched an air kiss Marianna's way. "I'm so glad we had some time together, Marianna," she said.

"Oh, I am too," Marianna replied. "I'm just sorry you have to go back so soon."

"Business before pleasure, sadly," Gavin said, his voice dripping with such sincerity that Lilah was surprised he didn't stain his Italian silk tie.

"I'm sure it's very important," Marianna said. "And you're sure you have everything you need?"

Gavin touched his briefcase with one hand. "Absolutely everything," he said. "Thank you again for your hospitality." He started toward the small plane. Lilah tossed another kiss Marianna's way and followed. A quick trip to the mainland, and they could turn over the Book. Once that was done . . . well, the world would never be the same.

And how many people can put that on their résumé?

With Faith leading the charge, the first patrol they'd encountered had fallen like dominos in an earthquake. The second had been a bit more of a challenge—Gunn's knuckles still hurt from taking a punch at a beast with skin like a brick wall. Fortunately its throat had been a soft spot and he'd been able to drop it. By the time the moon's reflection showed on the water, they were inside the compound.

He'd almost forgotten about the hunting party, still out there somewhere in the boonies, searching for them. His thoughts were occupied with trying to get into the compound, to stop those Wolfram & Hart scumbags from delivering the Book to Benedicta. Even by the low standards to which he held lawyers, those guys were evil. He'd been pretty upset with Angel when Darla had led him on a detour to the dark side, but one thing he couldn't entirely fault the guy for was locking all those W&H attorneys in a wine cellar with Darla and Drusilla. Sure, Angel had gone over the line that time. But if there was anyone who deserved to get bit by vamps, it was them.

But as they crossed the compound, heading toward the house, something felt wrong. There should have been more guards. He mentioned this to Wesley.

"Yes, but certainly most of them were sent out looking for . . ." He groped for the names. " . . . for Arle, and the rest of them. We've already encountered them."

"They'd still leave some kind of skeleton crew in place," Gunn suggested.

"Around here, that might be taken literally," Wesley pointed out. "But yes, I imagine so."

"Listen," Faith hissed. Everyone fell quiet. Then Gunn heard what she already had—the engine of an airplane.

"They're taking off!" Wesley shouted. "Arle, what's the fastest way to the airstrip?"

Arle led them across the grounds at a dead run. They encountered only a couple of guards along the way, and those were so startled by the sudden appearance of the creatures, along with the Slayer and her friends, that they didn't put up much of a fight. *Just means most of 'em are at the airstrip,* Gunn realized. *Making sure the plane gets off the ground okay. With the lawyers aboard. And the book.*

Then they topped a low rise. The airstrip was at the bottom of a gentle slope near the water's edge, washed in floodlights. He was right; there was a contingent of guards there, although not as many as he'd expected. Wesley had probably been correct that most of them had been sent out in search parties. *We can take the ones left over,* Gunn knew.

But it was too late to do any good. The small plane was already in motion, taxiing down the runway, picking up speed. And the airstrip was too far down the hill for them to get to before the plane lifted off. *If we had guns,* he thought, *we might be able to stop 'em.* But they'd left the guns of the creatures they'd defeated where they had fallen.

They all realized the hopelessness of the situation at once, it seemed. They stopped in their tracks, deflated as a balloon with the end untied. As they watched, the airplane lifted off, buzzed over their heads, then banked away toward the water. Toward California.

Toward Benedicta.

After a moment, Wesley turned to him. "Well," he said sadly. "That went poorly."

"What I was thinkin'," Gunn agreed.

Faith joined them. "We can still get back to the mainland

in time to help Angel stop it," she said. "We just have to find a boat or something."

"A boat," Wesley said. "What a good idea. At least we're still free, and we've managed to evade the hunters, right?"

"Not exactly," a voice said from the darkness. Suddenly a dozen flashlights clicked on, beams cutting the night from every direction. Some of the lights were mounted on rifles or machine guns, others held in fists. "We figured you'd show up here sooner or later."

They were surrounded.

The hunters had caught up to their prey at last.

CHAPTER TWENTY-TWO

In the nightswept desert, Angel finally broke free and lunged toward Benedicta. He only made it a couple of steps though, before something grabbed him by the ankles and threw him to the ground. Pain like fire began to spread upward through his body.

What he had thought were tendrils of brush were, in fact, the tiny grasping hands of hundreds of *menehune* emerging from the earth. Angel understood at once: Since Lohiau had ordered his little minions to attack his enemies, Angel was now an enemy . . . and they were attacking him with gusto.

So not good. One might be harmless, but many could kill. *Especially these guys,* Angel thought as he began to bat at them with his arms, work his feet lose so he could kick at them. *They're armed.*

Indeed almost every single *menehune* carried a small wooden stake like an army of well-accessorized vampire slayer dolls. They were raising and lowering them in violent stabbing motions as they grinned maniacally at nothing in particular. They were in thrall, under orders, and not interested in anything but cutting him to ribbons.

Angel worked hard at stopping them, but their sheer numbers were overwhelming. When he shook off one, five took its place. The pain was bad, but he could endure that. The bigger problem was, if enough toothpicks went into his heart, he would dust.

All he could do was struggle more and hit harder. His mind went back to the time when the Great Hunt had threatened Sunnydale; faery had accompanied the horned demon who led the Hunt, and he, Buffy, and the others had successfully fought against them. So it could be done.

He just wasn't sure how.

He kept fighting, smashing them with fists—*not pretty, that squishy sound*—rolling back and forth to crush bunches of them, doing whatever it took.

After an eternity he surged to his feet just in time to see yet hundreds more of the creatures swarming toward him. He was bleeding but hey, as a vampire, he would heal. But Escobar was on the ground about three feet away, and also covered with a writhing sea of the creatures.

Not good.

Angel pummeled *menehune* left and right as he waded through the stampede toward the man. Escobar was doing some serious damage himself, but he was sustaining more than he was dishing out. Then the man went limp, and Angel knew that for the human, the tides had turned. If Angel couldn't get him out of there, Escobar was going to die.

Fighting to Escobar's side, he saw with disgust that the *menehune* were everywhere—on Chaz's face, stomping on his eyelids, stabbing at his tongue and throat. Three of them were yanking at an ear and piercing the lobe.

Angel went vampface, staying that way as he grabbed up handfuls of them and tossed them out of his way like rag dolls. He had no idea there had been so many back in Lohiau's caves.

He kept focused, working on the tiny monsters in clumps, trying not to think about how many more there were to kill, nor about the fact that Benedicta was watching, and laughing, and that he and Escobar must fully expect more attackers if they survived this first wave.

Escobar must have sensed that help had arrived, for he struggled heroically to get back in the game. He groaned, then shouted from deep within his gut as he doubled his fists and swept at dozens of the creatures.

Then Angel heard gliding footsteps, bigger and steadier, and as he glanced up from the killing, he saw a swelling army of wraiths materializing beside Benedicta. The phantoms began floating toward him and Escobar, taking more substantial form as they did so. *Walking dead. Collusites will be next. And Night Marchers.*

Benedicta and Lohiau were definitely massing the forces of darkness against them.

Propelled by the increased threat, Angel doubled, tripled his efforts and got his fingers around Escobar's wrist. He hauled the man to his feet, batting at his body to shaking off more of the *menehune*. Then Angel half pulled, half dragged the wounded man behind him and they ran. Angel hated to retreat with Cordelia back there, but standing his ground and getting dusted wouldn't do her any good either.

A fireball screeched over their heads and crashed just inches from Escobar's body as Angel flung him to the left.

They were going uphill now, and Escobar, though winded, managed to put some real push into the scramble. More fireballs followed; at long last, Escobar started firing back, gunpowder and steel against magick.

Wraiths exploded; then the clearing erupted into flames that set up a wall between the two. Angel could see nothing, hear nothing but the blaze, and in the glare of the intense light, Escobar smiled proudly at him.

Then the two men fled into the darkness.

"You led a merry chase, I'll give you that." The voice was definitely Marianna's, emerging from the darkness beyond the flashlights. It sounded like she was climbing up the slope from the airstrip. Faith's hands twitched, so much did she want to silence that voice forever. Staking was too good for a bloodsucker like her. Better to separate the head and body, ideally with bare hands for maximum visceral pleasure. "I don't think anyone expected the hunt to last quite so long. It's so nice of you to walk right into our hands, here at the compound, so we can all sleep comfortably in the house tonight." She paused for a moment, then added, "Well, all except for you, of course."

She stepped in front of some of the hunters, so the crazily crisscrossing beams of light illuminated her. She was as lovely as ever, tall and strong, dressed in a gauzy, flowing outfit that caught and shimmered in the lights. Faith almost lunged for her; only the certain knowledge that if she did, the hunters would open fire and kill Wesley and Gunn kept her from doing it.

Wesley spoke up first. "Marianna, I'm not sure that you fully understand what's going on here."

Marianna laughed. "What is it you think I don't understand? Something about the part where you die at the hands of my friends?"

"Do you have any idea what those two Wolfram and Hart lawyers were up to?" he pressed.

"Lilah and Gavin? Something about a book, I gather. Their business is their own, not mine."

"That ain't just any book," Gunn put in.

"Not at all," Wesley said. "The book you're talking about is the Book of the Interregnum—one of the most awful, poisonous texts in the history of mankind. It's been sought after for centuries, by some of the true dregs of human history, who desired it to help them perform all manner of bizarre ritual. Men and women have been driven mad by reading just a few excerpts from it, according to the legends."

"This is all fascinating, Mr. Wyndam-Pryce, but what does it—"

"What does it have to do with you? You just let Lilah Morgan and Gavin Park fly out of here with the Book, or most of it at any rate. They're planning to deliver it to someone who's going to use it to summon the Beast of the First Blood, the original vampire on Earth. She plans to mate with it, and create a new race of powerful vampires."

"Benedicta," she murmured, and then she laughed. "I didn't know it was here, but . . . more power to them."

Faith couldn't keep quiet any longer. "There's always been a balance of power. Vamps on one side, humans on the other, Slayers, like me, in the middle, balancing toward the human side because you're so much stronger than they are, even though there are more humans than vamps.

"But if Benedicta's plan succeeds—if she can, in fact, bear the Beast's offspring—then there is no balance anymore. They will be the strongest—stronger by far than humans or traditional vampires. You'll be relegated to third class citizens. If you want to feed, you'll have to ask permission of Benedicta's brood—if they don't just kill you right off."

Marianna seemed to consider this idea for a moment. "I can see how that could be an inconvenience," she said. "Although I can't see why Benedicta would want me eliminated. She likes me. Her minions made me."

Marianna stepped back then, out of the lights, behind the hunters with their weapons at the ready. "These people are becoming tedious," she said. "I don't care to hear them argue any further. Give me a few minutes to get out of here, then kill them whenever you want."

Once the humans had spotted the landing strip, Arle, Zed, and a couple of the others had peeled off from the pack. They were on home turf now, inside the compound.

Instead of following the rest down toward the airstrip, they cut west, toward the buildings, running as fast as they could. There were only a couple of guards posted, and they—expecting any trouble to come from inside, rather than out—fell easily.

Once inside, Arle and his companions released everyone they could find and gathered them all in the dusty, open space of the biggest barn interior. There were probably thirty of them, all together. They ranged from the nearly human but decidedly murderous to abominations—one unnamed creature, for example, was nothing more than a gelatinous mass with no distinct features at all mounted on a wheeled wooden cart that it propelled by means of sticks that were actually inserted into its "flesh."

When they were all gathered and had been brought to some kind of order, Arle took center stage. "You all know me," he began, and then he explained what was going on.

He did a very, very good job of it.

CHAPTER TWENTY-THREE

Thirteen people with guns, against three—one a Slayer, the other two Gunn and myself . . . we've faced worse odds, Wesley thought. He caught Gunn's eye and gave the slightest tic of his head toward the circle of hunters. Faith noticed the motion as well, and cut her eyes in the opposite direction. *So that's settled, then. All we need is a cue.*

"How about now?" Faith asked calmly. She didn't wait around for an answer, though, but hurled herself in the direction she'd chosen. Gunn did the same, and Wesley charged toward his intended targets. Gunfire split the night, as tense fingers tugged triggers in a panic. Wesley heard the whistle of bullets hurtling through the air, and two of the hunters actually cried out in pain, caught in their own crossfire.

There's a certain satisfaction in that, to be sure, Wesley thought. A great deal of satisfaction, actually.

But he didn't have time to think about it for long, because he was suddenly tangled up in flailing arms and legs. He slammed into the nearest hunter, bowled him over, and landed on top of him. The hunter swung the butt of his rifle, catching Wesley in the gut and knocking the wind from him. Wes doubled over and the hunter managed to bring a knee up, shoving Wes off.

When the hunter turned the rifle around to point it at him, though, Wesley grabbed the barrel and yanked. Precariously balanced, the hunter fell over again. As he hit the ground, Wesley shoved the gun forward as hard as he could. Its wooden stock hit the hunter in the side of the head and he went limp.

Behind him Wesley heard grunts and shouts as Faith and Gunn both struggled with their initial opponents. Wesley spun around but couldn't make those battles out clearly— several of the flashlights had fallen to the dirt when they'd attacked, and their beams illuminated soil and shrubbery more than anything above ground level.

He hoped that in such close quarters the hunters would hesitate to use their weapons for fear of more crossfire injuries. Any advantage the guns might have given them was negligible, and they were probably not as accustomed to hand-to-hand combat as Wesley and his friends. Wes didn't have to go far to find his next opponent, another man who was coming toward him without a gun but with a big knife in his fist. It was a terrifying knife, with a long, sharp blade and a serrated top edge that looked like it would do a lot of damage if it went in and then came out again. He'd just have to avoid that. He braced himself to meet the man's attack, and caught the fellow's wrists as he moved close.

"I have been . . . hunting you for two days," the man got out as they struggled against each other. His accent sounded German. "Never have I put so much effort into the death of a mere human. The Slayer, yes, to be expected. But not you."

"Glad I was able to surprise you," Wesley replied. He still had the man's wrists, but the powerful German tugged his arms this way and that trying to break Wesley's grip.

He yanked himself to the right, and Wesley barely managed to hang on. Then, while Wesley was off-balance, he launched a kick at Wesley's midsection. Wesley turned and caught most of it on his hip, but it was still forceful, and he slipped, losing his grip on the knife hand. The blade flashed once in the moonlight as it swung toward him, and he was only able to dodge it by throwing himself flat against the earth. He rolled and came up a few feet away from the German, who advanced steadily, the knife still in his hand. He looked supremely confident, without the least bit of shakiness or hesitation in his movements.

Each time he came forward Wesley edged back, always keeping enough distance between them so the man would have to lunge to cut him. And if he did that, Wesley was prepared to take advantage of the move to knock him off his feet and gain the upper hand.

He hoped.

As they circled each other, Wesley always measuring the safe distance, they heard a horrible shriek of pain. *Definitely not human,* he thought.

He suddenly remembered Cordelia's vision, back in Griffith Park. She had seen a strange creature trying to kill Faith. But so far, none had—even the one that had been stalking her in prison was only trying to locate her. But an Enciardan demon would certainly qualify as a bizarre creature.

Finally his opponent feinted a lunge, and Wesley put his left foot down to stabilize himself as he prepared for the attack. But the ground beneath him was uneven—the hunter had backed him up to the edge of a ditch—and he went down to his knee. The hunter pressed the advantage, slicing the air toward him. Wesley raised his hands to block, knowing that at best he'd lose some fingers.

Except that a booted foot intercepted the man's arm, and the knife went spinning crazily into the air. "You gonna dance with him all night?" Gunn asked with a grin.

Wesley pushed himself back to his feet. The hunter was cradling his right hand, but some of the fingers stuck out at odd angles. Gunn had broken some bones. Wesley moved in with a left-right-left combination that dropped the hunter in the dust.

Faith joined them a moment later.

And they ran.

"Now we find a boat," Faith said. She pointed past the airstrip. "Docks are over there, right?"

"I believe you're—oh, my." Wesley stopped in midsentence. A troop of creatures, perhaps twenty of them, ran their way from the direction of the airstrip. He wondered if the monsters had seen them yet.

"There they are! Get them!" It was Marianna, leading her minions in the charge.

"I'm not sure I'm ready for another fight," he said.

"Don't got a lot of choices, seems like," Gunn responded.

"I suppose not." He resigned himself to another brawl, this one against veritable monsters. This one, he wasn't at all sure they could win.

"There they are!" came another shout. This one issued from behind them.

Just great, he thought. *Surrounded by these beasts.*

This group came on at a run—those of them who could run, at any rate. Others came at more of a shamble, or a roll. But they came. And as they got closer, the moonlight picked out a couple of familiar faces.

"That's Arle," Wesley said. "And Zed!"

"And a couple more that were with us during the day," Gunn added. "I think this bunch is on our side!"

Wesley, Gunn, and Faith simply stood there as the creatures reached them, enveloped them, and then passed them, continuing on toward the ones Marianna was leading up the slope.

"You appear to be right," Wesley said. "They are on our side."

"Then let's not hang around and watch," Faith urged. "We have a boat to catch. Right after we find one, I mean."

"Absolutely right," Wesley agreed. "I hate to let them fight our battle for us, but . . ." He watched the battle for a moment. It was savage, no quarter asked or given on either side. " . . . but somehow, I don't think they are. I think they're fighting for themselves, more than anything else."

"We got to get back to the mainland so we can do the same," Gunn pointed out. "Let's move."

They moved around the warring creatures and down to the docks.

There was a long wooden dock jutting from the beachhead of San Teodor, and tethered to it was a cigarette boat of sleek crimson lines—the same kind of vessel drug runners used to elude the Coast Guard.

"Looks like it's my lucky day!" Faith crowed as she pointed at the craft. She picked up speed and headed toward it.

Their footsteps clattered over the wooden dock. They moved without subtlety or stealth, and Faith had already reached the end of the landing before he could stop her.

"Rock it," she chortled. "This is so cool!"

"Now, let's hope someone left a key," Wesley commented sarcastically, still very wary.

"No problem if there isn't," Faith drawled. As Gunn drew alongside Wesley, she flashed him a look that Wesley interpreted as a gentle dissing of himself: *You can take the English guy out of the prep school, but you can't teach him to hotwire an engine.*

"'Cause, key," Faith announced, pointed at the ignition. Sure enough, there was a key. "Looks like it's someone else's really stupid day."

Without a moment's consideration, she climbed in and hopped behind the wheel, while Gunn took the single back seat, moving much more slowly than the Slayer. His movements were quite labored, and he was favoring his left side.

Broken ribs, maybe?

They both looked expectantly at Wesley.

"Hey, Grandpa, you comin' or not?" Faith challenged him.

Wesley didn't let her jibe ruffle him as he took in their

surroundings. In her eagerness to do the next doable thing, Faith had completely forgotten about Wes's earlier suspicions over entrapment. A boat, just sitting there like a weak plot point in a novel, was precisely the kind of trick a hunter might employ to bait his quarry. *And a simple bomb, wired to the ignition, would take care of all three of us at once.*

Unconcerned, Faith turned on the engine. It hummed like a Jaguar. She moved her shoulders with pleasure and gave the thing some throttle. Wesley turned his head slightly and scanned the empty sands. Beneath the roar the distant sounds of fighting were diminishing, and not simply due to the engine's decibel level. The battle was winding down. A massacre would also enhance today's fine fortunes—if the proper people and things were massacred.

He silently wished their strange comrades well before jumping into the boat.

Then he gestured for Faith to move aside and let him have the wheel. She did. Another small victory.

He looked questioningly at Gunn, who clenched his jaw and said harshly, "I'm good to go. So get it goin'."

Wesley grabbed the wheel as Faith cast off.

"Punch it, Wes!" Faith shouted triumphantly.

He'd take them where he could today.

Angel looked up at the moon and thought, *What's next?*

A few feet away Escobar was resting, crouched down, his feet under him and his hands locked across his bent knees. Always the hunter, he remained alert, ready to spring up and into action at any moment.

Escobar stared at him, and Angel realized he was wearing his true face—the demonic visage of the vampire. He morphed back to human features and Escobar visibly relaxed.

"We need to come up with a plan," the man said. "A new one."

"The old one isn't working out so well," Angel said dryly.

"Lohiau's treachery . . ." Escobar shook his head. "I should have anticipated that. I was lulled into trusting him because you knew him."

Angel nodded briefly. "I know," was all he said.

Now he was glad that Faith, Gunn, and Wesley weren't there.

The human race is going to need them, once the Beast and Benedicta mate . . .

"*Bien, escuchame,* Angel. They seem to be waiting to begin. Perhaps something's gone wrong. Let's speak of the new plan."

Angel gave his assent with a dip of his head.

"Cordelia is needed for their version of the ritual." Escobar took a breath. "We could try to sneak up on them and kill her before it happens. At least it will stop Benedicta, and—"

"No."

"But—"

Angel vamped. "*No.*"

"I don't understand you," Escobar said slowly. "Truly, I don't. You are willing to die for this cause. But you would rather jeopardize the entire mission—an entire race—than ask one of your men to do the same."

"Cordelia's not one of my men." *She's my friend.*

"I don't understand you," Escobar said again, more softly this time. "A vampire . . ." He put his arms around his legs. "They say you're different than the rest, but *so* different? A vampire is supposed to be a monster."

I know, Angel thought. *I am.*

And that hellbeast is not going to hurt Cordelia.

No one is.

They try, they'll meet the monster I am, just before they die.

CHAPTER TWENTY-FOUR

There was a lovely poem about putting to sea in a big green boat, but that was for children and other people who could sleep at night. Wesley wondered if under the new regime human children would be allowed to learn nursery rhymes.

For a speedboat, this craft is distressingly slow. Something must be wrong with it. Perhaps one of Wolfram & Hart's clients put a curse on it, rather than securing it more normally while its owner cavorted about trying to kill us.

"Yo, Wes, you okay?"

Wesley turned to stare at Gunn, exhausted. "Fine, Gunn. I was just worried about missing tea."

Gunn nodded. "'Cause for a second there I thought you were stressin' about, y'know, failing."

Wesley felt an overpowering urge to either laugh or weep.

he wasn't sure which, but he knew neither emotion would do him any good. He nodded to the back of the boat where Faith sat staring off across the dark water. By the light of the full moon, he saw her profile. She was not smiling.

"How's she doing?" he asked Gun.

"She'll live." Gunn winced, pressing his hand harder to his side. "Slayer. Plus, pretty edgy chick, you know what I'm saying? Tough. She's probably been through this kind of stuff a lot. Always lands on her feet, way I hear it."

"How're the ribs?"

"Feeling pretty messed up. Don't worry, though, they won't slow me down. The pain just pisses me off and you know what I'm like when I'm pissed."

Wesley allowed himself a small smile. "Maybe if things get really grim we should think about breaking some on your right side as well."

"How much longer are we going to be out here? I'm looking to get back on solid ground. Not much for that rocking motion."

Wesley glanced down at the gas gauge once more. He looked back up and met Gunn's eyes.

"Twenty minutes. We'll be there in twenty minutes."

"Cool. I'll clue in Faith," Gunn said, moving toward the end of the boat.

After Gunn was out of range, Wesley muttered, "Maybe more like thirty and probably a lot longer than that. Because we're running on empty now."

The cigarette boat was dead.

The three of us might as well be, Wesley thought.

"So, how are you at swimmin'?" Gunn asked Faith.

She moved her shoulders. "Good to go. You?"

He grimaced as he shifted his weight away from his damaged ribs. "A man's gotta do what a man's gotta do. Yo, Wes, you ready?"

Wesley slammed the storage bench shut. "Sorry, no life preservers. We'll just have to hope for the best and watch out for each other."

He and Gunn shared a look.

"More like I'll be watching out for your sorry asses," Faith bantered. She was unaware of Gunn's injury, since neither man had mentioned it to her.

The boat had finally run out of gas. They could see the twinkling lights of the harbor, but swimming with broken ribs . . . Wesley had done everything he could to ease the boat along, but in the end there just wasn't enough fuel to make it.

"All right then," Wesley said, "on the count of three?"

With a wild yell Faith dove into the water.

Wesley and Gunn turned to look at each other. Gunn gave Wesley a faint smile. They intoned together, "Three."

Then the two men jumped in.

In yet another reeking, bone-strewn cave in the ice-cold desert of grossness, Cordelia was so not loving her options.

Let's see, be possessed and killed or be possessed and then have to mate with that vampire skank.

How was she supposed to mate and have demon children with her anyway? She wasn't sure she wanted to know. Maybe "mate" was universal vampire speak for "suck your blood."

Or maybe it's some sort of ritualistic, spiritual sort of . . . oh, who am I kidding? I have no clue. Wesley might have parsed it together by now, but he's not here. No one is. They're probably all dead. And Angel left me.

Lohiau was celebrating the fact that he was a total immoral jerk with Benedicta and Bran, not with champagne, but some kind of transmissions to Benedicta's fans all over the world and in other dimensions. The Queen of the Mysteries was very sorry that she couldn't transport all her followers to the desert to be physically present for the big event. It was a huge disappointment to them and to her, blah blah. She was practically promising them they would be able to catch it on HBO.

Then Lohiau turned to look at her and she snapped her head away from him. *We trusted you. We put our hopes in you.*

She didn't cry. She wouldn't give the members of this very elite psycho club that pleasure. She was an actress after all, even if she wasn't making a living at it. She could suck it in. She could laugh when she wanted to cry, smile when she wanted to frown, or at least she could have if it weren't for the gag in her mouth.

She started to cry.

Benedicta, Speaker of Blessings, stood at the mouth of the cave and looked at the full moon. She saw images of her life—*my lives*—projected on the silver orb and actually felt a twinge of nostalgia for her brief existence as a weak, unquestioning little nun. She couldn't imagine why.

The only friend I had was Drusilla. I should look her up and thank her for Changing me. Then I'll stake her and feed the dust to my acolytes.

Simply because I can.

Soon I will live another new life. I will be the first and only one of my kind, and every other vampire will be a lesser being. Just as we are superior now to humans, I will be that much higher above all other vampires. And I will create a new race with the Beast.

I will truly be the Mother of All the Damned.

The moon beamed its joy upon her. She could feel it in her blood. So many years come and gone, so many moons, and still she could feel it. She closed her eyes, picturing it in her mind. She didn't have to look, she knew every shadow, every contour, always the same and yet always, deliciously new. When she could finally feel its power coursing through her body, rich and full as the blood that no longer flowed through her veins, she opened her eyes. She had seen it thousands of times and yet she still cried out with the beauty of it. There, glorious and shining, the full moon reigned, her companionable mistress of the dark. Deep inside in a place that had been dead for centuries, she ached.

"Is it not truly beautiful?" she whispered.

"It is that," Bran answered her quietly, respectfully, as he came up behind her. Another moment to watch and absorb and pray and then he nudged her from her reverie.

"The lawyers have brought the Book."

She turned and saw the two attorneys. One was a woman, the other a man, and they both looked very tired but also very excited and pleased. She wondered if they had any idea what they were helping to bring into the world.

"Are they staying for the Summoning?"

"They say they have to return to Los Angeles to take care of some other pressing work." He grinned at her. "I think they're terrified."

She turned her face to his and the moonlight glinted off her teeth as she passed her tongue over their tips. "Then maybe they deserve to live. Tomorrow their world will be very different."

He grinned at her, his eyes shining, and for a moment, it was like the old days, when they were in love and not sparring and jostling for position.

"Let them go. Then let's get started," she said.

She looked up at the moon and sighed happily.

Angel performed the first set of the Wu Shi style of tai chi to focus his mind and allow his body to heal. Best to be prepared, best to be strong. The moments he took here to reflect and rest might be the ones that would allow him to save Cordy when she most needed him and his strength.

Escobar came up behind him. The hunter's footsteps were so quiet that they might have been only the sounds of a sighing breeze. Angel did not have to hear his steps, though. Escobar's heartbeat pounded out a rhythm that Angel could have heard from a far greater distance. Then there was the smell of blood, both of man and beast, that emanated from him. Angel could feel the demon stirring inside and he willed it to stay quiet just a little longer. He managed to quiet it and waited for the other man to speak.

At last Escobar took a deep breath. "They're about to begin the ritual."

"How do you know?" Angel asked.

Escobar answered quietly, "I know."

Angel could read the hopelessness of their situation in the other man's eyes.

Escobar held out his hand to Angel. "Will you follow me into Hell?"

Angel clasped his arm just below the elbow, a warrior's clasp. "Not much on following. But since I'm heading in that direction myself . . ."

They smiled, wearily.

The cavalry was freaking out. Lorne didn't know how much longer he was going to be able to keep Fred from either going insane or leaping out of his fine automobile. Studebaker Hawks were classic, yet she had not said word one about how beautifully he had restored it.

"You did the right thing, kiddo," he said again. "I know it's hard, going outside and facing the world, but you're fine, see?"

They were almost there. Miraculously there wasn't much traffic that night, and no road rage. This neighborhood, teeming during daylight hours, was dark and silent at night, the only sounds coming from boats creaking in their slips and waves splashing against pilings. The air was pungent with the smell of the sea.

"We'll find a boat and go sail in and rescue everyone," he prattled on. Finding a boat wasn't the problem—they were everywhere, here. But finding a boat he felt comfortable piloting solo, while Fred, no doubt, hid belowdecks . . . that was proving to be more of a challenge.

Huddled next to the car door, Fred could barely manage a nod. Her fear was choking her. Angel had entrusted her to save the world, but it was all she could do to maintain her own composure. Lorne had seen unexpected flashes of valor from her, and knew that Angel was a good judge of character. If he trusted her to pull this off, then she could do it.

But watching her tremble against the far door of the Hawk, it was hard to see how.

Suddenly he saw a flurry of motion through her side window—three figures, it looked like, bursting from the darkness and lunging toward the car, arms out. An attack of some kind.

"Uh-oh, hang on, this could be trouble," Lorne said as he yanked the wheel and hit the gas. The Studebaker went into a skid. *Turn into the skid, or away from it? It's easy to remember when you're not sliding toward the ocean.* He had the presence of mind to pump the brake, though, and in a moment the car came to a reasonably gentle halt up against a chain-link fence.

The three figures lurched toward them. There was something strange about them, something almost familiar, but curiously misshapen. *Coming from a Pylean, that's saying a lot.* They were shouting something, but he couldn't make it out over the roar of the Hawk's motor and the Streisand CD in the deck.

Fred sunk down as though wishing the upholstery could swallow her. Lorne cranked the wheel, hoping to step on the gas again and pull away from the fence, but then Fred's narrow fingers closed over his forearm. "It's Wesley!" she exclaimed, beginning to cry all over again. "And Gunn and Faith are with him!"

Lorne inched his fabulous car away from the fence and popped open his door. The three heroes stood there, but with Gunn, "stood" barely applied. He was hunched over, in obvious agony. All three were dripping wet from head to toe and panting as if they'd just run a marathon. Strands of seaweed clung to Faith's hair.

"Funny meeting you here," Wesley managed between gasps.

"Not as funny as when you get the bill for cleaning my upholstery," Lorne answered, not smiling.

"Put it on our tab," Wesley said as he slid into the backseat. "How'd you find us?"

"Angel called," Fred explained, glancing at Lorne. "He asked me to come find you."

"And she called me, and I called two friends, and they called two friends, and so on and so on and so on." At Wesley's blank stare, Lorne said, "Never mind. We're here."

"Wow. This and the boat," Faith drawled. She tugged Wesley's amulet from beneath her shirt. "There just might be something to this after all, Wes."

Gunn and Faith climbed in beside Wesley, and Lorne pulled back onto the road. He studied Gunn in the mirror. Something was wrong and that had him worried. Tall, dark, and handsome was tall, dark, and broken. Gunn did not need to go to a supernatural rout in such terrible condition.

"Where to?" Faith asked.

Lorne looked at Fred, who answered, "Caritas, first. I forgot to bring the wall with the directions on it. Then we go to the desert."

"What she said," Lorne confirmed. *Good thing I filled the tank.*

Cordelia was terrified. She could smell her own fear and it was rank. Of course, it wasn't as rank as the goo they'd put all over her face or the stench of most of Benedicta's cult members. A devoted few had straggled in for the big event, and some of them needed to spend some serious quality time with Mr. Ivory.

She'd been twisting this way and that for hours, trying to gain some wiggle room and eventually escape from her leather bonds, but so far all she'd managed to do was peel off the top couple of layers of her skin where the straps chafed.

Then something even stinkier wafted in her direction. It was the Virgin Mummy of Heidelberg or whatever. *Great, that Virgin mummy thingy. After we went to all that work to find it, and they had it all along. Chaz, you big spaz.*

Bran laid the stinky mummy out on a clean white sheet on the ground and began to chant. Cordelia strained but couldn't hear his words. He waved something fine over the body that sprinkled down like some sort of pixie dust. Then he took a large stone, swung it over his head, and brought it down over the mummy's chest. The blow pulverized bone and cloth. He ground the stone farther into the cloth, turning the fragments into a powder that reminded Cordelia of some lost nights at Hollywood parties—*not that I ever partook of any drugs at them*. Within a few minutes he had finished his preparations.

Benedicta stepped forward holding a wooden bowl decorated with mirrors or something. The vampire scooped up some of the powder, and one of her groupies poured in something dark and red that Cordy guessed wasn't wine.

Benedicta raised the bowl in the place where the mummy had been laid out. "Dead, like her, immortal, like her, but definitely looking better than her," Benedicta laughed. She swirled the drink slowly before tilting back her head and downing it.

She licked at the red liquid running down the corners of her mouth. Suddenly she froze and her eyes bugged out; the bowl fell from her fingers and struck a rock on the ground with a ting.

Wow, is this neat or what? Cordelia thought. *She's gonna die!*

But Bran and Lohiau didn't look particularly concerned, so maybe no dying. Or the two men were in cahoots and wanting Benedicta to die.

The vampire grabbed at her throat with both hands and began gasping. Suddenly the mummy took form again, the dust regathering itself. Its hands moved as well and clutched its own throat in a macabre mimicry of Benedicta's movements, or like somebody using a VR glove to play Nintendo. Cordy would have screamed but the gag didn't allow for that much mouth movement.

Instead she watched in horror as both Benedicta and the Virgin writhed in seeming agony. At last the vampire fell to the ground and both were still for a moment. The mummy lay for only a moment before exploding from within, showering everyone close by, especially Cordy, with a fresh, rancid mist of bone and ash.

"I told you, y'all should have let me drive. We'd be there by now," Gunn complained.

"Yeah, I bet all we'd be is lost right now," Lorne retorted

"How about *I* drive? I'll get there fast and I'll stop for directions," Faith suggested.

"No!" everyone shouted at once.

"It's just that we don't want you to drive without a license," Wesley lied. "Imagine the trouble you'd be in then. I mean, in addition to being a fugitive."

"Plus we don't want to die," Gunn informed her.

"It might make the time fly quicker if we did some singing," Lorne suggested. Fred looked hopeful.

"NO!"

Benedicta was once again on her feet, fully recovered from her collapse after drinking her ancient mummy blend of delicious death Ovaltine. Now the vampire was chanting some mumbo jumbo about the end of one world and the beginning of another. *No joy there.*

Frightened, Cordy turned her attention to Bran. Not liking the wicked grin twisting his lips. Not liking him, either. *In fact she felt the hatred rush through her body. Oh, yeah, I am so going to kill him,* she thought.

". . . *posco vos Flamma!*" Benedicta shouted.

Suddenly a flame appeared out of nowhere and swooshed skyward before pulling back down into a bright, hot fire about two feet in diameter. The heat of the flames burned and Cordy's already parched throat became as dusty and dry as the desert she was in.

"Light and Dark, the first sign, the first part of Creation. Only this time, Darkness shall reign supreme!" Benedicta cackled.

Oh, yeah, the combination plate is missing a taco. She's definitely not sane.

Bran took on the second verse. "And now great sky, look down on us with favor. Make for us a new firmament that we might make a heaven out of hell! *Reduco novus Caelum!*"

Suddenly a strange red started to creep against the sky. Cordy felt herself sag in relief. *Serves them right for not knowing what time sunrise was. We at Angel Investigations pride ourselves on such thoroughness before we try to take over the world. But Pinky and the Bran here . . . what ineptitude.*

A strange prickling ran up and down her spine. *Wait a minute. The sun rises in the east. That light's coming from the west. Whatever that red light is, it isn't the sun.*

Bran saw her expression of terror and laughed in her face. Meanwhile his face started peeling off.

Cordelia passed right out.

"Okay, kids, met 'em on the highway," Lorne said, as he glanced in his rearview mirror.

In the backseat, Faith turned around to look through the window.

Oh . . . my . . . God.

Headlights had just joined them, merging onto their road from around a large mesa. But not just one set . . .

Dozens.

"We're dead," she muttered. She looked at Gunn and Wesley, and made a fuss. "All that work."

"Hey, you're such a wuss," Gunn shot back, crammed in beside her. But he was looking through the window too.

The headlights directly behind them flashed at them. Another set zoomed around that set and hit the sand, roaring up on Lorne's car. It was a 4-wheel drive SUV, and as Faith watched, the dome light inside went on.

Vamp faces peered back at the fivesome in Lorne's car.

"Damn," Gunn muttered. "We're dead."

Faith swallowed and her hand grazed her chest where the amulet hung. She said, mostly to herself, "Wish the thing had really worked."

Instantly she felt something sizzle through her like a warm rush of wind. Startled, she glanced at Gunn. His brows were raised . . . and there no bruises on his face, and his eyelids were no longer swollen.

"I felt something, too. Mainly what I felt was the lack of pain." He touched his ribs. "I'm healed."

"I am as well," Wesley offered, leaning forward.

Fred said, "It was like . . . like what I think hot flashes are like."

Lorne glanced at them in the rearview mirror. "What a relief. I thought I was going through the change, and I don't mean the change those fellows have already gone through."

Another SUV whined up beside Lorne on the opposite side. He craned his head to look first at the one on his right, and then the one of his side of the car.

"Pull over," Faith told him.

"You crazy?" Gunn said, scowling at her in disbelief "Belay that order!"

"Do it," Faith urged him. "I got a feeling . . . about that feeling."

"They're going to outrun us anyway," Wesley ventured. He leaned sideways, straining to touch the car's floor. "What I wouldn't give for one wooden stake."

Lorne sighed as the cars closed in. He put on his turn signal, and the vamp on his right moved over.

The car rolled to a stop. Fred said, "Um, if they get us . . . we'll be turned into vampires, right?"

But her question was not answered. Lorne was rolling down his window as the SUV on his left rolled to a stop and the passenger door of that vehicle opened. An enormous vamp climbed out, clad in a black-hooded robe.

"Hi," Lorne said cheerily, and Faith was reminded of all the many times she had been pulled over by the cops back in Boston, and had tried to sweet-talk her way out of a ticket. Sometimes it worked.

Sometimes it didn't.

The vampire approached, an enormous male in full game face—ridged brow, glowing eyes, fangs. The warm wind rushed through Faith again, and she tensed her muscles and put her hand on the door handle, ready to rumble.

"Hi," the vampire replied in a friendly, howdy-neighbor voice. "Are you coming from the Speaker of the Mysteries? We are so lost. Have they started the Ritual yet?"

Without missing a beat, Lorne chuckled. "*You're* so lost? We've been driving around for hours."

"Shoot. I came all the way from Montana for this," the vampire whined. "I *gotta* be there when the Beast shows It's the opportunity of a lifetime!"

"Yeah, I know," Lorne commiserated. "We're practically in tears ourselves."

The vampire sighed heavily. "We'll I guess the only thing we can do is—"

"Turn right," Faith said suddenly. The warmth suffused her, filling her with the knowledge. "Then keep going That's where Benedicta is." She looked hard at Gunn. "And a whole bunch of other . . . people. Some we know."

Gunn stared back at her, gaze to gaze. "You're right," he said slowly. "I know that too."

"Thanks," Montana said. He turned and dashed back to his car.

Faith touched the amulet. It sent an electric shock through her system.

"God bless ya, Wes," she said to him. Then to Lorne, "Punch it."

"Aye-aye, Captain," Lorne replied.

Faith grinned. "Five by five," she said.

"Long ritual," Angel observed.

The eerie magickal strobe lights had made finding Cordelia and company so much easier than it would have been if Benedicta and Bran had worked more discreetly.

The deep cover recon would have been almost fun, if the stakes—vampire humor—hadn't been so high. But Angel had to admit that he had enjoyed sneaking down the mountains and toward this cave with his predator's senses on high alert. There was a rush in going after a kill that was unmatched by anything else in his experience.

Yet more proof that Chaz Escobar and I are kindred spirits.

"Aren't they all long?" Escobar asked. They were squatting behind a boulder, watching the goings-on. "Have you ever been to a Lubber demon wedding? No, I imagine you haven't. They take so long you would swear that time has simply stopped."

"Yeah. Lubbers. Big on stopping time," Angel noted.

They watched for another long clump of darkness-loving chanting.

Then Escobar said, "As a matter of fact, this *is* a long ritual, longer than most. It mimics Creation but twists it and turns it into a kind of perversion."

Angel took that in. "So, what day are we on?"

"I'd guess they just finished the fourth."

"Well, it took a whole week, right? We've got time," Angel answered as he watched Cordelia. She was still bound and gagged, and she looked tired and scared.

"Just don't forget one thing."

"What's that?" Angel asked, his attention on Cordy.

"All the work was done in six days."

CHAPTER TWENTY-FIVE

"*Permitto quidnam subolesco minuo nobis!*"

Cordelia shook herself awake, grateful to be alive. She knew from past experience that fainting with a gag in one's mouth was very dangerous and could even be fatal. Not that she wasn't positive that dying would preferable to whatever was going to happen next . . .

Focus, Cordy. Find a way out of this mess.

It looked like Bran was waving around a bunch of leafy things, herbs, maybe. "Let all that grows bleed for us," Benedicta intoned. Cordy made a mental note to thank her sister for the translation.

"And now, Great Moon, fourth sign of Creation, rise up and take your place as ruler of this world," Bran said. As if a cue, the scarlet clouds parted and the moon shone down, bathing everything in an eerie light.

Lohiau looked at Cordy again—*the old perv keeps star
ing!*—and she looked away, just as determinedly. *I've go
nothing you haven't seen on a thousand hula dancers. Jus
maybe put together a little better.*

Take a picture, she thought. She was gagged, or sh
would have said the words aloud. *It'll probably last longe
than I'm gonna. Maybe even as long as this stupid ritual.*

The amulet around Faith's neck was glowing now. Where
lay against her chest, she almost felt branded. But it was
good kind of brand.

The car was sailing along, not touching the sand, ju
low-riding the air pockets. Vamp cars were all around then
their passengers hooting and honking, racing against th
full moon to bear witness to the ritual.

Cordelia didn't know what the vampires were planning o
doing with the seagull, but whatever it was it didn't look
be good for the bird. Bran held it above his head and circle
six times around a stone altar.

"Toto creatura sustineo nobis," Benedicta chanted.

Said the Great and Terrible Wizard of Oz, Corde
thought with giddy hysteria.

Bran drew a dagger from his cloak and slit the bir
throat. The blood flowed out and Benedicta caught it in th
same bowl. Cordy thought she was going to be sick an
only prayed that she could hold it down. Benedicta dra
half of the contents of the bowl as Bran laid the dead bir
on the altar. Then she poured the remainder of the bloo
over the body.

• • •

Benedicta smiled in delight at the taste the bird's blood left in her mouth. Ordinarily it would have tasted poorly, an unfit substitute for the human blood she craved. But not tonight. Tonight it was divine.

Eagerly she turned and signaled Bran to bring forth the goat.

Bran killed the goat and Benedicta drank its blood. Angel recognized most of the words, enough to understand that she was claiming all flesh as hers to be nourished from. He felt his stomach begin to rumble and he was painfully reminded of how long it had been since he had eaten.

Bright side: if I die, I won't be hungry.

With painstaking care, he and Chaz had continued to sneak closer to the ritual site. There seemed to be more spectators than there had been an hour before, and Angel had finally realized that they were spiriting themselves in magickally.

It was almost time to make their move. He judged the distance to Cordy, calculating how fast he could cross it. He tensed his muscles and prepared to spring.

Escobar stayed his attempt with a warning gestured. "There should be a third sacrifice," he whispered.

"What?" Angel asked, his concentration broken.

"The pages that I have reference three sacrifices but not what they are."

They can't sacrifice Cordy. They need her.

Escobar cocked his head. "So far there have been a gull and a goat. My guess is that the third will be a—"

"Goth."

"Pardon me?" Escobar asked.

Angel nodded toward the nightmare tableau—the unholy trio of Bran, Lohiau, and Benedicta; the blood on the altar; the stench of death; the onlookers, all of them vampires with leering faces and bad dental plans.

Now there was a girl, a child really, being led forward by Bran just as if there had been a leash around her neck.

The girl was dressed all in black. She had a pale face, and her eyes and lips stood out dramatically thanks to the black makeup she wore. Her hair was streaked black and hot pink.

A lost girl. One of many of the tribe who inhabit Los Angeles, who need someone to follow and something to do.

This one followed the wrong leader. And what she was going to do . . . was die.

Angel tensed and Escobar whispered, "Don't blow our cover so soon. There's nothing we can do for her."

There's always something we can do, Angel replied silently. He kept watching and waiting, so he could do it.

This is worse than church, Cordelia thought anxiously. *It just goes on and on and on. And, oh, no, they're not going to kill that girl, are they?*

" . . . this, our lovely sacrifice . . ."

Oh, no. No, no. Please, Cordelia begged silently, forgetting for a moment her own predicament.

Benedicta's voice carried through the cave and over the desert. The onlookers were getting more excited, milling and watching in the cold with growing tension. There were no chairs; maybe there hadn't been time to bother. Now Cordelia saw that in addition to vampires, demons were joining the party, and what looked to be ordinary people too. It never ceased to amaze her how many people joined the side of evil, particularly when the agenda was to kill people.

Now Benedicta said, "We summon forth the Beast of the First Blood. We give him wings to speed his flight, we give him the sins of the world to revel in and carry, and lastly we give him a human who worships the dark night and whose blood is pure. God made men in His image and so we shall remake them in ours."

Bran raised the dagger over his head and prepared to plunge it into the girl's breast. The victim was woozy; Cordelia figured he had given her something similar to what he'd given her, Cordelia, back during the good ol' ice-tong-in-the-feet days.

I so wish I could help you, Cordelia thought, tears welling in her eyes. She struggled at her bonds. No go.

She closed her eyes and braced herself for the death.

Then she heard a shout and popped her eyes back open.

Angel!

Sure enough, it was her guy. Bran had obviously begun to swing his arm down just as Angel rushed him and knocked him to the ground. Joy flooded through Cordelia and she mumbled through the gag, "Angel I'm here!"

And so was Hell. Demons opened their wings and dove for the intruder; vampires went fang-faced. They rushed Angel just as he gained his feet and whirled behind Bran.

That was when Chaz Escobar showed, and he had major weaponry. Within seconds his Rambo-like gun was strafing the cave with really cool and highly effective bullets or laser pulses or who knew what, except that it didn't matter because he was mowin' down the monsters.

"Yes!" Cordelia shouted ecstatically. Except gag, so even to her it sounded like "Ymf!"

Escobar opened his mouth and began to chant. Benedicta realized what he was doing and screamed, "No!" The Queen of the Mysteries took up her own chanting again.

Someone started shrieking, and Cordelia realized it was her. She had somehow forced the gag out of her mouth—maybe it had been done magickally—and she started making up for lost time.

As the battle sprang up around him like a fresh firewall, Angel concentrated on Bran. The sorcerer's game was off. Angel wasn't sure why—he suspected it was because he was draining himself by using magic to protect himself, Benedicta, Lohiau, and Cordelia from the battle—but he didn't mind why.

"You're pretty spry for an old man," Bran sneered as he swiped at the air with the dagger.

Angel barely moved. The dagger didn't come anywhere near him. "You're how old?" Angel grunted.

Then Bran did some magick and a stream of small fireballs soared toward Angel. But Angel managed to dodge all of them but one, which landed on his thigh and burned briefly. He slapped it out.

"Far older than you'll ever be," Bran said, as he quickly conjured another barrage. This time one of the fireballs hit Angel squarely in the chest.

But Angel was ignoring the pain. Cordelia loved him the more than anyone when he snapped back with, "Now, that's where I think you're wrong," and hurled Benedicta's boyfriend against the altar.

"Too late!" Benedicta shouted.

Angel turned in time to see that Benedicta had gotten to the little Goth girl. In the split second that her victory registered, she slit the girl's throat.

Taking advantage of Angel's distraction, Bran grabbed him around the legs, sending him crashing to the ground. The two fought wildly, each seeking an opening until a crack of thunder ripped through the sky directly above their heads.

Angel looked up in time to see Benedicta pouring the last of the girl's blood over the altar. She looked skyward, her face a study in ecstasy. "It comes!" she whispered.

Demons and vampires and all manner of unholy things, oh, my . . .

And as Wesley watched, Faith's amulet sent out streams of shimmering blue energy out into the desert.

One by one, the vampire-mobiles began to explode. Wheels squealed, horns honked, and *boom!* another one turned to dust.

Flashes of lightning ripped across the now bloodred sky. Thunder rumbled soon after. Gunfire and explosions echoed in the darkness.

Around Lorne's car, patches of sand exploded with the same blue energy, glowing and whirling; and each patch became a spectral warrior dressed in complete ancient Mesopotamian battle gear, from the leather skirt to the armor to the classically shaped barrel helmet.

And each was racing off to battle in a chariot driven by an equally spectral warhorse.

"Likin' this!" Gunn sang out. "Oh, yeah!"

"What I want for Christmas," Faith cried to Wesley, "is another one of these!"

As Angel and Escobar fought desperately against the odds, the Beast began to materialize on top of the altar.

Huge, black, and scaly, its purple-red eyes dripped ooze and its spiny back glistened with thick black liquid. Massive, misshapen arms and legs became shadow, then took form, then jerked and writhed like individual living creatures. Fangs protruded an inch from its lips. Something that could only be blood was oozing from pores all over its body and it smelled of the open grave.

Cordelia went fairly wild. She strained desperately against her bonds. She would rather tear herself limb from limb than be a host for that thing.

As it swung its head toward her she thought she was going to faint. *It's going to use me as a host and then it's going to completely take me over, change me into that and then make evil babies with that crazy vampire!*

It squatted grotesquely on the altar, still not completely solid, at least in this dimension. Then it stretched and grew, and without leaving the altar reached out with one taloned hand toward her cheek. She tried to scream. She tried to will herself to die, but there was nothing she could do. Everything began to go slowly black when suddenly something loomed closer to her than even the Beast, startling her.

Cordelia shrieked.

While Angel and Chaz Escobar fought the hordes of darkness, Lohiau swept in front of Cordelia in full kahuna regalia down to his feathered mask.

Addressing Benedicta, he raised his voice and proclaimed, "I have far more power than this woman. I beg for the honor of being host for the Beast of the First Blood. Take me."

Drawing near, blood smearing her face, the Queen of the Mysteries laughed in his face—or at his mask—and said, "You may look like a witch doctor, true. You may have learned a trick or two over the years. But you're not a Seer. The Beast cannot enter you."

With great ceremony, Lohiau grasped his mask and pulled it over his head.

"Oh, but I *am*," he informed her.

He looked at Cordelia, staring at her as he had been all night, and she gasped when she saw his eyes. They were completely black, and they seemed to spin like marbles as he looked at her.

Then she fell into something—a pit? a vision?—and suddenly saw a sort of old-timey movie in her head, in which Lohiau raised his arms to a big coconut moon and screamed, "Give me the power to defeat these damn Americans!"

Lightning flashed and the sky reversed, turning white with a black moon hanging in it like rotted fruit hanging from a tree. Another flash, and he was transformed into a far greater kahuna that he had been. He had gifts and abilities he had only dreamed of before.

One of them was the gift of Visioning.

Then Cordelia was back out of the pit, very dizzy and barely conscious.

"You should have told us sooner," Benedicta said angrily. "We have wasted so much time."

"I did. I told you that I foresaw your great reign," he replied evenly, "when I gave you the Chalice in the first place."

Benedicta glanced over her shoulder at the carnage and said, "Let it be done." She smiled at the truly revolting creature, who advanced on Lohiau and began to wobble, as if it was beginning to have trouble staying in this dimension.

"I invite you, my love," Benedicta said, gesturing to Lohiau. "Take him."

The creature hesitated for only a moment before it seemed to ooze right through the kahuna's skin and into his body. The old Hawaiian's wrinkled flesh rippled and distorted with the passing of the creature.

"I am the Beast of the First Blood. I have come to bring destruction." His voice was different now, fuller, with a kind of echoing undertone. He looked at Cordelia. "First I shall take lives to nourish me. And then I will create a new kind with you, Benedicta, and we will rule the earth."

The Lohiau Beast stared at her again.

"I shall begin with your life," he announced.

Oh, great, Cordelia thought, and real panic set in. Gagfree, no-holds-barred, big-time terror. She started to scream. Still bound in leather strips like an S&M mummy, she flopped around on the ground, jerking against the leather straps trying to escape. She felt the leather begin to give under her efforts, and allowed herself to think about the damage she was going to do once she was free. The only question was who she'd start with, Queen-bitch Benedicta or her pervy consort?

Before she could free herself, though, the LohiauBeast drew nearer, opening its fanged mouth.

"Seer," it said to her, and the word seemed to be very important to him.

Then she was surrounded by cold again, and she Saw:

Lohiau was explaining something to Angel—she listened—and she realized it was all a trap, one Lohiau and Angel had set for the Beast.

Lohiau said, "I will convince them to let me take the Beast into myself. I will create a void for my middle self, my uhane, which will act as a socket for the creature to plug in to. But I will route the control of my lower self, my unihipili and my kino to my higher self, my aumakua using cords of mana-loa. They will act as a bridge, if you can think of it that way, for me to contain the Beast, and to prevent it from moving unless I will it."

He went on, and Cordelia, in her vision-state, understood every word: the mana-loa was an ethereal conduit, and subject to attack. And the Beast would have access to his mana-mana, which might make him more dangerous. But the magician seemed confident that he could hold the Beast long enough for the ritual to work—and for Escobar to do his part. To kill him.

"And then, Angel, we will both be ended."

The vampire had argued with the kahuna not to sacrifice himself so, but the Hawaiian had remained firm:

"My friend, you gave me a gift when you showed me you were willing to die—you reminded me that life is only so good as it is spent."

The kahuna had gone silent for a moment.

"I have spent mine well. I have several students who will follow in my footsteps regardless of whether I fall tomorrow night. I have taught them well, and they will honor my spirit when they hear of my demise."

Cordelia blinked, the and LohiauBeast blinked back at her, releasing her from the vision. And she nodded back, her eyes filling with tears.

"I will take you in death," the Lohiau Beast said, advancing on the female Seer.

In her eagerness to watch, Benedicta drew closer, crowding them.

That was when the LohiauBeast pulled a wooden stake from its feathered cape, and staked Benedicta, Speaker of Blessings, the Queen of the Mysteries.

Benedicta stared down at her chest, her mouth open in complete horror.

CHAPTER TWENTY-SIX

Benedicta did not dust. At least not all at once.

She did, however, collapse to the sandy floor of the cave. *Gross, gross, gross!* Cordelia thought.

The formerly beautiful vamp lay twisted and decomposing, her hair and eyes nothing but fading ashes, her bones erupting through rice-paper flesh.

More gross.

Then Cordelia noticed that something seemed to be wrong with her own lower back. She felt a certain looseness there, as though something had—*broken.*

Horrified, she wiggled a bit more to test the extent of the damage, and realized that it wasn't *her* that was broken—

The leather straps that had been starting to work loose had finally given.

She got up, kicked at the grossness that had been Benedicta, and raced to the altar. She grabbed the Chalice and whirled in a circle.

Then the LohiauBeast threw back his head and shrieked like an unholy being.

"Run," he begged. "I cannot control it. I thought I would be able to, but—"

He advanced on her, raising the stake he had used to gut Benedicta, its point still dark and slick.

More hell broke lose.

Angel slashed at more of the red flying demons, popping them out of the air like blood-filled piñatas, *pap-pap-pap-splash—*

Twist.

—Bran was making some kind of magical gestures, pointing his fingers at the LohiauBeast—

Cordelia lunged forward and grabbed the stake. The LohiauBeast was powerful, though, and she couldn't wrench it from his hands. He continued driving it toward her breast. She had only slowed its progress, not halted it. Still, if she could slow it enough . . .

From nearby, Bran shouted, "No!" rushing to the aid of the LohiauBeast.

Cordelia saw another weapon. A large hunting knife, maybe eighteen inches long, lay on the sand nearby, abandoned by one of the combatants. She released the stake and rolled to the side. Her hand scrabbled across the dirt, then closed around the weapon's leather grip. She pushed herself to her feet.

The Seer gripped the big blade and lurched forward; her

first steps in several days were weak and stumbling, but she gained strength as she continued forward.

The old druid threw up his hands in a warding gesture, bringing a circular purple energy field up between them. If she had thrust straight forward with the knife, she would have probably been zapped. But this technique was better—Buffy had taught it to her, back in Sunnydale, when she'd been a Slayerette. Of course it had been shown with the intention that it be used with wooden stakes, but actors had to learn to improvise.

She feinted overhand with the knife, moving as if to drive it straight down through the druid's shoulder and into his heart—

And as the purple ward solidified, she altered her angle, bringing her elbow out and spinning it around changing from an overhand strike to a reverse slash and then a sideways stab to come in right under the ward. The meaty *thwack* as the blade forced its way between his ribs was intensely satisfying.

The druid crumpled to the ground, the rest of his gross skin turning a parchment yellow and sloughing off him in seconds, leaving nothing but a skeleton. Tendons and ligaments decayed then as if in a time-lapse video, allowing his bones to crumple to the ground and his black cassock to sink even further. Within seconds his bones began to disintegrate as well, leaving his clothes on the ground. He went even faster than Benedicta had; the power she'd amassed over the centuries preserving her, even in final death.

Cordelia eyed the black cassock on the ground. Was that *silk*?

Then the Beast came for her again, and there was no sign in its eyes of Lohiau anywhere.

Escobar had long since run out of bullets, but his electrically enhanced sword and gauntlet and his fighting techniques gave him an edge over the demons swarming them.

"Angel!" shouted Escobar as they battled beside each other, "I've got to get next to Lohiau! Benedicta is down, and the Beast is *mortal*! This is our last chance!"

The hunter sounded desperate and tired. Even *he* had to be wearing down after the long night of fighting. The vampire speared two Collusites and slashed at a serpent-shaped creature that ran for his legs before replying.

"Well, we'd better get moving then. You need some help, Escobar? Want me to carry you?"

The Spaniard grunted and shouted at Angel, "You are funny, Angel! Maybe I should carry *you*!"

The two laughed, and Angel felt good to be alive—or at least *aware*—and fighting for a good cause with a strong ally at his back.

What I wouldn't give to have the others here right now.

It certainly would help to have a few other swords, but more than that, it would have been nice to see his friends before Escobar killed the Beast.

I'll never know if they made it off San Teodor.

It was a hard thought, but it was just the way it was.

Angel knocked back a muscular demon that looked like one of Escobar's creations. The creature had four legs, all with huge feet, and two big fists attached to short muscular arms coming off a barrel-like torso. It looked like someone's idea of the perfect fighting machine, and it slugged him once, hard, before he could dispatch it.

The vampire and the hunter slowly worked their way toward the warded circle where the Summoning had taken place.

And they, too, were an endangered species.

Escobar grunted again behind him, and Angel spun quickly, lashing out instinctively to knock back a blow from a *menehune*. Escobar had taken a hit, but he wasn't down. The Beast of the First Blood had apparently gained quite a bit of control of the kahuna's *mana-mana*, and had immediately forced the little people to start attacking Angel, Escobar, and the few surviving creatures that the Spaniard had brought with them for the final attack.

Angel sliced the little creature's head off, sending it tumbling down the sandstone wash. Six more came running up to replace their lost fellow, and the vampire redoubled his attack.

He could feel himself weakening too, which was a bad sign. Escobar needed him to help make it to the warding circle. Time was running out.

He had to do something.

He needed to recharge his batteries, but he had no bottled blood with him, and the creatures around him would do no good. Sure, he was in the desert; with some time to hunt he could come up with a rabbit or a rodent, but there was no time. He needed a solution now.

So he thought about his friends. He thought about Cordelia, captured, helpless, her life endangered. He thought of Wesley and Gunn and Faith, somewhere in the Pacific. Lorne and Fred, on their way to find the others. All of them doing what they knew had to be done, in harm's way because he had put them there.

Most of them, he couldn't help. But Cordelia was nearby. He could do something for her.

At the thought of her, he felt new strength course through his weary muscles. With an unconscious roar, he took out three more Collusites with a single blow. Escobar could tell that something was different—their pace toward the Beast had increased.

"*Excelente*, Angel," he said. "We will taste success!"

One thing was certain though—he was much faster and more powerful than he'd been a few minutes ago. With his second wind, he was more aware of his surroundings: the cold night air, the gritty ground under his feet, the way it shifted and caused his body to flex and loosen in response, the sounds and the sights of the battle, all were digital-sharp and crisp, and everything seemed to move more slowly. Two Collusites attacked in tandem, one striking from the right with a mace while the other threw two large knives overhand. The demon's superior musculature drove the blades harder and faster than a normal human's ever could, blurring both knives into a single shape.

But not to Angel. He saw them flickering as if caught in a strobe, hilts and blades flipping as if in a poorly animated cartoon.

He sent the tip of his sword out and tapped one of the blades right where the brass guard arced down over the handle, hitting at just the right moment to alter the trajectory of the knife and send it down to glance off the mace-wielding demon's shins. This threw the creature's timing off, making it easier for Angel to slash its belly open with the backswing of his sword.

The other blade was too close to parry; he'd never cross the distance in time.

So he simply grabbed it, plucking it from the air like an errant Frisbee, hand closing over it at just the right moment, hand in place on hilt.

"Dios mío!"

It was Escobar. He'd seen Angel grab the blade.

The vampire didn't waste time answering, but threw the blade back at the demon, enjoying the momentary flash of surprise on the hell-spawn's face just before the handle of the knife suddenly sprouted from its torso, changing surprise to pain and dropping it in its tracks.

"I have never seen such skill before. Truly I am blessed to fight at your side."

A *menehune* threw a short spear at Angel, which the vampire parried. He lunged forward to impale the tiny man while he considered what to say to Escobar.

The vampire looked over at Lohiau, and saw the possessed kahuna fighting a battle that he could hardly imagine. What would it be like to have a powerful immortal spirit, steeped in centuries of power use, trying to devour your mind and spirit?

Actually, I know the answer.

And the magician had *known* that he would be facing such a creature, with himself as the battlefield.

"If we don't reach Lohiau in time, none of us will call this night blessed."

Escobar grunted, and they pressed forward, now only about a dozen feet from the kahuna.

Angel looked into the Hawaiian's eyes, and for a few moments saw recognition. Then the magician turned toward Cordelia, stake in hand.

He's losing! The Beast is taking control!

Angel started to shout a warning to Cordelia, but then Lohiau stopped, his left arm reaching out to grab his right. The stake fell from his hand, and then his arms locked.

The magician stood there, beads of sweat building on his brow, the strain on his body showing. Angel could see his chest heaving from the effort, every muscle straining as the war played out.

The Beast's minions slowed their attack as well. Plainly the creature possessing Lohiau was having to bring more of its will to bear on the rebellious body he was inhabiting, causing it to reduce its control on them.

"Now, Escobar! Start the ritual *now!*"

The two pushed through several attackers, getting closer and closer to their target. Escobar reached into a pouch and pulled out a wicked-looking spike that was thick with silvery runes. He began to speak words Angel had heard him rehearsing before—the words that would, when he killed the Beast, ensure the destruction of all vampires.

But at that moment, the LohiauBeast moved, a roar of triumph bellowing from his mouth.

Not the good kind of triumph, Angel figured. The Beast had won.

Time slowed, grew thick like molasses, as the Hawaiian's body underwent a subtle transformation. Angel's heightened senses picked it up immediately: The movement pattern was Lohiau's.

The LohiauBeast turned toward Cordelia. Angel was too far away, he couldn't possibly move fast enough to intercept the possessed kahuna. But Cordy showed no fear. She simply held out her hand, and the LohiauBeast put the Chalice into it. Angel looked on in wonderment. *Has she tamed it?*

Cordelia turned and slammed the Chalice against a tall boulder to her left. The movement seemed to take several seconds. Angel watched as the obsidian-faced Chalice splintered, small pieces flying to the left and right. The cup was destroyed beyond repair, no longer capable of being used for any ritual.

Lohiau's body staggered for a moment as the Beast within him let out a piteous scream, realizing that it was now trapped in this human body forever.

As it/he/they screamed, the kahuna reached down and picked up the jagged base of the cup and lifted it to shoulder height, his arm fully extended. He looked over at Angel and smiled.

Then the vampire watched, horrified, as Lohiau swung his hand in a short, whipping arc, flicking the jagged edge of the broken Chalice across his own throat and shredding it. The old man's arm dropped to his side and the stump of the Chalice hit the boulder, shattering as it hit the ground.

Blood spurted from the wound, gushing out in arterial bursts, a fine spray of red droplets misting up where it hit the ground. The Beast was in charge of what was left of the body now and tried to scream. But Lohiau had destroyed his own larynx, silencing its cries and ruling his own body to the end.

Angel hoped his friend had found some peace.

"Noooo!" Escobar shouted and rushed forward, thrusting the spike he'd made into the kahuna's body. Their few remaining allies kept the remaining demons and *menehune* at bay, but Angel couldn't be bothered to help.

He watched as if from a distance, and waited to die.

This was it, the end of vampires on the face of the earth, what he'd worked so hard to achieve. When the blood stopped flowing, he would die.

The end of me.

Part of him watched Escobar, desperately trying to complete his ritual before the Beast died, for what reason, Angel couldn't fathom. Dead was dead. With the Beast gone that was it. Game over.

Another part of him thought about his life. It wasn't the rushing life-before-his-eyes that he'd expected. Instead small moments came back to him, valuable gems he carried at all times but seldom cherished—

—a sunny day on the heath before the change, the feel of the warmth on his skin binding him to the world of the living, letting him know he was a part of things—

—the first time he'd seen Buffy, the day she'd been called to be a Slayer, the absolute wonder of watching her walk, seeing her spirit, her heart—

—the sadness he'd felt when he left Sunnydale for L.A., buoyed by the serene calm he'd felt at knowing it was the right path—

—*Darla.* What could be said, what could be felt about her?

All these thoughts drifted through his mind as he watched Lohiau die. The blood flowed slower and slower, the old man's heart pumping less and less blood, there being no more to circulate.

Cordelia . . . oh, Cordy . . . Cor . . .

All gone.

And nothing happened.

Angel stood there for a few seconds, confused. The Beast was dead, killed by Lohiau. Why hadn't he died?

Escobar's minions were all but wiped out in their effort to hold back the Beast's and Benedicta's thralls. A demon lunged at Angel, and survival instincts kicked in.

Figure out why you didn't die later—or die now from doing nothing.

He blocked the swing of the creature's sword and riposted, driving his blade behind the ugly's guard. Apparently the Beast had decided if he went so should everyone else, so all of his minions were suddenly attacking Angel, Escobar, and Cordelia.

The vampire was surprised to find that even though he'd been willing to face a peaceful death only moments ago, now that Lohiau had interrupted the ritual and saved him, he very much wanted to continue the existence he had. Of course, the world's other vampires would have been spared as well—which just meant he had to wrap up here, so he could continue taking them out one by one.

Suddenly the *menehune* joined them. Now that the Beast was dead, his hold on the little Hawaiians was gone. They poured out of cracks in the canyon walls, building human towers and pyramids, tiny phalanxes of defenders killing demon after demon.

"Angel! You need a hand?"

Gunn!

The vampire's heart soared, and he looked toward the sound of the voice.

Gunn, Wesley, Faith, Fred, and the Host were joining the battle, weapons swinging, magic flying.

They're alive!

They were not alone. Hundreds of phantom warriors surrounded them on chariots, joining the fray.

"You seem to have the situation well under control as always, Angel," said Wesley, swinging his fighting adz into the midst of a clump of demons, "but we happened to be passing by."

"You don't mind if we join in, I hope?" Faith inquired. The Slayer sprang toward a group of Collusites, knocking them over with her momentum before stabbing each one.

Gunn called out to Cordelia. "Nice outfit girl! Love that silk! Who'd you have to kill to get it?"

"Shut up, Gunn!" shouted Cordelia, slashing a demon that had grabbed her leg. "Nobody ever said you had a sense of style anyway!"

The team—his family—and their ghost warriors got to work, and started putting the remaining demons down like pancakes at an IHOP. The tide had turned, and Angel's team was back in play. Within a few minutes the remaining thralls and minions had gathered around a few lieutenants and retreated, taking the ashes of Benedicta and her consort away, as well as the pages of the Book of the Interregnum. Angel wasn't sure where they were going, but he had a strong idea that a certain law firm was about to have some visitors.

And not happy ones.

The Beast of the First Blood was dead, Benedicta and her consort were dead, and even though he had expected to be, Angel was just *not*.

It was a great day to be alive-ish.

And it looked to be a great morning too. The night was beginning to fade, its murky tone muted in the east by the distant approach of the sun.

Gunn must have been thinking the same thing.

"Yo, Angel, how 'bout we head home?"

Angel sheathed his sword and nodded. Getting away from the desert sun would be important in just a few minutes.

"Good idea, Gunn."

The vampire paused, and indicated Lohiau.

"But let's take him with us—he deserves better than this."

Gunn and Wesley moved over to get the body, and started for the road.

Escobar sat near where the kahuna had fallen, looking depressed.

"Look at it this way," said Angel, "we won—we just didn't get everything."

The Spaniard was morose. "It would have been the greatest kill of all time, and would have freed my Marianna from her curse. But you are right, Angel, we are done here."

The big hunter paused. "And I am glad you are still with us, for what that is worth."

Angel nodded. "It's worth something."

And it was.

EPILOGUE

San Teodor was a ruin.

There were dead demons everywhere; in the hot sun, they had begun to rot. The Escobars' fabulous home had been burned down; the wreckage still smoldered, scenting the air with sour smoke. All the trophies that summarized Chaz and Marianna's obsession for the hunt were gone.

There were wooden stakes, some finely crafted, others simple chair legs and fence posts. They lay atop piles of dust, testaments to their successful use.

"She must have been dusted," Gunn observed, passing his flashlight over the carnage. "We ain't seen no sign of her, and I'm pretty sure we took the only boat. Plane was already gone . . ."

"Maybe Lilah and Gavin came back," Cordelia said, "and rescued her."

"Couple of Escobar's faithful had 'em under surveillance," Angel mused. "They haven't left L.A."

A wind blew, ruffling Escobar's hair. There was white in it now, and he had aged.

The dust piles scattered in a gentle breeze that blew up from the shore.

Cordelia, Angel, Wesley, and Gunn had come with him. Faith had returned to prison, to finish paying that debt—as if she hadn't paid it a thousand times over, as far as Angel was concerned. Fred remained with Lorne in L.A. The nightmare was over, but Fred was still reliving it.

She's one of the bravest people I've ever met, Angel thought. Then he gazed at his friends and thought, *these are the others.*

The hunter lowered his head as if in prayer, and Angel thought, *The whole time all this was happening, he never succeeded in catching up to her. He never saw her again, never said good-bye. I wonder if, all along, he didn't put his heart into running her to ground. If he just couldn't bring himself to do it.*

He found himself thinking of Darla, and all that she had been to him. In her face gleamed his reflection, whether it be that of a savage vampire reveling in evil, or a tormented night creature burned with a soul.

There has never been another like me, he thought. *And I'm endangered every day. No whining, just fact.*

Wesley came up beside Angel and said, "We found the bodies of our allies. All dead." He looked around. "Everything on this island has perished."

"Except us," Cordelia said. "That's something." She walked over to Escobar, who was now silently weeping. She touched him on the forearm. "We're still alive."

Escobar raised his tear-stained face to the moonlight. "Yes," he whispered.

From the shadows of a canyon, a quarter mile away, Marianna echoed his word.

"Yes."

We will meet again, mi amor.

With a smile on her broad, lush lips, she blew her husband a kiss.

As many as one in three
Americans with HIV...
DO NOT KNOW IT.

More than half of those
who will get HIV this year...
ARE UNDER 25.

HIV is preventable.
You can help fight AIDS.
Get informed. Get the facts.

www.knowhivaids.org
1-866-344-KNOW